Kuji Furumiya
Illustration by chibi

Unnamed Memory I

The Witch of
the Azure Moon
and the
Cursed Prince

Once upon a time, there were five witches who had lived for many lifetimes and amassed immense power.
For hundreds of years, they symbolized fear and disaster.

...This is a story about the end of the Age of Witches.
It is also an epic fairy tale—the unnamed story of the fifth witch and a royal prince.

Contents

Unnamed Memory

The Witch of the Azure Moon and the Cursed Prince

I

Kuji Furumiya

Illustration by **chibi**

YEN
ON

NEW YORK

Unnamed Memory

Volume 1

Kuji Furumiya

Translation by Sarah Tangney
Cover art by chibi

UNNAMED MEMORY Vol. 1 AOKI TSUKI NO MAJYO TO NOROWARESHI OU
©Kuji Furumiya 2019
First published in Japan in 2019 by KADOKAWA CORPORATION, Tokyo.
English translation rights arranged with KADOKAWA CORPORATION, Tokyo through TUTTLE-MORI AGENCY, INC., Tokyo.

English translation © 2020 by Yen Press, LLC

Yen On
150 West 30th Street, 19th Floor
New York, NY 10001

Visit us at yenpress.com
facebook.com/yenpress
twitter.com/yenpress
yenpress.tumblr.com
instagram.com/yenpress

First Yen On Edition: November 2020

Yen On is an imprint of Yen Press, LLC.
The Yen On name and logo are trademarks of Yen Press, LLC.

Library of Congress Cataloging-in-Publication Data
Names: Furumiya, Kuji, author. | chibi, illustrator. | Tangney, Sarah, translator.
Title: Unnamed memory / Kuji Furumiya ; illustration by chibi ; translated by Sarah Tangney.
Description: First Yen On edition. | New York, NY : Yen On, 2020–
Identifiers: LCCN 2020041071 | ISBN 9781975317096 (v. 1 ; trade paperback)
Subjects: CYAC: Fantasy. | Witches—Fiction. | Kings, queens, rulers, etc.—Fiction. | Love—Fiction.
Classification: LCC PZ7.1.F976 Un 2020 | DDC 741.5/952—dc23
LC record available at https://lccn.loc.gov/2020041071

ISBNs: 978-1-9753-1709-6 (paperback)
        978-1-9753-1710-2 (ebook)

10 9 8 7 6 5 4 3 2 1

LSC-C

Printed in the United States of America

Unnamed Memory I

The Witch of the Azure Moon and the Cursed Prince

Character Profiles

Oscar
Crown prince of the kingdom of Farsas. Bearer of the legendary royal sword Akashia, which can neutralize magic.

Tinasha
Also known as the Witch of the Azure Moon. Lives at the top of a tower in the wilderness and is said to grant the wishes of those who climb to the top.

Lazar
Oscar's childhood friend and a royal attendant. A young man who has been through a lot in the service of his lord.

Als
A military officer of Farsas. The most capable person in the military and Oscar's sparring partner.

Meredina
A military officer of Farsas. Als's childhood friend and a woman who boasts incredible sword skills.

Kav
A mage of Farsas. A very inquisitive young man who doesn't shy away from Tinasha.

Kumu
A mage of Farsas. An older man who's the current royal chief mage.

Sylvia
A mage of Farsas. A beautiful blond woman who is sweet and kind but a little ditzy.

Doan
A mage of Farsas. A talented young man who is well-known to be the next in line for the position of royal chief mage.

Lucrezia
Also known as the Witch of the Forbidden Forest. Tinasha's friend who lives deep in a wooded area in the northeastern lands of Farsas.

A witch who lives in an azure tower.

A cursed prince.

If they could rewrite time, what would they do with such power?

This is the story of what happens when everything is overwritten.

▓ 1. A Curse and the Azure Tower

In the wilderness stood a tower of the faintest azure blue.

The surrounding land was sparse, adorned with only a few patches of grass. In the midst of that wasteland, a young man on horseback looked up at the lofty spire.

"So this is the tower where a witch lives." There was not one shred of excitement in his tone as he gazed at the colossal structure.

The young man had hair so dark it was nearly black, and he had deep-blue eyes—the same color as the sky after sunset.

The quality of his clothing and his graceful appearance spoke to an innate elegance. That was not to suggest he was frail, as his muscled body also exuded an aura of constant readiness. One who looked upon him would liken him to a commander on the front lines of a battlefield, despite his young age.

He was about to dismount and stride up to the tower when a voice whined from behind him, giving him pause.

"Your Highness, we really shouldn't…"

"Shut up, Lazar. What would I be if I faltered here?" Shaking his head in exasperation, he turned back around. The young man who had just been called Your Highness was Oscar, the crown prince of the kingdom of Farsas, the lands that extended east of the tower.

Oscar's retort to the attendant, a childhood friend he had brought with him as his only companion, brimmed with confidence. "After all, we managed to break out of the castle. Wouldn't it be pointless if we went back now? It's just some light sightseeing."

"No one goes to a witch's house for sightseeing!" Lazar protested.

A witch.

There were only five throughout the entire mainland. Perhaps owing to their tremendous power, they were treated as separate from everyone else.

The Witch of the Forbidden Forest.

The Witch of the Water.

The Witch Who Cannot Be Summoned.

The Witch of Silence.

The Witch of the Azure Moon.

These were the common names of the five. The witches appeared only when they themselves desired it, using their almighty magic to summon disasters and then promptly vanish. Over the last several hundred years, they had come to symbolize fear and calamity.

Of this quintet, the one who possessed the most powerful magic was the Witch of the Azure Moon. She had erected a suitably azure tower in the wilds beyond any country's borders and lived at the very top of it. It was said that she would grant the wish of any who could climb to the pinnacle of her great spire, but as word spread that such challengers never return from the tower, fewer and fewer people dared to even approach it.

Oscar and Lazar had come to this dangerous tower with a specific purpose in mind.

"I told you, it's just as dangerous as I thought. What will you do if the witch magnifies your curse?" asked Lazar.

"I'll deal with that if it comes. I don't have any other clues, do I?"

"There are still other ways... I'm sure if we look, we'll find something..."

Oscar listened to Lazar's pleading as he dismounted his horse. He took up the longsword in his saddle and returned it to the sword belt at his waist.

"You mentioned other ways, but none have been found in fifteen years. First, I'll meet this Witch of the Azure Moon and ask her how to break the curse. If this is a dead end, I'll go back to the Witch of Silence who cursed me in the first place and get her to undo it. Flawless, right?"

"It's not flawless at all," Lazar whimpered, sounding close to tears as he finally dismounted from his own steed. His skinny, gangly physique was wholly unsuited for battle. He wasn't carrying any weapons, but that was because the two had left in such a hurry. Lazar jogged after his lord, much like he must have done when they'd escaped the castle.

"Your Highness, I understand your feelings... But the reason no one's contacted the witches in fifteen years is because it's too dangerous! Any search for the Witch of Silence has been fruitless, and no one who's climbed the tower of the Witch of the Azure Moon has ever returned!"

"True. It does look a bit tall for taking the stairs," Oscar said.

The tower's walls were made of a blue-tinted, crystalline material that made the structure appear to blend into the sky. Oscar craned his neck to look all the way up toward the hazy, indistinct rooftop.

"Well, I'm sure I'll figure something out," he said.

"No, you won't! It's supposed to be full of traps! If something was to happen to you, how could I possibly return to the castle? What would I say?"

"Just act like you're really, really sad." Oscar shrugged and ambled off.

"Wait. I'm coming, too!" Lazar watched Oscar go and rushed to hitch both their horses to a tree before hurrying after him.

It had all begun fifteen years ago. One night, a witch's proclamation suddenly echoed throughout the castle.

"Never again shall you have children. Neither shall that son of yours. The blood of your family will tear a hole in a woman's stomach. The Farsas royal family dies with you!"

Oscar didn't quite remember the exact words the witch had said as she cursed them. What he did remember was the shadowy silhouette of the witch with the moon at her back. And how his father's arms had trembled as he held Oscar. At only the age of five, Oscar hadn't understood how serious such a pronouncement was. He had simply recognized that something bad must have happened because of how the color had drained from his father's face.

Oscar was the king's only child. This curse that threatened the lineage of the royal family was a well-guarded secret. Few knew of it, most of those being exceptional mages and scholars who'd been searching for years to find a way to break it.

In contrast to such a dark thing to bear, Oscar himself had been a bright, brave boy who'd mastered both swordsmanship and scholarship. Because of his brilliance and good looks, many had high expectations for his future, though they knew nothing of the curse. They would murmur *"In time, he'll be a king remembered throughout history."* If the curse wasn't lifted, however, all he'd leave behind would be an ill-fated name.

At the age of ten, Oscar came to understand what the curse meant and began searching for a way to break it. Unfortunately, no matter how many books he'd consulted or leads he'd chased down after practicing his sword-play, Oscar hadn't found even a shred of a clue to show for it.

Fifteen years had passed since that night.

This man who would become king someday had traveled westward, beyond the borders of his country, and now stood at the foot of the azure tower where a witch lived.

"Well, let's go," Oscar said.

"You can't just open the door so callously! Be more cautious!"

With Lazar shrieking in his ear, Oscar pushed open the double doors and stepped inside.

He looked around and found himself in a round, spacious hall. The center was an open atrium, and a passage on the right-hand side led up. It was not a staircase but a gently sloping path that hugged the wall and extended upward in a corkscrew shape.

Oscar craned his neck; the whole tower appeared deserted. "Looks just like the records said, I guess. At least the entrance does."

"Does this satisfy your curiosity?" Lazar asked shrilly.

"Let's keep going. C'mon, up we go."

According to the records left in the castle, the tower was fraught with several checkpoints. The witch would grant the wishes of those who made it past these challenges and reached the highest floor. Oscar's goal was to do just that.

Checking to make sure his beloved sword was still at his waist, Oscar set off with Lazar in tow.

There was no handrail along the passage, and Oscar could see that it led up to a round landing. Some sort of huge stone slab had been placed there, and Oscar headed for it as he climbed up the path. Lazar was trailing behind timidly.

"It's dangerous, so you wait there. I'll be back by sundown," Oscar called.

"N-no… I couldn't do that…," answered Lazar.

For quite some time, Lazar had been following after Oscar, starting with when Oscar had first escaped from the palace, and Lazar had ended up in some nasty situations because of it. Each time, he'd rained complaints down on Oscar's head, but it still didn't look like he planned on abandoning his reckless lord.

Oscar regarded Lazar and smiled faintly before turning to continue upward.

As the two approached the landing, they saw it was about the size of a small room. A list of numbers was carved into the stone slab in the middle. Oscar started to think of solutions as he strode up to it, and Lazar piped up in a quivering voice, "Your Highness…th-that's—"

"I'm thinking now. There's most likely some sort of commonality," Oscar said, cutting him off.

"Not that! The snakes! There are so many of them!"

"I see them."

The floor of the landing was overflowing with writhing snakes. There was no wall separating the landing from downstairs; what kept the snakes from escaping the landing was likely some kind of magical barrier.

Oscar remained undaunted. He crouched down and grabbed the head of one of the snakes that was sticking out into the passage.

"They're not venomous, so it's fine. They're just here to get in our way." He tossed it over his shoulder, earning a scream from Lazar. Oscar paid it no mind and stepped into the midst of the serpents. When he approached the stone slab, he put his hand on his chin and pondered.

The rock had been placed to obstruct the passage upward, so Oscar couldn't proceed. He mulled this over, ignoring the snakes winding around his feet, while Lazar let out little shrieks as he gingerly picked his way to his lord. This was most likely the first checkpoint. Oscar nodded, his eyes on the stone slab.

"I got it. This is a mathematical theory studied about a hundred years ago in a small country to the east. It was famous among mathematicians for being an unsolvable problem."

"Unsolvable?!"

"At the time, yeah, but someone figured it out around ten years ago. The witch in this tower really knows her stuff."

Oscar reached out and touched the slab. The spot where his fingers connected lit up with a faint white light. Following that trajectory, he input the answer, and then…

The gigantic stone slab crumbled into sand. At the same time, the snakes writhing at Oscar's feet vanished as though they'd been entirely illusory.

Astonished, Oscar gaped around the landing, which was now distinguished only by a mountain of sand.

"I see. So that's how things work."

"…Shouldn't we go home?" Lazar pleaded.

"No way. It just got interesting."

Lazar chased after his spirited lord as he continued the climb up the path. The top of the tower was still so very far away.

※

The wind that blew through the windows on the topmost floor was always somewhat dry. A voice called out in a large, disorderly room with books piled all over the floor.

"We have the first challenger in a long time, Master."

The person speaking from the doorway was a small child of about five or six years old, judging by appearance. This youth had pretty features but a blank expression, making it difficult to discern their gender. Their emotionless voice gave the odd child a doll-like quality.

The witch's child-shaped familiar looked at the table—no one was there. Atop the table sat a lone, steaming cup of tea. It had been there for over an hour but showed no sign of cooling.

The one person who should have been there was missing from this tableau. However, the attendant received a reply right away.

"A challenger? How rare. I thought everyone had forgotten all about this tower."

"There was one a month ago, too. They couldn't solve the first stone-slab puzzle and ran out of time," answered the child.

The traps in the tower were changed regularly, but ever since the first checkpoint had been set with its current challenge, not a single contender had managed to get past. Perhaps they hadn't thought they'd have to solve an impossible math problem right off the bat in a tower said to have the most difficult obstacles in the entire land. There also weren't many contenders to begin with, so it was no wonder the owner of the tower had misremembered.

The familiar reached with their mind to sense the challengers very far below them. "It seems like the ones this time around are making steady progress upward. Would you like to go take a look?"

"No. The real fun starts on this level, if they can actually reach it."

"Indeed."

Witches were beings better off lurking in the shadows of history. While this one's exact whereabouts were known, very few humans could actually make it past the tower's perilous checkpoints. The witch had no desire to reveal herself, content to wait for others to reach her.

She sang out in a clear tone, "Go, Litola. When our guests fail, be sure to take care of things."

"Yes, Master."

A dry breeze wafted in. The familiar she had called Litola disappeared, and the witch, floating upside down on the ceiling, cocked her head. She muttered to herself, holding an open book to her chest.

"Even if these two are advancing at the moment, no one makes it past the first guardian beast."

A double-edged sword pierced the lion's throat.

Oscar had expected a splatter of blood, but none came. The white lion, frozen in a leaping attack, tumbled to the floor like an automaton. Without sheathing his sword, Oscar took a closer look at the beast's huge body. It was even bigger than a horse.

"I thought this thing's fur was super-white, but it turns out it wasn't even real. I guess it's some sort of guardian beast animated by magic?"

"A lion this huge is terrifying, but the fact that Your Highness isn't scared of it at all is even more terrifying..."

"I'm just warming up. Wonder what'll come at us next..."

Exiting the hall where the lion had been, Oscar and Lazar were met by the tower's passageway again. Oscar looked down the open atrium in the middle of the tower. The distant sight of the ground floor was enough to make anyone feel light-headed, but Oscar peered at it fearlessly.

"That's a mortal fall," he remarked.

"Please don't get so close to the edge!" Lazar pleaded.

"You should've just waited for me at the bottom..."

When Oscar looked back, he saw Lazar edging nervously along the wall. With that attitude, he might never reach the top floor. Nevertheless, Lazar's face was desperate and determined as he cried, "I won't let you die alone here, Your Highness!"

"I don't plan on dying."

Oscar lightly brandished his sword. Along the ascent, he'd encountered countless traps and monsters in the guise of guardian beasts, but he'd cut them all down easily. They were about to reach the midpoint of the tower.

At first, his biggest worry had been the tower's height, but as a device had activated that brought them automatically to the next level after disarming a trap, that was no longer a concern. The traps, on the other hand, were clearly testing Oscar's physical strength, power output, judgment, and intellect. All of these were equally necessary to get past them.

"I guess normally you'd attempt this with a team of people," mused Oscar.

"No one's been fool enough to try to climb with only two..."

"The last one who made it all the way was my great-granddad, right?"

"I heard he went up with a party of ten. Although, His Majesty the former king was the only one to reach the top."

"I see…" Oscar pondered that, putting the hand not currently holding a sword to his chin.

About seventy years ago, Regius, his great-grandfather and the king of Farsas at that time, had reached the top of this tower and received the witch's assistance. However, that had apparently incurred some form of debt. Nowadays, it was a story told only to children as a fairy tale.

"It's been a walk in the park until now," Oscar commented.

"We should go home!" Lazar whined again.

"You can go home. You're useless anyway," Oscar quipped flatly as Lazar burst into anguished tears.

As they spoke, the next door appeared in front of them. From about the fifth floor up, checkpoints had occurred not on the landings connected to the passageway but in separate chambers.

Oscar opened the door without hesitation and saw, in the middle of the room, a pair of winged stone statues twice the size of a human. The sight would've made any child cry, but Oscar seemed content to offer his casual thoughts. "Those really look like they'd move if you get close to them."

"Without a doubt! They will move! Let's leave!"

"You should seriously wait outside…"

Oscar took a deep breath and readied his sword. As he did, the stony skin of the statues morphed into a bewitching black color. Their empty eye sockets glowed red. Spreading their enormous wings without so much as a sound, they flew up into the air.

Oscar signaled with his left hand, and Lazar rushed to plaster himself against the wall.

Immediately after that, one statue flew toward Oscar. The black monster swooped in fast, like a bird of prey diving after a kill. Just before its sharp talons could rip his body apart, Oscar leaped nimbly to the left. As if it had been waiting for that, the second statue chose that moment to swoop toward him.

"Oops."

Fending off its talons with his sword, Oscar slipped out from between the attackers and came around from behind. Effortlessly, but with phenomenal strength, he sliced off one wing from the first statue.

The wounded thing let out an earsplitting shriek. Oscar lifted his sword again toward the monster curled up on the ground. It had all happened in a flash.

※

"Master, the challengers have reached the stone-statue room."

Hearing her familiar's update, the witch smiled a little as she boiled water. "That's amazing. How many?"

"Two… No, in reality, one."

This fact should have been surprising, but the witch only lifted an eyebrow. For decades now, none had made it this far, no matter the size of their party.

It should have been impossible for one person to handle the stone-statue room. A challenger couldn't properly fend off two quick-witted and agile enemies who could fly without someone to distract one, allowing the first to fight the other. That room had seen more challengers drop out than any other.

"I thought I'd make some tea, but it looks like it's pointless now. Since our guest has made it so far, I suppose I should take out the fighting-spirit prize?"

"It looks like he'll clear that rather easily."

"…What?"

※

Dreadful shrieks echoed around the wide room. One monster with a sword stuck in its right eye was letting out a piercing cry. Its companion was already lying on the floor, its giant, motionless body slowly disintegrating into black specks that vanished into the air.

The remaining enemy was lashing out with its left arm as black ooze dripped from its right eye. Strengthened by the statue monster's rage, such a strike threatened instant death if it found purchase. However, the attack grasped nothing but empty air.

Oscar dodged the deadly swipe with his formidable reflexes and slashed down to cut the monster's neck. Its head hit the floor with a dull sound. The huge, headless statue swayed left and right and finally tumbled to the ground.

"So that's all there was to it? Pretty annoying."

Oscar flicked his sword to shake off the blood. He glanced back and saw Lazar giving him a relieved look. "I'm just glad you're not hurt…," he said.

"I would've been worse than hurt if I'd taken a hit from them," Oscar joked as he looked ahead. As the fallen statues disappeared, a spot in the back of the room began glowing faintly. The mechanism that would transport them to the next floor had begun to operate.

"Let's go."

Oscar set off for the device.

That was when the whole room began to shake violently.

"What's going on?!" Oscar shouted.

He looked around to see that holes had opened up all over the floor. The room caving in appeared to be part of a trap. The rest of the floor began slowly collapsing inward, too.

"Hurry, Lazar!" Oscar looked over his shoulder, then gasped in shock. There was a gigantic hole between him and Lazar, who was still against the wall. Lazar was stranded.

Oscar knew he could make the jump, but it was impossible for Lazar to leap that great a distance. Making a decision, Oscar turned on his heel to run toward Lazar. "Wait for me!"

More and more of the room collapsed, revealing the distant ground level. The path to the transportation mechanism had largely fallen away; little more than bits resembling stepping-stones remained.

Lazar raised his hands in front of him, urging his lord away. "Your Highness, please go on without me."

"Are you insane?! You're going to fall!"

"No, I'll be fine. I'm very sorry, but I'm heading back first," said Lazar. His face was pale, but he maintained a smile as he gave a deep bow. "Please go on ahead… With all my heart, I will be looking forward to the day you become king," said the attendant who had been a constant at Oscar's side for as long as either could remember. Lazar did not lift his head. His voice was quivering slightly but also held a note of tempered determination.

"Wait, Lazar!" Oscar sounded panicked. He stretched out a hand in vain. The next moment, with an intense roaring sound, the ground beneath Lazar gave way.

There were five floors left.

All of these featured abstruse puzzles or powerful monsters, but Oscar cut his way through each dispassionately. It was as if he'd climbed the tower alone from the start. Even with Lazar gone, Oscar had no trouble with battle. However, an indescribable sense of despondency plagued his whole body. Oscar imagined that when his great-grandfather had climbed this tower seventy years ago with a party of ten friends and had been the only one to make it to the top, he must have felt the same.

As the thought swirled about in his mind, Oscar at last reached the door to the top floor.

The thing that first caught his eye when he opened the door was the incredible landscape visible through the chamber's enormous window.

It was the top floor of the tower, after all, so the view commanded the far edges of the wilderness. The sun was just setting, and Oscar was speechless in the face of the grand, natural vista dyed in reds and purples. He had never gazed out at the land from up so high before. A gentle breeze blew in, ruffling his hair.

The room itself was large and messy. Along the walls, a variety of mysterious objects had been stacked haphazardly—from swords and boxes to jars and statues. Oscar could see a great many magical items mixed in as well. Aside from the jumble of paraphernalia against the walls, everything else resembled any ordinary person's room.

"Welcome."

A delicate, flutelike voice caught Oscar's ear. It sounded like it was coming from the blind spot farther into the chamber.

"I've made some tea. Come here."

Still holding his sword at the ready, Oscar advanced cautiously. Deeper inside, the space was still jam-packed with miscellany, just like the entrance had been. On the left-hand side by the window, he could see a small wooden table and a couple of steaming cups. He took a deep breath, steeling himself as he took another step forward.

She was standing there with her back to him.

"Your companion is sleeping on the first floor. He's not hurt," the witch said, turning around and smiling at him.

※

"It's nice to meet you. My name is Tinasha, although there aren't many people who call me by my name." Her smooth greeting was so airy it almost felt anticlimactic.

Oscar sat down in the chair she had indicated and began questioning her. "You're a witch? You don't look like it."

"How foolish to question a witch's appearance." Tinasha shook her head, finding Oscar's inquiry strange. To all appearances, she resembled a beautiful young woman of sixteen or seventeen. She wasn't wearing a black robe, nor was she some hunched hag. Clad in an ordinary dress made of high-quality fabric that looked easy to move around in, she took a seat opposite Oscar.

The witch possessed exceptionally good looks. Long black hair and porcelain-white skin. Her eyes were the color of the deepest darkness—night given shape. Her beauty was somewhat melancholy and yet serene, more striking than that of any of the young noblewomen Oscar had seen before.

"Have you used magic to change your appearance?" Oscar asked, voicing a naive doubt.

"You do ask the rudest questions. It's all natural," she replied.

"But you've lived for hundreds of years, and you don't have any wrinkles."

"I have lived many times longer than humans, yes. My body's growth has simply stopped, that's all." She brought a cup of tea to her red petal-shaped lips.

Oscar felt completely undone; this girl was so different from what he'd imagined a witch to be.

Apparently, Tinasha had expected such a reaction and smirked wryly as she urged the conversation forward. "So? Now it's your turn to talk, don't you think? You're the first one who's made it this far all on your own. You should tell me your name."

Oscar straightened up at the question. Nobility and majesty emanated from him naturally, transforming his whole bearing. "I apologize. I am Oscar Lyeth Increatos Loz Farsas."

When she heard his surname, the witch's eyes widened slightly. "Farsas? The Farsas royal family?"

"I'm the crown prince, yes."

"A descendant of Regius?"

"I'm his great-grandson."

"Wooooooooooowww," Tinasha said, looking him up and down with a scrutinizing eye.

"Come to think of it, you do look a bit alike...maybe? Although, you could see in his face how good-natured Regius was."

"Sorry for being bad-natured," Oscar quipped coolly, and the witch burst out laughing.

"I'm sorry. You're a fine man. Reg was too pure and could be a bit childish..." As Tinasha spoke, she gazed out the window, and for a moment, Oscar could see something more than nostalgia in her eyes.

Those black orbs unmistakably belonged to someone who had lived for a long time, and the emotions swimming in them convinced Oscar that this really was the Witch of the Azure Moon.

When Tinasha looked back at him, however, all those feelings vanished like they'd never been there. She was smiling like any other young woman would've. Oscar suddenly hit upon something to ask.

"Do you live here alone?"

"I have a familiar. Litola!"

In response to their master's call, Litola appeared soundlessly in the doorway. The genderless familiar faced Oscar and bowed.

"This is the first time we have met. My name is Litola. Your companion is under a spell and sleeping soundly, so I covered him with a blanket."

"Oh, thank you."

Lazar was safe, and so far, Oscar hadn't detected that Tinasha harbored any hostility. It was like they were just having a tea party. Oscar lifted the cup in front of him, and a comforting scent tickled his nose. Everything about this was all very far removed from the impression he'd gotten from the plausible-sounding tales whispered about this tower on the street.

"What happened to the people who came here and never went home? Did they end up in some mass grave?"

Tinasha openly scowled. "Don't just decide that people are sitting in holes. I don't want dead bodies in the tower. I arrange things in such a way that they don't die."

"If one of those stone statues landed a blow on them, they'd die."

"The moment a fatal wound occurs, they are returned to the first floor. After that, I adjust the memories of disqualified challengers and teleport them somewhere on the mainland. Most of my visitors are those seeking to test their skills or covetous of fame. I assumed they were ready to pay a price of that order, at the very least."

Tinasha's smile turned sweet and wholesome. As she sipped her tea, she exuded the dignity of the master of this tower. The elegance of her actions, coupled with her beauty, would have made it difficult not to mistake her for a member of the royal family. That is, if it hadn't been for the unusual surroundings.

As Oscar's eyes widened a little, Litola cut in. "However, in the case of those who came for things like wanting their deathly ill child healed, my master granted those requests even if the challengers failed."

"Don't speak out of turn." Tinasha looked embarrassed and averted her gaze from Oscar. The intimidating air she'd so confidently held a moment ago vanished, and now she looked even younger than she appeared.

Oscar's impression of the witch was constantly changing, a fact he found amusing. "It's hard to get a handle on you."

"It's fine if you don't." The sulky reply was adorable.

"Do you not go into town? I've heard the other witches appear before people more often than you do."

"Only if there's something I have to go out and get myself... I don't really want to thoughtlessly interfere in humans' lives, though. My power is not something that should be wielded on a whim."

"I see. If only the Witch of Silence could take a page out of your book."

Tinasha cocked her head at Oscar suddenly dropping another witch's name. "Does that have something to do with the reason you came here?" she asked.

"...Which is why I'd like you to lift the curse."

In response to her question, Oscar had explained the events of that night fifteen years ago.

Frowning, Tinasha had listened with her arms crossed. When he finished speaking, she let out a deep sigh. "Why did she give you a curse like that?"

"My dad doesn't want to talk about it, so I haven't asked. Apparently, it has something to do with my mom, who died before it happened."

"...I see." For a moment, Tinasha's eyes narrowed as if she had realized something, but before Oscar could puzzle over it, her expression returned to normal. She uncrossed her arms and lightly tapped her forehead with her index finger.

"I must inform you ahead of time that a 'curse' may not always be lifted."

"What do you mean?"

"What we call magic is organized under common rules and operates based on that, but a curse follows no rules. Language...is not just words; it also encompasses all nonverbal communication methods, like body language. But the words we choose carry the meaning we define for them, and pouring magic into that makes it a curse. Of course, this is different depending on the person who's cursed...so in extreme cases, if a way to break the curse is not defined at the time the words are spoken, even the caster cannot undo it."

"...So it can't be broken?"

"It can't, but on the other hand, curses aren't things of exceptional power. They block or bend the flow of natural energy, depending on the will of the individual. They don't have the power to kill someone directly. At most, they work in indirect ways...but they aren't unavoidable."

Feeling dubious about such an explanation, Oscar asked another question. "But isn't this curse pretty strong?"

"Yes, yours exceeds those normal limits. That's because what's been placed on you is not actually a curse but something more akin to a blessing or protection."

"What?"

Oscar was dumbfounded, and Tinasha got up from her seat. Leaning her slender body over the table, she reached out to him with a pure-white hand. Her skin was so pale, it made one think of freshly fallen snow. One look at the witch's fingers as they came closer, and Oscar couldn't move.

Her soft palm didn't touch him, though; instead, she grazed her fingers along his face without touching it. Quite suddenly, a red sigil emerged from the spot where Tinasha had nearly stroked him.

"What's that?"

"I've visualized the blessing placed on you. This is just one part of it, though." Tinasha pulled her hand back, and the sigil vanished as quickly as it had appeared. She sat back down.

"Blessings and curses are basically cast the same way, but the direction of power is different. You take the energy that's already here and boost it. In your case, you've had something fairly strong placed on you, owing to how much power the caster had. What's been cast on you takes advantage of that and will likely wrap any child you conceive in tremendous energy while in the womb, protecting it. A normal mother's body could not withstand such a thing."

Oscar was uncharacteristically taken aback by such an extremely novel explanation and sat there in shock. Across from him, the witch looked on him with pity.

"Um, so what you're saying is that, after all that, you can't undo it...?" Oscar asked.

"If I could analyze what's been cast on you, I could use magic to reduce the effects, but the enchantment has been a part of you for close to twenty years now... That's the Witch of Silence for you." As if squinting at something hard to see, Tinasha narrowed her eyes and focused her gaze on Oscar's chest. "I do feel so sorry for you, but..."

"Hey..."

An awkward silence fell. The heavy mood felt like it would last forever, but Tinasha broke it by jumping up and lightly clapping her hands together.

"Since you've come all the way here, I'll at least do what I can to help."

As she spoke, she brought out a shallow bowl of water from the depths of the room and set it on the table. Magical designs were carved the inside, and what little water it held sparkled in the light of the setting sun.

"Do you have something you can try?" Oscar asked.

"There's a simple countermeasure."

Sitting back down, the witch held her right hand over the scrying bowl. Ripples appeared on the surface of the water, though there had not been any wind.

"Because the issue lies in the fact that the mother won't be able to withstand the protective power the baby carries, you must choose a strong woman who can."

"...That *is* simple. Does a woman like that exist?"

"There are sure to be one or two somewhere on the mainland...most likely. I'm going to search with an emphasis on magical power and magical resistance, so ignore anything else."

The image of a faraway forest appeared on the surface of the water. Oscar clenched his forehead so tightly he was going to give himself a headache.

"What if it's someone's wife or an old woman or a child?"

"If she's married, she's off-limits, and we can't do anything about that. We can, however, fix old age with magic... If she's a child, then that's great; you can raise her to be just what you like! Age gaps of twenty years are normal in a royal family, after all," Tinasha replied brightly with a smile. "I haven't really started searching yet, though, so please be optimistic."

"Right..." Feeling like he really was going to get a migraine, Oscar held his head in both hands.

Regardless of the fair amount of hope he'd had in taking on the tower, Oscar's worst fears had been confirmed by the witch, and now this was happening. What's more, it seemed the one who'd placed the "curse" in the first place couldn't even remove it. Oscar was really in a fix. Were there truly no other options? Stewing over how he now had to be "optimistic," something suddenly occurred to him.

"Tinasha."

"Whoa! What?"

"Did that startle you?"

As if in response to her surprise, some water splashed onto the table even though she hadn't touched it. Tinasha wiped off her wet right hand.

"Because hardly anyone calls me by my name...," she answered.

"But you're the one who told it to me."

"I'm sorry." Tinasha took a cloth from Litola and mopped the water off the table. Folding the cloth, she again asked, "So what is it?"

"Ah, uh, what about you?"

Tinasha didn't seem to understand the question and was pointing at herself with a puzzled expression.

In response, Oscar restated his query more clearly, "Could you withstand the Witch of Silence's magic?"

"Easily, but... Wait..."

Tinasha finally understood, and her face visibly paled.

"Well then, that's sorted." Oscar resettled himself in his chair and drained the last of his tea. Tinasha jumped half out of her seat, face white as a ghost.

"Hey, hold on just a minute..."

"You're a sure thing compared to a woman who might not even exist. My wish as champion is for you to descend from this tower and be my wife." Oscar made the request with complete confidence, as though it were his right.

Tinasha froze, but soon enough, her small hands slapped down on the table. "I—I cannot do something like that!"

"You said you'd do what you could, didn't you?" Oscar drawled.

"There are limits! I can't!"

Amused, Oscar watched her yell herself blue in the face. "Are you actually married?"

"I have never been married."

"Are you seeing someone?"

"I never have."

"You said there were ways to fix old age."

"Yes, I'm old, but it's irritating to have you call me old! And that's not the point!" Tinasha was leaning over the table, her smile twitching. Cold sweat started to dot her forehead. "It's not wise to introduce a witch into the royal family's lineage. The royal council would all vomit blood over the idea."

"I'd kinda like to see that..." Oscar lazily dodged her desperate attempts at resistance, and the witch collapsed into her chair, exhausted.

"You're like Reg in a lot of ways, but you're also not like him at all... You've got some personality."

"Guess I'm bad-natured," Oscar replied calmly, earning a glare from Tinasha.

The witch shook her head and took some deep breaths. "In any case, the answer is no. If I let wishes like that slide, I'd be your great-grandmother."

Though imperceptibly, Oscar was surprised to hear those words but, at the same time, found them plausible. His great-grandfather, the one Tinasha had said was too pure, had probably fallen in love with this witch seventy years ago. Apparently, Tinasha hadn't accepted his proposal. Such circumstances differed greatly from the fairy tale about his great-grandfather that was told in Farsas. It interested Oscar somewhat. He wanted to ask for details, but since they'd only just met, that would've likely been impolite. Oscar swallowed his childish questions.

"My great-granddad might have backed down, but I'm not him, and that really has nothing to do with me anyway."

"What are you talking about? It wasn't okay then, and it's not okay now! That's a no all across the board!"

"Seventy years have passed, so how can you say no with such certainty? Be a little more flexible."

"There are limits to flexibility!"

While Tinasha was making a huge fuss, Litola reached out from beside her to take away the empty cups sitting on the table.

By the time the familiar returned with a fresh pot of tea, Oscar and Tinasha were still arguing back and forth.

Oscar was calm but completely unwilling to back down, and the witch appeared quite mentally worn out.

Finally hitting her limit, Tinasha sighed. "Ugh, if you're going to be this unreasonable, I'm going to alter your memory and send you back to your castle!"

"I don't think what you just said speaks well of your character."

"That's my line!" Tinasha stood up, and with a smile, she extended her right hand toward Oscar. Something was gathering in her palm. The mood of the room changed in an instant.

"Hey, hey, I'm gonna fight back." Oscar had been acting nonchalant but finally got to his feet and drew his sword. When Tinasha saw the hilt of the weapon, she made an obvious face.

"Why are you walking around with something like that? It's a national treasure."

"Things like this were made to be used."

The well-polished, double-edged blade drew Tinasha's eye and sparkled like a mirror. Antique decorations ornamented the handle of the weapon. The royal sword Akashia, passed down through the ages in Farsas, was the only sword in the world that had full magical resistance.

There was a legend that, a long time ago, nonhuman creatures had pulled the sword from a lake and gifted it, but the story had never been confirmed. The weapon had been around since Farsas was founded and, until recently, had hardly ever been used in combat. It was only worn by the king on formal occasions. Oscar treated the weapon like one of his personal belongings. It was clearly something any mage would regard as their natural enemy, and Tinasha, as a witch, was no exception.

Looking sour, she hesitated awhile longer before dispelling the magic she'd started to summon.

"Urgh. Let's talk this out a bit more."

"I couldn't agree more. Calm down."

As they both took their seats again, Litola refilled their teacups. Tinasha used her hands to brush back bits of her hair that were starting to come undone.

"You are oddly stubborn. You really should give up."

"I could say the same about you..." Looking pensive, Oscar brought his cup to his lips. Just then, he remembered something. "That's right. I heard that seventy years ago you spent some time living at Farsas Castle."

"For about half a year, yes. I taught magic and grew flowers. It was fairly interesting."

Oscar felt like he could believe that, though he had a hard time imagining it, and tilted his head in contemplation. "Was that my great-granddad's wish?"

"No," Tinasha answered, smiling at him, her eyes crinkling. Based on how clipped her reply was, it was obvious she had no intention of telling Oscar what Regius's actual wish had been.

Oscar lifted an eyebrow a little at that, but he saw the meaning of her reply and didn't press further. Instead, he proposed a different wish of his own. "How about this: Leave here for a year and live with me in Farsas. That's my request as champion. Could you accept that?"

Tinasha looked taken aback by the unexpected demand. When she considered their extended back-and-forth, however, she thought it a considerable compromise. One year wasn't very long for a witch like Tinasha. In the blink of an eye, she flashed back to her fond memories of the sights of Farsas. The witch took a deep breath, and as she exhaled, she made her decision.

"Fine, then. I'll come down from this tower as your protector. For one year, starting today, you and I have a contract."

She lifted her arm, and one white finger stretched out toward Oscar's forehead. A faint white light emanated from her fingertip before passing through the air and disappearing into his forehead. Oscar pressed his fingers to where the light had touched him but didn't notice anything strange.

"What did you do?"

"It's a mark. To start with."

Tinasha rose with a smile, stretching both arms high above her to loosen her stiff body.

"If I'm leaving the tower, we'll have to close off the entrance. Litola, take care of it."

"Understood."

Litola left the room, and Oscar stood up as well.

Dusk had already fallen, and the last streaks of light colored the valley in the distance. Oscar came to stand next to Tinasha. He was a lot taller and looked down at her with an evil smile.

"If you change your mind partway through and decide to stay in Farsas permanently, that's fine with me."

"I won't."

And so, the Witch of the Azure Moon became the protector of the crown prince of Farsas and appeared among the people for the first time in close to seventy years. Little did she know that a story that would strum the strings of her own fate was just beginning.

※

"Lazar! Wake up!"

The young man jerked awake reflexively at the sound of his lord's voice and found himself in the shade of the same tree the horses were hitched to just outside the tower. Lazar took in his surroundings before looking up at Oscar, who was right behind him.

"Huh? Your Highness...? Wasn't I just...climbing the tower...? It's already dark?"

"Enough. We're going home. Get up."

Puzzling over the fogginess in his mind, Lazar got to his feet. He undid the horses' ties. "You're ready to return?"

"Yeah, my business is finished."

Lazar thought that was strange but led his horse out anyway. As he did, he noticed for the first time that someone was standing in his lord's shadow. When the young, beautiful girl noticed Lazar's eyes on her, she smiled like a flower blooming. Her black hair and white skin seemed to be traits of some unknown country, and her powerful dark eyes completely sucked him in.

"Your Highness, who is…?"

"She's the witch's apprentice, and she's leaving the tower to live in Farsas for a while."

"My name is Tinasha."

The girl bowed politely, so Lazar hurried to lower his own head in kind. Although Oscar had said she was leaving the tower, she wasn't carrying a single bag. Lazar found that odd and approached his lord to whisper in his ear. "If this is the witch's apprentice, does that mean you met the witch?"

"Yeah, I did."

"She didn't eat you up?"

"Do you want me to hit you…?"

Oscar swung up into the saddle and offered Tinasha a hand. Lazar still looked worried. Oscar started to say something to his attendant before grimacing a little. "It was an…interesting experience. In a lot of ways."

Looking bitter for some reason, Oscar pulled Tinasha up into the saddle. With her petite stature, she settled easily in front of him before lowering her long eyelashes.

Perhaps because of her hair and eyes, Tinasha's beauty called to mind a clear night. She looked entirely at home in her current position—like she'd been by Oscar's side forever. Lazar was entirely captivated by the pretty picture the two painted. Oscar frowned at his childhood friend.

"What's up? Didn't you want to go home?"

"Oh, y-yes… Sorry."

Lazar rushed to mount his own horse. The sun had set, and night was fast encroaching. Tinasha gave a wave of her hand, and a small light emerged just past the horse's muzzle.

Oscar voiced his admiration for the orb illuminating their way. "Magic, huh? That's convenient."

"I can do this anytime. Feel free to ask whenever you want to burn something."

"No need. All you have to do is stay near me," Oscar replied smoothly, and Tinasha looked up at him in dismay. She soon recovered, closing her eyes and smiling.

As Lazar watched the two of them, he suddenly got the faintest hint of a premonition—one that told him that, from here on out, things were going to get very muddied.

"Let's go, Lazar."

The horse carrying Oscar and the girl broke into a gallop. Lazar took up his own reins and cast a final glance back at the tower.

In the dim light, he could see that the door that had once been there had disappeared. In its place was the same smooth, azure surface that made up the rest of the structure.

▉ 2. Countless Mentions of the Past

At the moment, the mainland was home to four powerful countries, known as the Four Great Nations.

As one of these four, Farsas was the large region in the center.

It had been founded during the mainland's Dark Age and was widely perceived as a military power, both due to its symbol of the royal sword Akashia and the royal family's steady seven-hundred-year reign.

Even during peacetime, those who served the castle carried out meticulous drills and trained nearly every day.

"…How diligent they are. It hasn't changed at all."

Tinasha surveyed the soldiers' field from the walkway along the outer walls of the castle.

In a huge open clearing on the grounds, the soldiers had been performing mock battles, likely part of their regular drills. As two fought one-on-one, the others clustered to the side to observe.

Leaning on the stone wall, Tinasha watched them. Though easily mistaken for just a pretty girl, she was actually the witch extolled as the most powerful in all the mainland. Seventy years ago, this was a fact that everyone had known, but this time when she entered the castle, she'd kept her true identity hidden.

No matter what Tinasha herself was like, witches were generally beings to avoid. There was even a small country that incurred the wrath of one around three centuries earlier and had been destroyed overnight. It was understandable that the general populace would fear them.

It was Tinasha who proposed concealing who she really was. Oscar had approved, and so her assumed identity was that of an apprentice mage.

The white fingers she ran through her hair were adorned with numerous power-sealing rings so that other mages wouldn't pick up on her magic. She was also wearing power-sealing earrings that bore magical designs.

"Ngh…" A sudden, strong gust of wind blew a cloud of sand into Tinasha's eyes. She rubbed them as they watered, when someone addressed her from behind.

"So this is where you were."

Tinasha turned around to find Lazar there, holding a book. She smiled and greeted him.

"Hello. I was just taking a walk around the castle."

"Yes, you can see the training grounds from here."

Lazar came to stand next to her and looked down at the training drill. Tinasha pointed to one of the soldiers who was fighting.

"That one has been winning every match and must be quite strong."

"That's General Als. He's young, but he's the most talented of the generals. Just last month, he led a small platoon and wiped out a gang of weapon bandits."

Just as Lazar said, the red-haired swordsman did look to be the same age as Oscar. Als flipped up his right hand, and the sword of a soldier he'd been fighting flew into the air. His slender opponent clutched her wrist in pain and appeared to be saying something.

"That one lost, but she also seems to be pretty good… Is she a regular soldier?"

"Her name is Meredina. She fights under General Als, though I think she'll be commanding her own unit soon."

"Wow."

Tinasha narrowed her eyes to get a better look at the female soldier. At such a distance, however, all she could see was the woman's bright blond hair.

Farsas had no restrictions on gender when it came to occupations. People could do just about any job as long as they had the talent and the desire. That was why Tinasha wasn't too surprised to hear Meredina was a woman, although such a talented female soldier was rare.

"She can be a little rough around the edges, but she's a kind person," Lazar added, smiling at her. He seemed unaware that he himself was actually the kindest person around. Tinasha broke into a grin, too.

"Is it fun to watch the mock battles? I would think mages would have little interest in this sort of thing," remarked Lazar.

"In the past, I used to do swordplay. I had some free time…"

When Lazar heard that, his eyes widened in surprise, and he glanced at her petite frame. "Are you actually quite strong…?"

"No, I'm not, which is why I couldn't get very good. Let's see… I could probably beat that woman from earlier. But that general, hmm…probably not. I think I'd lose."

It was hard for Lazar to tell from Tinasha's lighthearted tone if she was being serious or making a jest. In the end, he didn't press the matter any further.

Back on the training grounds, Als was sparring with a different soldier. His opponent was backing away in fright, and there were what sounded like jeers coming from the surrounding troops. Lazar adjusted his grip on the book in his arms.

"His Highness is stronger than General Als."

"He is?" Tinasha sounded astonished, and Lazar turned to look back at her.

"Why are you so surprised? There's no one stronger than him in the whole country. I mean, at the tower the other day, he… Hmm?"

Lazar cocked his head in confusion. He knew something had happened at the witch's tower, but when he tried to recall what it was, he found he possessed absolutely no concrete memory of it. On the other hand, Tinasha's face was frozen, and she was at a loss for how to react.

"Stronger than that general…? Hmm… Really?" she wondered aloud.

"Really. He's got natural talent, of course, but despite his appearance, he actually works very hard. He's always been eager to study any subject, and he absorbs things quickly."

"Wow…"

"Why do you keep reacting like that?"

"No—no reason…" Tinasha looked displeased, frowning with her arms crossed. "This has made me want to take up a sword for the first time in a while."

"Um…why?" asked Lazar.

Tinasha didn't reply, merely nodded to herself. Such an inexplicable reaction made some doubts start to gnaw at Lazar, but he had to be off for the library.

Left alone at the castle walls, Tinasha murmured to herself, "As expected of a tower champion. I'll have to be sure not to let my guard down around him."

Even so, if push came to shove, she could force him to surrender. She was a witch, after all.

Tinasha thought on the matter for a while until she remembered the royal sword, made a face, and sighed.

Farsas was warm year-round, but it did have a summer that lasted two months a year, where the days were hotter than the rest. It also had a very mild winter. Tinasha had arrived right at the start of summer, and the castle city awaited the fast-approaching Festival of Aetea, a celebration of the mainland's chief god.

One night, Oscar was walking along a corridor while reading a thick stack of reports when he noticed a black-haired girl approaching from the opposite end of the hall.

"Well, if it isn't Tinasha."

"I haven't seen you in a while," she said.

The witch had run up to Oscar when he'd called to her. She was as petite as ever, and he patted her head as if she were a young child.

"It's been about a week. How's the castle? No one's been mean to you, have they?"

"I'm not a child. Everyone's been quite kind, although I have gotten some stares."

"Because we didn't hide the fact that you came from the tower. If you run into any problems, let me know."

"I'm fine."

Tinasha didn't appear to be heading anyplace in particular and fell into step with Oscar. "Is that your work?"

"Yeah, some diplomatic stuff and the arrangement of security for the festival. It's not done yet, and I'm having some trouble." Flipping the edges of the huge stack of papers, Oscar grimaced. At his side, Tinasha's eyes widened.

"You do that, too? I thought you just lounged around the court all day."

"You really do say some rude things without batting an eye, don't you? ...Last month, my uncle, the prime minister, died. We're temporarily short-staffed, and it's work I'll have to do eventually, so I don't mind."

"I'm surprised you're so diligent!"

"Listen here..."

As they bantered back and forth, they reached the door to Oscar's room. He'd been so busy, he'd ignored the witch for an entire week. "Do you have some time?" Oscar asked. "I want to hear your report on what you've experienced this week."

"When you put it that way, you make it sound like I'm your spy... I haven't found any suspicious people in the castle."

"I see... I just wanted to hear about your daily life."

The two weren't always on the same wavelength when they talked, a fact that had been true since the moment they'd met. When the pair entered the room, Tinasha rephrased her answers.

"I'm just doing normal royal-mage work. There are a lot of different jobs posted in the mage area. I just pick the ones I like and complete them. I can also freely attend lectures and do research, so it's pretty fun."

"It *is* the mages' job to do research, after all," Oscar added.

For that reason, the royal mages had been furnished with a rather lavish budget. In exchange, they gathered up jobs both inside and outside the castle, divided them up, and took care of them. Creating magic potions, medicine, and magic tools were part of their responsibilities.

Within the spacious room, Tinasha floated up into the air lightly and hugged her knees.

"With the festival coming up, I've been assigned a task on that day. I'll be in charge of lighting."

"Lighting? What will you do?" Oscar asked, looking through documents on festival security. Soldiers were to take turns doing security rotations during the celebration, and the general had drafted a report summarizing their shifts and positions for the prime minister to approve. With no prime minister at the moment, Oscar was in charge of the final approval.

Tinasha created a white light in her hands, showing it to Oscar. "I'll make light sources like this one using magic and place them in the castle moat, like underwater lights. Won't it look pretty once it's done?"

"Ah, so that's how it's done. I always thought they buried lamps or something."

"It's easier to do it with magic."

Once Tinasha had floated high enough to reach the ceiling, she flipped over so she was hanging upside down.

Oscar looked up at her, exasperated. "You really are a witch."

"You're saying that now?"

He'd never seen a mage levitate without using an incantation. Floating magic was fairly difficult to begin with. What's more, Tinasha was wearing magic-sealing ornaments all over her body. Oscar started to worry if Tinasha would be able to keep up her facade.

The witch snapped her fingers, and the candlestick on the far wall lit up.

"However, to maintain the light, it must not fall outside the range of the caster's power. Normal mages can only light the lamps of one or two shops at most."

"What about you? Can you maintain it no matter how far away you go?"

"Mmm, I can keep it up from anywhere in the city, even with the sealing accessories. I'm planning to take in everything the festival has to offer!"

Oscar glanced at Tinasha's happy, smiling face and very much felt like messing with her. "All right, I'll go talk to the chief mage and give you some more annoying work to do."

"Stop it! I'll cry!"

Oscar pretended he was going to leave the room, and Tinasha desperately pulled on his jacket to keep him from doing so.

"They don't really trust newcomers anyway. That's why they didn't give me a more important job," Tinasha explained.

"Well, I guess that's true. I was only kidding anyway." Oscar grinned.

Tinasha puffed out her cheeks at him, but he ignored it and sat down to get back to checking over his many documents. "You seem pretty excited about it. Have you not been to a festival before?"

"It's my first. The last time, I arrived just after the festival. I really regretted it, so I still remember it clearly."

"You could've just come back another time after you'd left."

"I promised not to return to Farsas until after Reg died."

Tinasha floated up toward the ceiling again. The hem of her white robe filled with air and fluttered out. Oscar looked up from his papers and caught sight of her.

"I wasn't in any mood to ask about his death, either, so after that, I forgot all about the festival." She smiled just like a young woman, but there was a curious lack of emotion in her expression. As she tumbled in midair, she looked like some beautiful fish that had freed itself from everything but had been left behind.

Oscar was about to call her name without thinking when Tinasha suddenly clapped a hand on his shoulder.

"That's right. I had something to discuss with you. It just wasn't important, so I forgot."

"Something to discuss? How could you forget about it?" Oscar asked.

"It's about your safety."

"My safety isn't important?!"

"You're pretty strong already...," Tinasha retorted, looking thoroughly annoyed. "Anyway, we've made a contract, so I'm going to honor it. On the day of the festival, though, I'm going to be busy wandering around, so let me cast some more defensive magic on you."

"You're asking if you can slack off?"

Oscar wasn't sure if this offer had been motivated by anything, but it didn't seem to be. It wasn't like Oscar had climbed the witch's tower in pursuit of protection anyway. He tidied up his papers and set them on the table before looking up at her.

"All right, what should I do?"

"The spell is a little complicated, so I've already assembled it."

With a happy glance, Tinasha flew down to land in front of Oscar. Then, she interlaced all ten fingers and pressed her palms together before bringing them in front of his eyes. Instantaneously, five rings made of thin red lines floated into the air between Tinasha's hands and Oscar. They were all intricately intertwined, impossible to unravel, and after a moment, they morphed into a huge magical sigil.

Oscar barely managed to suppress a cry of wonder at the sight. The sound of the witch's chanting filled the room.

"*May this last the length of the contract. Let three times and two worlds be specified…*"

Mages did not normally require incantations for simple magic.

If floating was representative of what was normal for Tinasha, all she had to do was concentrate or wave her hands to do magic that ordinarily required an incantation. This was the first time Oscar had heard her chanting a spell. Such a long recitation meant that the witch was about to cast something extremely powerful.

"*Melt away the words that should be destroyed at the source, and the rain that was formed will disperse their meaning… All circles come back as circles… Follow my rules for all that may appear.*"

When her chant ended, the slowly rotating, tortuously woven sigil converged and melded into Oscar's body. Surprised, he turned his hands over to look at both sides but could see no traces of the crimson mark.

"That's amazing."

"Mm, that should be good. It has a semipermanent effect," Tinasha explained. She took a moment to even out her tense breathing. "That magic will nullify just about all incoming attacks, regardless of physics. It can't protect you from things like poison and mind tricks, though. Be careful. It'll fade away if I die, too. On the flip side, it can't be undone by anyone else as long as I'm alive."

"This sounds almost like cheating."

Undoubtedly, there were quite a few eager people who would pay any price to receive such incredible protection.

But they would most likely go their whole lives without having such a spell cast on them. Oscar was suddenly reminded how powerful an ally he possessed.

But Tinasha merely smiled in the face of his astonishment. She walked over to the wall and sank into a sofa. "You made a contract with a witch. This much should be expected."

"Expected, huh? …I just wanted you to marry me," Oscar objected.

"And didn't I reject you?!" snapped the witch.

"Even if I don't die, I still need an heir—or we're all in trouble."

The argument was sound, and Tinasha looked discouraged. She wouldn't meet Oscar's eyes; she must have understood that, too. With a little sigh, she crossed her slender legs.

"When you say you need an heir or you're all in trouble… Aren't there others of royal blood? I thought you had lots of relatives."

"I do, but they don't have any children. When I was four or five, there was a strange rash of kidnappings. In the end, dozens were lost. Several of my cousins were among those who disappeared. I currently have no younger relatives of royal blood."

Oscar took up a water pitcher and poured its contents into a cup. He watched the witch as he took a sip. She looked astonished. Though she'd only just sat down, she leaped to her feet and bounded over to him.

"Did they find out the culprit behind those disappearances?"

"No, it's still a mystery."

"Did the Witch of Silence come before or after that?"

"After my mom got sick and died, so…yeah, it was after." Oscar had to think for a moment, reconciling private records with his own memories from childhood.

Just then, a splitting pain lanced through his head.

Image of a witch
against the moon
A curse
A voice
Sharp nails
Ripped apart
Covered in blood

Shapeless images and wordless fragments flashed through his mind. All too soon, though, they disappeared as if they'd never been there. Oscar shook his head, brushing off the foreign sensation that had pierced his brain like thorns.

"What happened?"

"Nothing… I'm fine."

"You must be tired. You look like you haven't slept in a while." With concern tinging her words, Tinasha reached out to place a hand on Oscar's cheek. Her cool touch was comforting, and he could feel the tension melting from his shoulders.

Oscar grabbed Tinasha's tiny hand and grinned. "I slept for three hours."

"I don't think that counts." She gave Oscar a horrified look and grabbed his arms to force him to his feet. Tinasha started dragging him toward the bedroom. Ordinarily, her slender arms and light body shouldn't have been able to budge the much taller Oscar, but she must have used magic because she effortlessly moved him along. Ultimately, he ended up sitting on the bed.

"Hey, I still have to organize my papers." Oscar looked up at her from his spot on the bed, clearly discomfited. Tinasha had to suppress a fit of laughter.

"If you get some sleep, you'll find you can finish much faster."

"I don't think so…"

"See, aren't you sleepy?" She tapped his forehead.

Just as he registered that she'd done something to him, Oscar fell into a deep sleep.

※

"Children disappearing and a curse to end the bloodline…? What in the world happened, I wonder."

Tinasha fell into deep thought again after forcing the man with whom she'd signed a contract to sleep. To her, fifteen years ago was still rather recent in her memory. Perhaps because she'd been holed up in her tower, however, she had no knowledge of these events. Thanks to the kidnappings and the actions of the Witch of Silence, the Farsas royal family was in danger of extinction.

Were it any other royal family, they would've simply adopted a child from distant kin as their new heir. Unfortunately, that option was not available to the kingdom of Farsas. The royal sword, the symbol of the country, was inherited only through direct lineage.

"This is a pretty thorny situation..."

What was the Witch of Silence thinking, bestowing such a curse on this family? Tinasha was curious but knew that the other witch wasn't someone who would readily tell her if asked. If Tinasha really wanted to know, she would need to be prepared to either lose her own life or kill the other witch—both of which were beyond the bounds of this contract.

Which was why, instead of digging up the past, Tinasha was going to clean up the current problem instead. She was confident her power was capable of accomplishing that much.

She pulled out the stack of documents Oscar had left and quickly perused them. Here and there, she could find corrections the young prince appeared to have written in by hand, and she grinned.

"He does seem to be quite capable. I'd expect nothing less of a hard worker."

In Tinasha's long life, she'd seen many decision-makers, but Oscar held the potential to become a wiser ruler than them all. That said, as long as he was cursed, his future was up to Tinasha, his protector. Taking advantage of the fact that he was in an ensorcelled sleep, Tinasha petted his head as she leafed through the documents. Once she'd put them in order, she disappeared from the room without a sound.

When Oscar awoke, the witch had already left.

Looking at the clock, he saw that only an hour had passed. Yet he must have slept deeply, because for some strange reason, he felt refreshed in body and mind. He sat up in bed and shook his head lightly.

Glancing over at the side table, he saw that his paperwork was lying there in a stack.

Reaching over to check the documents, he noticed a new sheet had been added to the top. In what was clearly Tinasha's handwriting, the page neatly summarized the parts Oscar should review as well as other salient points.

"I really can't get a handle on her," he murmured.

Even though she lived like a recluse, she apparently had a good acumen for clerical work. Snorting a little as he glanced through the papers, Oscar took up the stack and left the room.

※

Everyone in the castle went about their preparatory duties, and before anyone knew it, the big day had arrived.

The castle city was packed with people first thing in the morning, and strains of the performers' music floated among the crowds.

The townscape was elegant, with rows of stone buildings. Light refracted through the colored glass inlaid on hanging signs, glittering like a rainbow. There were many foreign guests from outside Farsas milling around the historic streets, heightening the hustle and bustle of the already prosperous Farsas castle city.

This was the 187th Festival of Aetea held in the 526-year history of Farsas.

"This is so fun," Tinasha said to herself, holding up a little porcelain cat in front of her eyes.

With the festival having finally arrived, she'd been out exploring the city by herself since morning. Wandering the streets, Tinasha happily took in the bookshops and traveling minstrels. It had been some several dozen years since she'd been in such a huge crowd of people like this. Having received the porcelain cat as a freebie, she placed it in her waist pouch.

Tinasha would have liked to keep playing to her heart's content, but as long as she served the court, that meant she had work to do. She took note of the setting sun and returned to the castle moat to assume her post.

Ramparts and a moat encircled the magnificent alabaster castle. Festival stalls lined the road in front of the moat, and tons of people were strolling about. Slipping out from the crowd, Tinasha stood right before the moat and lifted a hand.

"Let there be light."

The incantation was quick, a mere handful of words. A white ball of light rose from the witch's hand and dived into the water. Now submerged, the luminous orb split into five spheres and spread out to evenly spaced positions in the moat. People passing by let out cries of joy at the pale, flickering light rising from the waters.

The mages stationed in other locations must have done their lighting at almost the same time, too, because the ramparts suddenly seemed cast in a bluish glow. When Tinasha glanced at the station next to hers, a mage in a robe noticed her and approached with a wave.

"How'd it go? You're new, right? It looks like you did a good job, though."

"It's all due to the mages' tutelage. Thank you, um…?"

"I'm Temys. Nice to meet you." The man held out his right hand. His arm was covered in black markings—magical sigils. On the inside, Tinasha was surprised at the rarity of the designs. On the surface, however, she smiled and shook his hand.

"I'm Tinasha. It's nice to meet you."

"I'll be around here for a while, so let me know if you need anything," Temys said.

"I will," she answered.

Temys gave a friendly wave and wandered off. Though the lighting was done, Tinasha would have to keep them going late into the night. As she watched the seemingly endless supply of people go by and wondered what to do with her time, an unknown man's voice called out to her from behind.

"Best not to leave. You'll get drawn into something annoying."

"What?" She whirled around, but all she could see were the crowds of revelers. Tinasha had no idea who had spoken or if, indeed, they'd even been speaking to her. Then she saw a young man in a traveling cloak backing away, trying to blend into the masses. He was accompanied by a silver-haired girl. No sooner had Tinasha noticed them than they vanished into the throng of festival goers.

"…A mage?" She'd only seen him for a moment, but he had appeared to be suppressing his own magic. Tinasha brought a sealing ring–clad finger to her chin. For an instant, she considered going to question him but soon thought better of the idea.

"Well, it is Farsas."

It was a festival day in the number one country in the entire land. There were bound to be some oddballs about. Tinasha herself, as a witch, was the oddest of them all. She pulled herself together and left her post, heading over to inspect a stall emanating a lovely, sweet smell.

During a festival that attracted attendees from inside the country and out, security was considered the most important consideration.

Whether acting as guards for important guests and locations or directing the flow of traffic in the streets, the security team had to possess split-second decision-making and vigilance. Which was exactly why Oscar had appointed only those who had proven their worth in battle.

Amid the excited hustle and bustle, a man wearing a sword complained, "Festivals sure must be nice. I'd love to have a drink."

"We're on the clock."

The tall man dawdling through the congested streets and the woman with perfect posture next to him could not have appeared more dissimilar. Both, however, had the same smooth gracefulness as they made their way through the crowds.

The emblem on the tall man's waist and on the well-postured woman's chest denoted affiliation with the castle. It was the proof that they both had higher status than a commander. The red-haired, affable, and baby-faced young General Als turned to the woman, his childhood friend, and asked, "Actually, where's His Highness?"

"In the castle. Working." Meredina, the female officer with the authority to command a platoon, answered without pausing to look at Als. The woman's face bore gentle and beautiful features. Only her blond hair, cut cleanly to her shoulders, gave her the appearance of a soldier.

"This year, we don't have any official guests from other countries, so we don't have too many guards assigned to specific people. We just have to do a good job of patrolling... Do you understand?" Meredina asked.

Als, who had been eyeing some salt-grilled pork strips, shrugged when he heard that. He and Meredina had grown up in town together, but perhaps because of their differences in personality, she was still always scolding him.

Although, if mischief within the castle was ranked, Oscar was much more of a troublemaker than Als. The crown prince loved to go off on his own, and he regularly sneaked out of the palace. Though he was supposed to be inside the castle during the festivities, whether he'd actually stay there was an entirely different matter.

"Hey, is anyone with His Highness?" Als asked.

"He said he didn't need any guards. I wish he'd trust us a bit more, but…" Meredina trailed off.

"I think he needs a babysitter more than a guard… But yeah, he probably doesn't need anyone protecting him. He's strong." Als shrugged before he realized something, and then he clapped his hands together. "Oh, did you want to be his guard, Meredina?"

"No, I didn't say that." Meredina pouted the same way she had since childhood. Als knew she had feelings for their commander, the crown prince.

The stars were visible in the bright night sky while the pair walked along the main avenue and approached the castle moat.

A startling scream cleaved through the droning buzz of the festival goers. Als and Meredina took off running toward the sound of a woman's high-pitched cry. She had both hands planted on the bank of the moat as she stared at the water.

"My son… My son has…"

"Did he fall in?!"

She looked up at Als with a face that seemed drained of blood and just nodded in shock.

"Als!"

Meredina grabbed his collar. He shrugged off his jacket and unbuckled his sword belt before diving right into the moat. Though illuminated for the festival, the water still proved to be dark and murky. Squinting, Als swam to the bottom.

The moat was about four men deep. The lack of a current made it easier to swim, but it also made the water cloudy. Als's vision was obscured by illuminated clumps of mud, and as he looked around, he began to panic. Just when he thought he should return to the surface for a breath…

A hazy, glowing ball of light suddenly grew in size.

It expanded rapidly, eating up the dark until the field of vision beneath the waters of the moat looked no different than on dry land in daytime.

Als boggled over what had just happened, but he kept searching and finally spotted a boy of about two years old floating some ways away. He grabbed the child's unconscious body and kicked his way back up to the surface. When he finally breached and took a deep breath, cheers erupted all around him.

"Meredina, help."

Als lifted the child up, and Meredina hauled the boy out and began tending to him. "It's all right. He has a pulse, and it looks like he didn't swallow much water," she said, consoling the child's ghostly pale mother.

"Th-thank you so much!" The woman was in tears as she thanked them both, hugging her child. A physician came running up and, soon after, departed with the parent and child. It was best to have the boy examined just to be safe, after all.

Als watched them go as he wrung out his sodden clothing. "Ah... It's a good thing I didn't drink..."

"Of course it was."

"It was hard to see down there; I was getting pretty worried. Oh, actually... Which mage made these lights?"

"That would be me. I deeply apologize for my carelessness."

In response to Als's loud question, someone in the crowd lifted a pale hand. Tinasha came forward, and as Als caught sight of her, he fell into a trance for a moment. He wound a wet strand of hair around his fingers.

"Oh, no, I didn't mean you were negligent... You really helped me by making the light brighter. Thank you," he managed after a moment.

Tinasha said nothing and bowed her head. Looking past the girl, Als saw that the robed mage stationed next to her had noticed the commotion. He lifted a sigil-inscribed hand as their gazes met.

As the crowd of onlookers began to disperse, Meredina held out Als's sword belt. "For now, go get changed."

"Yeah...okay."

Als and Meredina set off for the guardroom. Once they were a safe distance from the moat, Als shouted, "That was a shock! Who was that beautiful girl? Has she always been in the castle...?"

"Apparently, she's a mage who was in the witch's tower. His Highness took her as his companion," Meredina muttered in hushed tones, like she was talking about something ominous.

"Oh right! I heard about that. I see. No wonder."

"What's no wonder?"

Als shook his head, sending the water droplets clinging to his hair flying. Meredina got caught in the spray and frowned, looking annoyed.

"No, it's just that I didn't think His Highness was the type to hang around women, so it surprised me to hear that... But it's totally understandable in this case."

"What's totally understandable?!" Meredina snapped.

"Getting jealous?" Als needled.

Meredina punched the general in the back as hard as she could.

As the festival wore on into the night, Tinasha floated in the sky above the castle and gazed down at the city below her.

Filled with multicolored lights, the city was like a jewel box laid out on a jet-black cloth. The hem of Tinasha's black dress fluttering in the breeze, she blew on the paper bird in her hands. The little folded thing was a decoration sold at a festival stall, and its white wings quivered slightly.

"Tinasha!" Oscar called out from below. She saw he was standing on the castle walkway and slowly descended to him.

"You've got good eyes," she said.

"Everything around you looks kind of fuzzy and bright."

"What? How?" Tinasha hadn't been using any magical camouflage, but she'd purposely changed into a black dress so she wouldn't be as easily spotted from the ground. Curious, she looked down at her own outfit, and Oscar laughed.

"You sure you don't want to walk around the festival? You were looking forward to it so much."

"I already have. And I'm keeping up my lighting, too. While I was at it, I made an air barrier so no one will fall in the moat."

"Why?"

Evidently, no one had reported the moat incident to Oscar yet. He gestured to the witch casually. "I've managed to reach a stopping point in my work, so I thought I'd go out for a bit. I'll show you around the city."

"I do hope this isn't you trying to escape the castle. You really shouldn't. It'd mean that advance security plan the guards set up will go to waste."

"I escape every year, so I'll be fine."

"Wow…"

Tinasha thought it likely this careless disposition of Oscar's is what had led him to the witch's tower with only one companion.

Floating soundlessly down to Oscar's side, she blew again on the paper bird. The toy wasn't unusual in Farsas at all, and Oscar watched in amusement as she played with it.

"Whatcha got there?"

"All the kids were playing with them, so it made me curious. It's fun," Tinasha said, kissing the bird. Somehow, the action had apparently given the toy life. It gave a big flap of its wings and flew off into the night. Tinasha watched the paper bird soar farther and farther away before her eyes softened as she took in the nighttime scenery.

"The city is so beautiful. It almost doesn't seem real that there are tons of people down below all those lights." She gave him a gentle little smile, and Oscar stroked her hair languidly.

"Was it worth it coming down from the tower?" Oscar asked.

"Yes," replied Tinasha.

"Then I'm glad." The way Oscar spoke made it sound like he was the one looking after her. Tinasha giggled and tried to float up again, but Oscar suddenly reached out a hand to drag her back down.

"Hey! What are you—?" Tinasha started to protest when, past Oscar's shoulders, she spied Lazar running in.

"Your Highness! We have a problem!"

Oscar and Tinasha exchanged a puzzled look at Lazar's flustered state. Lazar noticed Tinasha and cried out in surprise, "Miss Tinasha, so this is where you went! Everyone's been looking for you!"

"What?" Tinasha looked guilty, and Oscar patted her shoulder.

"This is what you get for playing around. I bet you're in for a lecture."

"Now's not the time for that! Someone's been killed!"

"What?" Both Oscar and Tinasha were stunned.

※

Lazar led the other two into a back alley, one that people hardly ever traversed. In the dim light of the dead-end street, Oscar could make out a small gaggle of soldiers and mages.

"Can I see the body?" asked the prince.

"Your Highness…it's this way."

Kumu, the royal chief mage, materialized from the crowd. He motioned for Oscar to come closer and lifted a black cloth that had been spread on the ground. What lay underneath was no longer recognizable as human. It had been reduced to a charred lump of meat.

"Urgh…"

Starting with Lazar, all who caught sight of the cadaver covered their mouths and backed away—save Oscar. Tinasha's eyes softened as Oscar calmly inspected the formerly human corpse.

"Do we know who this is?" Oscar questioned.

"The mage Temys. We identified him from his ornaments; they survived the burns."

"Oh!" At Tinasha's cry, all eyes turned to her. Oscar looked down at the witch with a conflicted expression.

"Did you know him?" he asked.

"He was stationed next to me today. He came to say hi."

"Yes, which is why we were searching for you, Miss Tinasha. During the three minutes between Temys's lights disappearing and his body being found, your lights were lit, but you were nowhere near the moat… Exactly where did you go during that time?" With the festival revelry beginning to die down, Kumu's question echoed clearly and decisively.

Temys's lights had gone out sometime after the child had been rescued from the moat. Right around then, Temys's girlfriend had shown up at the moat to pay him a visit, but he'd been absent. Since his shift was not yet over, she'd guessed he was somewhere nearby. However, he was nowhere to be found. Three minutes later, his body was discovered in an alley a short walk from the moat.

"I look pretty suspicious, don't I?" Tinasha asked.

"You're probably the number one suspect," replied Oscar.

Oscar and Tinasha whispered to each other in hushed tones as they trailed behind the other officers and mages on their way to the royal audience chamber. Curiously, although both agreed Tinasha was likely under suspicion, Oscar didn't sound worried at all for some reason.

"Well, if push comes to shove, we'll just tell them who you really are."

"I think that would land me in hotter water than if I was the actual culprit…"

"It'll be fine. I'll protect you."

Even though she was really a witch, Oscar had begged her to come back with him. He had no plans of pinning unnecessary guilt on her—she didn't seem the type to harm others anyway. Tinasha was a girl who found delight in a simple paper toy. To no small degree, that was how Oscar saw her.

As if to reassure the witch, Oscar patted her on the head. The gesture was no different from what one would have done to a child. Tinasha glared up at him in protest but said nothing.

After a trek down a long corridor of the castle, the assembly of soldiers and mages reached the audience chamber. They entered with heads bowed, fanning out in front of the throne. Tinasha stood in the center, while Oscar placed himself at the side of the king's seat.

The king entered the room. He was a comparatively young king, being somewhere around fifty years of age. He resembled Oscar, but his demeanor was milder. In his gentle eyes, Tinasha could find traces of Regius, the king with whom she'd made a contract in the past.

"So you are the mage my son has brought." The king gazed steadily at Tinasha, and she accepted the look with poise. "Have we not met somewhere before?"

The abrupt question caught Oscar and Tinasha completely off guard, though neither let it show on their faces. Ever since the Witch of the Azure Moon had left Farsas seventy years ago, she had never again made an appearance until now. Perhaps Regius had once described to this king the tale of how a witch he'd made a contract with had fought in battle for him. Now was not the time to consider such things, however.

Tinasha gave the ruler of Farsas a brilliant smile. "No, this is the first time we've met. My name is Tinasha." She swept one leg beneath her as she curtsied deeply. The graceful motion charmed the entire court. The king's head was still inclined to one side as if something was still nagging at him. Whatever it was, he did not raise it. Instead, he merely surveyed each person spread out before him, from left to right, before his gaze landed back on Tinasha.

"A mage has been killed. Were you involved?" asked the king.

"No. I had nothing to do with it," she replied immediately, her voice firm. Sighs could be heard in the crowd, and people began to murmur.

The king looked up at Oscar, who was standing next to him. "I leave this to you. Choose a good team to help you and take care of this."

"I understand."

The king stood and exited the chamber through a door in the back. All present bowed deeply at his retreating figure.

Oscar and the magistrates left to handle the remaining festival business, while Als and others involved in the situation gathered in another room. Seated around a table, they went over the state of the body and the time line of events in rapid succession.

Surrounded in the center, Tinasha simply received the oncoming questions, neither flinching nor growing defensive.

"Don't you think it's incredibly suspicious that you weren't at your station?"

"Where were you, and what were you doing?"

"Are you even capable of magic that can serve this court? Those lights weren't lamps or something, were they?"

"Oh, they were magic lights. I got a good look at them," interjected Als, raising his hand. "Partway through, they got bigger and brighter. I saw them up close. There's no mistaking it."

This was the first word anyone had spoken in Tinasha's defense, and the rest of the group was speechless for a second. Meredina broke the awkward silence by adding, "When that little boy was drowning, Temys was still there."

"Ah yeah, I remember seeing him. His hood was up, and I couldn't see his face, but he waved at us. I definitely saw the magical black sigils on his arms."

"B-but even so, if she was using magic to keep the lights going, then she must have been nearby. That's the issue. Maybe she traded places with another mage?"

Listening to the assemblage speak as if she wasn't there, Tinasha suddenly recalled something that had happened while she was among the crowd.

"Best not to leave. You'll get drawn into something annoying."

If that warning had been meant for her, then the situation had developed just as the mysterious person had said. Maybe that mage had even known that Temys would be killed. Tinasha fell deep into thought while suspicious gazes converged on her.

"You're rushing to a conclusion. She's a mage from the tower. It doesn't seem unreasonable to think she'd know things we don't," offered the aging Chief Mage Kumu as he stroked his dark-skinned, shaved head and considered Tinasha. "Making lights bigger and brighter after they've been created isn't a simple thing in and of itself. These balls of light were originally made with the intention of being maintained for several hours. None of us besides her have the ability to adjust them in response to an unforeseen event. It shouldn't surprise you that she can maintain them from a separate location, too."

Tinasha was a little moved by the older man's more flexible demeanor. It was just what she expected from a mage who had been known as Farsas's Rock for decades now. Tinasha's familiar had sometimes brought stories of his strength and astute judgment to her in the tower. At the same time, Tinasha began wondering just how much of her own hand she should give away.

It was then that the door opened, and Oscar entered.

"What happened?"

"We were just about to question her—"

"What were you doing and where?!"

Kumu's explanation was interrupted by the mage who'd gotten held in check earlier suddenly pressing Tinasha for an answer.

The witch's dark eyes glanced at the man who had made the outburst. Something deep and unknown lurked in those eyes, and he stiffened.

Oscar answered readily, "She was with me. Lazar saw her, too."

The alibi immediately got the room buzzing.

Kumu's eyes widened, and Meredina's face twitched for a moment. Als noticed the woman's brief movement and shrugged.

Oscar, responsible for the ripple through the room, merely looked around at them, not at all concerned with the shock of his subjects.

"Don't waste time insisting she's guilty. She's not the one who did it; I can vouch for that... Tinasha!"

"Ah yes." Grimacing, the witch stood up and showed her open hands to everyone in the room. "It's true that, as Master Kumu said, I use a slightly strange kind of magic. I'm particularly good with light spheres and spiritual-type magic... So that's why I can do things like this."

Tinasha manifested a sphere of light in her hands. The luminous orb bounced up to the ceiling, then slid over to the window, edged out through the gap, and flew off into the night. Its light continued glowing until it got so distant that none present could even see it anymore. Everyone in the room let out gasps.

"It was irresponsible of me to leave my post. I'm aware that it's unavoidable that you will suspect me because I did. I truly am very sorry." Tinasha bowed her head low in apology, and everyone in the room shifted uncomfortably as they watched her.

Oscar let the moment pass before addressing Als, the only one who appeared unaffected.

"Als, I want you to look into this. Meredina, you help him," he ordered.

The two soldiers exchanged looks before bowing respectfully.

※

Having their orders, Als and Meredina headed back to the alley for one more look a short while after midnight. As they walked along, they found the castle city far emptier than it had been. Meredina glanced back at the castle, its visage stark against the night.

"Are we sure she didn't do it? Even if she did make those lights, she still left her post, which just makes her even more suspicious."

"So you think His Highness is covering for her, Meredina?" Als asked. Putting aside personal feelings, it was only natural that she'd suspect Tinasha. Als gave a little shake of his head. "Well, it's definitely a possibility, but I don't think so. It's true that she was with His Highness; Lazar confirmed it. But I admit I do feel a little...uneasy."

"Uneasy?" Meredina turned to look at the general.

"It's just a hunch, but something about her makes me think she's...scary."

Als's words were so out of place that Meredina burst out laughing, but she quickly realized he was serious. She stared at him. "You're serious? Why?" she asked.

"I am. Earlier, a mage tried to get closer to her but froze stiff."

"What? That happened?" Meredina apparently hadn't been watching Tinasha at the time. It was likely no one else had noticed, either.

Als had sensed a pressure emanating from Tinasha, one that felt like it pierced the skin. The girl's dark eyes had seemingly held the depths of night. The force from them had been unmistakably real. If Tinasha had really wanted to kill someone, Als didn't doubt she was capable, regardless of who or where. Nor did he doubt she had the power to do it inconspicuously or right out in the open.

"I wonder if His Highness knows about that..."

Als had sunk deep into thought when he noticed a mage farther down the road and raised his head. The small-statured mage approached the two soldiers and bowed.

"I apologize for the wait."

His name was Kav. He was the one who had first examined the victim's body. He and Kumu had just performed the autopsy, and as he fell into step with Als and Meredina, he began explaining the results of the postmortem.

"The cause of death appears to have been poisoning. Some not yet incinerated vomit was still in the alley, and we detected poison in it. It's an old type of magic potion known as limath, a tasteless and odorless liquid. Those who ingest it vomit, and their whole body hemorrhages until they bleed from the nose. Death comes within minutes."

"Is this poison easy to obtain?"

"It's something one could make with the right instruction. You might be able to find it for sale somewhere, but not in Farsas."

"So just as an example, could any of our mages make it?"

"Around half are capable. That said, potions are my specialty, but I wouldn't use limath if I wanted to kill someone. It's an old potion. The ingredients are hard to obtain, and the procedure is troublesome to perform. The magic involved in making it also takes a heavy spiritual toll... Nowadays, there are poisons that are far simpler to make."

"I see!" Using a finger to flatten out his scrunched-up brow, Als asked Kav another question. "So what about how the victim was torn apart and burned?"

"The victim was dismembered after death. The head, arms, and legs were all severed, and the torso was cut in two. It looks like an ax or some other downward-swinging tool was used to dissever the body. Some parts took just one cut, and others required multiple. After that, the corpse was incinerated. He was doused in oil and then set on fire."

"Horrible."

Only guard soldiers were at the scene of the crime, but it had been close enough to the festival that the breeze still carried the sounds of laughter and harp music from nearby streets. However, the murder had taken place in a blind spot in a dead-end alley. There were no windows overlooking the narrow street, giving it an isolated feeling from the surrounding festivities. Peering down at the scorched ground, one could still catch the scent of death wafting silently in the air.

"Who found the body first?"

"One of our mages. They were searching for Temys. His girlfriend found him, too, and went half-mad. Right now, she's resting inside the castle."

"With what happened to him, that's understandable," commented Meredina, hugging her arms like she'd caught a chill. She looked up and realized that Als wasn't next to her anymore. He'd gone back a little bit and was peeking out onto the street.

"Als? What are you looking at?"

"Well... I want to look inside the moat, too. It's already dark, though, so it'll have to wait until tomorrow. We'll check out the moat, talk to some people, and then go report to His Highness."

"Wait, do you already know who did it?" Meredina asked.

"Nope, not at all," came the general's swift reply.

Kav and Meredina looked disappointed, but Als looked up at the starry sky. "Why do you think someone would've dismembered and burned a corpse? Any ideas?"

"Some sort of ceremony?"

"Because they had a grudge?"

Meredina and Kav gave different answers at practically the exact same time, and Als shook his head at both.

"What I suspect is a body swap or an easy disposal method... Well, let's head back for today. It's about time I have a drink and get to bed." Rubbing his neck, Als sauntered off at a quick pace. Meredina rushed to catch up with him, with Kav following.

"Hey, what kind of a person was the victim?" asked Meredina.

"You mean Temys? If I had to say... He was a lucky guy. He was a fast learner and had a real way with women. The man was friendly and responsible, so it's not as though he was despised."

"Which means it'll be pretty hard to pin down a motive."

Als, walking ahead of them, let his impressions slip. Adding to her friend's train of thought, Meredina asked, "What about aside from his personality? Did anyone have anything to gain?"

"If we're talking about inside the castle, I can't think of anyone who stood to gain from his death. To begin with, all the royal mages research different areas... We're not fighting over promotions or anything, either."

While both served the court, the army, with its emphasis on collective behavior, and the mages, with their emphasis on individual behavior, had fairly different cultures.

"What did Temys research?" Als inquired.

"Magical lakes and spiritual magic. As for the former, he mainly worked with the lake in Old Druza," explained Kav.

"What are magical lakes? Lakes made of magic?"

"They're called lakes, but they don't have any water in them. They're places where magic has pooled underground with considerable density. There are a number of them scattered across the mainland. The major focus of Temys's research was the magical lake in Old Druza, the site of the war from seventy years ago. He went there about once every month."

"The war... There are stories about a witch who fought some kind of demonic beast during that conflict, right?" asked Meredina.

One unforgettable part of Farsasian history was the war with Druza that erupted seventy years back. Druza had quite suddenly attacked with a fleet of mages. Their magical strength had made it a hard fight for the army of Farsas at the time. In the face of such a fierce attack, Farsas lost much ground to the invading enemy.

Worst of all was a giant magic weapon that Druza had procured known as a demonic beast. This beast appeared suddenly on the front lines and boasted overwhelming destructive power. Druza's weapon mowed down the Farsasian army. In the face of such a strong adversary, Farsas had been at a complete loss. Its generals and mages alike had fallen into despair.

However, Regius, the king during the time of the war, had called the most powerful witch to the front lines. She fulfilled the wish of the one who had made a contract with her, eliminating the terrible magic weapon. With their greatest advantage lost, Druza was defeated, and Farsas triumphed. Victory came at a price, however. After suffering such heavy casualties, Farsas took thirty years to truly recover. Druza, defeated and already contending with political instability, declined rapidly and broke apart into four small countries.

Als frowned at the mention of the historic battle and the infamous magic weapon. "I heard rumors the beast isn't actually dead, though. Isn't it dangerous to go somewhere like that?"

"That's why he was going. If the seal on the demonic beast really is about to come undone, its effects would be seen at the magical lake," Kav explained.

"Hmmm… If that really has something to do with the murder, this is really getting big. I can't even begin to imagine the culprit now," remarked Als.

"You sounded pretty confident that you knew who it was a little while ago," Meredina retorted.

"I only said it was suspicious. And I was only talking about how it was done. I have no idea who actually did it." Als shrugged, like he was out of ideas.

Meredina sighed in exasperation. Regaining her composure, she turned to Kav. "What about his other research topic, spiritual magic? Was he a spirit sorcerer?"

"No. Spirit sorcerers are extremely rare. What's more, they're very insular. We have many mages who can use spiritual magic, but no pure spirit sorcerers," answered Kav.

"Really? What's the difference?" Als inquired.

"The magical strength is completely different. Spirit sorcerers excel at controlling nature. Just a platoon of them would be more than a match for a traditional army," Kav explained.

"Oh wow, that's amazing," said Als.

"On the other hand, there's little record of them. By nature, they must be pure, as it's a requirement of their magic. If they are no longer pure, they will lose their power. That's why they live in small, reclusive groups and don't often intermingle with outsiders. Evidently, Temys was doing experiments in an attempt to analyze their spirit magic. The sigils on his arms were spiritual magic, too."

"Oh yeah, those. He sure was passionate about his research." As Als recalled the black sigils covering the man's arms, he and his companions at last reached the castle gate.

"We'll make our report to His Highness tomorrow. Thanks for lending us your expertise, Kav," said Als.

With that, the three of them went their separate ways.

A fragrant smell of tea pervaded the royal study. It had been brewed by the crown prince's protector, a witch. Tinasha set a cup down on the desk, grumbling to herself. "I come down from my tower, and all of a sudden, I'm the suspect in a murder... Truly, no good can come from being on land..."

"You didn't do it, so act more confident. If anyone says anything, I'll deal with them," Oscar offered.

"That will just damage your reputation."

Although he was the crown prince, if Oscar went too far, there would almost certainly be backlash. Tinasha wondered if she shouldn't just tamper with the memories of everyone involved in order to avoid the issue altogether. Oscar, on the other hand, had a mountain of paperwork to take care of after the festival and appeared busy working on things entirely unrelated to the murder case. Tinasha tidied up the teacups and crossed her legs as she floated about in midair.

"Anyway, I'll handle my own problems. If this blows up, I'll be the one to clean it up," she said.

"I have a feeling it'll get messy if I leave it to you, though. You'll adjust everyone's memories or something," Oscar speculated idly.

"How'd you know what I was thinking?!" Tinasha snapped.

"So you really can do that..." Oscar looked shocked, but it wasn't a bad last-resort option. The witch floating in Oscar's room made no attempt to deny it, and he winced.

"In any case, I'll handle it, so just sit tight. I signed the contract, so I have to take that responsibility," he said.

"Responsibility? I'm only here in the castle for a year. I don't care if I have a bad reputation."

"You say that, but you're going to be queen in the future," Oscar reminded her, as if chiding the witch.

"I will not! Don't make up a future for me!" Tinasha denied the assertion wholeheartedly, and Oscar burst out laughing. She rolled her eyes at him. "How serious are you about that anyway? It's exhausting to get dragged into your jokes, so please stop it."

"Don't worry; I'm serious about all of it. You may be a witch, but you're a good person. I don't think I'll ever suffer a dull moment with you as long as I live. It's perfect."

"That's your reasoning?"

Tinasha didn't enjoy people pursuing her with eyes full of adoration or worship. The reasoning "because it sounds fun" hardly sweetened the deal, either. In fact, it was even worse, because Tinasha had no idea how to reject something that unusual. She felt at her wit's end, and Oscar turned back to his paperwork.

"Anyway, do you have any ideas who did it? The murder case, I mean," Oscar asked as he scribbled some things.

"Mm... A lot of things don't add up. We don't have any conclusive evidence, though, and it would look suspicious if I got too involved," Tinasha admitted while still floating overhead. What was bothering her now was that warning she'd gotten only a short while before the mage had turned up dead. That mysterious man might've been involved, but he'd been given ample time to flee the city by now. Tinasha regretted not chasing after him.

Oscar grinned like he could see everything the witch was thinking. "Well, you can trust me. I've left it to a capable team."

"You're terrible for making your officers solve a mystery." Tinasha wasn't certain Oscar had heard what she'd said, because the door to the study had loudly opened at the same time. Oscar and Tinasha exchanged a glance, and the latter flicked her right hand—vanishing instantly. She had probably cast invisibility magic so as to avoid complicated inquiries. Oscar was impressed at how quickly she'd managed it.

Als entered the room, stood in front of the desk, and gave his summary of the investigation. Once Oscar had heard the gist, he grinned teasingly.

"Do you know who did it?" he asked.

"We know how they did it, more or less, but not who," Als stated flatly. Curiously, his response seemed only to please Oscar even further. The prince's grin widened.

"Then tell me how they did it. Oh, but only once everyone's here. I want to see their reactions."

"Understood."

Als left, and Oscar spoke to the seemingly empty room. "So there you have it. You should come, too, Tinasha."

There was no reply, but Oscar felt like he could sense a sigh right next to him, and he laughed.

Everyone involved in the case gathered together in a seminar room normally used for practicing magic. Among those in attendance were people close to the victim or with some sort of indirect connection to him. Temys had no blood relations. The only person there who didn't work at the castle was his girlfriend.

Oscar sat at the very back, with everyone else scattered around him in a circle. Tinasha stood behind Oscar outside the circle, almost leaning against the wall. On the opposite side sat Temys's girlfriend, Fiura.

Oscar, who was leading the meeting, cast his gaze around the assemblage. "All right, it looks like everyone's here. I'd like to hear General Als's report on the investigation and any current leads." The introduction was short. Oscar quickly yielded the floor to Als, who was waiting by the prince's side. Als took a step into the circle.

"First, I'll go over what happened the day of the murder. After Temys created his light spheres for the moat, he spoke with Miss Tinasha. Sometime after that, a child almost drowned in Miss Tinasha's area of the moat, causing a mild uproar. Temys was also spotted nearby, though I think I was the only one who noticed him. I definitely saw a mage who waved at me from a short distance away."

Als lifted his right hand, re-creating Temys's gesture at the time.

"After that, this young woman, Miss Fiura, came by and noticed that Temys was not at his post. She asked the nearby mages about him, and by the time everyone realized he was missing, his light spheres had vanished. In the ensuing search, Temys's body was found. It was determined he was murdered in the approximately thirty-minute window between when the light spheres went out and when his body was discovered. Miss Tinasha, who was missing during that time, was suspected accordingly. However, is it really possible to murder someone and incinerate their body in under thirty minutes?"

Als exchanged a look with Kav, who left for the neighboring room.

"Wondering this, today I went diving in the area of the moat that Temys had been assigned to. I never thought I'd be taking a swim in the castle moat two days in a row, let me tell you... But it was not a trip taken in vain."

Kav returned, holding what looked to be an ordinary lamp. Its one peculiarity was that it was enclosed inside a large glass sphere.

"I found six of these set positioned at the bottom of the moat at regular intervals. The glass looks like it was made with magic. Of course, a regular glass sphere would be sealed off, keeping out both water and flames. However, because it's made of magic, the lamp can be lit from outside the surrounding shell. Isn't that right, Master Kumu?"

"...Yes."

"Judging by the air inside and the wax, the flames appear to have simply naturally extinguished after enough time passed. We never got any reports about Temys's lights going out and getting relit, so the lights were likely these from the very start. Temys had told Miss Tinasha, 'I'll be around here for a while.' Meaning that, even though he was supposed to be at his post for the entire festival, he did actually plan on leaving partway through. It was not Miss Tinasha but Temys who did not use magic for their lighting duties."

All members of the assembly gasped. Oscar crossed his legs, listening while keeping a sharp eye on everyone's reactions. Tinasha had her eyes closed, content to only listen.

"This discovery tells us that Temys was not in position, even though his lights were lit. So when did the murder take place? If you'll allow me, I'd like to put forth my own theory."

Als closed his eyes for a second, organized his thoughts, and then continued.

"The murderer probably had a meeting set up with Temys in advance. They prepared the lamps ahead of time and buried them together. After Temys pretended to create his magical lights, he left his post to go meet with the murderer. After that, he was poisoned in the alleyway. When he was killed, there was still some time before the candles were due to go out. Unfortunately for the killer, something unexpected happened...the incident with the little boy almost drowning."

Als glanced at Meredina. She gaped back at him, her eyes wide.

"Let's suppose that, at that time, Temys was already dead. If you turned the corner out of the alley where the body was found, you would glimpse the moat, just a short distance ahead. The murderer likely chose that alley for that very reason, its proximity to the moat... But when the culprit heard the commotion caused by the child falling in, they probably panicked. If a person dived in after the boy, there was a chance they'd discover that Temys's light globes weren't magical. Even if no one noticed, there was also the risk of someone observing Temys's conspicuous absence. As such, the murderer hurriedly put on Temys's robe and went to the moat. There, they saw that the child didn't fall into Temys's section and, pretending to be Temys, waved at me. I have to admit, it was a clever way to turn a crisis into an opportunity."

"Well, hold on." Kumu held up a hand, cutting Als off. All eyes turned to him. "I don't mean to interrupt, General Als, but the murderer held up an arm, didn't they? A mage would have been able to tell that the markings didn't belong to Temys. Why would the culprit have run such a risk?"

"That's what I'm saying...they held up an arm. The body was dismembered, remember? The murderer brought the severed arm with them, concealed beneath their robes." Almost the entire room was speechless at Als's revelation. Such calculated violence sent shock waves through those gathered in the seminar room. Meredina's green eyes widened, and she let out a little sigh.

"After that, the murderer returned to the scene of the crime and removed Temys's other limbs to hide the fact that they'd taken an arm. And to make it harder to determine the time of death based on how dry the blood was when the body was discovered—or perhaps to make it more difficult to discover the use of poison—they doused the body in oil and burned it."

Als dropped his gaze to the floor, looking somewhat indifferent as he continued.

"Looking at it that way completely changes how we narrow down our suspects. Whoever did this was someone close to Temys, someone who had to have been absent until his false lights had burned out, and then was quick to assert an alibi afterward to cover their tracks. We can make a guess based on that, but that's as far as my investigation and impressions go." Als turned and offered a bow to Oscar before returning to his seat.

An atmosphere thick with suspicion settled over the room. From its midst, Oscar said, "Thank you for your hard work. Does anyone have any ideas?"

The awkward tension grew weighty. None dared to claim innocence or cast doubt on another.

Oscar shifted his gaze to one person in particular, as if he'd known the answer all along. From about halfway through Als's report, this person had appeared strangely calm, keeping their eyes glued to one spot on the floor. As Oscar was deliberating over how to bring this up, he heard the delicate voice of his protector call from behind where he was seated.

"You're a spirit sorcerer, aren't you? Or at least, you used to be, I'd guess. You're the one who gave Temys those markings, right?" Tinasha asked, and Temys's girlfriend, Fiura, looked up.

A spirit sorcerer was an extremely rare type of mage. When Tinasha identified Fiura as one, the whole room burst into an uproar. Kumu was the one to vocalize the thoughts of every other mage in the room. "How is it you know that?" he asked Tinasha.

"I could tell... Because I'm one, too. I can tell by looking at someone if they're a spirit sorcerer, even if they aren't one anymore. Also, Temys's sigil markings were so complex and difficult to apply that only a spiritual-magic specialist could've done them. I'd assumed there was a spirit sorcerer in the castle who I just hadn't met yet, but it seems I was mistaken." Tinasha cast a sad look in Fiura's direction. "Did you give your purity and power to him? Did you come to regret it?"

Fiura met Tinasha's darkness-filled stare head-on. Her own eyes were brimming with a kind of hollow determination. After a long bout of silence, she smiled at Tinasha and began speaking.

"I never... I never thought I'd meet another spirit sorcerer after leaving the forest and coming to this strange land. I miscalculated. You must be a powerful spirit sorcerer if you can discern what I am just by looking at me. I'm sorry you ended up as the primary suspect." Fiura's eyes were as calm as the most placid lake. There was a clear resignation within them, one that had pervaded her whole body, like that of an elderly person who knows their time had come and is ready to go.

"I don't plan to talk about most of it. I also won't try to justify myself. I just... couldn't bear the condescending look in his eyes when I couldn't use magic anymore. I couldn't handle his superiority complex, and every time I looked at him, I saw the protections I had put there and how shortsighted I'd been... I hated it. I killed him out of respect for myself. Nothing more, nothing less." Fiura spoke as if to herself, desiring neither understanding nor sympathy.

"So in the end, the body was dismembered after the drowning incident was resolved," Meredina said.

She, Oscar, Kumu, Als, and Tinasha had gathered in the crown prince's study. Fiura's questioning had concluded, and she had been temporarily imprisoned.

As Tinasha added hot water to a teapot, she replied to Meredina's remark. "Magic that produces markings like that—and it's not just limited to spiritual magic—will be effective for as long as the caster is alive, at the very least. In her case, the sigils continued to function even after she lost her spirit-sorcerer magic. Since she's the one who cast them, she was probably able to transfer a portion of them to her own body, even though her magic was gone."

"Why didn't you notice it was a woman's arm?" Meredina chided, and Als groaned.

Kumu interjected soothingly, "The marks on the arm were the more striking feature; it's not surprising that's all he noticed. Besides, Als also saw the wave from a distance."

"No way she cut the arm off after noticing the disturbance at the moat. There wasn't enough time. I guess that means all she prepared in advance was what she needed to burn his body to disguise the fact that his markings were gone," Oscar reasoned. He uncrossed his legs and accepted a plate of snacks from Tinasha.

Als looked even more frustrated and confused. Meredina ignored him and kept asking questions. "Then why did she cut up the body? If she'd just left it how it was, she might have gotten away with impersonating him."

Tinasha offered an answer. "I think it was all a gamble on her whether the impersonation would work. She couldn't retrieve the lamps submerged in the moat, so she must've considered the possibility that someone would sense that she wasn't really Temys. If the body was cut up by the time it was suspected that the person who'd waved wasn't really Temys, then she had a chance. But if he wasn't dismembered, then only a spirit sorcerer could've been responsible. No one else could've transferred the markings or drawn new ones. As a proud spirit sorcerer, Fiura wanted to avoid drawing suspicion from any potential brethren. In this case, that was her downfall, however, as it's what led to us realizing she'd impersonated Temys."

"You fell for it hook, line, and sinker," said Meredina archly, and Als was unable to meet the woman's gaze.

Oscar grinned and attempted to mediate. "Don't bully him. It's only because of his work that we were able to solve the mystery. What's more—we did so quickly, which really helped."

Once again, Als bowed low. Despite the truth having been revealed, Kumu still looked displeased.

"But Temys came to me to discuss his plans to marry Fiura. Did he really think so low of her?" Kumu asked.

"No one can say if he actually did or if it was more the workings of Fiura's mind," Oscar said, bringing everything to a close. The prince scrawled a signature along the papers spread out before him.

Kumu, Als, and Meredina departed from the study after their discussion, each returning to their work. Quietly, Tinasha cleared away their cups as she muttered, "Why am I doing the job of a lady-in-waiting?"

"Because you make good tea, I suppose," Oscar teased.

Tinasha set the tea-laden tray down on a stand by the wall, looking not at all satisfied. "What will you do with Fiura now that you've caught her?"

"That's for my dad to decide... But she won't be executed right away. I think the mages have a lot they want to ask her."

Tinasha looked down at her own hands. The witch's expression was one of pity. "I suppose there are reasons why spirit sorcerers never come to the city."

"Are you okay? Let me see your hands," Oscar interjected.

"Don't avoid the subject. I'm not exactly happy about it, but everyone's convinced that I'm important to you. I'm going to make sure not to do anything that will reveal my identity."

"I knew you cared."

"No, I don't!"

Oscar let out a big belly laugh and began work on a fresh set of documents. When he went to dip his pen in the adjacent inkwell, he suddenly remembered something and looked up.

"Come to think of it, if you're a spirit sorcerer, does that mean all your power will disappear if you lose your purity?"

Tinasha, now wiping down the table, smiled as if to say, *Oh, so that's what you're asking.*

"There's some truth to it, but it's also kind of an old wives' tale. In reality, having sexual relations does make it easier for your soul to become impure. It will require a much greater amount of magic than before to perform spiritual magic, but that's all. When that happens, the majority of sorcerers end up being left unable to use spiritual magic altogether. If it were an easier kind of magic, it would be a different story, though... That's why it's likely Fiura mixed the limath used in the murder herself; its magical composition is pretty simple."

Tinasha cut herself off there. She finished wiping the table, folded the cloth she'd been using, and went to place it on the tea tray. Now empty-handed, she returned to the study desk and sighed.

"The amount of magic I have is totally different from someone like her, so I don't think it would affect me much. It's not like spiritual magic is the only type I can use anyway. Although, the really big spells might start giving me difficulty."

"Oh, that's good," Oskar remarked rather casually.

Tinasha finally realized what Oscar had been hinting at, and her jaw dropped. Flustered, she came around behind the desk and went right up to him.

"No, that was a lie just now. It'd be a big problem. A huge one. I wouldn't be able to use magic at all."

Paying no mind to her desperation, Oscar broke into a wry grin.

"Even if that were true, it wouldn't matter. I'd take responsibility and protect you."

"No!"

Their quarrel came to an end when an abrupt pounding erupted at the door to the study. A soldier hurriedly entered. Between gasping breaths, he managed to say, "The woman we locked up for murdering a mage has killed herself!"

Oscar heard Tinasha inhale sharply.

Kumu and Als had beaten the prince and the witch to the small room where Fiura had been confined. She was lying facedown in its center. Her right hand was clutching a small bottle, and flecks of blood were spattered around her body.

"It looks like she took limath, the same poison used in the murder. She wasn't eating, so there was no vomit, but she bled from her eyes and nose."

"Didn't you check her belongings beforehand?"

"We did, but she didn't have anything on her at the time…"

While the soldier on duty explained the situation, Tinasha got a closer look at the bottle Fiura was holding. She reached out and scooped up the drop clinging to its rim.

Everyone else was clustered around Oscar, so none noticed what she was doing. Tinasha let out a low humming chant and began concentrating on the magical composition of the poison on her fingertip.

Oscar left the room after giving everyone their orders. Tinasha had been waiting for him and beckoned him over. He bent down to listen, and she stood on tiptoe to whisper in his ear.

"You should take one more look around Fiura. She wasn't the one who made the poison. She probably has a coconspirator… That—or there's a mastermind with a different goal entirely."

Oscar nodded sagely and went back to the door to instruct the soldiers on what to do next.

Left alone, Tinasha let out a deep sigh before leaving.

*　　*　　*

The follow-up investigation revealed that a suspicious-looking old man had been visiting Fiura for the past month or so. It also came to light that an unfamiliar old mage had been walking around the castle the day Fiura committed suicide.

When the two accounts were put together, everyone concluded that both were the same person, but no one could track down the enigmatic elderly man in question. The case was left unresolved, leaving Oscar uneasy about the whole thing.

Tinasha took Fiura's remains and went to bury them in some faraway forest. Whatever Tinasha saw in the lonely mage who threw away her power for a man and killed him out of pride, she didn't say.

▮ 3. The Transparency of Night

One sunny afternoon, a young woman floated above the spires of Farsas Castle.

Technically, she wasn't that young at all. This was Tinasha, the Witch of the Azure Moon. She was the one who represented the Age of Witches, an era that had stood unchallenged for three centuries. Tinasha's title was rumored to come from the fact that, long before she lived in the tower, she would only appear on nights when the moon could be seen unobstructed, though this was never confirmed.

Her hair had gotten mussed by the wind, and as she patted it down, she received a report from her familiar. Tinasha had been receiving these updates since long before she'd ever lived in the tower, and not one of them had ever been good. She'd received so many over the years that their details had begun to blur together.

Narrowing her eyes, she gazed out at the horizon. She felt like she could see her azure tower—small and distant on the horizon.

"Until next time," she said.

She stroked the neck of her gray cat familiar, and it purred happily. Tinasha wondered if everything she'd been doing this whole time had been for naught. It seemed almost certain. A deeply self-deprecating smile appeared on the witch's face. Still, she released her familiar back into the world. The creature's job was to look for a particular person who was probably already dead.

※

Court mages spent most of their working hours attending lectures and working on their personal research, but in addition, they also had to take on and fulfill small tasks that came from all over.

These tasks were posted in order of difficulty on a wall in the hallway outside the lecture hall every morning. Normally, only mages could see them, but right now the crown prince was examining the postings with interest. He motioned to his protector at his side.

"Tinasha, this one looks fun. You should take it."

"Why are you the one deciding…?" Tinasha pulled a face. This was the most powerful witch on the mainland. With her level of magic, she could complete any of these requests easily. Oscar knew that as he picked up one and began reading it.

"Looks like it has to do with setting up transportation arrays in the city. Says it'll take about a month. That means you can go exploring."

"It would be for work, not pleasure," Tinasha added, plucking the paper from Oscar's hand. She read the details with rapt concentration, but for all intents and purposes, she appeared to be just a beautiful girl. Passing mages caught sight of her and stared in fascination. When Oscar noticed, he smirked to himself about it.

It had been five years ago that he had first decided he would visit her tower.

At that time, Oscar had devoted himself to his studies and sword practice, trying to cope with the curse placed on him. When he heard the story of the tower and the promise that its master would grant a wish to someone who climbed to the top, it had sounded almost too good to be true.

Ever since that day, meeting the witch of that tower had been Oscar's foremost goal…but the witch he'd met was nothing like what he'd imagined. She looked like a young woman instead of some horrid old crone. She also wasn't crafty or unreasonable, as Oscar might otherwise have assumed. She was mouthy, but that was part of how she showed that she cared deep down. Oscar placed his hand on the head of this much smaller girl.

"It sounds interesting, so I'll go with you. I think you'll get abducted if I let you do it alone anyway."

"I am not a kitten; I'll be fine! Don't take advantage of the confusion to slip out of the castle!" scolded Tinasha.

"You say that, but…if something happens, it'll be too late."

Tinasha's breathtaking beauty and slender frame were enough to invite unwanted attention. If Oscar took his eyes off her and she landed in danger, as the one who'd signed the contract, he would be responsible.

Keenly aware of Oscar's obvious worry, Tinasha rolled her eyes in exasperation. "I'd like to have a serious chat with you about just how you see me."

"How I see you? There's nothing wrong with my eyes."

She was kind, smart, and not particularly selfish. That already qualified her to be queen. In addition, being with her was fun. Perhaps because she wasn't a citizen of Farsas, she was unreserved in her interactions with him. It was refreshing.

…Which was why all that was left was to wait for her to change her mind about marrying him. The prince made no secret of those intentions, and Tinasha sighed.

"Well, since you've gone to the trouble of picking it out, I'll take on this job. But you are to stay in the castle. I can handle it alone."

"Ah, hey!"

Oscar shot out a hand reflexively, but Tinasha disappeared without any incantation. Perhaps she'd teleported? Some mages who had seen it happen from a distance were stunned in amazement at what Tinasha had done.

Left alone, Oscar scratched his temples before turning back. There was no time to ponder how Tinasha had made her escape; he had mountains of work to attend to. Their little exchange just now had been a nice change of pace, however. Oscar looked out the window, up at the cloudless sky.

Then, he set off with a spring in his step, leaving some astonished mages staring after him.

Lately, it seemed Farsas was getting hotter with each passing day.

Amid the boiling-hot air of the training grounds, Als was sparring with the young soldiers. Whether because it was only a week after the festival and everyone was still spent or a consequence of the heat, the soldiers' moves were sluggish. Als was debating whether to let them take a break or give them a lecture when he spotted someone approaching from the castle. Realizing who it was, he was overcome with surprise.

"Miss Tinasha, are you here on an errand for His Highness?"

"Why would *I* be?" She had her long hair pinned up and was dressed in lightweight clothing, easy to move in. Her leggings came to the knee, revealing the bare skin of her calves, which were so strikingly pale, Als worried the girl might suffer sunburn.

"I'm done with my work, and I'm feeling a little pent-up frustration from my daily routine. I'd like to get in some exercise, so if I won't be in the way, I'd like you to spar with me."

"Is His Highness messing with me again?" Als asked, clearly surprised.

"I wonder where he gets that from." She shook her head vehemently, clearly irritated.

…It was already well-known in certain circles that Tinasha was Oscar's favorite and that he involved her in just about everything.

Some thought it cute; others thought it was pathetic. Kumu and the other mages fretted over how Tinasha might lose her power to Oscar, after they'd finally lucked out and gotten a spirit sorcerer in the castle and everything.

Als grimaced, aware that his soldiers were distracted by the sight of her slim figure standing among them. "I was just about to call a break, so I'll spar with you."

"Thank you."

Giving his people leave, half the soldiers in Als's command returned to their main stations while the other half stuck around for the show. Tinasha borrowed a practice sword from one of them. Feeling relieved that Meredina was off duty, Als grabbed one, too.

"Have you used a sword before?"

"A little, in the past."

"I'm surprised." Als lifted his sword and began slowly swinging down at her, warming up as he did.

Tinasha met his strikes once, then twice. Her intuitive, fluid movements were those of a fairly talented combatant. Gradually, Als sped up his attacks, and Tinasha met them all with ease.

...She might be better than Meredina. Als felt a chill run up his spine imagining the unhappy face of his childhood friend.

Perhaps because of her combative personality, Meredina always tried trading blows with him head-on, but Tinasha never took a strike full-on. Instead, she'd divert the direction a little and let it graze off. She must have known very well that her small stature gave her a disadvantaged fighting style. As she did this, Tinasha was waiting for the moment when her opponent's stance weakened.

If this were a real fight, she would've seized her opportunity and instantly rushed to run her opponent through. Of course, had it been a real fight, Als wouldn't have given her the chance in the first place.

Still, Tinasha was undoubtedly a much trickier sparring partner than the other soldiers. Als whipped his sword faster through the air as that thought struck him. The soldiers who'd stuck around just for fun were now standing aghast at the young mage's skills.

"...Maybe I'll test her a little."

Als poured even more strength into his grip—so much that if he took a blow, his hand would go numb, and he'd drop his weapon. Powerfully, he brought his sword down at Tinasha.

The slender girl didn't dodge the attack, however. Stepping forward to meet him, she sank into a lunging posture and slanted the angle of her blade. When Als's powerful strike came rocketing down, it glanced off the top edge of her weapon as she parried it to the left.

Immediately thereafter, she took another step in and drove her left elbow into Als's wrist.

What Tinasha's counterattack lacked in power it more than made up for in speed. It was perfectly aimed for his joint, and he almost dropped his sword. As he rushed to get a better grip on his hilt, Tinasha pointed the tip of her blade to his neck.

"...!" With a sword tip in his face, Als immediately used his left hand to push it aside by its flat edge.

With the pass Tinasha had poured her body weight into evaded, she sprang to the right, her upper body still crouched. She dodged Als's next horizontal swipe.

Tinasha jumped another step back, creating some distance between the two of them, before turning back to grin at him.

"That was close." With her devilish smile, Tinasha appeared not unlike a black cat prowling the night. Als just shook his head in shock.

"Those aren't the moves of someone who's only done a little swordplay... You're good enough to quit the mages and join up with us over here."

Such nimble movements indicated that Tinasha had done far more than just taken a few lessons. She likely possessed real battle experience. The way she could move spoke to a great deal of it.

"Thank you." Tinasha gave him a big smile. Als could only shake his head, crestfallen, sensing something unfathomably deep in that grin.

※

The mage's voice echoed throughout the lecture hall.

"Four hundred years ago, with the destruction of the Magic Empire of Tuldarr in a single night, a portion of magical techniques were lost to us. But nowadays, the majority of verified magic is shared among us. We can, therefore, say that the starting point now is ensuring that each spell caster has a strong grasp of their individual knowledge. The first step to using magic is becoming aware of yourself as a glass jar filled with liquid, interacting with the world as an individual while utilizing that magical composition to affect natural phenomena."

Around twenty people were gathered for the morning lecture, an introduction to magic.

Sitting in the very back row, Tinasha was listening raptly when a door in the back opened and Kav entered the room. Noticing Tinasha, he waved and sat down next to her.

"Interesting lecture?"

"Very much so," Tinasha answered, twirling a pen between her fingers. She had no memory of learning magic from someone prior to becoming a witch. Listening to theories like this was quite novel for her.

However, noisy footsteps came from above, interrupting the lesson. The lecture hall was located in the atrium, designed in such a way that those on the walkways of the floors above could look down into the room. Someone upstairs was creating a rather disruptive uproar while sauntering about.

Tinasha watched, wondering if it was some kind of emergency, and a garish, greasy man came into view. He walked to the back and began unloading a steady stream of complaints on the magistrates. The noise put the lecture on pause for the moment, and everyone craned their necks to look up and observe. The greasy man paid no mind to his spectators, walking out without glancing once at the lecture hall below.

"What was that about?" Tinasha whispered, and right as Kav was about to answer her, the lecture resumed. They fell silent to listen.

It wasn't until three days later that Tinasha finally heard the answer to her question.

Crown Prince Oscar's quarters occupied a block deep within the castle. No sooner had he entered than there was a rapping at the window. Dumbfounded, Oscar opened it to find Tinasha standing on the balcony. He invited her in.

"You can use the door, you know."

"I don't want to. If someone sees me, the rumors will just get worse…"

"I think it's a little late for that."

Tinasha entered, looking sour. "You're back pretty late today," she commented.

"Someone's arrived at the castle who tends to make a lot of work for me… Oh, I have what you asked for, by the way."

Oscar went to his table and presented Tinasha with a stack of papers that had been resting on it. Contained within the documents was information on the research of the recently murdered Temys, which Tinasha had been wanting to study. The tall sheaf of papers detailed everything from his published studies to his top-secret, unannounced theories.

"Thank you," Tinasha said, accepting the reports and starting to leaf through them.

"Seems we still haven't been able to find the old mage who was sighted with Fiura. We're still looking for him, but..." Oscar trailed off.

"We can safely suppose that he broke into the castle and gave her the poison, but that's an awful lot of effort for merely interfering in a personal entanglement," Tinasha reasoned. That was why she'd grown curious about using Temys's research to unravel the mystery. As Tinasha perused the documents, she continued: "The truth is, there's someone else who seems slightly suspicious to me. It could just be my imagination, though."

"Someone suspicious? Who is it?" Oscar pressed.

"During the festival, I received a warning from a mage passing by. He said, *'Best not to leave. You'll get drawn into something annoying.'*"

As she explained about the man who'd passed by near the moat, Oscar frowned. "Another weird story. But it doesn't seem like the same guy spotted inside the castle."

"No, he wasn't," Tinasha agreed.

The stranger she'd seen by the moat had been a young man about Oscar's age. He had light-brown hair and had been with a girl with silver hair. The mage seen with Fiura was older and had a hood pulled down over his eyes.

Regardless, Tinasha remained wary of the mystery man she'd met during the festival because his magic had been concealed. His true magical ability was nowhere near hers, of course, but still most likely surpassed that of an average court mage. That was why the thought of him bothered Tinasha so, even though she'd pushed the memory to a corner of her mind the past few days.

"I have my familiar looking for him. When he turns up, we can get some answers out of him."

"If he has nothing to do with any of this, he's in for a nasty shock. Being interrogated by a witch from out of the blue is likely pretty startling," Oscar quipped.

"I don't care. I can just erase his memories," Tinasha retorted. There was no such thing as being too careful. She didn't consider herself weak, but she'd resumed sword practice to be able to handle any unforeseen circumstances. If Oscar died now, that would be the end of the Farsas royal line. Tinasha wasn't so indifferent on the matter as to be able to just watch that happen.

The witch wore a serious expression, and Oscar grinned at her before pouring a cup of water from a pitcher. He brought it to his lips but pulled it back quickly. He stared at the liquid suspiciously.

"What is this? It's oddly sweet."

"What?" Tinasha put down her papers and came over to look at the cup of water with him.

"Is it sugar water?" Oscar asked.

"It shouldn't be…," she replied. Tinasha had a bad feeling. She looked up at Oscar, her face twitching. "Did you drink it?" she asked warily.

"Just a sip. But I don't feel any…" Oscar broke off there, staring at Tinasha without blinking. His steady gaze made her uncomfortable, and she took a step back.

"Wh-what? What is it?"

"Nothing…"

Oscar thought for a second, a hand over his mouth, before pointing to the documents on the table.

"You can take those with you. Leave me for today," he said, turning away. The prince was acting unmistakably strange, and Tinasha couldn't help but approach him, pressing for answers.

"Why? You're being a little weird. Look at me and tell me the reason." The witch floated up a few centimeters, grabbing Oscar's shoulder and shaking it. "What did you drink? Throw it up."

"It's fine. Just leave."

"Your neck is going to get a crick."

Oscar was still turned to the side, and Tinasha took his face in her hands, forcing him to look at her.

There was a beat of silence, and Tinasha had the briefest notion that her face was reflected in the prince's blue eyes. Unconsciously, she leaned in closer to see if it really was.

As she moved in, Oscar wrapped his arms around her. His large hands threaded through her hair. He drew her close and pressed a kiss on her lips.

She was speechless. Calmly, she pulled back and blinked slowly.

"What was that? Some kind of joke?" Tinasha asked.

When Oscar let her go, Tinasha floated softly to the ground. He gave her a light pat on the head, his face twisted in a frown.

"I'm feeling kind of riled up. I think that was some sort of aphrodisiac."

"…"

A heavy silence settled over the two. Tinasha was half-frozen in shock for a bit before she snapped out of it and yelped, "I—I didn't do it!"

"That'd be quite an unpredictable turn of events if you had—and pretty damn funny, too. Too bad." Oscar sounded almost disappointed.

"It's not funny at all!" Tinasha snapped.

Oscar sat on the bed, and as Tinasha looked the prince over, her mind worked fast to come up with a countermeasure. If it was just an aphrodisiac, then the best course of action was for her to leave as he'd asked. However, there was the risk that it was a potion with some sort side effect, too. In which case, it could be fatal later if the dosing wasn't treated immediately.

For the time being, all Tinasha could do was analyze the magical composition of the liquid. She decided to do just that, but the witch suddenly found that her arms were caught, and she was pulled down onto the bed.

"Hey, cool it."

"This is why I told you to leave," Oscar said. His face was scrunched up as if in pain, and his voice was absent its usual teasing tone.

Tinasha broke into a cold sweat seeing him like this for the first time. She twisted her body to roll out from under the man pressing her down, but the difference in their statures was too great. She couldn't budge.

In times like this, the best thing to do is blast off into the air and knock him out cold, thought Tinasha just as Oscar, with a very intent look in his eyes, came in close and kissed her right earlobe.

"I just realized something…"

"What is it?" she asked, looking back coldly at him.

"I don't need to hold back here. There's nothing in my way."

"There is! I am! I'm going up to the ceiling!" she cried.

"Do what you want." His voice was low and rough, and his handsome face was coming closer and closer.

Tinasha sighed a little, closed her eyes, and pressed her forehead against Oscar's. She poured magic into the point where their skin touched. The magical composition of whatever was running through his veins took the form of a sigil floating in the air.

Three rings. Very strong, but a simple construction nonetheless.

The moment she concentrated hard, putting power into those rings, they shattered without leaving so much as a trace.

Once she climbed out from under Oscar, Tinasha picked up the water pitcher that had started all this.

"This is why I told you that I couldn't protect you from poisons! You need to be more careful. I'm going to taste it now."

"If you get affected by the aphrodisiac, I won't stop you," Oscar teased, seemingly back to normal.

"Potions have no effect on me!" Tinasha flushed in anger. Then, for as much as she'd yelled, the witch grew very calm, and her head tilted doubtfully. "In any case, we have no idea why you were dosed with this... It really is just an aphrodisiac."

"I have an idea who it could be. No proof, though," Oscar said, looking uncharacteristically disgusted. He crossed his legs on the bed, and Tinasha sat down next to him with the water pitcher in hand.

"Then we'll have to get some proof," Tinasha offered, humming a short incantation to infuse the remaining amount of aphrodisiac with a magical form. The liquid reacted almost immediately and floated up into the air as wispy filaments that formed a three-dimensional shape.

"Wait a moment. This will deduce who created this stuff." Tinasha added a further incantation to the three-ringed form.

"You can do that?" Oscar asked, rather surprised.

"Whoever made this probably thought no one would be able to reverse it and discover their identity. This spell died out a long time ago, and I'm probably the only one who knows how to cast it now."

Each time Tinasha hummed a little more of the incantation, the shape gradually changed form and spun in the air.

"By the way, if the person who cast this is someone I don't know, I won't be able to tell who it is. Look… Oh, wait…"

Tinasha got her answer, and her face clouded over even more as she stared at the rotating shape.

※

Even with an unexpected annoyance, Oscar could not shirk his many responsibilities. The best he could manage was getting rid of the people who were piling on more irksome matters. As he processed documents in his study, Tinasha handed him a cup of tea she'd made, and he thanked her for it. There came a quick knock at the door. The person Oscar had asked for had arrived.

"I've come at your summons." Kav, a potions expert, stepped timidly into the room.

Oscar held out a glass of water to him. "You know what this is, don't you? Don't drink it."

Kav stepped forward and took the glass. He stared at it in puzzlement as he sniffed it. Tinasha watched with amusement as the blood drained from his face.

"Why do you have this, Your Highness?"

"Someone put it in my water pitcher."

"Wh-what?!" Kav yelped in astonishment, looking back and forth from Oscar to Tinasha. Oscar placidly withstood the man's gaze, while Tinasha frowned and nodded. Kav caught her meaning and turned to her, bowing extremely low.

"I must apologize deeply! I never thought it would be used for this purpose! Miss Tinasha, how can I ever atone for this?"

"Ah, no, you don't have to apologize that much."

"But this is the strongest one! Even just a sip will destroy all reason!" Kav insisted, looking stricken, and Tinasha whirled around to look at Oscar with wide eyes. She gave him a slow clap.

"Wow! Such self-control!"

"Go on, keep praising me." Oscar found the action rather adorable and endearing, but he turned away to face Kav.

"So who asked you to make this?" he insisted.

Kav hesitated a little before he admitted through gritted teeth, "Duke Pasval. Your uncle..."

It was exactly the answer Oscar had been expecting. He felt a headache coming on.

※

Kevin, the reigning king of Farsas, was the oldest of three siblings.

He had a younger brother and a younger sister, but they had both already passed away. His younger brother, the former prime minister, died from illness only a month ago. His sister, youngest of the three, had always possessed a weak constitution. She'd died only a few years after getting married. She was devastated by the loss of her children in the kidnapping incidents that had rocked Farsas, and her health had rapidly declined.

Her husband, Duke Pasval, was well-known as a materialist. He'd taken his late wife's inheritance and built a house in Colas, outside the castle city. There, he was rumored to be living an openly self-indulgent, debauched lifestyle, but for some reason, he'd returned to live in a mansion in the city ever since the festival. Not only that, he came to court, despite not being summoned, to whisper complaints in the ears of those on the royal council. He made sarcastic, cutting remarks to Oscar and often created more work for him.

While everyone gossiped about Pasval behind his back, they nonetheless treated him courteously in person. He was still related to the royal family after all, if only through marriage.

That night, Pasval returned to his mansion. With a bottle of liquor in hand, he listened to a report from one of his servants.

"Do you know if the drug has worked yet?" he asked.

"It was perfectly placed, but we don't yet know that much...," the underling replied.

"Well, whatever. Just gotta sit tight and wait for the results."

Dismissing his subordinate, Pasval poured some of the amber liquid into a silver cup. Already a little drunk, he laughed in amusement.

"That damn brat and his spirit sorcerer. Right about now, he should be reeling from digging his own grave, and if what I heard is right, the woman'll die. So much the better."

"…What, exactly, have you heard?"

A voice spoke from behind him, and Pasval turned around, startled. Outside the room's large window, a clear azure moon hung in the darkness.

A young woman stood at the foot of the window, illuminated by that cold moonlight. Her skin was so white and her looks so striking that she resembled a doll, but she wore a cruel smile.

"I'd like to know," she added.

Her voice was as cutting as a cold blade. An instinctive fear lanced through Pasval, pitching his voice high and shrill.

"Wh-who are you?! How did you get in?"

The pale girl lifted off the ground lightly, floating over until she was standing directly in front of the duke. Her jet-black locks swayed as if underwater. Her dark eyes seemed to pierce him through.

"Allow me to introduce myself. I am the witch Tinasha. I am called the Witch of the Azure Moon… Yes, your nephew often scolds me for coming in through the window. I do apologize."

"W-witch…?"

"I'm sorry I'm not an ordinary spirit sorcerer."

At those words, Pasval finally understood that this was the spirit sorcerer he'd laid a trap for and that she wasn't just some mage. His knees gave out, and he collapsed weakly into a chair.

"Why is a witch…?"

"What have you heard?" The question was asked with sweetness tinging its tone, but Tinasha's appearance gave no indication of her true, terrifying strength. Once displeased, she could reduce someone to ash in an instant.

Pasval gasped in reply and said, "He's got a witch's curse on him… All women involved with him will die, apparently…"

"If it was *all* women involved with me, there would've been a lot more deaths by now."

A new voice, that of an exhausted-sounding young man, entered the room. Pasval turned to find his nephew-by-marriage standing by the wall.

"H-hey, when did you get in?!"

Arms crossed and leaning against the wall, Oscar ignored Pasval and addressed the witch. "I told you that you shock people when you come in through the window."

"I don't care. It's convenient." Tinasha bent down and picked up the papers scattered on the floor. The report contained a detailed investigation into castle personnel, as well as national and international policy, but had no record of confidential information.

"So, Uncle, who did you hear that from?" Oscar drawled.

"Did the drug not work...?" Pasval asked.

"Did it work...? Did it not work...? Either way, I think I might've done something I regret, to be honest," Oscar joked.

"What, missing your chance when I lifted the spell?" Tinasha cut in coldly. She floated over to Pasval, creeping her white fingers along the nape of his neck. "Who told you about that curse? If you tell us, we'll leave," she said.

"I—I don't know! I didn't get his name, either! Some old mage!" Pasval cried, retreating into a fetal position. Tinasha and Oscar exchanged a glance.

"Do you think it's the same guy?" Oscar asked.

"The chances are high... Looks like he's beat us to the punch," Tinasha replied. The witch floated over Pasval's head and glided past to land next to Oscar.

"I don't really understand what he wants to accomplish. What's the connection between this and the other incident?" Oscar mused. With one hand on his chin, he considered possibilities. He used his other hand to stroke Tinasha's hair. Her eyes fluttered closed, like a cat happy to be petted.

The man hiding in his chair watched the scene and shouted desperately, "If the witch is here, that means the curse is real! Serves you right! You and your father's bloodline ends here! Just die already!"

Tinasha's eyebrows raised. She lifted her arms and began weaving a spell, but Oscar held out a hand to stop her.

"Even if that comes to pass, it's nothing for you to worry about, Uncle. Just go back to your house in Colas," Oscar said over his shoulder as he headed for the balcony from which he'd entered.

Pasval hurled more abuse at his nephew as he left. "Once you're dead, this country is mine! You'll pay for the many mockeries I've suffered!"

Oscar did not respond to the provocation. It was like he hadn't heard anything at all. As Pasval began cackling madly and loudly, the witch looked down on him with scornful eyes. She drew near and whispered in a clear, decisive voice, "His bloodline will not die out. Why do you think I've come here?"

Pasval stopped mid-cackle and stared up at her. Silhouetted by a halo of moonlight, she wore a bewitching smile.

"His bloodline will not die. And you... *You may never again enter this city... That's* final."

Eyes huge, Pasval gaped at her. Then, he flopped back into the chair limply, like his strings had been cut. He just sat there shivering, lacking even the energy to look up.

Tinasha eyed him icily, then followed Oscar out onto the balcony.

"What did you do?" he asked.

"That's how you cast a curse." She smiled, her eyes narrowing. It was the expression of someone strong and secure in her power to control the fates of others. "Let's go back, Oscar. Our business here is done."

Tinasha held out a hand. Oscar took it, and the pair floated into the air. Gaining altitude, they soared across the night sky. Like a little kid, Oscar's eyes were fixed on the spectacle below him.

"It's fun using transportation magic, but flying is so new and exciting," he said.

"To use transportation magic, you have to know the coordinates of your destination, or it won't work. I certainly don't know the coordinates of every location in the city," Tinasha explained. Then, she sighed unexpectedly, and Oscar looked over to her in surprise. After a pause, she muttered, "You've really got a nasty uncle there."

"Oh, him? Well, we aren't blood relatives. I'm grateful for that, at least."

Oscar had thought Tinasha was feeling bothered over not knowing many places in the city yet, but it turned out she'd sighed because of his family circumstances. However, no matter how many annoying and stomach-turning things cropped up, all of it was Oscar's burden to bear alone. He couldn't share the load with anyone, nor did he intend to try. He'd long been prepared to live his whole life that way.

Grimacing a little, Oscar met Tinasha's worried gaze.

"I can sympathize with you a little more now... I'll definitely do something about your curse," she said.

The look in Tinasha's eyes was so unlike the one back in the mansion. Oscar felt his heart skip a beat. As this witch in the guise of a girl looked over at him with clear, bright eyes, he felt a fondness welling up within him.

"What? Do you want to marry me now?" Oscar asked.

"I'm talking about finding another way!" Tinasha snapped back in the same way she always did, and Oscar burst out laughing. His heart felt lighter, and he inhaled, deep and easy. His momentary gloom had passed.

First thing the next morning, Pasval fled the city in great haste. He locked himself in his home in Colas, never to reemerge.

▌4. On the Shores of the Lake

The earth was dry and cracked. Reminiscent of the lands surrounding the witch's tower, the desolate area had been shrouded in perpetual fog for seventy years.

This was the site of the battle between Farsas and Druza, where the giant magic weapon referred to as a demonic beast once went on a rampage. A young man wearing a robe gazed out over the dried-out expanse that mages called a magical lake. The silver-haired girl standing next to him looked up at her companion.

"What's in a place like this, Valt? It's definitely thick with magic, but…"

"You can't see it, but it all starts now," he answered, running a hand through his light-brown hair.

They were outside the Farsas castle city, but Valt was still concealing his magic. He'd put a fair distance between himself and the witch, but there were others in this land. To ensure the path to their destination went smoothly, he'd lent a bit of help and guidance, but he didn't want anything more to be expected of him. Valt would only risk stirring up trouble with his own magic as an absolute last resort.

"She should be noticing it right about now. Let's see what she's got."

"The Witch of the Azure Moon? Will she really come all the way out here?" the silver-haired girl asked.

"She will. She has eyes all over the mainland. Especially out here," Valt answered. He looked up at the sky. The gray cat that raced among the clouds was the witch's familiar. That was how she searched all across the land. The witch being unable to give up on the man was her destiny. That's how Valt knew she'd notice a tipping of the scales like this right away.

"We'll have to hide in the clouds for a little bit, too. I don't want to go toe to toe with her," Valt said. Though his magic far exceeded that of the ordinary mage…and he held memories no other person could, any of the witches could easily twist him into surrendering. Such was the gap of strength between them.

"The only one who could face off against a witch head-on and kill her is the Akashia swordsman."

"By Akashia swordsman, do you mean the crown prince of Farsas? Are you going to make him kill her?"

"He can't right now. He can't beat her yet."

Which was why things were still stagnant. The poor witch's wish remained unfulfilled, and the scales of the world were yet untipped.

"Let's go, Miralys," Valt said, taking the girl along and leaving the wasteland behind. The gray fog grew even thicker, cloaking their ever-more-distant figures.

※

The light of a clear summer sky shone down on the castle training grounds yet again. Tinasha was cooling off in the shade, her sword set aside, when Als came to sit next to her.

"You've made major progress. Or maybe it's just your senses returning to you," he remarked.

"Do you really think so? Thank you," Tinasha replied.

After their first match, she'd started regularly showing up at the training grounds to get in some practice. Als recommended some times to drop by—all of them being when he was free and Meredina was away—but his childhood friend might have picked up on that. He felt bad for Meredina, but because the soldiers' morale went up whenever Tinasha came by, he welcomed the mage's visits.

Tinasha had her arms folded over her knees, and her head was resting on top of them. "How long do you think it'll take me to be as good as him?" she asked.

"Do you mean His Highness? That's been impossible for as long as I've been practicing a sword. I've never beaten him once."

"What? Really?" Tinasha asked, looking up at him with big, round eyes. The sun caught her dark orbs, making them sparkle like black quartz.

Als nodded, retying his boots. "Really. This is just between us, but I was pretty upset after the first time we sparred. I'd kind of looked down on him, thinking royal blood couldn't be anything special."

"He's that strong...," Tinasha said, trailing off and glancing up at the sky as she sighed. Clouds were streaming rapidly by; the winds up there were likely pretty quick.

"Lately, His Highness has been fairly good about staying in the castle, but until recently, he was always sneaking off with Lazar to who knows where... That wasn't too dangerous in and of itself, so I let it be. When I heard he was going to the witch's tower, though, I thought he'd lost his mind. It was pretty surprising to see he'd come back in one piece."

"I heard he crushed the tower's guardian beasts easily," Tinasha said.

"Are we sure he's human?" Als muttered.

They both sighed. Als combed back his red hair so it wouldn't get in his way. "Couldn't you just use magic? Can you not use it at close range or something?"

"Normally, I have a barrier up, but don't forget that he carries Akashia with him," reminded Tinasha.

"Oh...right, yeah," Als said.

The royal sword that granted absolute protection from all magic. It had been two years now since Oscar first armed himself with the enemy of all mages.

"I guess it's impossible," Als concluded.

"It really is," sighed Tinasha. The general made it sound so final that she felt a little panicked.

Als apparently took notice and gave her a pitying look. "Isn't it still possible to get him to train you?"

"Mmmm... I don't really want to show him my hand just yet. I still don't know how things are going to turn out."

"I see, I see..." The youngest general in Farsas tilted his head thoughtfully. "Yeah, I think it's impossible," he reiterated.

"Noooo!" cried Tinasha. She looked even more anguished than she had a moment ago. For an instant, Als thought she'd fainted from the agony of it all, but she'd merely sagged listlessly to the ground.

Finished with practice, Tinasha was walking along a connecting passage when someone called out to her, and she stopped in her tracks. No one else could hear the voice that had spoken. Tinasha went outside and walked up to the base of a huge tree in the gardens.

"Litola."

"I'm glad you appear well, Master. You've been blessed with a good contract holder," said Litola.

"You think so?" Tinasha asked.

Litola, sitting in the upper branches of the tree, jumped and landed on the ground silently, then bowed. "You seem like you're having much more fun now than you used to."

"I suppose it is fun, but... Well, it's not bad," the witch said, shrugging as she made a face.

In reply, Litola frowned a little. "Shouldn't you just marry him? It doesn't look like things will change in a year or even a hundred."

"They'll change, they'll change. Besides, I have no desire for a spouse," Tinasha said, waving her hand dismissively.

At this very human gesture, Litola bowed their head respectfully. "I've said too much. Please forgive me. I have completed my assigned investigation, so today, I've come to report."

"All right, go ahead." The curtain hiding Tinasha's emotions fell from her dark eyes. Her gaze was like a completely still pool of water. This was her witch's face, the one very different from the expressions she normally showed Oscar and Als. Silently, Tinasha listened to the report. She clicked her tongue in irritation when Litola finished.

The witch appeared in Oscar's study just as he and Lazar were taking a break to play spinning tops. Her sudden intrusion caught both men off guard.

She wasn't wearing her usual mage's robe or fluttery clothing but a form-fitting magical costume made of black fabric inlaid with sigils. The outfit hugged her curves, and the cut was one not seen in Farsas, lending her a strange, commanding presence and an eye-catching charm. Over it, she was wearing a cloak, yet again inlaid with magical symbols.

Perhaps most unusual of all was a slender sword that hung at Tinasha's hip. Crystal-embedded wrist braces adorned her hands, and belts affixed to her waist and legs held other items that resembled weapons.

In all likelihood, this was her battle ensemble.

Oscar was quick to pick up on this and rose to his feet. "What's happened? Why are you dressed like that?"

"I'll be heading out for two or three days," she replied curtly, turning to go. Oscar grabbed for her wrist, barely catching hold of it.

"Wait, wait. Where are you going?" he demanded.

"Does it matter? I'll come back safely," she said.

"It doesn't look like you're just going out to play. You've taken off all your sealing ornaments."

To keep up the guise of an apprentice mage, Tinasha normally wore a number of rings and earrings designed to seal her magic. If a normal mage wore even one such item, they wouldn't be able to cast spells anymore, yet Tinasha wore close to ten while working as a court mage. That was just how powerful she was, but now she'd removed all her shackles.

She made to leave the room, but Oscar pulled her back toward him. Lazar rushed to close the door, blocking her exit.

"At least tell me where you're going. You made a contract with me. You can't just go off and leave," Oscar pleaded.

Tinasha glared in reply. She looked completely unlike her usual self, and Lazar was clearly unnerved by it. Seeing that Oscar wasn't cowed at all by her flashing eyes, the witch reluctantly admitted, "The magical lake in Old Druza."

"Old Druza?" Oscar repeated, but he quickly understood. "So that's why that mage was killed."

"What? What? What are you talking about?" Lazar was utterly confused, unable to follow the conversation.

Oscar explained, still gripping the witch's wrist tight. "The guy who was poisoned used to make monthly trips to study the magical lake in Old Druza. Someone who didn't want him doing that egged his girlfriend on to kill him, right? Pasval was sent to the city to stir up confusion among the royal council and buy time."

Tinasha nodded, confirming Oscar's guess. "Waves of powerful magic are coursing through the magical lake. I'm going to go investigate and see if someone's up to something. Is that acceptable?" she asked, imploring with her eyes for Oscar to release her.

Oscar shook his head. "Give me an hour. I'm coming, too."

"What?" Tinasha went agape, but she quickly regained her composure. "That's not necessary. Rather, the prince should not be roaming about."

"What do you think you're doing going alone? Under the terms of the treaty, that land belongs to no country, but in reality, Farsas controls it. If something happens and you're the only one investigating, I won't have enough of a reason to get the country involved."

He made a good point, and Tinasha's face softened just a little. She maintained a fierce glare on Oscar, however. "If I take you along, it's going to be an even bigger problem."

"I'll assemble a capable team. Fifteen should be good for an investigative mission," Oscar reasoned to himself.

"I am not obligated to protect anyone besides you," she warned.

"I understand," came the prince's flat reply.

Oscar hadn't hesitated at all, and Tinasha was left speechless. The prince hadn't wavered, to an almost enviable degree. He'd made a purpose-driven snap assessment. Surely, this was what made him worthy of the throne—the mark of a strong warrior who could take everything in and stand tall.

Tinasha inhaled deeply. Her thoughts were paused, but in their place, an infinite number of memories filtered past her mind's eye. Sights and sounds she'd lost. Herself as a child. A country on the verge of ruin. Countless... people she'd made contracts with who were no longer alive. It was like the last lingering traces of her sentimentalism. All of it, she could never get back. What about this moment had sparked such thoughts?

As Tinasha stared at this man before her, she spoke hoarsely. "One hour... I won't wait any longer."

"That's all I need," Oscar said, finally releasing her. He left the room to begin getting everything ready.

Exactly one hour later, a group of fifteen, including Oscar and Tinasha, had gathered. Soon they would step onto a transportation array that would bring them to a fortress on the northern border. There were nine soldiers, including Meredina, and four mages. Everyone had protested Als going, saying that the castle would be lost without him, so the general had stayed behind. For that same reason, Chief Mage Kumu also wasn't part of the group. Both of them had shown up to see everyone off, though, perhaps out of worry.

Tinasha was standing in a corner still looking a little sullen. While they waited, one of the mages in the party came to say hello.

"My name is Sylvia. I think this is the first time we've spoken. It's nice to meet you."

She had glossy blond hair and a cute face. The mage looked to be around twenty years old. She exuded a kind of natural warmth that helped melt Tinasha's irritation.

Breaking into a smile, Tinasha replied, "It's nice to meet you, too."

"Um, is that a dragon?" asked Sylvia. She pointed to the red dragon the size of a hawk perched on Tinasha's shoulder. The dragon in question yawned, paying her no mind.

"Yes. But it's not really used to people, so be careful."

"Wow... I've never seen a dragon before," said Sylvia.

"Tinasha!" came a man's loud, well-projected voice. There was only one person in the whole castle who referred to her that way with no "Miss" before it. Summoned by the one with whom she'd contracted, Tinasha nodded at Sylvia before running over to him. Oscar caught sight of the dragon, and his eyes widened.

"What's that?" he asked.

"When I was planning to go alone, I summoned it to ride there," Tinasha explained.

"That doesn't look big enough to carry a passenger," Oscar observed, ending their conversation there. He then addressed the group.

"We're going to investigate the magical lake in Old Druza. We don't know what's going to happen, so be careful. Also, do what she says," Oscar ordered, reaching around the dragon to place a hand on Tinasha's head. The dragon looked up at Oscar curiously.

The order caught Tinasha off guard. "Is it okay to say that?" she hissed.

"Well, we can't explain the full story," Oscar replied quietly.

"You're so strange," Tinasha said. Regius had been a little strange, too, but Oscar was in a league of his own.

Tinasha glanced over at Sylvia, who appeared somewhat troubled. As she did, the witch also caught sight of a sour-faced Meredina. She then took in Als, Kumu, and Lazar in turn, all of whom were wearing concerned expressions. Finally, she looked up at Oscar, who smiled a little when he felt her gaze on him.

"It'll be fine. I'll handle it." His voice was a pleasant hum.

Tinasha inhaled deeply and closed her eyes. As she did, memories of the day she'd left this castle to fight against Druza flashed through her mind.

"Let's go, Tinasha. I need your power."

The recollection was ephemeral, like a bubble on the water's edge. No one from that time was still alive. Everything eventually flowed on, leaving Tinasha behind. Yet she was still stuck in the same place. That was what she had chosen for herself.

Tinasha lifted her face. Her long eyelashes fluttered open, and she gave everyone such a beautiful smile that, for a moment, enchanted them all.

The sentimentality overflowing from her eyes was nothing but pure, crystal-clear loneliness. A light that loved and adored the fleeting lives of mortals. Oscar was stunned by it for a short while. Sensing him gasp, Tinasha turned to look up at him. "What's wrong?" she asked.

"Ah… Nothing." The prince averted his gaze, and Tinasha was left with no idea what he was thinking.

"Let's go," Tinasha said, re-centering herself.

As she spoke, the transportation array began to move.

Having been teleported to the northern border fortress of Ynureid, the party borrowed horses and crossed the national border to ride for Old Druza's magical lake. The entire environment was still cloaked in gray fog year-round—something many assumed to be some sort of lasting aftereffect of the war seventy years earlier. Visibility was poor, but the group relied on the magic sunk deep into the ground to guide them.

After riding for an hour, the hazy landscape at last began to demonstrate some observable change.

At the vanguard, galloping along side by side with Tinasha, Oscar frowned. "What a view. Looks like someone's nightmare."

Every so often, a tree would appear with twisted, spindly branches and a crooked trunk. Nothing but these leafless, snakelike trees and fallen rocks surrounded them; it looked like another world entirely.

Tinasha replied without turning toward Oscar. "It was pretty much destroyed seventy years ago. This is actually better than it looked back then, but it'll take another two centuries for it to completely self-purify."

"So we're not even halfway there. It must've been pretty bad at the time, huh?"

The witch riding next to Oscar was the one who'd brought a close to that historic battle. Tinasha patted down parts of her hair that had gotten mussed in the wind. "Yeah… It was incredibly tough. That beast isn't remembered as a terrible magic weapon for nothing, after all. It was everything I could do just to seal it away."

"If even you couldn't beat it, doesn't that make it pretty damn strong? Did they really deploy something like that in battle?" Oscar wondered.

"It couldn't be fully controlled. I think they just dropped it into the conflict and let it go wild. I'm glad I decided to seal it, though. Considering the situation, if we had fought it head-on, the carnage would have been gruesome."

Tinasha speaking so candidly about a war from so long ago while looking like a beautiful young woman made it sound like a fairy tale; it didn't feel real. She looked up at the fog-covered sky. "The magical lake is right up ahead... Even so, I think the horses are almost at their limit. Any more, and we'll ride them to exhaustion."

Tinasha was right. The horses' strength and speed had been starting to wane. They were probably more sensitive than their riders to the surroundings. The party had no choice but to hitch their mounts to nearby trees and continue on foot.

As they walked, Tinasha murmured a light incantation and lifted her hand. Oscar sensed that the air surrounding him had changed and looked around.

"What did you do?" he asked.

"I set up a barrier. The miasma was growing thick." After she'd commented on it, Oscar noticed that everyone was looking somewhat pale and unwell. With Tinasha's barrier in place, the group quickly recovered.

Oscar, who hadn't noticed anything out of the ordinary at all, pointed to his own face. "Was I spared the effects because of your protection?" he asked.

"Correct. I can protect you from the miasma without lifting a finger," Tinasha answered, grinning.

Behind her, a young mage named Doan muttered, "Temys's reports didn't mention any miasma..."

"Maybe something's happening."

"I'd like to avoid any sort of historic events in the making...," Doan said, shaking grit out of his dark-gray hair. He was widely seen as next in line to be chief mage, but considering his crafty tendency to keep his talents hidden, he acted more like a worldly bureaucrat. He made no secret of his mild concerns.

Oscar answered, "You don't get to be in something like that just by thinking about it anyway. I should know. I used to wish I could be in one all the time as a kid." Doan looked visibly disheartened at that reply smacking of adventurous curiosity, and Tinasha gave a little sigh.

They were almost at the magical lake.

It was a wasteland, stripped of water and grass. The same thick murk blanketed everything, making it hard to see more than ten steps ahead. The cracked earth was bone-dry, but every so often, invisible ripples undulated slightly above the ground like waves.

Oscar stared at one ripple that slipped past his feet. "This is my first time here… Are these waves normal?"

"More or less," Tinasha answered. She then began reciting another spell, a longer one this time. In response, a giant circular design spread out on the ground. When she finished her incantation, red threads floated up from the outer edge of the circle. They knit together above the design, forming a half-sphere-shaped cage.

"Don't go beyond this and wait here for a little while. I'm going to go take a look around," she ordered.

"Ah, wait, Tinasha," Oscar said, grabbing after her arm immediately, but the witch had already floated into the air. In an instant, she'd disappeared into the fog.

Doan watched her go, murmuring, "Just what is she…?"

"She's a bit of an eccentric. I want to bring her back…," Oscar said. He'd followed Tinasha in the hopes of preventing her from going off alone, but he'd lost sight of her. He wanted to go after her, but the fog made that difficult.

However…since he alone had Tinasha's protection, he could probably leave and move around just fine. Oscar glanced down at the royal sword at his waist. Meredina took notice and was just about to say something when there came a cry from another soldier.

"Th-the fog!"

When the group turned to look, high waves of thick fog were rolling in. In an instant, they had poured into the barrier, making it impossible for anyone to see. Screams pierced the air, and disorder threatened to take over.

"Stay calm! Don't move!" shouted Oscar.

Even if they couldn't see anything, they only had to stay inside the barrier. Such was the logical conclusion from the man who knew Tinasha's true identity. The strange mist, as if mocking Oscar's orders, seemed to thicken. It was freezing cold. Just as Oscar was about to click his tongue in annoyance, he heard the distant, high-pitched scream of a girl echo from somewhere in the distance.

"Tinasha?" Oscar only hesitated for a second. He shouted to his subordinates, "Stay here! I'll be right back!"

"Your Highness!"

The prince stepped out into a sea of fog, unsheathing his sword. He advanced through the floating gray sea in pursuit of his protector. The farther into the gloom he traveled, the more he felt the air around him warping.

After some time had passed, the fog finally thinned out a little. Oscar noticed a figure up ahead and made for it, but someone caught hold of his hand from behind.

"Your Highness... You can't."

"Meredina? You followed me?"

Meredina, the army officer, was holding on to Oscar with a desperate expression. She shook her head, deathly pale. "It's a trap. Please come back."

"I know that, but...," Oscar protested.

He was aware it might be a trap. Even so, if Tinasha was in danger, he couldn't leave her to such a fate. He had gone out knowing that he alone could endure the strange fog.

However, Meredina showed no signs of relenting. Acquiescing in the face of her stubbornness, Oscar pointed to the figure up ahead in the fog. "Okay. Then I'll go back after I check out who that is."

The small-statured silhouette stood totally still. Based on that, it couldn't be Tinasha. However, Oscar reasoned that if he didn't check to see who it was, then their whole fact-finding expedition was pointless.

Meredina reluctantly released the prince, following behind him. Proceeding cautiously through the fog, the two reached the hazy figure. Its back was to them, and after Meredina got a good look at it, she let out a yelp of surprise.

"This is unexpected," Oscar commented.

As if reacting to their voices, the figure slowly turned. It was a skeleton wearing a battered suit of armor.

Tinasha took a lap in the sky above the magical lake, releasing her magic to scan the landscape. What she could see through gaps in the fog suggested nothing unusual, but the unconcealed miasma and unusually powerful magic waves indicated obvious irregularities.

"Maybe it's underground..."

The witch returned to the barrier she had created but instantly noticed that something was amiss. A few people were missing, one of them being her contract holder.

"Miss Tinasha!" Sylvia half shrieked at her, and Tinasha flew over to the mage.

"What's happened? Where is His Highness?" she asked.

"Th-the fog suddenly pressed in on us... We could hear all sorts of voices from outside the barrier. He told us all to wait here and..."

"..."

This was the enemy who had laid the groundwork to thoroughly obstruct the investigation in Farsas. It should've been no surprise they'd do something to the investigative team, too. The enemy had probably robbed the group of sight, used noises to create confusion, and teleported whoever left the barrier to random places. It was Tinasha's fault for having not taken precautions against such actions, but she'd thought things would be fine if she only left for a short while. Now she was cursing herself for having not had the foresight to knock Oscar unconscious.

One would've never known she was blaming herself by her words, though.

"That...idiot...prince!" Tinasha was shaking with rage, and the others eyed her fearfully.

Desperate to soothe her, Sylvia said, "His Highness was worried about you, Miss Tinasha. He should be back soon..."

"I really need to give him a stern talking-to!" Tinasha spat, swallowing her irritation and opening both hands to weave a spell with no incantation.

"I'm going to detect their location. I don't think they've gone far," she explained.

Tinasha would have noticed if anyone had been teleported beyond the wilderness. Just as she anticipated, she sensed the location of people. She'd warned Oscar that she wasn't obligated to protect anyone but him, but in reality, Oscar was the only one Tinasha trusted would be fine without her coming to his aid. The same could not be said for the others the enemy had scattered. If she didn't retrieve them fast, none could say the kind of danger they could find themselves in.

While Tinasha repeated the detection spell, she manifested three small balls of light in her hands to both illuminate the way and provide protection. She sent them out into the air, where they flew along until one hit something and flew back.

"What?" Tinasha said, surprised. It had made a metallic clank. Several shapes emerged from the fog.

Though wearing armor and carrying swords, they were unmistakably not alive. Sylvia caught sight of their empty eye sockets and let out a high-pitched scream.

"D-dead bodies! Skeletons!" she cried.

"Whoa, they really are dead," Tinasha muttered.

Countless corpses, their flesh having long since rotted away, staggered toward them.

Inside the barrier, the mage Doan frowned. "That armor has the crest of Druza on it. Some of them have Farsas crests, too."

"Ghosts from seventy years ago…"

The casualties of the war had been colossal, and many soldiers had been hastily buried on the battlefield. Someone had raised up their bodies. The shambling things were reaching for their swords, as if they didn't know they were dead. Ever so slowly, the animated dead came to surround the investigation party from all sides.

An army officer spoke up with a decision. "Let's fight back. Those who left won't be able to return at this rate."

"…I suppose you're right," admitted Tinasha.

They could stay holed up inside the barrier, but that would mean giving up on retrieving those who'd gotten lost.

Tinasha unsheathed her sword and gave an order to the dragon on her shoulder. "Nark, go find Oscar and bring him back! He's the man with blue eyes who was here earlier. He has a mark on him, so you'll recognize him, okay? If he's with anyone else, pick them up, too. Don't eat them!"

The dragon gave a cry, and its neck and tail warped as the creature grew and lengthened. It expanded until its scarlet body was the size of a horse. Throwing a sidelong glance at the stunned group, the dragon flapped its wings and soared off into the fog.

Tinasha didn't even bother to watch the dragon depart. Instead, she stepped outside the safety of her barrier. A skeletal warrior stabbed at her, but Tinasha sent the creature's weapon spinning off into the air, then used her own sword to lop off the corpse's head.

"Once everyone's back, we retreat. Hold them off until then," Tinasha ordered.

"I'll back you up," Sylvia said, running up behind Tinasha. The others made their own battle preparations.

The ensorcelled dead gradually tightened their ring around the group. Soon after, the sound of slashing steel erupted from amid the horrifying spectacle.

There was no apparent end to the dead soldiers they cut down. The approach of shuffling footsteps echoed in the humid air. The stench of mildew and dirt was overwhelming, as was the temptation to retch.

Meredina fought back the urge to shriek as she fought. Had she been alone, she might've already joined the undead ranks.

After barely managing to fend off a longsword attack from overhead, she staggered back from the impact. A different sword darted out of the fog, aiming for her side. She was unable to dodge it, but another blade repelled what would have been a fatal strike.

"You okay?"

"Your Highness... Thank you," Meredina said.

Oscar had also been pressed into the battle with no end in sight, but he hadn't even broken a sweat. His steady presence was reassuring, and Meredina took a breath. At the same time, a bitter feeling prickled her chest.

"Let's force our way through and go back. I'm sure she's safe."

"I think so, too, but technically I'm kind of her protector," Oscar answered, his gaze searching through the fog for Tinasha.

His words sounded like he only felt a sense of duty toward her, but Meredina knew it was more than that. She bit back a sigh of grief. She was positive Oscar hadn't realized it himself. At the moment, he simply appeared to feel he had to protect the girl he'd brought along.

Looking at the circumstance from the outside revealed something more, however. Like the clear smile Tinasha had flashed Oscar when they left the castle...and how it had drawn him in instantly.

Up until this point, the prince had most likely regarded Tinasha as no different from an adorable kitten. He spent the most time with her but cared little for her exotic looks or magic. Meredina was probably more aware of those attributes than Oscar...and she was tortured by secret feelings of inferiority. It had only gotten worse when she'd learned her rival had gone to Als for training and was even better with a sword than Meredina herself. She knew there was no need to compare herself to this woman, but she couldn't help feeling a sense of defeat just by knowing that such a nemesis existed.

Still, Oscar had to have known something when he saw that smile, too... Perhaps that Tinasha wasn't a defenseless child under his protection but, rather, someone he'd spend the kind of time with that he wouldn't spare for anyone else.

"It's all right, Your Highness. By now, I'm sure she's returned and is waiting for you."

"Meredina," Oscar said, grateful for her words.

It probably wouldn't be much longer. Meredina's lord was perceptive and would soon realize his own feelings. Until that happened, while he was still unaware, all she could do as his subject was warn him against it. Pushing down her bittersweet feelings, she took up her sword again.

"I'm sorry to be a burden on you. I'm going to clear a path," Meredina declared. She knew that when she saw Tinasha again, she'd feel irrepressibly jealous. However, she was an army officer. She had to stick to her duties without being led so casually astray. If she didn't, she'd be letting down her old friend—Als.

The animated corpses swung their swords at Meredina. She advanced, trampling fallen armor underfoot.

The ring around them was never-ending, and Oscar spoke up apologetically just as she began to panic. "Sorry I caused you some trouble."

A flash tore through the atmosphere.

Without a sound, the dead soldier that was about to attack Meredina collapsed. Then, all its compatriots in the area fell flat on the ground in kind. Shocked, Meredina looked at Oscar.

One swipe of his sword had ripped through the fog. As he broke the shambling corpses, mowing them down ruthlessly, a sword tip drove for his empty left hand. However, even though he was weaponless, something shattered the sword the instant before it touched his hand.

"What…was that…?" Meredina asked.

"Let's just keep this just between us, but I have a protective barrier that can neutralize almost any attack. Sorry for dragging you into this."

"What?" Meredina was stunned, but feeling an enemy attack coming, she lifted her sword to deal with it. As she jogged after her lord to catch up with him, she heard the sound of huge wings beating from the rear.

The fog dispersed instantly. Aware that something had landed behind her, Meredina turned into the heavy winds and saw two fiery-red eyes gazing at her.

"…A dragon? A real one?" Meredina said, incredulous.

"It got pretty big, huh…? Looks like people can ride it," Oscar noted.

In response to their remarks, the magic dragon answered with a shrill cry.

"Now all that's left are His Highness and Meredina!"

"Don't look away!"

Angry roars sailed up into the air from the battlefield as Tinasha fended off attacks with her sword while spreading out her magic to search the landscape.

The lake overflowed with magic, but that alone wasn't enough to ensorcell these dead bodies and get them walking. There had to be someone, somewhere, controlling them. Tinasha had to find out who—and fast.

Whoever the ringleader was must have been aware of that themselves, because they seemed to be constantly on the move. Their location was difficult to pin down.

Tinasha cut off the arm of a dead soldier that was attacking Sylvia. The tattered appendage flew through the air, falling into the fog.

"Th-thank you!" Sylvia said, gasping in surprise.

Tinasha smiled at her. "Don't worry about it. Just a little longer."

Then, as if in response to its master's voice, a sharp cry came from overhead. The crimson dragon spread its wings, catching an updraft and descending slowly. On its back were a man and a woman. The man jumped off the dragon's back before it even touched the ground.

Tinasha regarded him coldly. "You're due for a scolding."

"Sorry," he apologized.

"Everyone, get inside the barrier!"

Upon that order, the group retreated into the red semisphere. The dragon landed inside it, too, Meredina on its back. The walking corpses tightened their perimeter even further. Tinasha sheathed her sword and began chanting a spell.

"*Recognize my will as law, transformer that sleeps in the earth and flies in the sky. I control your flames and summon you. Know my command to be every concept of your manifestation.*"

A ball of flame appeared in the witch's palms. She took it in her right hand.

"*Burn!*"

In an instant, the conjured fire grew blindingly bright. The scorching ball became waves of flames. With a thunderous roar and fearsome power, tongues of crimson lashed out in all directions.

After only a moment, the rippling fires consumed the swarm of animated dead, reducing them to cinders. Voiceless screams of deathly agony swept over the wasteland while hot winds blew into the barrier.

Sylvia had instinctively turned her face away from the impact, but when she opened her eyes, she saw nothing but level ground beyond the barrier. All that remained of the army of bodies was a burnt smell wafting through the air.

"I guess that's all it was. Finally cleared that away," Tinasha said, dusting off her hands. The others were stunned by the sheer force of her magic after witnessing it at such close range.

Meredina dismounted from the dragon, eyeing Tinasha fearfully. She felt like she finally understood why Als had called Tinasha terrifying.

Oscar was the only one who was calm. He surveyed the area and let out a low whistle. "The fog's totally gone; that's great."

The flames had engulfed the entire stretch of land, dispersing the thick mists. Now the blasted acreage was completely unobstructed. Oscar turned back and patted the witch's head.

"Tinasha, one zombie survived the fire," he observed.

Some distance away stood an old man in a mage's robe. He was so emaciated, he could've easily been mistaken for a skeleton, and he stared at the party with sunken eyes.

Tinasha noticed him and frowned. "It looks like he put up a defense."

The old mage caught her gaze on him and spoke in an unexpectedly sonorous voice, "It has been a while. I didn't think I would see you again during my lifetime."

Starting with Oscar, everyone cast a questioning look at Tinasha, but she ignored it. She looked at the man dispassionately, and he continued.

"Glimpsing that outfit and your beauty nearly fooled me into believing I'd gone back seventy years. Witch of the Azure Moon, are you doing this again in memory of the man you loved?"

The man's words made everyone except Oscar and Tinasha let out a sharp gasp. Sylvia was astonished and panicky, while other soldiers put their hands up in the air for no reason.

Behind Oscar, Meredina spoke in a quivering voice, "Witch... Is that true?"

"It is," answered Oscar, sounding sullen for some reason. Tinasha, for her part, paid no mind to the actions of those behind her and faced the old mage with an entrancing smile.

"You've gotten quite old. At the time, you were just a child. You haven't just gone bald, you've completely dried up," she commented, and the old man laughed loudly.

He rubbed his head, little more than skin and bones now. "I should be long dead. Not everyone is like you."

Tinasha snorted lightly. "You've come to resemble your master both in speech and appearance... It's disgusting."

"My master whose head you cut off? That's quite the compliment." Dramatically, the strange old man spread both hands wide. Recognizing that for the challenge it was, Tinasha casually drew her sword and walked out of the barrier.

"Since we've met again, how about I take your head, too? You can get down on your knees and thank your master for sacrificing himself." The witch's smile was chillingly cruel and beautiful.

Tinasha swung her slender sword. With a crackling sound, blue lightning coiled around the blade.

But before she could take another step forward, the old mage vanished like the fog that had only minutes earlier pervaded the place.

"I am not strong enough to fight you, so I'll be taking my leave now. Perhaps you should return home soon, too. Or maybe that only comes after a death or two, hmm?"

His presence disappeared in a cloud of throaty laughter. Once it died out, a silence fell over the group. Tinasha was lost in thought for a short while, but soon enough, she stowed her sword and turned back around.

She stuck her tongue out childishly. "He got away."

"Someone you know?" asked Oscar.

"In the war seventy years ago, he was one of the Druzan mages who controlled the demonic beast."

"The demonic beast...," Oscar mused, hand on his chin.

Tinasha returned to the barrier, and Sylvia addressed her hesitantly. "Um... Miss Tinasha, are you really the Witch of the Azure Moon?"

"Sorry for keeping it a secret. I didn't want to scare anyone," Tinasha admitted. No traces of the cruelty she'd so easily adopted just moments before remained on her face. Her current smile held faint tinges of loneliness. Sylvia's heart ached seeing it. At the same time, the mage felt a little ashamed of how she'd been afraid of witches without knowing much about them.

"Ah, I…"

"No, no. Witches are scary creatures. Don't worry about it," Tinasha reassured, cutting Sylvia off with a shake of her head. The witch gave her a sunny smile that was lovely and also somewhat distant. Sylvia swallowed what she had been going to say.

Oscar looked up and spoke. "Let's go back for now. We need to prepare forces and equipment."

The crown prince's decision put everyone at ease. Staying where they were would only lead to more undo eeriness.

Party members checked in with one another, then started on the trip back. Thankfully, the ground visibility was much better now.

Oscar put a hand on the head of the witch at his side. "The horses didn't get burned, did they?"

"Probably not…" She gave him a worried smile. Perched on its master's shoulder, the now-little dragon yawned.

The horses were indeed alive and waiting where they'd been left. The fog was still thick in that area. Without delay, the group set off on horseback, returning to the fortress of Ynureid. Oscar and Tinasha rode side by side.

"Do you think their goal is to bring back the demonic beast?" Oscar asked.

"In all probability, yes. It's quite annoying," Tinasha answered.

From behind, Doan the mage piped up. "Isn't it possible that they're building something else?"

"I'm afraid not. There seem to be some misunderstandings… They did not create the demonic beast. It would be the end of the world if ordinary humans could build something like that. Most likely, a core of some sort entered the magical lake, and it absorbed each wave of magic as it came… After hundreds of years, that became the demonic beast," Tinasha explained.

"So all they did was control the beast?" Doan pressed.

"The entire point is that they were unable to fully control it. Honestly, I don't know why they want to stir up trouble."

As they were talking, the fog gradually began to clear. After riding for a while, the spires of the fortress came into view on the horizon.

Upon reaching that point, though, Tinasha slowed her horse and came to a halt.

"What is it?" Oscar asked.

Tinasha dismounted and gave the reins to a nearby soldier. "Continue on with everyone else. I'm going back in."

"What are you talking about?" Oscar demanded, dismounting in kind and approaching her.

The witch's reply was calm. "I suspect the enemy wants us to take this opportunity to retreat and prepare. They're trying to undo the seal as quickly as they can. I'm not going to give them the time to do that. I'm attacking now. That bag of bones might have thought he got away, but I'm going to chase him down." She held up the back of her right hand. The crystal on her wrist brace was vibrating a dark red, as if it held a flickering flame. Oscar was struck speechless.

He glared at his protector. "You... Did you wear that with the intention of doing this all along? It was never your aim to just go out to investigate."

"Of course not," Tinasha fired back instantly. There was no emotion in her eyes.

Oscar caught hold of her slender wrist. "I'm going, too."

"Not again!" Tinasha cried, feeling utterly exasperated. She pulled a sulky face, looking very much like she wanted to give Oscar a piece of her mind. In an attempt to free herself, she lifted off into the air and looked down at him, but Oscar held firm.

"You are infinitely capable, and I admire you for wanting to do everything yourself. However, as a future king, you need to learn to use those around you a bit more," Tinasha advised. As a mother would have, she placed a hand on Oscar's cheek. He glanced fondly at that hand but quickly returned his gaze to Tinasha's own and still did not yield.

"I know, and I'll be mindful of that. But I can't right now. I don't intend to use you like that," Oscar said.

"Isn't that why you brought me from the tower?" asked the witch.

"No," Oscar replied.

"Reg would have let me go," Tinasha reasoned.

"I don't care." Oscar tightened his grip. The demonic beast that slept beneath the earth was something Tinasha had only managed to seal away. Back then, she'd had the king of Farsas and his army. There was no way Oscar was going to let her try it again alone. At the same time, however…he knew that was just his excuse.

Seventy years ago, Tinasha had almost certainly battled to protect the others. She'd said there had been no choice but to seal it away—which meant she'd done it to prevent further loss of life on the battlefields. Thus, even if Oscar followed her here, they'd just be repeating the same mistake.

Even in the face of such rationale, Oscar didn't want to let her go alone. "Their target is Farsas. I can't make you bear this responsibility alone," he asserted.

"I have my own reasons pertaining to that… I really can't allow you to go," Tinasha replied, giving the prince a pained smile. It was an expression identical to one she'd had in the castle.

Her long, glossy locks fluttered, though no magic enchanted them. Slowly, she blinked her obsidian eyes.

Whether Tinasha was recalling a specific event in the past or merely losing herself in the thoughts of her many lifetimes was difficult to discern. She gave Oscar a gentle smile. "Our contract is only for one year. Please don't be shy about giving me the annoying work."

"Tinasha…"

"I can bear your burdens quite easily," she added, almost singing it out.

Oscar's words caught in his throat at that. All the burdens he'd carried his whole life. His royal blood, his duties, his curse—she knew all of them and told him to hand them over, smiling as she did so. Tinasha was insisting that none of it was heavy for her to bear and that Oscar should make use of that.

The witch's eyes, the color of a moonless night, bore into the prince's. "Oscar, I've made a contract with you, and as long as I'm your protector, I promise to return to you no matter where I go or what I do. I will not die before you. I swear it." Her promise sounded close to a wedding vow.

Oscar stared back into Tinasha's eyes. It felt like he was gazing into a bottomless abyss. He had been naive to think of her as just a clueless young woman. Just how many more years had she seen than him? It was impossible to imagine. He had no way of catching up now. In fact, all he knew for certain was that he had no hope of closing that distance.

Oscar bit back a sigh. Gently, he released his grip on Tinasha's wrist. "All right. Go," he conceded.

Tinasha gave him a soft smile. She lifted her left hand, and the dragon on her shoulder gave a cry and flew into the air. It grew even larger than it had before, expanding until it rivaled the size of three small houses.

"I hope you'll put a little more faith in me from now on. Regardless of how I look, I've never once been defeated," Tinasha said.

"Then I'll be your first," Oscar quipped.

"...I need to look into some countermeasures first, so give me a little time..." The scarlet dragon extended its neck, and the beautiful witch climbed onto its back.

Tinasha and her mount made for a fantastic sight, like some fairy-tale painting. All who beheld the scene let out an instinctive sigh of admiration, their fear of witches mixed in with their admiration of Tinasha the person. As Meredina looked up at Tinasha, she felt a curious warmth filling her heart.

The dragon dropped back to the ground a little, hovering in front of everyone for a moment. Its huge left eye, seemingly lit with flames, stared at the assembled soldiers and mages. Tinasha was checking her equipment.

"Hey, when you come back...," Oscar started.

"When I come back?"

"Do you want to get married?"

"No! And don't make it sound like I'm going to die!" Tinasha snapped back the same way she always did, laughing.

She gave the dragon a light slap, and it took off for the magical lake in a cloud of dust. The dragon and its rider disappeared into the fog.

※

Druza lay to the northwest of Farsas. During the war, Druza had been the first to attack. At the time, the nation had been suffering from bad harvests and hoped to acquire its neighbor's large tracts of land and abundant natural resources.

The Farsasian army put up a good fight in the face of such a sudden invasion. They pushed back the enemy forces with a staunch show of military might. After only a week, it seemed the conflict would end. It was then that Druza awakened the demonic beast sleeping within the magical lake and set it loose on Farsas.

The giant magic weapon lay waste to the Farsasian army. Such an unprecedented strategy was felt all across the mainland. However, the decision to use the demonic beast had been a rather arbitrary one put into practice by a group of mages. In reality, the magical weapon could not be completely controlled, and just as many Druzans were crushed beneath the monster's claws. The miasma that surrounded the beast also seemed to poison the earth, reducing the battlefield to a foggy, barren wasteland for many years to come.

Casualties of the demonic beast rose beyond two thousand on both sides. Everyone despaired in the face of its overwhelming power, but the monster was finally sealed away by the witch who had been accompanying the king of Farsas.

After that, the witch had killed almost all the mages who had loosed the beast, and those who escaped her slaughter met their ends at the hands of their fellow Druzans.

From there, the demonic beast slept underground, and the fog-covered land finally knew peace, at least on the surface.

After the passing of seven decades, the very same witch who had defeated the beast had come to this land once more.

"Hurry and break the final spell on the seal! There's no time!" the old mage shouted as soon as he returned to the underground cavern.

"Right now? But the control spell isn't completed...," a young mage replied in surprise.

"I don't care! Start the incantation for breaking the final spell! The witch knows!" commanded the old man.

"She does?!" The younger mage seemed to have grasped the gravity of the situation. He ran into the depths of the cavern. Coughing, the old mage followed.

"…I'm not going to let it end here," he muttered.

After the war, Druza had broken into a number of smaller nations. The old man's hometown now belonged to the most destitute of all the shattered pieces of Druza. That was why he was going to use the power of the demonic beast to reunify Druza, destroy Farsas, and save his birthplace. In pursuit of that goal, he'd offer up his own life and those of his comrades' countless times over.

"…I'm not done yet; we're only just getting started…"

Dragging along his stiff and creaky body, the old mage finally arrived at the spell-breaking site. More than ten mages were already gathered there. All were united with the same desire, though different reasons had led them to it.

Just beyond this cavern floated a bluish-white pattern of spells—one so intricate it hardly looked man-made. This incredibly detailed multiple-configuration spell was the very seal the witch had constructed to end the war. Beyond it, within an enormous cave…was a giant, closed eye.

The eye was black around its edges, and its tremendous size made it difficult to discern it for what it was, unless viewed from a distance. Long silver fur lined the beast's enormous body, most of which was veiled by the dark cave and couldn't be distinguished. The only visible parts of the great monster were those illuminated by the seal, but the creature must have been the size of a small castle. When seen in full, the beast resembled a giant wolf, from its eyes to the shape of its snout.

Its immeasurable magic filled the air, making its presence nearly impossible to ignore. The sleeping beast was enigmatic—dreadfully so. To awaken this fearsome creature, five mages had already begun chanting the incantation. The old mage left them to look down into the cave. He asked a mage kneeling behind him, "How long will it take?"

"We'll need three days…," replied the mage.

"Three days… It'll take about that long for the Farsas army to arrive. That should be enough time," said the old man.

"I understand," answered the kneeling mage. Then came the sound of something tumbling onto the ground. Puzzled, the younger mage looked to where it had originated.

The freshly severed head of the gaunt old mage was lying on the ground.

"Wh-wha…?" The startled younger man could barely get a word out before he felt something cold at the back of his neck. He died before even realizing what had happened.

The tragedy was over in a flash.

A mage in the shadow of a rock, concentrating on his incantation with his eyes closed, realized he didn't hear his fellow mages chanting anymore. Suspecting something, he looked to where they had been…and his mouth fell agape in horror.

A pool of blood was spreading across the ground. His comrades were facedown in the crimson pool. The head of their leader, the old man, sat severed on the ground. Its face was fixed in an incredulous expression.

"Wha…?"

The mage who had been beneath the shade of the rock clapped a hand over his mouth. The stink of blood in the air assaulted his nose, and the scene was so gruesome that he felt dizzy.

What terrified him most of all was the sight of the young woman standing at the center of the ocean of blood. She held a sword dyed deep scarlet. The frightening woman grinned when she spotted him.

"Guess I missed one," she said cheerfully, and a paralyzing terror gripped the man. He collapsed, unable to speak.

The diminutive yet no less commanding young woman approached him casually. "What's wrong? Don't you want to undo the seal?"

Stammering, the man nodded. The girl's dark eyes opened wide, and she smiled.

"Then I'll open it for you." She swung her sword at the wall, shaking off the blood clinging to the weapon before sheathing it. Then she lifted a hand to the seal. Amid the thick stench of blood, what stood out most was that the mysterious young woman appeared to be backlit by moonlight.

"Sing, old admonition. Let the chains created long ago rot with my command…" It was a clear, resonant incantation.

While the seal was active, none could approach the demonic beast. The same was true for the witch who'd first put the spell in place. She lifted her right hand and unraveled the complicated seal. Off to the side, the mage stared at her, pale as a sheet.

The pattern was made up of seven smaller spells. One by one, they came undone as the witch's hands worked. After only a few moments, the spell pattern disappeared.

Very slowly, the beast's eyes began to open.

※

No sooner had the investigation party passed through the gates of the fortress of Ynureid than a sudden quake made the ground lurch beneath their feet.

Spooked, the horses whinnied frantically. Their riders looked back and heard heavy rumblings echoing from the direction of the magical lake. Such a sound suggested some sort of cave-in or collapse. Sylvia blanched.

"Just now, was that…the demonic beast?" She sounded almost too afraid to even ask.

His people looked panicked, but Oscar said nothing. He eyed the wastelands with a sharp gaze for a few seconds before shaking his head lightly and giving an order. "Let's get inside. We don't want the horses running off."

"But what about Miss Tinasha…?" Sylvia asked.

"She told us she'll be fine. She'll handle it," Oscar assuaged.

Undoubtedly, none, including Oscar, really knew of Tinasha's true form, the strongest witch in the whole mainland—an embodiment of overwhelming power.

After the Dark Age that had plagued the land for eons came the current era: the Age of Witches. It had been dubbed so because Tinasha and her fellow witches used their power to direct the course of history.

If a witch was angered, she could destroy a country overnight. That was something even little children knew, but until now, Oscar had never considered Tinasha to be that same sort of creature. He knew he'd learn of it someday, however. That was what it meant to have signed a contract with the Witch of the Azure Moon.

While the rest of the group continued milling about, Oscar rode through the gate and dismounted. Doan took notice and turned back to look.

"What is it, Your Highness?"

The immediate area beyond the gates to the fortress was flat and stark. Any trees near the gate had been cleared to ensure an unobstructed line of sight when looking out from the front of the bastion.

Oscar glanced around before suddenly unsheathing Akashia. In one motion, he kicked off the ground, advancing several steps in a flash. The blade of his mighty weapon cut through the air with frightening speed.

To all others, Oscar appeared to be slashing at nothing, but a bit of dark-gray fabric stained with blood suddenly fluttered from out of thin air. Doan, who'd been watching, immediately understood and let out a gasp. Akashia had cut open an invisible barrier, revealing the robe of the mage hiding inside it.

"Who are you? Are you with that old mage, too?" Oscar demanded.

"...Dammit. I knew you had good instincts, but I didn't expect this," said the young man, looking down at his torn robe and laughing. He had a youthful face and light-brown hair. His similarly colored eyes were filled with anxiety. After getting a good look at him, Oscar recalled something.

"You're the one from the festival, aren't you? So you've been following us since parting ways with Tinasha. Have you been keeping an eye on her this whole time?"

"Of course not. She'd catch me right away. She's actually been trying to track me down." The man's comment revealed he was aware Tinasha was looking for him. Someone who could discern a witch's actions and escape was more than an average enemy.

Imperceptibly, Oscar shifted his balance of gravity, taking a firmer stance.

Clutching his belly, the man gave a pained smile. "Relax. I only wanted to give you some advice."

"Advice?"

"Yes, it's something your protector is dying to find out. I'd appreciate it if you could pass on the message. I'm sure she'll be pleased."

"More likely she'll just get mad at me. If there's something she wants to know, she's more than capable of finding it out on her own," Oscar fired back, and the man's smile stiffened. He appeared about to say something but clearly thought better of it, sighing instead.

"It really is…so annoying how both of you are like this. You're too smart for smooth talk. That's why I always end up having to use backhanded forms of attack," he said.

"Stop joking around. Are you the one who killed our mage?" Oscar pressed.

"All I did was tell them to avoid an investigation. They decided how to do it. My role is always telling someone what to do. *How* they do it is up to them."

"You sure do talk in circles. Do you mean to say you're not with the Druzan mages?"

This man was clearly a mage, and he also gave off an unpleasant aura. Tinasha had said the man she saw at the festival was concealing a fair amount of magic—perhaps that was the reason.

"I belong to no country. Strictly speaking, I am not your enemy, either. I merely have business with the witch."

"I see. So you have some score to settle? In that case, die here." Before Oscar had even finished speaking, he rushed the man. His sword, one that could slash through all magical barriers, was now leveled at the brown-haired mage.

However, the blade never found its mark, hitting a rock that had appeared suddenly out of thin air and bouncing back. As Oscar's eyes widened in surprise, his opponent wove a transportation spell. A second before Doan's own capturing spell could reach him, the man disappeared.

Doan ground his teeth in frustration over barely missing the suspicious mage. "I'm very sorry, Your Highness… I couldn't catch him."

"No, don't worry about it. What's with this rock? Where did it come from?" At Oscar's feet lay a large stone about the size of a cat. It had seemingly formed out of thin air to block Akashia.

Doan explained with a bitter expression, "He transported it from wherever it was before. A pretty quick-witted move."

Akashia could dispel any magic but was only slightly stronger than a normal sword when it came to ordinary physical objects. Someone who knew that and could adapt to it was a tricky adversary indeed.

After checking to make sure the man had truly left, Oscar shook the blood off Akashia. "I'd intended to kill him…"

So long as his goal was Tinasha, Oscar wanted that man removed. At the very least, Oscar reasoned he should've been able to stop him while Tinasha was battling the demonic beast.

Yet all he'd been able to achieve was a first blow. Judging by the feel of the cut, Oscar knew he hadn't inflicted a fatal wound, but it hadn't been a glancing touch, either.

Doan shook his head. "Even if he has that injury tended to, he won't be able to make any moves for a while."

"So I managed to ground him. Next time, I'll finish him off," Oscar promised.

Another tremor rippled through the ground, and Oscar looked in the direction of the magical lake. Fog had wrapped around the spot like a gigantic cocoon, and his witch was somewhere inside.

※

Amid a cloud of fumes, Tinasha floated in the sky and looked below her.

The force of the demonic beast's awakening had caused a violent cave-in. Most likely, the surviving mage and his dead brethren were now buried there.

Tinasha called to her dragon as it circled the sky. "Nark, it's going to be dangerous until this is over, so stay back."

The dragon heeded its master's order and made off into a distant cloud of dust and fog.

Rubble on the ground was gradually clearing away. In the middle of the magical lake, a giant silver wolf lifted its head and glared at Tinasha. A red stone was embedded in its silver-furred forehead. Hostility glittered in its crimson eyes as the gigantic creature fixed them on the little witch in the sky.

Tinasha smiled beatifically. "It's been seventy years. Did you sleep well?"

This first encounter between the two since the war was sure to bring death upon one or the other. The demonic beast must have known that as well as Tinasha did. Its silver fur began emanating a faint glow in preparation for battle. Its pure quantity of magic might've rivaled that of Tinasha's fellow witches.

"Still, a mage's strength isn't measured only by their store of magic," Tinasha said, lifting her right hand. In response to the action, a ball of light appeared above it.

The blindingly bright sphere quickly expanded and began to emit an earsplitting noise. Lightning sparked out in long filaments that swirled around the glowing orb. The demonic beast loosed a booming howl in response.

Menace seeped into every available space. The demonic beast opened its mouth and released a powerful shock wave. Tinasha leaped to the side, dodging the beast's preemptive strike. Without a moment's delay, she hurled the ball of light at her opponent's still-open mouth.

Right before the sphere reached the beast's maw, the creature ducked. The white light impacted on the creature's forehead. Its long silver fur somehow absorbed the sphere—sparking as it diffused the attack.

"Just how fluffy is this thing...?" Tinasha muttered.

One reason she'd had such trouble with the demonic beast seventy years ago was because of its high resistance to magic. Anything other than an all-out attack wouldn't so much as scratch it. Had Tinasha used any attack powerful enough to overcome such incredible defense, the humans of the gathered armies wouldn't have escaped alive. That was why she'd chosen to seal it.

"I knew it would be, but this sure is tricky," Tinasha grumbled as the demonic beast tried to mow her down with its sharp claws. She only narrowly avoided the swipe. Flying through the air, Tinasha dipped toward the beast's feet. She pulled out a cylinder that had been attached to her leg and snapped the tiny lid off. A red ball rolled out onto her palm, and she poured a spell into it.

"Grow full, my definition…"

A second swipe of the great wolf's claws was fast incoming. As Tinasha leaped off the ground to avoid her demise, she threw the spell-imbued red ball at the beast's hind legs. The ball tore through the beast's silver fur with the precision of a knife. It burrowed itself deep, embedding into the flesh beneath the beast's hair. A moment later, the creature's leg exploded in a spatter of blood and flesh.

A howl of anguish rent the air. The beast sought Tinasha with eyes of dreadful fury. It spotted its foe standing on top of the magical lake. Hoping to tear her to pieces, the gigantic wolf opened its jaw wide.

"Oh no you don't."

As the beast's gigantic maw loomed, Tinasha erected a defensive barrier to withstand the attack. Floating up into the air again, she looked at her opponent's shredded hind leg and saw that the mangled flesh had already begun knitting together. Silver fur sprouted over the freshly healed wound.

"Seventy years has done little to slow your recovery," Tinasha complimented sarcastically. She then shook another red ball out of the cylinder. Flipping over in the air, she took aim at the beast's forelegs this time. The targeted spot burst apart with a muffled sound.

"If the Witch of the Azure Moon hadn't been with King Regius seventy years ago, the demonic beast might have ravaged all the way to the castle city."

Most scholars agreed with this postulation made by a famous history book.

In terms of characteristics, the demonic beast possessed a magic-resistant exterior. What's more, its huge body was endowed with inexhaustible physical stamina, the muscle power to flatten forests, and astounding resilience. Such capabilities were more than humans could have hoped to contend with and allowed the monster to wade through tens of thousands of soldiers.

Even those countries that had remained neutral in the Druzan invasion of Farsas were in an uproar as they scrambled to take any sort of measure they could to combat this walking nightmare.

In the end, they'd worried for nothing. A witch in service to the king of Farsas had appeared on the battlefield and sealed away the beast only a half day after its first appearance. With her work done, the witch then vanished from Farsas.

Perhaps she had sealed the rampaging monster not just for Farsas but for the safety of every other country, too. This incident drove home to the people just how almighty a witch's power was, all over again.

Seventy years had passed, and the very same witch had appeared once more on behalf of another contract holder to do battle with the demonic beast.

"Ooh, close call."

The creature's claws grazed through Tinasha's black hair. For a while now, the two had been exchanging barrages of deadly attacks. Tinasha had even used up seven of the exploding balls. Eventually, the beast's silver fur had started absorbing the attacks, simply causing ripples in its coat as if nothing had happened.

Tinasha, on the other hand, was starting to pant from the exertion of flying around with no time to rest. She leaped up high to dodge another claw swipe, then looked down on the beast from the air again.

"I didn't plan on getting tired so quickly... But I can't do anything about my endurance."

There were limits to Tinasha's slender body, even if she was a witch. Sweat collected in little beads on her forehead and neck. Her hair was sticking to her skin, and she tossed it over her shoulder, muttering self-deprecatingly that "The real test starts now. Will we have a repeat of what happened last time?"

No matter which way things went, one of them was still going to perish.

Tinasha sucked in a deep breath and began an easier incantation. *"Rise. The cage that imprisoned you lays still in the dark. What you see are only these seven shackles."*

In response, the red balls embedded in the creature's flesh shot through it and began glowing. The beast let out a howl of pain as light spilled forth from several spots in its body.

"A tranquil blindness that seeks no meaning. Sleep in the cave of stupidity that you rejected."

The magic light pouring from the seven balls morphed into innumerable threads, winding around one another as they bound the beast and began weaving into a giant spell. Though the great wolf struggled to escape, the netlike configuration twined flexibly around its giant body and refused to yield.

Once the spell was complete and the beast netted, Tinasha finished the incantation and caught her breath.

"Sorry, but you'll have to die this time. You have nothing to gain from staying here."

The towering beast had come into the world a magical creature and had only been awakened to serve as a tool of war. Its life had been terribly warped. It had become an unsustainable existence. Tinasha looked at the beast with pity in her eyes. The thing had never wished for itself to be this way. Then, she began to chant the spell that would, at last, kill it.

"*Recognize my will as law, silencer that fills all spaces. Without my words, you have no power. May the light of death be the definition...*"

A huge array made of light appeared above Tinasha's head. The circular spell pattern revolved slowly as it began sucking up magic from the magical lake below. A frightening amount of power congealed above her.

As light surged into the formation, the beast took notice and looked up. Hatred burned in its fiery eyes and met the witch's own dark gaze. A low growl issued from its muzzled mouth, shaking the earth.

Bloodlust and emptiness. The two embodiments of dissimilar feelings stared each other down.

Seconds of silence stretched out, feeling like an eternity... Then, suddenly, the beast sprang up, breaking through its bonds and charging for the witch.

"...!"

Tinasha instantly shrugged off her cloak, tossing it at the hungry white fangs. Woven of magic, the cloth filled with air and billowed out. The defense array embedded into the fabric activated, erecting a wall of light. Undaunted, the beast's teeth penetrated the barrier without so much as a moment's pause. The demonic beast's huge snout closed in on Tinasha and snapped her up before she could escape. Its teeth lodged deep in her slim belly. She was trapped in its jaw.

"Ahhhh!"

Shock and blinding pain bent Tinasha's body like a bow. She swallowed all other anguish, but in return, her mind went blank. The beast opened its mouth to bite down on her again.

Tinasha began to lose consciousness but refused pass out. If she did, the spell she'd initiated would disappear. If she didn't hold her ground here… everything would have been for naught.

The beast's maw gaped wide as Tinasha wielded all the strength in her body to kick at its teeth. A spell glowing at her toes shattered the alabaster fangs. She used the momentum of the recoil to escape its jaw.

Tinasha clutched her left hand to her stomach, where a deep wound had started oozing copious amounts of blood.

"This is the end," Tinasha declared. Outstretching her right hand above her head, a brilliant light began gathering in her palm. The spell she let fly grew to the size of the lake and swallowed the giant silver beast.

The earth rumbled with a thunderous boom. A great flash of light erupted from the magical lake; it was so intense, it was visible not only from the fortress of Ynureid but from the castle city of Old Druza as well.

A white luminescence rent the sky, and faraway cities trembled and shook. An inhuman howl of resentment echoed in the air, ringing in the ears of all who heard it.

Despite such strange occurrences, none of the citizens of Old Druza dared to approach the magical lake. Though it was now a stateless territory, it was still the site of many bitter memories.

It was thus that the legacy of an old war vanished in secret.

※

The sun was slowly setting, and the winds in the fortress smelled dry.

Meredina had gone out onto the ramparts of the fortress. There she found Oscar, still waiting.

"Your Highness, shouldn't we return to the castle…?" Meredina asked with some reluctance.

Oscar had been gazing out at the faraway wastelands but turned to face Meredina. It'd been around two hours since they'd seen the strange light from the magical lake, and Oscar had been standing out on the ramparts all the while. It was starting to get dark, and lamps were being lit all around the fortress.

Oscar shook his head. "No, I'll wait a bit longer."

Meredina looked like she wanted to say something but kept silent and left him to it. Oscar turned back to gaze upon the wilderness.

…In reality, he'd thought of going out to check on things many times over by now. In the end, though, he couldn't bring himself to do it.

As the contractee, part of his job included trusting in his protector, the witch. He hadn't brought home some powerless girl locked in a tower; she was the embodiment of overwhelming strength. One who stood in the shadows of history. He knew better than to confuse her for anything less.

"Reg would have let me go."

Tinasha's words were redolent of long-past days of which Oscar knew nothing.

"My great-granddad, huh…?"

Had she loved him? Oscar had never even met the man. He considered asking Tinasha if she'd ever met his great-grandfather again… As he thought, his face twisted in a bitter smile over how he was already acting like Tinasha wasn't coming back.

…There were still ten months left until the contract ended. Oscar had plenty of time left to ask.

He looked up and caught sight of a dark shadow. The distant thing was fast approaching, and Oscar recognized it as Tinasha's dragon. It was flapping its huge wings as it approached the fortress. Unconsciously, Oscar let out a sigh of relief. The dragon looked like it was coming right for him, only slowing once it was directly overhead.

Oscar couldn't see the dragon's back but called out, "Tinasha? How did it go?" He didn't doubt that she'd been victorious, but no reply came from atop the winged creature.

"Tinasha?" he called. All of a sudden, worry overtook Oscar, and he leaped up onto the dragon. Keeping his balance, he took in the scene and was struck aghast.

Lying there was his witch, covered in blood.

The color drained from Oscar's face in an instant. He lifted Tinasha up, not taking his eyes off her as he shouted, "Somebody help! Call a mage!"

"Your Highness? What's happened?!" Meredina, who'd been waiting nearby, came running.

Oscar saw Sylvia behind her and called her over. "Sylvia! She's hurt!"

Tinasha's whole body was caked in blood, but the worst of it was her stomach. Her clothes had been torn open around the midsection, and bits of what looked like meat were sticking to it here and there. Tinasha was breathing, but it was questionable how long she could hold out in her current condition. Oscar set her down, and Sylvia screamed at the sight.

"B-bring her to my room!" she cried. "I'll treat her right away! Meredina, get some gauze and hot water!"

"Got it! Your Highness, take her to that room!"

Yelling out directions, the two women sent the entire fortress into an uproar as they ran off. Cradling the witch in his arms, Oscar set off as fast as his legs would take him. The dragon shrank itself and followed.

Surprisingly, the process of healing Tinasha didn't take all that long. Sylvia exited the room, wiping her hands. She bowed gently to Oscar, who had been waiting outside.

"I examined her thoroughly, but she didn't have any major injuries, though I treated the smaller ones…"

"No injuries? What about her stomach?"

"That appears to have healed on its own. I don't know what things are like internally, however…"

"I see… Thank you," Oscar said. His whole body sagged with relief.

Sylvia smiled at the prince's expression of gratitude. "Because she'd bled so much, I'd thought it was a serious injury, one that wouldn't be able to be fully healed. It's a good thing that wasn't the case. I've cleaned the blood off her body and placed her ripped clothes and other equipment to the side."

"Excellent," Oscar said with a nod. Nark the dragon landed on his shoulder, holding a huge red crystal in its mouth. The prince petted its head.

"Can I go in?" Oscar asked eagerly.

"Go right ahead, though I don't think she'll wake up until she's done recovering her magic." Sylvia bowed to Oscar as he walked past her into the room.

Tinasha was lying on the bed with her eyes closed, wearing a peaceful expression. He checked to verify she was breathing and placed a hand over the blanket covering her stomach to make sure that was fine, too. Only after receiving confirmation of both did he exhale.

"You really...really had me worried," he admitted, reaching out to stroke her cheek. It was warm and firm.

In the end, Oscar spent that night at the fortress. Of the investigative party, Meredina and most all the other soldiers returned to the castle ahead of the prince. Two guard soldiers as well as Sylvia, Doan, and the other mages remained, in case Tinasha's condition worsened. Oscar had asked them to stay, hesitant to move the severely wounded witch.

The night passed without incident. By the next afternoon, Oscar was working in a chamber in the fortress while waiting for Tinasha to recover. Doan had been patrolling the grounds and was presently giving his report.

"There was no trace of that mage last night. I reinforced the fortress wards, but this is still a completely unfamiliar enemy..."

"For now, it's enough. So long as we prevent him from coming near until Tinasha recovers. We can discuss the next move with her once she's awake."

The suspicious mage seemed to know a fair amount about Tinasha, so she would need to be apprised of things. At the moment, protecting her was paramount.

Oscar deliberated over whether he should go check on her one more time. Just then, a woman's cry came from Tinasha's room.

"What?!" Oscar stood up.

It hadn't been the witch's voice. Expecting some kind of attack, Oscar dashed over. Sylvia was standing in front of the entrance, her face rather red for some reason.

"What's wrong?!"

"Ah, Your Highness... No, I'm sorry. It's nothing. Please wait a moment." Looking oddly panicked, Sylvia blocked the door.

Suspicious, Oscar pushed her aside. "I'm going in."

"Your Highness! Wait!" she called to stop him, but he ignored it and entered regardless. There, Oscar was met with a sight that confounded his senses, and he froze in place.

On the bed, Tinasha was sitting up, half-naked. That, however, wasn't the shocking part. It seemed that, overnight, her black hair had grown long enough to touch the floor. Strands of inky locks spread out all over the room.

Tinasha noticed Oscar and pulled the covers up over herself. Smiling stiffly, she didn't look anything like the girl he knew. She appeared very nearly twenty now.

Glaring at the prince, Tinasha grabbed the pillow behind her. "Don't come in until I'm dressed!"

Oscar dodged the hurled pillow and took his leave without a word, closing the door behind him. Unconcerned, Nark yawned from his place on Oscar's shoulder.

"What the hell...?"

"That's why I told you to wait...," Sylvia muttered, a hand over her face.

Tinasha emerged with a frown, wearing a change of clothes borrowed from Sylvia as she dragged her long hair behind her.

She was still every bit the breathtaking beauty she'd always been, but now that she looked a few years older, she'd gained a cool serenity and a sensual charm.

Her long eyelashes drew one's gaze and gave the witch a sorrowful look. The sense of eternity in her eyes was a mystery in and of itself, captivating anyone who looked upon her and robbing them of a sense of time. Oscar gazed wonderingly at her, staring into her eyes, utterly fascinated.

For a long while, he said nothing. Tinasha scowled in annoyance. "What is it? You're acting creepy. Say something..."

"Uh..." Hesitantly, Oscar reached for Tinasha. When he petted her head the way he usually did, she closed her eyes like a cat. This really was the same witch as before.

Feeling reassured, Oscar asked, "What in the world happened out there? How did you end up like that?"

"My internal organs were severely damaged, so I repaired them by drastically speeding up my body's rate of growth. My hair is much too long now." As Tinasha spoke, she whipped out a dagger and brought it up to a spot along her hair.

Sylvia rushed to stop her. "I'll do that! You sit down."

"What? I'm just going to cut it off."

"Let me! Do that!"

"Okay…" Tinasha conceded, sitting down obediently in a chair, and Sylvia began carefully combing out the obsidian locks.

Oscar sat down opposite Tinasha. "So is everything all right now?"

"Yes, I'm fine. I just suffered a bit of blood loss."

"Yeah, I really thought you were dead. Will your appearance go back to normal?"

"It won't. Like I told you in the tower, my appearance isn't fabricated by magic. My body's growth has stopped, that's all. I suppose I could use a spell to look the way I used to… Do you prefer young women?"

"I definitely don't," Oscar replied emphatically. In fact, the way she looked now was much more attractive to him. Taking her mental state into account, this was much closer to who she really was. Her more-mature-looking eyes suited this form well, and Oscar gave an internal sigh of relief.

Nark jumped from Oscar's shoulder to Tinasha's lap, and she stroked its back.

"Oscar, it appears it's fond of you now. Look, it's like it's giving me this."

The dragon dropped the red stone in its mouth into Tinasha's palm. The jewel-like thing was a little smaller than her hand, and she tossed it to Oscar. He caught it in midair and stared at the crimson stone. There were marks on it that suggested it had been carved from something larger.

"That's the demonic beast's core. It looks like Nark could only pick up half of it, though. It's just an ordinary jewel now, so no need for alarm."

"The demonic beast's core… Wait, you defeated the demonic beast?!"

Oscar knew Tinasha had gone out with all her battle gear, but he hadn't expected her to really go that far all on her own. The prince was dumbfounded, and Tinasha's eyes narrowed as she smiled.

"I didn't want to have to go through the trouble of sealing it a few years down the road again. Oh, the bodies of the mages who wanted to break the seal are all buried underground. Sorry I didn't retrieve them."

"I don't care about that… Just…don't act so rash next time."

"That was nothing!" Tinasha argued.

"You got seriously injured," Oscar replied matter-of-factly, and the witch stuck out her tongue at him.

Oscar sat up straight and rephrased himself. "You saved us. It was because of you that we didn't suffer any casualties. Thank you."

If those mages had gotten their way, the carnage would have been unfathomable. Thankfully, this witch had taken care of it before that had come to pass. Her big black eyes opened wide as a broad grin spread across her face.

"It was no trouble. I'm a witch, after all." Paying no mind to the burden Oscar bore, his protector beamed.

Sylvia's little pair of scissors did their work well, cutting the witch's glossy-black hair back to its previous length.

▌5. Falling into the Water

She'd taken a light sleep to refresh her body. Perhaps because the slumber had been so gentle, she was visited by many dreams. In them, she saw memories of a distant past too jumbled to put in order.

There was a vision of herself as a child, as a witch, an infinite number of selves in an infinite number of forms. Before the many sights, she felt akin to a traveler in a desolate wasteland walking all alone.

All of the various people she'd signed finite contracts with had long since lived and died. She was the only one who kept going on, alone. No, perhaps she liked to think she was going on, but in reality, it was more like being stopped in place. All was as it had been the day she'd lost everything…

Then, someone touched her hair, and consciousness returned; light shone in her eyes.

A brightness surrounded her, but she couldn't yet fully awaken. A warm hand slowly ruffled her hair. The gentle touch instilled a feeling of safety… The sensation had her falling into a dreamless repose.

When her body finally felt recovered and she at last awoke, Tinasha hugged her knees to her chest and tilted her head in confusion.

"…Oscar?" She couldn't remember why his name was on her lips, but she recalled the warmth she'd felt in her chest…and blushed a little.

※

In the fortress's study, Oscar immediately drafted a report detailing the recent occurrences, adding in the information he'd gotten from Tinasha.

Once they returned to the castle and he handed it in, it would be over. He looked up and beckoned to his protector, who was close by.

"What is it?" she asked, approaching with a dubious expression. Oscar hoisted her up easily and settled her on his knees. Her delicate body had felt so heavy when she was unconscious, but now she was so light, it seemed inhuman. Tinasha was always floating in the air, so perhaps she'd reduced her weight with magic.

Held on his lap like a child, Tinasha stared at him with her round eyes. "What are you doing…?"

"Ah, the way you look now just makes me want to hold you," he answered.

"…"

Tinasha frowned, but Oscar paid it no mind and combed his fingers through her neatly trimmed hair.

"I told the group who returned ahead of us to keep quiet, but considering how you look now, we can't really hide the fact that you're a witch anymore. Are you going to use a spell to restore your old appearance?"

"No, it no longer matters. It would be hard to keep people from talking anyway."

"I see."

"I've also gotten tired of calling a certain idiot prince Your Highness, so this works out well."

"Tired of it, huh?"

Tinasha crossed her dainty legs, allowing Nark to flutter down into her lap instead of wandering around the room. The sunlight filtering in from the window warmed Tinasha's milky-white legs.

"The fog around the magical lake was due to the beast, so it should clear up soon. Someone should go out to check on it once every three months. Oh, but there was a cave-in, so tell them to be careful," instructed the witch.

"Will the magical lake dry up?" Oscar asked.

"The lake is the traces of powerful magic scattered around the land there, so…even if a little was consumed, it will absorb magic and vitality from the surrounding land and restore itself pretty quickly."

"So that's how it works," Oscar said, rubbing Tinasha's bare toes. Playfully, Nark tried to grab his fingers.

Tinasha folded her arms, falling into thought. "But that mage you stabbed bothers me. I guess this means he's the one who put the whole idea of releasing the demonic beast into the mind of that old geezer?"

"Most likely," replied Oscar.

"What business does he have with me to go to such an extreme? It's so annoying. I wish he'd show himself." Tinasha pouted.

"I mean… He's not because you'd kill him, right?"

"How dare you think of me that way. I would kill him, though," the witch said as if it were the obvious choice—exactly why her opponent was erring on the side of caution. Based on how he'd acted, however, it was very possible that he'd continue making indirect advances. Dealing with him was going to be much more difficult than just handling a direct challenge.

Undeterred, Tinasha decisively stated, "In any case, he's after me, so I can't cause any trouble for you. The next time he lays a trap, I'll take care of him for good."

"I understand how you feel, but don't overdo it. It worries me when you do things all on your own," Oscar said.

"…I'll be careful going forward," Tinasha agreed, hanging her head a little. She must have been aware that she'd worried him.

Oscar smiled, and Nark flew to his shoulder. Then, he asked the question he'd been meaning to get to for a while. "Oh right, what kind of guy was my great-granddad?"

"…Where is this coming from? Why do you want to know that?" Tinasha responded with questions of her own.

"Ah, I'm just curious. That old guy said something about him, didn't he?"

The old mage had called Regius the man she loved. Tinasha looked ready to faint from distress.

"Aaaauuughh! There were a lot of people who had that same mistaken impression at the time. Please believe me when I say it wasn't like that at all!" she whined.

"Farsas fairy tales say that's how it was, too, you know," Oscar added.

The story of a king and a witch was told to children far and wide. Even

Oscar himself had heard the tale. In it, Tinasha had been made out to be more witchlike, which was why Oscar had been surprised at the sight of the real article.

"I knew there must be stories like that, but I also knew they would make me angry so never bothered to listen to any."

"A king begs for help, and the witch demands that he marry her and give her his kingdom in return…," Oscar started.

"Noooo!" Tinasha wailed.

"After the war ends, the king agrees and holds a wedding, but the witch disappears without a trace."

"A few bits are correct, but it wasn't like that at all!"

Some small portion of Tinasha's magic was starting to leak as a result of her frustration, because a nearby windowpane began making a strange creaking sound. Mentally exhausted, Tinasha heaved a huge sigh while Oscar stroked the back of her neck.

"I suppose I always figured it was something like that," Oscar said as he continued brushing his fingers along the witch's nape.

Suddenly, Tinasha jolted up and began fidgeting in his arms. "That tickles! Stop it already," she demanded.

"Ah, sorry. I guess it was a bit much." Oscar let Tinasha go, and she silently floated up. Nark also took off, following her. She welcomed the little dragon into her arms and crossed her legs in the air.

"Reg was…to put it succinctly…a stupid king."

"…"

Regius Kurus Lar Farsas, the eighteenth king of Farsas, was crowned at the tender age of fifteen after his father's sudden death. He was a straightforward youth, just and upright. Never was he particularly suspicious of others, nor was he one to quit when things got tough. He was thought of as a good king.

"We first met before Druza invaded. He'd climbed the tower, so I asked him what his wish was, and he suddenly asked me to marry him…"

"How absurd," Oscar added.

"Someone else I know did the same thing…," chided Tinasha.

Pretending not to hear, Oscar beckoned to Nark. The dragon flew over to him as Tinasha idly flipped around in the air and rolled her eyes at Oscar from above.

"Well, I might have understood if he'd had special circumstances like you! But he didn't! So I lectured him about how a witch could not become queen, but—"

"Then you demanded his kingdom…" Oscar cut in again.

"I didn't need it!" Tinasha objected, wondering if perhaps Oscar's habit of offering candid commentary came from his great-grandfather.

"So then what happened?" Oscar asked, hoping for the story to continue.

"I turned him down, but he clung to me for two days."

"…"

"I'd gotten fed up and was mad. Then he suggested something else. *I don't want you to leave my sight until I die.* I don't even understand why he came to the tower…"

"That…is really stupid." Oscar suddenly felt like he'd asked Tinasha something he shouldn't have. Despite feeling a stress-induced headache over his ancestor's idiocy coming on, he pressed for more. "Did you accept?"

"With conditions. In exchange, I said I would do nothing for him and not come to his rescue. If he did ever request my help, that would become a new clause in the contract, and I would never show myself in front of him again."

"And then the demonic beast showed up," Oscar surmised.

"He was *extremely* reluctant to make the request. I think he came to the decision relatively quickly, though."

"I'm sure the royal council didn't want the part about it all hinging on his personal whim going down in the history books…"

Perhaps that had led to the council twisting the facts and spreading the fairy-tale version that had survived until this day. They certainly had unknowingly created a lot of trouble for Tinasha. In midair, her hands shook.

"I wish things had ended there!" Tinasha squirmed.

"There was more…?"

"The contract had ended, but because my relationship to him hadn't been part of the agreement…"

"Hmm?" Oscar cocked his head.

"A w-wedding, of all things… He threw it together out of nowhere… Even sent a wedding dress to my room…" Tinasha was trembling.

"…"

Oscar massaged his temples. In addition to a headache, he was starting to feel a bit dizzy.

"I stood him up, of course. And I never saw him again."

"I feel like I just bore witness to a darker side of history I wasn't meant to know about," Oscar moaned.

No wonder Tinasha had called Regius a stupid king. Oscar finally understood why she hadn't wanted to talk about her contract with his great-grandfather when he'd first met her.

"Still… I didn't hate him or anything. Even though he was stupid. I thought of him like family."

Tinasha looked down. A wealth of emotions flickered rapidly through her eyes.

Oscar couldn't help but wonder: If she hadn't been a witch, would she have accepted the king's proposal? It seemed a ridiculous supposition. What kind of life would she have lived if it had been true?

"I got on nicely with the woman who later became queen…your great-grandmother. She was smart and quick-witted and probably reined Reg in a bit. You're a little like her." Tinasha cut off her reminiscing there, landing softly in front of Oscar. She laid a hand along his cheek and gazed at him with her big round eyes.

The way she stared gave Oscar the feeling she was watching scenes from something long past.

With her true identity now in the open, reactions were mixed when it was announced that Tinasha would be returning to the castle.

Because of the fairy tale about her, quite a few people disapproved of her position at Oscar's side, but those who had interacted with her more or less accepted it without protest. A fair number of disagreements arose, but no one shared them openly. Tinasha merely gave anyone who disapproved a sort of forced smile.

Oscar reintroduced Tinasha to his father, the king, as well as the few other people who knew about the curse. They gathered not in the audience hall but in a sitting room deep in the castle. The five guests included King Kevin, Minister of the Interior Nessan, veteran General Ettard, Chief Mage Kumu, and Lazar. Tinasha had accompanied Oscar, and the guests listened to his explanation with a range of different expressions.

Oscar concluded his summary of everything that had happened with: "So I plan to make her my wife."

"You will not! What a terrible explanation that would be if I hadn't said anything!" Tinasha exclaimed. Because of their height difference, she had to hover slightly to grab Oscar and shake him.

The king stood, attempting to pacify her. "My son has said something reckless. I do apologize. This explains why I felt like I had seen you somewhere before. A long time ago, I stole a peek at my grandfather's journal, and tucked in the pages was a portrait of you."

"If the journal is still around, I'd like to ask you to dispose of it...," Tinasha murmured, face red as she landed on the floor.

The king turned to more pressing matters. "How are you progressing with my son's problem? Do you think you'll be able to solve it?"

A perfectly reasonable question, but the witch gave the king a pained smile. "I've started analyzing the curse to try to disable it. That's why I was asked to come live in the castle."

"No, I asked you here so I could have a year to talk you into marrying me," Oscar admitted rather bluntly.

"Excuse me?! This is the first I'm hearing of it!" Tinasha snapped.

"Based on how the situation stands, it's the only reason that makes sense," said Oscar.

"What doesn't make sense is that option being open to you in the first place!" The witch fumed, flushing with anger, and Oscar burst out laughing.

Oscar didn't look like he planned to reply, and all Tinasha could do was curl her hand into an angry fist before turning back to the king. "...I am analyzing the curse, but the Witch of Silence is much, much more knowledgeable about these things than I am. It looks like it will take several months for the analysis to be completed, and even once it's finished, we might not be able to expect to fully break the curse. One way or another, I will deal with it, so please rest assured."

"If it doesn't work, you can take responsibility and marry me," quipped Oscar.

"Don't imply it won't work!" Tinasha started shaking him again.

Ettard observed this and murmured to Lazar next to him, "They do appear to be quite close…"

"They are," Lazar replied.

"Ugh… What in the world kind of introduction was that?" Tinasha sighed. The mentally draining meeting had left her sapped of all strength, and she was now slumped over a table in the castle lounge.

Oscar said shamelessly, "None of that was a lie. What did you take issue with?"

"There are still some things you shouldn't say, even if they're true! Especially since I'm not going to be marrying you!" Tinasha shouted.

"You say that now, but if you can't break the curse, you don't have any other option, do you?"

"…I'll figure something out. I'll introduce you to another witch or something."

"Wow. That's certainly one solution…"

In other words, Tinasha would present a different queen candidate to Oscar. Exempting the Witch of Silence who cursed him in the first place, there were still three other witches.

Tinasha massaged her temples, head in her hands. "One is too dangerous, so that's a nonstarter, and it's impossible to communicate with another, but the last might work. She has a lot of issues personality-wise but is very beautiful, and I think she'll like you."

"Do you really think I'm going to change my mind after you've described her like that?"

It wasn't that Oscar was uninterested in the other witches—but only as famous historical figures. In terms of marriage, there was no one more attractive to him than the witch sitting right next to him.

Oscar concluded firmly, "I don't need you to introduce me. I prefer to enjoy my time bothering you, so I'm fine."

"Don't bother me, idiot! Be more mindful of the position you're in!" Tinasha shouted as she got up, stomping over to make tea. As she did so, Lazar and the mages Kav and Sylvia stopped by, and the five began chatting.

"A ghost in the castle? Seriously?" Oscar was rather incredulous at a story Lazar had brought up.

"As of now, it's just a rumor. A number of people have seen a woman who appears to be soaked to the bone walking the halls at night. After she passes, the floor is sopping wet," Lazar said.

"That sounds difficult to clean up," Tinasha commented indifferently, but Sylvia looked pale with fear. Evidently, the lovely mage was not good when it came to ghost stories.

Across from her, Kav stared into his teacup before looking up. "I heard about it from another mage, too. Apparently, the ghost looked him in the face without saying a thing. He was terrified and closed his eyes, but nothing happened. When he opened them, no one was there, just a dripping-wet corridor."

"Ahhhh!" Sylvia cried, covering her ears and putting her head on the table.

The witch patted her shoulder with a pained smile. "Ghosts don't exist. Souls have a type of power, but after death, it scatters naturally. It's impossible, even for witches, to maintain a form and a consciousness after death."

"Really?"

"Really. If there really is something walking the halls, you can rest assured that it isn't human."

"Ahhhh!" Sylvia shrieked. The witch frowned, sticking her tongue out in chagrin.

Oscar objected, "Not human? So you're saying something has sneaked into the castle?"

"Most likely. It could be a demonic spirit or some other type of fiend. Not having seen it, though, I can't say..."

"What's the difference between a demonic spirit and a demon?" Lazar, who was not a mage, piped up with a simple question.

With a smile, Tinasha answered him. "There isn't a clear dividing line between them, but demonic spirits are generally plants and animals that were transformed after contact with strong magic or a miasma—or the acquisition of demonic blood. These entities usually cause trouble for humans. The demonic beast in Old Druza is a rare example of something that came into being from a jewel, but roughly speaking, that was a demonic spirit, too."

Abruptly, Tinasha fluttered her fingers in the air, and a silver wolf appeared there. After yawning wide, the wolf winked out of sight again.

Tinasha continued her explanation. "On the other hand, demons are a type of being that have always been the way that they are. Demon sightings are pretty common, and we often lump together the various different types, like water spirits, fairies, and succubi. True high-ranking demons, however, are rarely spotted and are completely different from the ranks of demons that coexist with humans."

Kav added, "In the Dark Age, high-ranking demons were evidently worshipped as gods. The most well-known is probably the water god of Nevis Lake. Speaking of powerful demons that interacted with humans, I wonder if that's what the mystical spirits of Tuldarr were?"

"The ancient Magic Empire of Tuldarr? The one that was destroyed in a single night?" Oscar asked, recalling his history lessons, while Lazar sat there, blank with shock.

Kav nodded knowledgeably. "According to legend, twelve high-ranking demons were sealed away in Tuldarr. At the time, they were called mystical spirits. When the royal heir succeeded the throne and became king, he selected one to three of them to be his familiars. That said, this is merely an old story, likely to be false. It's virtually impossible that multiple high-ranking demons could be put to use like that."

Tinasha made a wry face listening to the magical history lesson. "For those types of beings, the higher their rank, the less interested they are in human affairs. There's just too much of a difference in power between them. Think about it this way—would you spend much time on an insect?" the witch inquired glibly, and the others exchanged glances.

Oscar's curiosity was piqued. "What's the difference in power between you and those high-ranking demons?"

"I could defeat them easily. Although, I would have some trouble against the strongest of them."

"Hey," Oscar chided. Tinasha's comment was basically a backhanded sleight against those present.

The witch's eyes narrowed cheerfully as she smiled. "Anyway, that's why I don't think whatever's been sighted in the castle is a high-ranking demon. I'm sure I would've noticed if something like that had slipped in."

"I wonder what it could be… Either way, we'll look into it later," Oscar said. He glanced at the clock and stood up. "Time for work. Tinasha, what are your plans?"

"I'm going to go clothes shopping. My old ones don't fit me anymore. Sylvia said she'd take me around."

"Oh yes… Yes!" Sylvia cried out too loudly. She seemed to be trying to shake off her lingering fear.

"Those two stand out when they're together," Kav whispered to Lazar, taking note of how beautiful a picture the two women painted together.

Perhaps Oscar heard that, perhaps he didn't, but he turned around to look at them. Sylvia still looked white as a sheet, and he said to her, "Pick out something in black or white."

"All right… Why?"

"Because I'll like it."

"Who cares?!" the witch snapped, calling up a little ball of light in her right hand and throwing it at Oscar as he left the room. Before the light sphere could hit his back, the protective barrier that Tinasha had placed on the prince repelled and dispersed it.

Without turning around, Oscar laughed and sauntered out the door. Tinasha scowled after him, running a hand through her long black hair as she signaled to Sylvia.

"Come on, let's go. You don't have to take what he said seriously. I'll pick out my own clothes."

"Ah, okay…"

Tinasha set off down the hall, lifting both hands and stretching. When she was in her younger form, her physical body appeared to be about sixteen years old. Now it was closer to nineteen. She hadn't grown that much taller, but she sported some new womanly curves. Clad in a mage's robe, Tinasha looked up at the sunny sky out the window.

"Farsas is bizarrely hot, so this will be a good opportunity to get something a bit cooler to wear."

"You do get used to the temperature living here, after a while…," Sylvia murmured in reply, still sounding dispirited. She realized Tinasha was staring at her with widened eyes, and she waved a hand in front of her own face. "Um, I'm really not very good with ghost stories… I'm sorry."

"Don't worry about it. Everyone has something they can't handle." The witch waved a dismissive hand.

"Do you, Lady Tinasha?" Sylvia asked

"Don't call me that…," Tinasha replied.

Far out the window, the soldiers were out on the training grounds. Tinasha made a face as she watched them trading sword blows. "A long time ago, yes, but I suppose the longer I've lived, I've just gotten worn down… At the moment, I would say the only thing I don't like is to be put to bed."

"What's that? You mean, like when a parent puts their child to bed?" Sylvia asked, head cocked in confusion.

But the witch just smiled and didn't elaborate. Instead, a bitter look came over her face as she recalled something else. "And I'm not good at dealing with Oscar. I have no idea what he's thinking. He seems to mistake me for a cat or something he's picked up off the street…"

No matter how Tinasha looked at it, that was exactly how Oscar treated her. It was almost like he viewed a witch as just another type of cat. She had fully expected his perception to change slightly after she defeated the demonic beast, but it had done little to change their relationship. It felt altogether too anticlimactic.

Tinasha did little to hide her baffled emotions, and Sylvia appeared stumped. "It looks like you two get along perfectly to me."

"Wha—? Perfectly…?" The witch stammered, falling into silence with a very dissatisfied expression, and Sylvia burst into bright laughter. It seemed she'd managed to forget her fear of the ghost rumors.

✻

"There's a ghost?"

For two or three days, the strange apparition had been the talk of the castle. Rumors abounded in the garrison and made Suzuto, a young soldier, pause while polishing his sword.

"Ghost? That's the first I've heard of it."

"It just started happening recently, after you got back from visiting your family."

"Oh? That *is* recent, then," Suzuto said, nodding in acquiescence. Until just three days ago, he'd been visiting his parents in eastern Farsas. It was a beautiful bit of land bordered by forests and lakes, but after joining the royal army, he hadn't been back to visit in three years. He'd used his leave to go visit his parents and stop by an old castle near a lake while he was in the area.

He returned to cleaning his weapon, but one man snickered and said, "That's right, have you seen the witch yet? Man, what a sight. Well, she was already a looker before."

"I haven't seen her since I got back."

By "the witch," Suzuto assumed the other man meant the young mage who sometimes came for sword practice. The crown prince had said he'd brought back an apprentice mage from the witch's tower, but in reality, she herself was the witch.

She was an embodiment of the kind of power only possessed by five beings in all of the mainland—the stuff of fairy tales. It was strange for Suzuto to think someone like that truly existed and lived in the same castle as him, but that was all. He had no intention of acting on his curiosity.

In contrast to Suzuto's uncaring attitude, his fellow soldiers were getting rowdy and excited. "You've *got* to see her. She's the very definition of a seductive beauty who could bring ruin to a country."

"And His Highness is head over heels for her, too, so Farsas'll be under the witch's control soon."

The soldiers chattered and laughed, and Suzuto finally looked up from his work. He eyed them coldly. "You're all awful. You talked to her when she came by, right? Wasn't she pleasant enough?"

"Well, she was, but..."

All at once, the reckless, idle gossip faded away; the wind had gone out of their sails.

※

Despite the safety afforded by the castle, its corridors were dim and spooky at night. Light from the candelabras evenly spaced along the walls flickered faintly, casting long shadows on the figures of two people as they made their way down a hallway.

Lazar looked to his lord, who was moving a step ahead. "What will you do if you run into the ghost because you were up this late working...?"

"Tinasha said there are no such thing as ghosts, didn't she? If anything, it'll be a demonic spirit."

"That's even worse..." Lazar gulped.

Oscar brought a hand to the hilt at his waist. He was carrying a simple sword for self-defense. He generally didn't carry Akashia inside the castle, but with all the rumors running around, perhaps it was time for him to start. He was deliberating on the idea when Lazar piped up again with more criticism.

"I mean, you're always trying to handle everything yourself, which is why Miss Tinasha—" Lazar suddenly stopped, and Oscar heard his friend tumble onto his bottom.

"Don't just fall over for no reason," Oscar teased.

"It was more like I slipped on something..." Lazar held a candle up to his hand that had touched the floor.

His palm was very clearly wet. Oscar's eyes widened. Lazar opened his mouth to scream, but before he could, a woman's cold arm reached out from behind him and pulled him tight against her.

"Tinasha! Wake up!"

The witch was in bed in her chamber when a man burst in and grabbed her arm.

The rooms the current king had granted her were the same ones she'd used the last time she'd stayed in Farsas. Regius's order had kept them furnished exactly as they had been for over seventy years. Others had only entered them for regular cleaning. Tinasha had felt a complex series of emotions churning inside her when she saw the quarters.

Dragged from her peaceful bed, she rubbed her sleepy eyes.

"Mmm, Oscar... What is it?"

She opened her dark eyes to find she was being carried like a child in Oscar's arms. The moonlight pouring in from the window gave his face a pallid sheen.

"Lazar is...dead?" Oscar answered.

"Why is that a question?" Tinasha frowned.

She soon understood. By the time Tinasha rushed over after hearing what had happened, a small crowd had gathered at the scene. Lazar was lying in a corner of the hallway, and while he had no exterior wounds, he appeared unconscious, and his body was cold as ice.

As soon as Tinasha caught sight of him, she murmured, "His soul has been taken."

"His soul...? Can he be saved?" Oscar asked, and the witch bit her lip. Calling magic to her hands, she placed them on Lazar's body.

"I will maintain his body, but...after three days, his soul will disperse. We need to retrieve it quickly." Tinasha asked the soldiers in the vicinity to carry Lazar to a different room.

"I can do a quick search, but I'm sure his soul isn't in the castle anymore... To put it simply, something must have carried it away. Did you see the ghost?"

"I saw it. It was a woman with green hair and bluish-white skin. She dodged my sword. It was like trying to cut through water," Oscar recalled.

"A water spirit, then..." Tinasha looked back to see a puddle in the corridor and frowned. "Go ask everyone in the castle if they've been near any bodies of water lately. Water spirits do not normally leave their homes. There must be a reason it's come here."

"Got it."

The witch ran after Lazar as he was carried away. Oscar went off in the opposite direction to gather people together.

*　　　*　　　*

While there weren't many soldiers in the garrison at such a late hour, each one present was shaken awake and questioned.

Suzuto was naturally summoned as well. After he mentioned something to Als, he was sent elsewhere in the castle—separate from his fellow soldiers.

Suzuto did not normally enter the castle proper. When he and Als entered the room Als had led him to, the first thing that caught his attention was the bed placed along the front window. Someone appeared to be sleeping on it, and a woman with familiar-looking black hair was standing at his side with her back to Suzuto.

"…Good, you're here," came a man's voice to his right. Suzuto knew that voice very well, so he gave a respectful bow in that direction.

"Go on, then," Oscar, seated in a chair, urged.

"Y-yes, Your Highness. A few days ago, when I went to visit my parents, I stopped by a nearby lake. As I was wandering around exploring, I came across a dry water fountain nearby. There was a stone blocking off the water faucet, so I—"

"Removed it," Oscar finished.

"Yes."

"Did anything strange happen then?"

"No, nothing. A little water came out and got on my hands; that's all."

Oscar crossed his arms and glanced over at the window. "Tinasha, what do you think?"

"I think that's what caused it," Tinasha answered, turning around. Suzuto caught sight of her and fell speechless. Her silky black hair, porcelain-white skin, and eyes the color of darkness filled the dim room with a strange magnetism.

Her ethereal beauty was such that she seemed to be the very personification of a bright-azure moonlit night. Suzuto understood why his fellow soldiers had made such a fuss over her.

"That fountain was originally connected to the lake bottom where a water spirit dwelled. The stone was sealing her away," explained the witch.

"So when the seal was broken, it opened up to the lake bottom?" Oscar asked.

"She probably came here via the water that landed on Suzuto, although I don't know why she took Lazar away."

Startled for a moment at hearing his name come up, Suzuto remembered that this was the same girl who had attended combat practice with him. He felt a jolt of fear upon the sudden mention of Lazar's name.

"Um… Did I do something bad…?" he asked nervously.

"I'll explain it to you later. For now, we need to head out. You'll guide us to that lake," ordered Oscar.

"Y-yes!" Suzuto said, bowing, and left the room with Als.

Oscar stood and walked over to the bed to gaze down at Lazar's face. His childhood friend remained in his strange, deathly sleep.

"Hold on, friend. I'll figure this out," Oscar muttered.

His voice was so quiet that Tinasha looked up at him with concern. "You're going?"

"Who else would?" asked Oscar.

The witch looked to Akashia, belted to Oscar's hip, and gave a little sigh. "Your protective barrier can't defend against the psychological spells used by demonic spirits and fairies, so be careful. Trust your senses. Don't fall prey to some illusion. And…," she said, trailing off.

"What?" Oskar pressed.

Tinasha hesitated for a long time but finally said, "If your life is in danger, I am your protector and will come to your aid. In such a case, I will be unable to keep Lazar alive… Do you understand?"

Oscar didn't show the slightest lack of composure. He looked down at her and patted her head. "I do, so don't look so down."

Tinasha looked terribly forlorn, practically on the verge of tears. She said nothing, though, mustering a tiny smile.

"This will be a cinch," Oscar declared, tearing his gaze away from Lazar's pallid face and leaving the room.

Under the moonlight, Oscar, Als, Doan, and Suzuto left the castle on horseback. Suzuto rode at the vanguard, galloping eastward. The lake in question was normally a three-hour ride away, two if they hurried.

When they emerged from the castle, something that looked like a huge bird came swooping down from the darkness. Oscar drew his sword before quickly realizing it was Nark. The dragon gave a cry before settling on Oscar's shoulder.

"Wh-what is that?" Suzuto stammered, pointing fearfully at the first dragon he'd ever seen.

Oscar scratched Nark's neck. "Just something a certain worrywart sent."

Tinasha had never approved of Oscar sneaking out of the castle. Very likely, she didn't want him going out alone to face an opponent against which her barrier might be ineffective. Taking care to keep Nark from falling off, Oscar urged his horse on faster.

The four ran the horses without stopping. By the time they arrived at the shore of the lake, dawn was already breaking.

Pausing there, Doan marveled at the gorgeous scenery. "This is...amazing."

Woods bordered the western half of the huge lake. The eastern half backed up to a cliff, on top of which was perched an old castle. The crumbling structure's gardens stretched down to the base of the cliff, half submerging the fountain. White pillars rose out of the water, giving the place an almost spiritual feel.

Faced with such a wondrous sight, Oscar remarked casually, "Tinasha would love it here."

"Since we're here, shall I record the transportation coordinates, Your Highness?" Doan asked.

"That would really come in handy, thanks," answered Oscar.

Doan started the incantation to learn the coordinates, while Suzuto stared intensely at the lake.

"Wh-when I came here before, the gardens hadn't sunken into the lake like this..."

"..."

The other three were silent, and it hit Suzuto just how grave a mistake he'd made.

At the time, he hadn't thought much of what he'd done. The stone stuck in the fountain had just bothered him for some reason. All he'd wanted to do was remove it and make the fountain nice again.

Oscar seemed to pick up on his subject's feelings and dismounted his horse to reassure him. "Don't worry about it. We'll figure this out. Should we start by diving into the lake?"

"No, I feel a strong magic coming from the nearby forest. Let's begin there," Doan said. Nark alighted from Oscar's shoulder and flew toward the woods, as if confirming the mage's hunch was right. The humans followed after it on foot.

The forest was dense and dark; the rising sun could hardly penetrate the gloomy atmosphere beneath its leafy canopy. Nark followed no path as it fluttered this way and that through the woods. To provide a traceable way back, Als led the group and cleared a path with his sword as they went.

"Your Highness, please watch your feet."

"This magic is very strong... Almost like a fog," Doan commented, though the remark was lost on the other three members of the party, as they were not mages. Warning one another not to get separated, the group proceeded deeper into the forest.

Eyeing the thickly growing trees above his head, Oscar asked Suzuto, "That castle belonged to a lord of old, didn't it? Is it abandoned now?"

"The people who live in the area don't go near it. Growing up, there were all sorts of terrible stories about the place," Suzuto explained.

"Like what?" Oscar asked.

"There's a story about a girl who lives in the lake. The lord had a son, and when the son met this beautiful girl, he asked her to marry him. But she said no, because she wasn't a human. However, the son didn't give up, and they were married. Soon after that, though, the son fell in love with another woman, and the girl returned to the lake in tears."

"How disgusting," Oscar remarked.

"I feel the same way...," Suzuto admitted.

"But hmm, a girl who lives in the lake..." The prince pondered the idea.

Tinasha had postulated that the culprit was a water spirit, and now that he'd heard this story, he had all the more reason to be wary. For some unknown reason, an inhuman woman had set her sights on Lazar. They had three days to get his soul back, but they hadn't even lost a day yet. With things as they stood, Oscar felt confident they wouldn't lose Lazar.

Oscar and Lazar were childhood friends who had been raised in the castle together. They knew each other better than brothers. Oscar recalled the way Lazar always smiled so innocently as he followed him around. "He really got the worst of it this time... Why does he always tag along with me...?" Oscar murmured to himself self-deprecatingly as remorse tugged at his heartstrings.

Lazar, who was petrified of ghosts, had been abducted by one right before Oscar's eyes, and he hadn't been able to do anything about it. The prince gritted his teeth, feeling angry with himself.

As he was lost in thought, he ran into Nark, who had turned back around.

"Hey, be careful," he said reflexively.

Peeling the clingy dragon off his face, Oscar took another look around and realized that, at some point, he and Nark had gotten separated from everyone else.

"Uh-oh..."

Something must have happened, and the two had become separated while Oscar wasn't paying attention. Als had been clearing the brush as they made their way through, but when Oscar turned to look back, he only saw overgrown foliage.

"This isn't good... Als will be all right, but I'm not so sure about the other two."

Doan and Suzuto were both capable, but anything seemed possible in a place like this.

As Oscar wondered what had become of his companions, he drew his sword to clear the way. For the time being, he'd keep heading in the direction Nark indicated. Oscar felt grateful to have his little dragon guide.

Suddenly, Oscar heard splashing at his feet. Looking down, he saw that a small amount of water pooled between the outstretched tree roots. It appeared the ground ahead was slowly being swallowed by the lake. Oscar stepped more carefully going forward.

Sensing something, Oscar ducked down. As his instincts had indicated, an unknown object whizzed over his head from behind. It stopped on a branch ahead and let out a high-pitched squeak. Oscar examined it and found it was a green-winged pixie of some sort. It resembled a bat. He could hear a group of chattering voices coming from behind him as well.

"So they've decided to show themselves," he whispered to himself.

Oscar held Akashia ready, checking his footing again with regards to the tree roots and flooded ground. No sooner had he prepared himself than the pixies flew at him.

First, Oscar merely held up his left hand. Just before the pixies would've crashed into it, they found themselves repelled by the prince's protective barrier. The pixies staggered in the air, and Oscar quickly cut them down, along with the one that had attacked earlier. Then, he took a step back, dodging yet another diving at his flank. Having missed its target, that pixie went flying off into the trees. In the meantime, another struck.

There was no end to the waves of attackers, and Oscar was constantly on the defensive. Dodging pixies and branches, the prince picked his way through the forest while cutting down anything in his way. The deeper he advanced, the higher the water rose, until it lapped around only the tallest roots.

By the time Oscar's boots were nearly submerged, there were almost no pixies left in pursuit. When the prince finally paused to catch his breath, Nark launched off from his shoulder to fly lazily forward.

"...Destroy the barrier."

That had been the dragon's original mission. Obeying its master's order, Nark breathed fire into the air.

The forest erupted in flames. Heat swirled up, causing the surface of the water to quiver. Oscar scrunched up his face against the red tint searing his eyes. All too soon, the flames went out. Once they did, he was surprised to see an unnatural break in the trees had appeared.

The branches of the trees on either side were entwined, forming what looked exactly like a small door. It was unlike any Oscar had ever seen before, and he let out a cry of wonder.

"Wow! Where did that come from?"

This must be the psychological magic Tinasha had nagged him to be careful about. Impressed, Oscar crossed through the tree-made door and found himself inside a small clearing. A layer of clear, ankle-deep water covered the flat ground, and trees encircled him on all sides. Atop a piece of driftwood in the center sat a beautiful green-haired woman along with Oscar's childhood friend.

"Lazar!"

When his name was called, Lazar slowly turned. He looked perfectly real, but Oscar knew the man's real body was still waiting back in the castle. Even so, the prince couldn't help but reach out to his friend. "I've come to take you back. Let's go!"

"Your Highness...," Lazar murmured, and worry flashed across the face of the woman at his side. Her pale-blue arms wrapped around him. Lazar stared at the woman's sad expression, and there was a calmness in his eyes.

He looked back at Oscar, then lowered his eyes and shook his head. "I deeply apologize that you had to come all this way to look for me... But I will not be returning. I'm sorry."

Lazar's reply was not at all what Oscar had been expecting. For a moment, he doubted his hearing. Frowning, Oscar retorted, "What the hell? Wait until your soul and body are reunited before making jokes."

Oscar was certain it had to have been a joke. Surely Lazar didn't understand his predicament.

Gripping Akashia, Oscar took a step forward. Startled, the woman clung to Lazar. He squeezed her hand reassuringly before climbing down from the piece of driftwood. Then, he came forward, keeping the woman covered behind him.

"Please wait, Your Highness. She was betrayed by her fiancé. He promised to marry her, but he ended up with another woman..."

Oscar made a face. If the fairy tale was true, then he sympathized with what she'd experienced. Despite whatever pain the spirit had suffered, though, it was no reason to abduct Lazar, even if she truly was the victim here. The prince's friend was just being too sympathetic.

"Then she should abduct that guy instead," Oscar snapped.

"It happened hundreds of years ago. You saw the state that old castle is in, right? He's long dead. But to her..." Lazar paused, looking back at the spirit.

She caught his gaze and smiled at him. In her smile was all the compassion of a lost child who had finally been found. It belied her character and her soul, worn down over the hundreds of years she'd spent searching for the man she loved, yearned, hated, and waited for.

Lazar looked at her smile with fondness in his eyes. Oscar could sense an unwavering kindness from his friend, but he only felt anxious.

"...You'll die if you stay here," Oscar said.

He had long known that Lazar's kindheartedness would get him killed one day. However, Oscar had always believed that, as long as he was by Lazar's side, he could prevent it. He'd never imagined Lazar would reject his help.

Lazar looked at his lord and gave him the same sort guilty smile he'd often shown in the past. "I don't mind. She's been all alone for hundreds of years, wanting to die but unable to... Wanting to kill him but also not wanting to... I want to save her. If I can't do that, I at least need to give her some comfort."

It was clear Lazar was determined to help this spirit, even to the point of sacrificing his own life. Such was the strength of his character, which was undoubtedly why the woman had been drawn to him.

Oscar started to panic. "Don't get a big head. Is that really something you should be doing?"

Though the words were harsh, Lazar merely smiled. He met Oscar's gaze and asked, "Don't you feel anything when you look at her, Your Highness?"

Oscar had no idea what he meant by the question and pondered it for a moment before understanding.

Alone for hundreds of years.

Human, but also inhuman.

Lazar was implying that this miserable water spirit, possessed with tremendous magical power and existing entirely alone...was akin to Oscar's witch.

Oscar let out a sigh.

He closed his eyes.

In his mind's eye, he remembered the sorrow he'd seen in the witch at the top of the tower and her lonely smile before she'd left for the magical lake. Tinasha exposed such feelings very rarely, which was why Oscar saw her as a regular girl who needed his help. He was well aware that she wasn't that at all, of course. Tinasha was very different from ordinary humans.

Oscar opened his eyes and tightened his grip on Akashia. He walked over to the woman gazing at him with childlike innocence in her eyes. He glanced at Lazar standing next to her. The man looked unspeakably sad.

The look in Lazar's eye was one Oscar would not forget for the rest of his days...but some things were not up for debate.

"I'll listen to your complaints back at the castle."

There was no reply. The woman smiled happily.

The ending of a fairy tale was always merciless and abrupt.

Oscar lifted his sword.

※

A group of people was waiting at the castle gates when the party returned.

Wearing her witch outfit, Tinasha caught sight of Oscar and nodded. "Good job out there. His soul came right back," she said, smiling. Nark flew over to her shoulder. The tiny dragon appeared quite proud of itself, and Tinasha stroked its little head.

On the other hand, Als handed the reins of his horse to a soldier and grumbled, "Meanwhile, I went around the same spot in the forest over and over... I could have cried."

"You were caught fast in an illusion."

"Urgh..."

Doan and Suzuto, who'd suffered the same fate, looked equally disheartened.

Oscar expressed his appreciation for their efforts. "In any case, we saved him. I'll take care of the rest, so you all go get some sleep. Tinasha, where's Lazar?"

"Same spot you left him. I'll stop by later, too," she answered.

"Got it."

Apparently, Tinasha still had business to take care of. She hummed an incantation as she departed through the castle gate. Oscar watched her leave, then headed for Lazar's room.

As he walked, Oscar did not hesitate. He had chosen this himself. Showing regret here would only prove he was ill-suited to rescue others. Therefore, without the slightest change of expression, Oscar strode into the room where Lazar had been kept.

Lazar noticed him walk in and sat up in bed. "Your Highness…"

"You can lie down," Oscar said.

Likely as a result of having his soul taken, Lazar's movements were still jerky. Still, he staggered out of bed to kneel before Oscar and bowed his head low.

"I deeply apologize…for my conduct."

"I don't intend to apologize…and you don't need to, either."

Even though they'd walked such a similar path, they were different people. Oscar knew that, which was why they could be friends.

Lazar didn't lift his head. Instead, he said tearfully, "Starting tomorrow… I will once again serve you with everything I am."

"You rest until you've fully recovered your strength," Oscar ordered bluntly. Despite the sternness of the command, the prince's voice was tinged with his affection for Lazar—the affection he rarely voiced despite their closeness.

"He's still not fully recovered, so don't disturb him," Tinasha said. When she'd come in carrying a round bowl, Lazar was already asleep again.

Eyeing the cloth tied over the bowl, Oscar asked, "What were you up to?"

"Strengthening the wards around the castle. We weren't able to capture that suspicious mage, so I'd like to prevent any further intrusions. As long as I'm here, no one will be able to enter the castle anywhere other than the front entrance."

"…We're really beefing up everything with you around…," Oscar noted.

Just how many changes would the castle undergo during the witch's stay? Oscar had some apprehensions, but none of it appeared to be a big deal to Tinasha. She made the action seem as trivial as adding sugar to tea. It was commonplace, over in a flash, and only the memory remained. Just like how she'd left the castle seventy years ago.

Oscar stared at his protector. "You sure you don't want to marry me and live here permanently?"

"I'm sure! …Where did that come from?" Tinasha replied, sensing something different than Oscar's usual teasing in his words.

He gazed sincerely into her dark eyes. "Aren't you lonely living all by yourself for hundreds of years?"

The question sought to probe at the deepest part of the witch. Tinasha was stunned for a second before making a wry face. "Well, I'm a little lonely, but it's unavoidable." The look in her eyes seemed to be wondering what had prompted such a question.

In those eyes, Oscar saw a bit of sorrow and harshness.

Unlike the water spirit who'd disappeared into the forest, this witch had never even had anyone to lose. No one to keep in her heart forever, unable to let go. That was why she could go on for ages and ages with nothing but beauty, calm, and solitude.

Tinasha saw the fleeting lives of humans as distant things. While she might feel sad to say good-bye to them and watch them die, it wasn't enough to drive her mad. Her immense power, her loneliness, and her harshness were what made her a witch. Doubtless, she was aware of her own rigidity.

"Tinasha," Oscar started.

"Yes, what is it?"

"You can come to me for anything, at any time."

If someday Tinasha tired of everything leaving her behind while time was frozen for her, Oscar wanted her to know she could come to him. He'd welcome her the same way he always had.

"If you decide you want something that won't change, I can be that for you. I want you to remember that."

"Seriously, where is this coming from? Your constant stubbornness is really starting to concern me," Tinasha answered with a wide grin. Her skin was just as pale as it ever was, and the witch seemed incapable of being tied down by anything.

Oscar felt a sudden urge to reach out and grab her.

6. A Dream in the Forest

There was nothing in the wasteland after the fog cleared.

Magic indelibly stained the earth in places where none dared travel. Five such magical lakes dotted the mainland.

"Do you know how long this magical lake has been here?"

"No," replied the silver-haired girl—Miralys—frowning a little.

A week ago, a heavy fog had blanketed this land, but all was clear now that the demonic beast was dead.

The wind carried traces of grit and magic. The girl stood in front of the man next to her to guard him from it.

"You should go to sleep. Your wounds may be healed, but you're not back to normal yet," she said.

"I can't help it. The wound came from Akashia." It wasn't a fatal blow, but he'd been injured by the so-called Mage Killer. Further complicating things was the fact that the man had used transportation magic shortly after, leaving his magic in tatters. He'd managed to heal himself, but it was a stretch to say he had recovered. Valt smiled self-deprecatingly at how heavy his body still felt.

"But this resolves one thing. Now that the demonic beast is gone, she bears a little less sorrow," Valt said.

"Do you mean the Witch of the Azure Moon?" asked Miralys.

"Yes."

The witch had eliminated the beast just as Valt had predicted she would. The next challenge was appearing before her without dying. He didn't want to make an enemy of her, but no matter what useful information he brought her, she likely wouldn't listen.

If it were anyone else, Valt could manipulate them however he wanted. However, the witch would never trust him because he knew things he rightly should have been beyond him. No matter how eagerly she wanted to learn what he knew, she wouldn't work with him because she didn't know the source of that information.

Which was why he'd been forced into a neutral role where he would string her along.

"Magical lakes are the vestiges of powerful magic. Made by humans, they are now independent of their creators. They are very much not products of nature, though few people are aware of that," said Valt.

"And the witch is one of them, right? But why do you know about it?" asked the silver-haired girl.

"Because I once served her."

Unsurprisingly to Valt, Miralys's eyes widened at that revelation. By the time Valt was born, Tinasha had already become known as the witch in the tower. He'd attempted the climb but never made it to the top.

It was from there that the witch's story would truly begin.

"Now we have a secret weapon. It's fortunate she was severely wounded after she slayed the demonic beast. Otherwise, I never would've gotten my hands on a certain something."

Valt was covertly raising an incredibly useful secret weapon. The only trouble was that it had a kind of exhaustion point, but it was better than nothing. There were lots of strong people in the world. It was crucial to have weapons with which to oppose them when their paths crossed.

"All right, let's get going. Like you said, I need to rest for a bit," Valt said, clapping the girl on the shoulder and turning back.

However, he suddenly stopped in his tracks.

"Valt?" Miralys asked.

Finding it strange that he'd paused, the silver-haired girl looked up. Someone else was in their presence. An unknown voice called to the pair.

"That's quite the interesting story. You have a lot of magic. It makes you a rather noteworthy mage."

Something about the smooth, clear voice made Miralys uncomfortable. The sound felt like it was coming from terribly far away, seeming both there and not. Still, its tone was kind, even though it put her a little on edge. She peeped over Valt's shoulder. He was still frozen in place.

There Miralys saw a young man with long hair as white as snow.

His striking good looks exuded an air of nobility, and he had a gentle expression on his handsome face. However, the fine lines of his features gave him a somewhat sickly appearance, and his eyes glowed with an odd determination. He gave no clue as to his identity, but something about the stranger filled Miralys with an ominous feeling—whoever he was, she didn't like him.

When Valt replied, nervous tension tinged his voice. "Why are you here? Was it so important that you made the trip alone?"

"I wanted to take care of the puppy that was here. But the little girl did that already, didn't she?"

Miralys understood he was referring to the Witch of the Azure Moon, and her face drained of color. Who was this man, to refer to the strongest, most powerful witch in such a manner? She wanted to ask, but Valt already seemed to know.

Keeping Miralys behind him, Valt answered, "Yes, she destroyed the demonic beast, so it would be best if you didn't go out on needless excursions. She is constantly…searching for you."

"I know she is, but it's not time yet. We are not ready to welcome her, after all. When the time does come, I plan to go out and greet her. I'm sure she'll be so pleased."

"Pleased? *Her?*" Valt's tone was unusually dour, which surprised Miralys. Feeling uneasy, she started tugging on the hem of his robe only to have him reach out and stop her.

The white-haired man sounded bemused as he answered, "She will be. She's wanted to meet me forever."

"…You're so insolent toward her, no matter the time line," Valt spat. Miralys didn't understand what he meant.

Evidently, neither did the white-haired man. He cocked his head curiously like a child. "No matter the time line? What does that mean?"

"Just talking to myself. I'm simply an onlooker. In any case, it appears we have nothing in particular to discuss, so I'll be taking my leave soon." Valt patted Miralys on the shoulder and moved to turn around.

Behind him, the white-haired man spoke up again. "For an onlooker, it does sound like you've been up to some trouble."

"Nothing of importance. I merely placed things on the right track. That's what family does for one another," Valt shot back.

"What if I said I couldn't let this slide?" asked the white-haired man.

In an instant, the air between them turned cold. The man held out his right hand to Valt and Miralys. A pale light overflowed from his palm. Even magicless Miralys could sense that the spell was unusual. She tried to alert Valt, but before she could, he said, "Miralys, run."

His voice was hoarse. A smear of black was slowly surfacing on his chest.

Before she could register it as blood, the man began laughing. She could no longer see him, but his voice echoed. "To me, that girl is irreplaceable. I don't need any extra interference from here on out."

"Valt!" Miralys screamed. The searing-white light swelled larger.

Before it could burn everything away, Valt quickly drew a transportation array and pushed her onto it. Miralys realized what he was doing and reached out for him.

"Wait, Valt!"

The array swallowed her up before she could grab him. Suddenly, Miralys's surroundings grew distant. She screamed for Valt as he rapidly vanished from sight.

Thus, a mage who had stood on the sidelines of history was taken off the stage—irrationally and abruptly.

The cat running through the air caught sight of the woman standing on a castle spire and descended toward her.

Tinasha reached out a slender arm, and her familiar alighted on her hand. She received its report and frowned. "They found his body…"

The rather unexpected bit of information had Tinasha scratching her head. According to her familiar, the mysterious young mage who had been acting suspiciously had died within the magical lake in Old Druza.

"Oscar said he didn't give him a mortal wound... Did something go wrong with his recovery?"

In any case, this was a mage who had the power to outwit Oscar. She didn't think he could be killed that easily. Surely there must have been some sort of blunder.

"But if this means we don't have to worry about him anymore, I suppose there's no problem." Tinasha heaved a sigh skyward, then listened to the rest of her familiar's report. It proved as unsatisfactory as ever. A bittersweet smile crossed her face.

"I understand... Then you can go."

It had been the same result many times over now. A journey just to search for a person Tinasha couldn't find. A resignation incorporated into her life, like waking and sleeping.

Standing atop the tower, she stared out at the world...believing the answer she was searching for was out there somewhere.

※

In the hall just inside the castle door, bolts of colorful cloth were laid out over a great table. The court ladies were in high spirits as they rummaged through the rolls of beautiful fabric. Ladies young and old grabbed at material that caught their eye and chatted as they held it up to themselves or to their friends.

A traveling cloth merchant had brought a myriad of fabrics of all materials and colors. He came to the castle four times a year with a special selection of his wares to display. Almost all the ladies at court who could afford to have dresses tailor-made had been looking forward to this day.

Sylvia the mage was no exception. She entered the lounge in a very good mood. Approaching the witch who was busying herself with a book, Sylvia pressed her hands together in supplication. "Hey, Miss Tinasha, would you come look at fabrics with me?"

"Didn't I just buy some clothes?" Tinasha answered idly.

"Oh, come on, don't be like that. There are lots of rare fabrics from other lands," Sylvia pleaded.

"Hmm." Reluctantly, Tinasha closed her book. She sipped from the cup in her hands.

"Let's go! I'm interested to know what your measurements are!" said Sylvia, rather excitedly.

"Why?" Despite the protest, Tinasha got to her feet grudgingly, like a child being taken to the doctor.

The witch was wearing a short white dress she'd just purchased the other day. Her shapely legs peeping innocently from the hem had drawn the eye of every man she'd passed so far that day. Tinasha was a truly ethereal beauty. Her slim and elegant body now exuded a gracefulness her stiff teenage form had lacked. Secretly, Sylvia wanted to know just how narrow those willowy hips were.

In sharp contrast to Sylvia as she tugged Tinasha along excitedly, the witch's feet were dragging. She wanted to seize her chance and teleport away but knew Sylvia might cry if she did.

Just then, two men appeared at the end of the hallway. One of them called out to her, "Tinasha!"

It was the man she'd sworn to protect, accompanied by his attendant. Tinasha had a bad feeling, but with Sylvia pulling her toward them, she resigned herself to following.

Oscar handed the book he was holding to Lazar and turned to face his guardian witch.

"This is perfect timing. I was just about to have Lazar go get you. Let's go look at fabrics."

"I don't need any new clothes..." Tinasha already looked exhausted, and Oscar patted her head lightly.

"I want to know what size you are," Oscar stated matter-of-factly.

"You, too?!"

Tinasha now sorely regretted agreeing to go.

"Miss Tinasha, your waist is so small!"

"Kinda wish your bust was a bit bigger, though."

The high-grade fabrics reserved for the royal family were laid out in a separate hall from the one occupied by the court ladies. Tinasha flopped wearily onto a couch in the corner of that private room after undergoing what felt like ages of measuring.

On the other hand, Oscar and Sylvia were examining the list of measurements the tailor had written down and sharing their thoughts rather freely.

Tinasha, exhaustion writ large on her face, grumbled at them, "It's my prerogative to have whatever kind of body I want…"

"Now, let's pick out some fabrics. For starters, let's go with this one…and this one, too." Ignoring the witch's objections, Oscar picked up some bolts in front of him. Starting with a fine black silk that would go well with her hair, he picked out several and handed them to the tailor. The witch eyed him coldly throughout the process.

"Why are you ordering me clothes…?" Tinasha complained.

"It's what I'm into. It'll be fun to dress you up," Oscar replied.

"Please get that out of your system some other way…," urged Tinasha.

She knew the crown prince had many stressful responsibilities, but she still didn't want to get drawn into his weird means of amusement.

Oscar observed how disheartened she looked. "Got it. Then do you want to go out into town? I'll pick out some clothes for you there instead."

"That's not what I meant! Settle down!"

Tinasha had set up solid wards around the castle to prevent any trouble, but they were meaningless if Oscar left on his own. Resigning herself to the activity, Tinasha stood up and went to grab a bolt of glossy white fabric.

"I'm paying for this myself, so I'll make my own choices," she asserted.

"Suit yourself. I'll place my own order using your measurements." Oscar shrugged.

"…Do what you want." Tinasha hung her head dejectedly, but then she remembered something and grabbed Oscar's sleeve.

"What?" he asked, a little surprised.

"If you make me a wedding dress, I will curse you…"

Oscar burst out laughing, most likely remembering Tinasha's past mishaps.

※

"Hmm? Is Miss Tinasha not here?" Lazar asked, poking his head into the lounge several days after the whole clothing ordeal. Doan was the only one there. Lazar had come there looking for Tinasha because it was a spot she frequented often when not in her quarters.

"Lazar, haven't you heard?" Doan replied quickly. "She said she was going back to the tower to air out her magic implements and wouldn't be back for two days."

"N-no…I hadn't…"

It had been three months now since the witch had first arrived in Farsas. In all that time, aside from the excursion to the magical lake, she had never been away from the castle for longer than a day. She normally spent her time attending the mages' lectures, practicing on the training grounds, reading and researching, or making tea for Oscar and getting teased by him. A fairly carefree lifestyle, all things considered.

If she was gone…

"Will the prince be in danger?"

"Of course not," Doan answered, not looking up from his spell book.

The witch's protective barrier was active no matter where she was. Even without his protector, Oscar was more than able to defend himself. Lazar felt relieved when he remembered that, but he forgot to count himself as a part of those who safeguarded the peace of the castle.

Two hours later, Lazar was on horseback, trying to leave the castle by the back gate for some reason.

"Really, let's give up on this! If Miss Tinasha finds out, she'll be very angry with you!" he pleaded.

"That's why I'm going, isn't it? If she were here, I'd be getting an earful," Oscar retorted.

"I thought you'd been cured of that recklessness of yours!" Lazar complained.

"It's all right every once in a while, isn't it? If you don't like it, stay home and mind the fort."

Hanging his head upon hearing his lord's cold words, Lazar nevertheless urged his horse into a gallop to follow him.

Everything had started an hour earlier, when Oscar stopped on the last page of one of the various different reports he'd been reading.

"Lazar, look at this."

"What is it?"

The tray he'd been given in hand, Lazar headed for Oscar's desk. With Tinasha gone, the tea that day had been made by a court lady's maid. The crown prince's new attendant stood against the wall looking nervous. Aware of her gaze on him, Lazar placed a cup of tea on the desk before picking up the document Oscar had indicated.

"Let's see…people have been going missing from a village near an eastern forest since last week…then two to three days after disappearing, their dried-up bodies are found in the woods… What is going on here?!"

"You wanna know, right?" Oscar grinned.

"…No," Lazar answered flatly.

He had a very, very bad feeling about this. Oscar seemed to take no heed and continued anyway. "Nine people have died already. The place isn't even that far from here."

"I'm not the slightest bit curious!" Lazar cried.

"How about we go check it out?" Oscar suggested, seemingly unaware of his friend's objections.

"Listen to me, please…" Lazar planted both hands on the desk and slumped over it in dejection.

Since Tinasha's arrival, it was common knowledge that Oscar had a bad habit of sneaking out of the castle—and not on walks or to go sightseeing. He only went to dangerous places like the lairs of demonic spirits or archeological ruins riddled with traps. Each time, Lazar accompanied him against his better judgment and felt his lifespan grow shorter and shorter with each excursion.

Now the witch, who Oscar had met during the most dangerous of those outings, was absent. Though the prince derived great pleasure teasing her to death every day, it seemed he had thought up something reckless to do while she wasn't around to tell him no.

Lazar envisioned the danger ahead and the witch's wrath to come later and felt the blood drain from his face. He wished he'd gone on a vacation like she had.

※

The village of Byle stood at the foot of a mountain to the northeast of the castle city. Right outside the village was a deep forest that led to the mountain. So dense were the trees of those woods that the place was dark even in broad daylight.

Oscar and Lazar arrived at the village before dusk and interviewed the villagers under the guise of investigators from the castle. They'd chosen to conceal their true identities to avoid creating any undue commotion. The first man they approached was cutting wood in his garden, but once they struck up a conversation with him, he sat down on his pile of wood.

"The first one said he found something in the woods... He wouldn't say what it was exactly, but he was darn excited over it. Jus' when I thought he sure did disappear fast, turns out *that* happened to 'im."

"That" referred to the body being found dead and dried out. It was clearly a sign of foul play of some kind. Lazar still wanted to go back before they got themselves too involved, but based on previous experiences, he knew it was futile.

After getting the stories of nearly all the other villagers in Byle, Oscar, as enthused as Lazar had expected, said, "Right, let's head into the forest."

"Ugh, just unbelievable... What do you plan to do if something happens?" Lazar asked.

"Tinasha said that mage who was doing suspicious stuff died," assured Oscar.

"So because he died, it's okay for you to act recklessly? I see..."

More than the prince's safety, the real issue was his attitude. Undaunted, Oscar replied blithely, "If something hits my protective barrier, Tinasha will find out, so I'll have to dodge everything that might come at me."

"Let her find out, then," said Lazar, thoroughly nonplussed.

Facing the witch was far preferable to turning up as a dried-up husk.

Tinasha would absolutely be incandescent with rage, but she got mad at him regularly anyway.

Lazar let out a heavy sigh but followed Oscar into the forest regardless. While the woods were thick, there was a thin trail the villagers regularly made use of. However, Oscar and Lazar had been told that, because of the recent unnatural deaths, few villagers went into the woods anymore.

"I wonder how big this forest is…," muttered Lazar.

"The map says it's about ten times the size of the village," Oscar answered.

"There's no way we can search that whole area."

"People from Byle are the ones who've been dying. The spot has to be within walking distance from the start of the trail," Oscar pointed out.

Without any better leads to go on, Oscar and Lazar headed for the east side of the woods—a spot the locals had previously frequented. Medicinal herbs grew deep in the forest, which many villagers sought out to pick and sell for good prices to mages.

Soon, Oscar and Lazar arrived at a clearing amid the many trees. Lazar inspected the grasses that grew abundant there. "I really can't tell which of these is the medicinal herb," he said.

"Yeah, it all looks like wild grass to me."

A villager or mage would know which herb was useful, but Oscar and Lazar had no connection to magic and couldn't so much as guess at the right plant to pick. They ventured deeper into the grassy meadow, taking wide strides so as to step on as few plants as possible.

"If only the herb had flowers…it'd at least be easier to spot…," muttered Lazar.

The pair stood surrounded by a sea of verdant colors. Lazar turned his head this way and that and finally caught sight of some little white flowers only slightly farther ahead. As he drew closer, Lazar realized they weren't flowers at all.

"…A pearl?"

The conspicuous plant first resembled a cluster of flowers, but a closer look revealed that it was laden with tiny pearls. Lazar reached out for it, doubting his eyes. Sure enough, the pale little spheres were hard to the touch.

"Your Highness! These are pearls!" he called.

"Are you stupid?" Oscar asked, turning around and glaring at Lazar from a short distance away.

"No, they really are..."

"That's even stupider."

Oscar drew Akashia, and Lazar's jaw dropped at the unexpected reaction. Then he felt something odd at his feet. He looked down...and froze.

A green vine had wound itself around Lazar's ankle several times over while he'd been distracted. The thing lifted its tip, as a snake would have done with its head, and began slithering away.

"Aaaaah!"

"Idiot!"

Lazar let out a scream as Oscar dashed after him, slashing at the creeping plant with Akashia. The prince grabbed his attendant and pulled him from the vine's grasp.

Tossed onto the grass, Lazar turned back to look at what had grabbed him and gaped in shock. "Wh-what is that?" he asked, fear in his voice.

"Some kind of...bizarre plant?" Oscar answered, unsure himself.

Wriggling on the ground was a giant mass of pearl-covered vines. The strange thing writhed in pain as if it had a mind of its own. Seemingly in retaliation for Oscar's attack, it shot out a thick tendril at Oscar and Lazar. The vine Oscar had severed was still squirming on the ground.

Lazar scrambled back, hand over his mouth. "So this is what killed everyone?"

"Probably. I guess it sucks you dry once it gets ahold of you," observed Oscar.

The tentacles had a giant pearl-like thing at the root, surrounded by green petals. While the size was different, it was obvious the small pearl grasses were of the same type. Amid the swaying vines, Oscar took a breath.

"I wish Nark were here. It'd burn this to dust," he said.

"Miss Tinasha would find out...," Lazar reminded him.

"Yeah, that's the tough part. If I piss her off, I'll go straight to the doghouse."

"If you're aware of that, then just behave yourself and stay in the castle."

Even as he cracked jokes, Oscar slashed at the vines creeping toward him. The attacks were relentless, but he was so good that they never touched him. Oscar narrowed his eyes at the huge pearl.

"Something's off about that pearl. Lazar, stand back."

Four vines were left. Their ends were poised for attack, as if locked onto their target. Oscar seized his chance and leaped for the root. Two tendrils lunged for him, and he cut them both down at once. He ducked to dodge a third coming from the side. Once it whizzed by, he lopped it off at the base.

That was when the last vine came barreling toward him head-on. But just before it could reach the barrier placed around Oscar, it met Akashia's blade. The razor-sharp, double-edged sword split it right down the middle.

Without pausing, Oscar approached the giant pearl and stabbed his sword into its lustrous center. The pearl-like thing quivered and trembled. Almost immediately, some sort of purple liquid erupted from the cut.

"Wha—?" Reflexively, Oscar jumped backward and avoided the spray. The purple fluid gushed from the deflating pearl, rapidly flooding the clearing.

"Damn, it's poison! Lazar, we're getting out of here!" cried Oscar.

The now-vineless pearl began to emit a fog the same color as the liquid. The toxic vapor hissed from the thing and encroached upon the two men. Before Lazar could obey his lord's orders and retreat, a terrible nausea overtook him, and he clapped a hand over his mouth.

Breathing became painful, and his forehead broke out in a cold sweat. With his vision swimming, Lazar fell to his knees.

"Lazar!" Oscar cried.

Just then, the clear voice of a woman rang out through the forest. "What are you doing?"

Lazar could barely make out the shadow of someone floating in the air. Consciousness left him as he was overcome with relief at his apparent salvation.

"You must have some strange tastes to come all the way out here. Isn't this where a bunch of people died?" the woman asked, sounding amused.

"Well, what are you doing in this forest?" responded the voice of a man. He sounded somewhat vigilant and curious. It was a voice Lazar knew very well. He tried to think of who it was, but his head was pounding.

When at last he opened his eyes, Lazar found himself in a house. The building couldn't have been very big, because he could see the underside of the roof. Blinking, Lazar sat up and saw his lord sitting at a dining table.

Across from Oscar was a woman Lazar didn't recognize. She carried a kind of dramatic beauty about her, with curly light-brown hair, amber eyes, and ivory skin.

"Oh, you're awake?" She asked after seeing that Lazar was up. Gently, she waved a hand at him. After hearing the question, Lazar realized he'd been lying in a bed.

Oscar glanced over at his friend. "How are you feeling?"

"Your Highness, I...," Lazar started.

"There was some kind of poison in the air," Oscar explained. "Sorry I didn't notice it quick enough."

The mysterious woman rose from her seat and offered Lazar a glass of water. Thanking her, he took a sip and felt the cold liquid wash down the sides of his throat. He sighed deeply.

"Thank you very much... Um, and you would be...?"

"Me?" the woman asked, pointing to herself and grinning with amusement. "I'm Lucrezia. Though most don't call me by my name. Everyone knows me as the Witch of the Forbidden Forest."

Shocked, Lazar stiffened. The witch grinned wider, clearly even more thoroughly amused by his reaction, while Oscar gave a chagrined sigh.

Lucrezia's house was deep in the forest, in an area normally impenetrably concealed behind a barrier.

Here and there inside the wooden house were rows of dried herbs and glass beakers for processing them. Bookshelves occupied one wall, packed tight with what looked like tomes of spells. The glass cabinet next to the shelves housed teas and bottles containing unknown substances.

"Your place looks like an apothecary," Oscar noted.

"I research magic potions and medicines. That thing you cut down earlier seems like it will make for a good specimen. It was growing in a part of the forest that most people don't usually venture into. My guess is someone got curious and explored a little farther than they should have. It pursued the villager back to a spot closer to the village and stayed there, sucking dry anyone who came near, growing bigger and bigger."

"So the first victim unknowingly caused all this," reasoned Oscar.

"I've never seen one so big before. I'm excited to see how much fluid I can extract from it." Lucrezia sounded utterly thrilled, leaving Oscar unsure how best to respond. Lazar got out of bed, looking wholly disheartened.

Lucrezia turned her attention back to her two guests and noticed that Oscar hadn't touched his tea. Tilting her head in confusion, she asked, "Oh, are you not going to have any?"

"If I did, a certain someone would yell at me for being too careless. Sorry."

"I see… So Tinasha hasn't changed, then."

"You know her?" Oscar's eyes widened a little.

Lucrezia gave a mischievous smile. "Of course. I've known her ever since she became a witch."

Oscar felt no small degree of shock upon hearing those words.

"Became a witch."

That meant that Tinasha wasn't born a witch; she became one sometime after. Given her appearance when she'd stopped growing, that must've meant she'd become a witch shortly before turning sixteen.

What was she before that? And why did she become a witch at all? A flurry of questions whirled about in Oscar's mind.

"She's the only one who could have put that protective barrier on you, so I knew it had to be her. What's she doing now? Is she still holed up in that tower?" asked Lucrezia.

"No, she's acting as my protector," Oscar answered.

"Ooh, so you climbed up the tower? And here I'd thought she'd made it a bit too difficult…"

"His Highness climbed it virtually alone," Lazar chimed in.

"What? Really?! That's amazing." Like Tinasha, Lucrezia didn't seem particularly witchlike, though in an entirely different way. The way she spoke was frank, open, and guileless.

Oscar had always thought of all witches as beings like the one who'd cursed him—the Witch of Silence. To him, they'd all been creatures who bent the land to their capricious whims by way of their astonishing magical powers. However, Lucrezia was not at all like that. Her demeanor was disarming enough that even Lazar was starting to relax and smile a bit.

Still, Oscar couldn't quite shake his apprehensions. She'd dispelled the poisonous vapors in the forest and invited him into her home where she'd cured Lazar. But that wasn't enough for Oscar to forget that he barely knew this woman or to ignore the fact that she was indeed a witch. Trusting her implicitly seemed foolish. Tinasha had described the three other witches, excluding the Witch of Silence, as *"dangerous," "impossible to communicate with,"* and *"having a lot of issues personality-wise."* Which of them was Lucrezia?

The witch's amber eyes sparkled as she gazed at Oscar. "So what did you ask for in the contract? Do you want to become king of the world?"

"I don't think she would grant a wish like that...," Oscar answered.

"That's true, but it's not impossible with her protection and that sword you've got. Wouldn't you agree?" Lucrezia narrowed her eyes. Her smile lingered, but it was edged with the kind of immeasurable darkness befitting a witch as she kept her gaze locked on Oscar.

Unshaken, the prince bore the weight of her stare calmly. "I may be strong, but I can't win a war alone. I've no desire to go out and do such a thing anyway."

"...Is that so? Then what did you wish for?"

"Who can say?"

Oscar refused to give a proper answer, and Lucrezia looked disappointed. She pouted like any other woman would've, dissolving the tension in the air. "I was only curious. Maybe I should go ask Tinasha myself. I haven't seen her in decades."

"His Highness wants to make Miss Tinasha his wife," Lazar said rather glibly.

Oscar almost fell off his chair. He'd been so careful, and now it was all ruined. He looked over to see Lazar partaking of a cup of tea with an innocent smile.

Before Oscar could chastise his friend, the witch's laugh cut him off.

"Ah-ha-ha-ha-ha-ha-ha! I see, I see! Thank you," Lucrezia trilled, pounding on the table. Apparently, she found it so utterly hilarious that tears came to her eyes, while Oscar sat there looking as sour as vinegar.

"...Well, she turned me down. Which is why she now acts as my protector," explained Oscar.

"Ah-ha-ha-ha... I'm sorry. Still, it worked out well enough for you, all things considered, right? I bet it's pretty tough having her around, though," Lucrezia said.

"I don't know if I'd say that," Oscar replied.

Lazar leaned forward intently. Evidently, he'd completely let his guard down around Lucrezia. Oscar added another item to the list of things to lecture him about once they got back to the castle.

Lucrezia stirred sugar into her tea as she said, "It must be tough. She's been a spirit sorcerer forever, so she's laced up incredibly tight. She's friendly enough, so she'll warm up to the people she lives with pretty quick. But she'd never take a lover of any kind. She's got a lot of baggage."

"Do you mean with the king of Farsas?" Oscar asked, wondering if Lucrezia was hinting at his royal great-grandfather—the man who'd previously held a contract with Tinasha. Lucrezia burst into fresh peals of laughter.

"Oh, that was one of the biggest mistakes. I laughed so hard at the time. He was just so pushy, and she was so tired of it. Still, I wonder if he might've actually succeeded had he been a bit cleverer... No, no, there's no way," she concluded on her own, slapping her knee.

Despite having just laughed herself silly, Lucrezia's normal smile returned quickly to her face. "How about I help you out? Do you want any aphrodisiac to take with you? Normal potions won't work for her, but the ones I make use special plants. They'll probably do the trick."

"...No thanks, I'll manage on my own," Oscar said, leaning slightly against a chair. This new witch was hard to get a handle on. Things were going in a completely different direction than when Oscar had first met

Tinasha. Had Lucrezia's status as a witch emboldened her to try to foist an aphrodisiac on him?

Lucrezia's smile gave away nothing of her true intentions. "If you win her, you'll have the world in the palm of your hand."

"Like I said, I don't have any interest in that."

"…I see." Without making a sound, Lucrezia got to her feet and extended a long finger to Oscar.

Reflexively, the prince's hand shot to Akashia's hilt. Before he could draw the sword, however, Lucrezia floated into the air above the table. She placed her right hand on Oscar's cheek, gazing into his blue eyes. On her beautiful face was a gracious smile.

"In that case… I'll give you something more interesting than an aphrodisiac." Lucrezia's words carried the inflection of a threat.

Oscar started to draw his sword, but the Witch of the Forbidden Forest merely landed softly on the floor. Her amber eyes gazed into his own for only a brief moment, but he frowned, feeling like something had flickered inside his mind.

Lucrezia giggled. "Ooh, so scary. Unlike Tinasha, I'm not good at fighting, so could you let this slide?"

"I'm not sure." Oscar's hand remained ready on his blade.

"Y-Your Highness… She did save us, and no one else from the village will fall victim to that plant thing, so let's call it a day and head home. Miss Tinasha is sure to be worried," Lazar pleaded, attempting to assuage the building tension despite clearly being flustered himself.

"…Yeah," Oscar replied. He straightened up, refusing to take his eyes off Lucrezia all the while. The witch gave him a mesmerizing grin.

"Come by again anytime," she offered. Something about her openly beguiling expression was unmistakably witchlike.

The pleasant scent of tea pervaded the study.

A day had passed since Oscar and Lazar had returned from the witch's forest. The latter brought in a stack of documents before closing his eyes to inhale the sweet aroma.

He'd long since gotten used to the sight of a beautiful black-haired witch passing a cup of tea to his lord. Lazar was captivated by her graceful movements, only snapping out of his trance when she turned around.

Tinasha stared at him curiously. "Why are you just standing there?"

"Oh, er, no reason."

Lazar rushed to deliver the papers to his lord. Ever since Oscar's uncle—the previous prime minister—had passed away, Oscar had inherited his former duties as well as a portion of kingly authority. All kinds of reports came from both within the castle and without. Oscar was the one who reviewed and approved them all, excepting only the most important documents.

After briefing the prince on this latest set of papers, Lazar turned to Tinasha and asked, "Did you get everything aired out without any trouble?"

"Yeah, I managed, somehow. I've got a lot of things that are tricky to deal with. So much so that I can't leave the job to my familiars. Sorry for being gone so long."

"Oh, not at all. Feel free to take as many holidays as..." Lazar trailed off. He'd nearly said *Take as many holidays as you'd like* before he froze after remembering the danger he'd wound up in because Tinasha had been gone. Still, that wasn't her fault, and after a moment, he completed his sentence.

Lazar's pause didn't appear to rouse Tinasha's suspicions, but Oscar cast a scowl at his friend from behind the witch's back.

"Was there any trouble while I was gone? Anything you needed my help with?" asked Tinasha.

"N-not particularly...," said Lazar, his voice wavering.

"Nothing," Oscar confirmed flatly.

"That's good, then."

Tinasha gave them a full, gorgeous smile, and Lazar breathed an internal sigh of relief. Oscar may have seen right through him, because he stood up and clapped Lazar on the shoulder as he passed by.

"Come outside with me."

"Ah, okay."

Don't say a word was written in Oscar's eyes. On their way back from the witch's forest, Oscar had warned Lazar, "You need to be less trusting. And don't tell Tinasha we met that witch." Oscar was likely worried the witches would end up in an argument if Tinasha found out he nearly drew his sword on Lucrezia.

The prince stared into Lazar's eyes, searching for confirmation, and Lazar offered an awkward smile. Oscar gave a little nod. Perhaps he knew that Tinasha's own eyes were glued to his back. He looked over his shoulder at her.

"What's up? Do I have something on my back?" Oscar asked as nonchalantly as he could.

"No, nothing, but… Oscar, are you sleeping well?" Tinasha's question was rather unexpected.

"Yeah, no problem. Why?"

"…I suppose it's fine, then," the witch answered, though she still looked skeptical.

Oscar grinned and reached out a hand to her. "Since you're here, you wanna come, too?"

"Why should I? It's your work."

"For a change of pace, I'm going to go see if the mages are working on anything interesting. Come with me," Oscar said, urging Tinasha to follow.

"Allow me to remind you that I've given up my identity as a court mage already! That's why I'm here, making you tea!"

"If you want a commission, I'll give you one. How about you pick one of the jobs that was too difficult for the others to handle?"

"Are you just looking for a fun diversion?!" Tinasha snapped, but she followed him out of the room anyway. Perhaps she felt the prince really couldn't be left to his own designs.

The door slammed shut. Lazar felt a stomachache coming on and sighed.

As it was already afternoon, few jobs were left unclaimed on the board.

The crown prince and his witch standing side by side at the job board made for a most unusual sight. Passersby did double takes while Oscar checked the dates on a few slips and pulled two of them off.

"These two have been up for more than five days. Brewing potions to keep in reserve and restoring classic literature tomes... Kinda boring," Oscar commented.

"Give me those. I'll do them. You get back to your work," Tinasha said.

"Tinasha..."

Oscar had probably been hoping for something involving going out and exterminating a demonic spirit or the like, but a task like that was better suited for soldiers. The prince knew the reason there were only a few jobs left was because the court mages were so very capable. He wanted to protest but decided to concede this one and patted Tinasha on the head.

"Then I'll leave them to you; sorry. If there's anything you need, just put in a request," said Oscar.

"Understood," Tinasha replied.

With a bittersweet smile twisting his face, Oscar turned and departed, appearing as the very picture of irreproachable nobility as he did. Their little break must have reinvigorated him. Tinasha watched him go.

"...Weirdo."

He was unlike any of the people she'd signed a contract with before. It truly seemed he did not care at all that Tinasha was a witch.

That didn't mean Oscar regarded her as a regular human. It was more that he'd readily accepted she was a witch and wasn't afraid of her. Tinasha didn't know whether to pity the prince for being thickheaded or praise his courage.

Opinions on his attitude within the castle were mixed. Quite a few people criticized him for keeping a witch by his side as if it were completely normal, to say nothing of the fact that everyone knew the story of the fairy-tale version of Tinasha. Even though that tale was inaccurate, it was the account most people knew—and all they had to go on.

Despite their misconceptions, Tinasha made no attempt to correct them. People like that would never come around to the idea of befriending a witch. To them, Tinasha was some kind of creature that operated wholly differently than them. Trying to dispel or change their impression was an entirely futile effort.

This was why Tinasha normally lived in the tower. It ensured she only encountered those ready to meet someone like her.

"But he brought me down from the tower. He really has some strange tastes."

Tinasha tore off another job request. When she placed it in her robe, a man at the end of the hall waved to her. "Miss Tinasha! May I ask you a question?"

"Oh, Kav. What is it?"

One of Tinasha's mage acquaintances had found her and come running over. There were still quite a few people in the castle who avoided her, but starting with Kav, more and more of them had been interacting normally with her.

Tinasha glanced through the potions recipe book he was carrying, then identified the problem spot.

"The spell procedure here and the third sequence should be flipped. It'll get overwritten, and you won't derive the right result. Also, it might be good to use a substitute for the catalyst… Like this and this…"

Nodding, Kav took notes on all the witch's suggestions. Tinasha checked over the corrections.

"If that doesn't work, come to me again. Although, really, Lucrezia's the only one who would be able to say for sure. I'm sorry," Tinasha said.

"No, you've really helped me. Thank you so much. Is this Lucrezia an acquaintance of yours?" asked Kav.

"I suppose you could call her that. She's an eccentric who's good with potions and psychological magic."

"An eccentric… What kind of person is she?"

"…It's better not to ask," Tinasha said firmly with a very serious expression. There were quite a few things in the world one was better off not knowing.

Tinasha's first day back passed uneventfully. Mentions of another witch had been well concealed.

"Oscar, are you sleeping well?"

It was at least the second time Oscar had heard this question. He considered it for a moment, still unsure why Tinasha was asking.

Early in the morning, the witch had caught him just as he was leaving his quarters. She eyed him suspiciously.

"I'm sleeping just fine. I don't feel tired or anything," he answered.

Oscar stroked Tinasha's soft hair. Suddenly, a strange image came to his mind for a brief moment, stopping his hand in midair.

Skin as white as snow, eyes the color of darkness, and lips as red as a flower petal. A face so beautiful that a mere smile would be enough to captivate any who beheld it, though that visage was frowning with incredulity. It was the face of Tinasha, Oscar's protector, a face he'd come to know quite well…but for an instant, Oscar felt like he'd recalled a different, more flirtatious look in those eyes. Something in his memories felt a bit strange.

"Oscar?" Tinasha called.

"…No, it's nothing. Just had a weird sense I'd done this before…"

"You're half-asleep. You need to get more rest."

"I told you, I'm sleeping just fine… Oh, Tinasha, I had a gift for you." Oscar suddenly recalled something and returned to his room. He quickly returned holding a small box. Tinasha received and opened it, finding a small crystal ball inside. She gave Oscar a bemused look, head cocked to the side.

"Yesterday, you went to heal a kid in town who was injured, right? The mage who completed the request didn't give a name, but the family came to the castle to express their thanks in person. It's from them," Oscar explained.

"What are you talking about? I don't know anything about that," Tinasha said.

"Do you really think there's any mistaking your appearance?" Oscar asked.

"Next time, I'll put on a disguise before going out," the witch replied. She turned away to sulk, and Oscar burst out laughing. Tinasha was kindhearted, but she often avoided openly associating with people because of what she was.

Oscar patted the head of his little protector. "Either way is fine. You should do what you want."

"If I can do what I want, then I want to go back to my tower," Tinasha quipped.

"Not that," Oscar fired back, making a sour face. She flicked the crystal ball with a finger.

"I don't think this is meant for me, but I'll go ahead and take it. I'll enchant it with something. Maybe a spell to force you to sleep."

"Why do you want to put me to sleep that badly?"

Ignoring Oscar's retort, Tinasha floated into the air and vanished without a trace.

"She's always just disappearing like that…," Oscar said, shaking his head ruefully as he headed for his study. The strange momentary thought that had given him pause had been forgotten.

Tinasha reappeared in front of Lazar as he was in the midst of his attendant duties. The man had been hiding something from the witch for a few days now, and he practically screamed when he noticed her lying in wait for him in the hallway. Flustered, he greeted her as normally as he could.

"G-good morning."

"Good morning. I actually had something I'd like to ask you about."

"O-oh yes?"

Smiling, Tinasha approached Lazar and gazed up at him with her dark eyes. Meeting the witch's gaze felt like she was boring into your soul, and Lazar broke into a cold sweat. If she asked him about what happened while she was away, he didn't trust himself to lie.

Thankfully, Tinasha inquired about something completely different.

"Is Oscar sleeping well lately?"

"Wha…? I think so. He's not staying up late or anything like that."

"Really?"

"Really."

Feeling a bit let down for some reason, Lazar wondered what could have prompted Tinasha's question.

The witch thought about the answer for a moment and then posed another query. "Any romantic meetings lately?"

"What?! Who are you asking about?" Lazar exclaimed.

"Oscar," Tinasha clarified.

"…No."

Lazar had to wonder what she was actually asking after. He spent much of his time each day with Oscar but couldn't think of anything out of the ordinary that had happened recently. The prince didn't seem sleep-deprived, and aside from the witch before him, there was no special woman in his life.

Tinasha looked pensive, tapping a finger on her chin. "Hmm… There's really no one?"

"No, no one. Are you jealous?" asked Lazar.

"Save the sleep talk for when you're asleep," Tinasha retorted, not batting an eye. Lazar felt a rush of sympathy for his lord.

"You know… His Highness has a lot of good points…"

"I know he does, but that has nothing to do with it. No one would ever let him marry a witch in the first place. Please get him to stop."

"I'm really sorry, but His Highness is the type who won't quit even if he's held back."

"Don't let someone like that outside the country, then!" the witch scolded, yelling as she often did. Her more serious expression quickly returned, however. "In any case, please tell me if you notice anything. Try not to do anything that'll get him excited," she said, then vanished without a sound.

Lazar, finally released from Tinasha's intimidating aura, let out a soul-deep sigh of relief before setting off for the crown prince's study at a trot.

The lounge of Farsas Castle was a rectangular room facing the hallway and had been designed to be used by any castle staff.

Sylvia, Doan, and Kav happened to be in the lounge on their afternoon break. Everyone was sipping tea and reading as they liked. Other mages typically spent the entire day at lectures and magic practice, but these three were highly talented. Often, they would spend time after work continuing their own research. However, they also enjoyed spending their breaks striking up idle chitchat.

No sooner had they concluded one topic of conversation than Tinasha appeared. As soon as she saw the three of them, the witch pulled out an old book from under her arm and presented it.

"Here you are, Doan, the book you asked for," she said.

"Whoa! You really did track it down. I heard it was destroyed a long time ago," Doan said, accepting the volume with a mixture of shock and joy on his face. The battered old spell book was a rare tome said to no longer exist.

Tinasha pulled a chair over and joined the three mages at their table. "I have quite a few of those. If there's anything else, just let me know, and I'll find it for you."

"Thank you!" Doan said, ecstatic.

The witch gave him a smile in return, then glanced at the hallway as the sound of footsteps gradually grew louder. A girl in the garb of a lady-in-waiting was passing by. She was a lovely lass with light-blond hair. The young woman gave no indication that she noticed those in the lounge as she sauntered past.

Sylvia noticed Tinasha staring at the girl. "Do you know her? I think she's an apprentice who arrived at the castle recently."

"Mmm. Her name is Miralys. She waits on Oscar a lot lately, and Lazar has been instructing her," Tinasha replied.

"I suppose she can learn a lot about her job that way. Although, Oscar doesn't seem to like having ladies-in-waiting attend him, so there haven't been many in the past," Sylvia said.

"I think he's had his reasons. And I have a guess as to why she's been assigned to wait on him," Tinasha added.

"You do?" Sylvia asked.

"But it has nothing to do with anything, so never mind. More than that, I'm worried about how Oscar's been in bad health for the past few days. I think he might be sleep-deprived, but he keeps insisting he isn't."

"What, really? But he hasn't looked sick," Sylvia exclaimed, sounding surprised. Doan and Kav looked up from their spell books, too.

For her part, Tinasha slumped back against her chair and crossed her legs. Her posture wasn't usually so careless, and it seemed to indicate she was in an exceptionally bad mood.

"He doesn't appear to be aware of it, but his life force is flickering. I wish he'd be serious about taking care of himself... If he has a girlfriend, he should just go ahead and date her outright."

"What?" all three mages chorused in astonishment.

"A girlfriend?!"

"I didn't think he had anyone."

"It *is* a bit unthinkable."

Everyone in the castle knew how important Tinasha was to Oscar. And those close to Tinasha knew she didn't mind the prince's feelings one bit.

Naturally, they couldn't even imagine Oscar getting involved with another woman.

Though all three mages had expressed their incredulity, Tinasha shook her head. "There are strong traces of perfume on him. I think it's from a woman. I guess he doesn't notice the smell."

Sylvia, Kav, and Doan exchanged glances. Doan raised his hand a little before speaking. "I saw him today, but I didn't smell anything like that."

"What...? It's pretty noticeable if you're near him... Wait," Tinasha interrupted herself, freezing in place. Unconsciously, she bit down on the finger she'd had against her chin. Something dawned on her, and then, slowly, her face transformed into a mask of rage. The three mages watched with bated breath. They could sense a huge amount of magic amassing within Tinasha's slender body. The table they were sitting around began to creak, although the witch wasn't touching it.

Emerging from what appeared to be deep thought, Tinasha clicked her tongue. "Sorry, something just came up," she said, vanishing immediately thereafter.

The three mages who'd watched it all happen looked to one another.

"That was scary..."

"No cheating on her allowed, that's for sure..."

"What in the world...?"

After witnessing the storm that was gathering, Sylvia, Doan, and Kav each felt pity for the one about to be caught up in it.

The maelstrom crashed upon its unsuspecting victim in brilliant comeuppance.

"OSCAR!"

With a thunderous peel, the door exploded open, and Tinasha blew in, her face contorted with anger. It was not Oscar's first time seeing her so furious, but it was a rare occurrence. The prince looked up from his burrow amid countless stacks of papers. He had a bad feeling about this.

"What's wrong, Tinasha?"

"Don't 'what's wrong' me!" She flew through the air, grabbed his head in both of her hands, and forced him to look at her. She hadn't put much force into the action, but Oscar could feel Tinasha's hands trembling with anger. "Why didn't you tell me you met Lucrezia?!"

"…Dammit, Lazar…" Oscar threw a glance at his friend, who was pale-faced and standing next to the door. He raised his hands up as if to say *I couldn't help it!* Tinasha must have wrung the truth out of him earlier… Oscar had anticipated this but still couldn't help but sigh. It'd been a losing battle from the start to think Lazar could've ever lied to a witch.

Tinasha looked like she was about to fly into a rage and destroy the room, but Oscar met her fearsome gaze. "I didn't tell you because I didn't think it was a big deal. Sorry."

"If you think meeting a witch is no big deal, then every danger of the world must be a cakewalk to you!"

"They might be, yeah," Oscar replied.

"You have a serious problem when it comes to understanding danger! I told you that I can't guard against psychological magic! It's great that you're so confident in yourself, but I'm not going to be responsible if that gets you killed!"

"…I'm sorry," Oscar muttered, then exchanged a glance with Lazar. "Killed?"

"I'm just glad we're in time," Tinasha said, sounding thoroughly put out.

In an ancient country to the east, a much-beloved queen had died. Her king grieved the loss deeply, and he saw her every night in his dreams thereafter. The king had many imaginary rendezvous with his beloved, but each time, he would wake and mourn reality. One day, he finally passed away in his sleep.

The people wept, saying the king had followed his queen into death.

"What a sad, moving story…," Oscar said.

"Yes, if it had really been the queen who'd appeared in his dreams," retorted Tinasha curtly, playing with a strand of ink-black hair.

The prince picked up on something unsettling in her words. "What was it, then?"

Oscar and Lazar were drinking tea at the table in Oscar's study. Although Tinasha was still thoroughly indignant, she'd made them some tea—perhaps she'd calmed down a little. The beverage seemed to taste slightly more bitter than usual, though Oscar noted that perhaps that was just his imagination.

"Probably a demonic spirit or the interference of a mage. Whatever it was, it appeared under the guise of the dreamer's lover and slowly robbed him of his life force through sexual union. When done properly, the victim usually dies in a week."

Today marked the fifth day since Oscar and Lazar had met Lucrezia. Both men had kept quiet about the very thing that had put Oscar in danger.

"I don't know if she used a succubus or dream demon to do this for her, or if she manufactured the whole thing with magic, but you probably had a dream like that every night for the past few days. Lucrezia likely set it up such that you'd have no memory of it when you woke."

"It's actually kind of a shame I can't remember," Oscar quipped.

Tinasha glared coldly at the other two in the room, but Oscar didn't flinch.

"How could you tell?" he asked.

"The smell. There's a strong floral scent, like ladies' perfume, coming from you. Which is why I thought that you must have gotten a girlfriend…"

"I didn't. Wait, do I really smell like that?" Oscar exchanged puzzled looks with Lazar, while Tinasha snapped her fingers.

"Apparently, no one but me can detect it. She must've made it so that I'm the only one who can smell it, that pervert."

Pervert referred to Lucrezia, evidently—choice words for someone who seemed to be an old acquaintance.

Of course, sparing time debating such words was only possible because the worst-case-scenario had been avoided. Having very narrowly avoided death, Oscar reached out to twirl some of Tinasha's hair in his fingers.

"So what should we do?" he asked.

"I'll break the curse tonight. There are already some fluctuations in your life force, so there's a chance I could kill you if I broke it through external force."

"I see."

"Which means I'll need to forcibly smash it from in the dream."

"So it's going to be by force either way," Oscar concluded.

Tinasha clicked her tongue, an expression that said *What does that have to do with it?* on her face.

Lazar piped up anxiously, "Is there no other method?"

"Theoretically, I know of several others, but…" Tinasha trailed off. Something in her eyes suggested the other methods were less preferable. One look at Tinasha, and Oscar understood, removing his hand from her hair.

"Got it. We'll leave everything to you. We're counting on you."

Night seeped in from the huge window. The moonlight cast long shadows in the room, and an all-consuming stillness pervaded the place.

Enveloped within that silence, a woman sat on a bed. The man lying next to her tugged lightly on her glossy black hair. She frowned at him. "What is it?"

"Nothing, I just can't sleep," he replied.

"I don't care. Go to sleep."

The man let out a big sigh, staring up at the bed's canopy. Only he and his protector, the witch, were in the room.

She was wearing a dress made of multiple layers of thin black silk. Backlit by the moonlight and with her face cast down looking somber, she appeared more a work of art than a person.

"I can put you to sleep with magic, but she might have set it up so that something happens in the dream if magic interferes with your sleep. I wouldn't put it past her, so it's best if you fall asleep naturally. Once you do, I can intervene."

"I'll do my best," Oscar said, closing his eyes and sinking into his own darkness. No matter how he tried, however, he couldn't get the idea of Tinasha waiting impatiently at his side out of his mind, and he was unable to relax. Finally, he asked, "Is Lucrezia good at this type of magic?"

"This—and potions. She's better than me at both," Tinasha admitted.

"So witches have their strengths and weaknesses, too."

Oscar had his eyes closed, so he couldn't be certain Tinasha had smiled at that, though he was fairly sure he'd sensed it.

"We do. On top of a basic mastery of all magic, we each specialize in something. And we can't allow anyone else to surpass us in our fields…"

"What's your specialty?" Oscar probed.

"Attack and defense, as well as raw power," replied Tinasha.

Oscar opened his eyes to see a self-deprecating smirk on her face. That power was why she was known as the strongest. Despite such strength, Tinasha was hardly one to flaunt it in front of others. She never left her tower without a reason; she seemed to know that too much might would lead to nothing.

Tinasha stroked Oscar's hair, hoping to soothe him to drift off, and the prince closed his eyes again. Still, sleep refused to claim him, so after a short while, he grabbed her hair again.

The witch looked annoyed as she peered down at him. "Can I bring you a nightcap?" she suggested sarcastically.

"No, I'm good," Oscar answered earnestly.

"I suppose I have no choice." Once again, Tinasha slowly stroked Oscar's hair. Parting her red lips, she began singing softly.

It was a song he'd never heard before, but the lyrics made it sound like a lullaby.

Dark of night, stars are far
Beloved child in my arms
One thousand safflowers, the azure of the moon
Holding your little hand, I'll send you off to the path of dreams

The witch's voice was deeper than usual, with a comforting, gentle lilt to it.

Perhaps the song was foreign. Regardless, the strange melody filled Oscar's mind. Tinasha's pale-white hand continued stroking his hair ever so gently, and he slowly faded off to sleep.

※

The next thing Oscar knew, he was standing in front of an unfamiliar building. A pair of double doors were set into the front of a great white mansion. He turned back to see a fog curling around a forest behind him.

Oscar tried to call for the person who'd been at his side until just a moment ago but realized he couldn't remember their name. He shook his head, but it felt like it was filled with cotton. He was having a hard time thinking.

"What's going on…? What am I…?"

Puzzling over all the strangeness, Oscar reached for the door. At a single touch, it swung open silently before him. Almost drawn inside, he stepped into the mansion and saw it was a house furnished of the same white material as the exterior. It was very pretty but utterly deserted, with none of the lived-in feel a home should rightly have had.

A sense of familiarity coursed through Oscar as he took in the sight of the place. Only now did he remember that he'd been coming here every night.

He climbed the main staircase and proceeded deeper into the mansion. Someone had been calling for him for a while now.

Before long, Oscar saw a pale door at the end of a long hallway. He opened it to find a spacious room. Like those before, the room was entirely white, and against the back wall sat a bed hung with silk curtains. He approached it slowly, parting the gauzy fabric.

The woman sitting on the bed turned around like she'd sensed his presence.

…Her long, glossy black hair was spread out all across the bed. Her ivory skin blended into the room, hidden under a thin negligee of the same color. With eyes the tint of the deepest darkness, her beauty appeared ethereal.

"Oscar…"

Now that she'd found him, she smiled softly. She held out two impossibly slim arms. He reached for her and drew her delicate frame into his embrace. Very carefully, as if handling something that would shatter, he hugged her tight.

"Tinasha."

"So distasteful…," someone muttered in a tone of utter disgust. The words seem to whisper themselves in Oscar's ear.

He let go of the woman in his arms to look her in the face, but she only cocked her head with a bemused smile. A sweet light filled those big, round eyes. Oscar cradled her face in his hands, and her expression softened.

Knowing her smooth skin well by now, Oscar's left hand glided along Tinasha's slender neck. He bent to place a kiss there but realized that, all of a sudden, his hand's grip was tightening.

"Oscar?" She looked up at him in puzzlement. Oscar found it strange himself, but in the next moment, his eyes opened wide with shock. All on its own, his left hand was starting to tighten around her neck, and his right hand had joined it.

"My hands are—"

No matter how hard he tried, he couldn't remove them; they didn't belong to him anymore. Instead, they squeezed the woman's throat with the clear intent to kill. Her beautiful face screwed up in pain as she cried out, "Oscar… Stop… Save me…"

Her small hands scrabbled at his frantically. Seeing her like that, Oscar felt sweat pour down his own neck. An indescribable jolt of fear washed over him.

His nails bit into Tinasha's thin nape.

"Please… Save me…" Her fragile voice sounded in his ears. Tears welled up in her dark eyes. The stress was so great, Oscar bit his lip hard enough to taste blood.

A dizziness overtook the prince. His body wouldn't move—frozen by something unseen. The woman's neck was in his hands. There was a surging fear growing within him, as he knew what would happen next.

"Stop… Stop it!" Oscar's cry rang throughout the pure-white room, but it did no good. Reflexively, he closed his eyes and heard the dull sound of bones breaking. The woman's head lolled. At last, he could move his hands, and her body crumpled.

Oscar lifted her limp figure with trembling arms. Her dark eyes had lost their luster. Like dull marbles, they provided only the thinnest reflection of the surrounding room. The dead girl's faintly parted lips would never move again.

"...Tinasha?"

With unbearable emotion, he clutched her lifeless body to his chest.

Finally, the world broke down.

Oscar jerked awake, only to find himself soaked in sweat. Glancing to the side, he saw the black-robed witch looking at him with annoyance plain on her face. Seeing her now after his dream brought on a mix of fear and relief. He could still clearly feel the sensation of the woman's neck snapping in his hands. In an attempt to drown out the tactile memory, he interlaced his hands tightly.

"Good job. All your stolen life force has been returned to you." Tinasha's voice had a distinctly chilly tinge to it. This was the same voice that had spoken to him in such a soft tone from within the dream, but it was commanded by a wholly different person now.

Oscar took in a deep breath, exhaling slowly. He used both hands to brush his hair up and back.

"Don't...make me kill you...," he managed.

"That wasn't me."

"Even so."

The prince's blue eyes met the witch's dark ones. Her lips quirked up in a cruel smirk. "I'm a witch, and you possess Akashia; you really might have to kill me someday."

Pale moonlight shone down on the two of them.

To Oscar, the pale glow seemed to suck the warmth out of the room. "Are you being serious?"

"Of course." Tinasha smiled, narrowing her eyes—her witch's grin.

Though Oscar understood that the young woman sitting next to him was the same one who'd been at his side these recent months, there was an unbearable feeling of distance between the two now.

He reached out to touch her, but she floated away before he could.

"I'm going to give Lucrezia a piece of my mind. I'll be back tomorrow," she announced.

"Wait!"

"Good night, Oscar," Tinasha said, promptly disappearing. Left alone with the moon and the shadows it cast, Oscar felt a thick unease and loneliness pervade his room.

Sipping a glass of liqueur as she percolated a potion, Lucrezia chuckled to herself when she sensed a familiar presence enter her barrier.

"Lucrezia!"

"It's been a while, Tinasha. Oh my, have you grown? Lucrezia greeted her with a face as gleeful as a child who'd successfully pulled a prank.

Lucrezia's old friend answered with a sullen tone. "What are you playing at? There are limits to distasteful pranks, you know."

"I thought you'd undo it right away, but I guess they didn't tell you about me. Good thing I added the scent."

In sharp contrast to Tinasha's glower, Lucrezia appeared to be in an excellent mood. "What was really distasteful was how you broke the curse. I didn't think you'd force him to break her neck."

"It was quick, easy, and it made me feel better," Tinasha offered.

"I wanted the curse to be broken in a sexier way…" Lucrezia pouted.

"Who would use sexual techniques for that?!" Tinasha yelled, and the Witch of the Forbidden Forest clicked her tongue in disappointment.

Lucrezia cared little for the life of one human when it came to her capricious whims. She poured a glass of liqueur for her guest and set it on the table. Tinasha sat down and took a sip. Normally, she didn't like dulling her reason and almost never drank alcohol, but she made an exception when with a friend.

"I know you're aware that he's my contract holder, so what in the world were you doing?"

"You've given him quite the protective barrier. It's very intimidating. I just thought it would be nice to say hi to you after so long," Lucrezia explained.

"Don't half kill someone to say hi," Tinasha replied.

Amused, Lucrezia laughed out loud, then set some homemade treats on the table. "So? What happened to him?"

"He got mad at me over the neck-breaking thing."

"Well, I can see why... It does leave a bad taste in your mouth."

"I wouldn't underestimate him. He holds Akashia," Tinasha chided sharply, but Lucrezia only shrugged.

If the world ever called for the end of the witches, all mages knew that the bearer of Akashia was the best person to lead such a movement. Tinasha was well aware of Oscar's skill, knowing it could very well be enough to slay a witch.

Which meant, all the more, that he shouldn't get any closer to witches than necessary. It was especially out of the question for him to marry one.

"But isn't he handsome? Better looking than Regius, I think," Lucrezia teased.

"There are a lot of reasons why you shouldn't compare him to Reg," Tinasha answered.

"That's such a waste, though. Can I have him?"

Originally, Tinasha had planned to introduce Lucrezia to Oscar as a potential bride, though only if he agreed to it.

Tinasha waved her hand dismissively and then recalled the time she'd proposed the idea. "...I knew it wouldn't work."

"What? Are you regretting saying no?" Tinasha's friend smirked at her, but she shook her head and denied it.

"No. What I meant was that I knew adding a witch into the royal bloodline wouldn't be a good idea."

"Ah, so I was right to think that something interesting's been going on." Lucrezia's words seemed to suggest she knew about Oscar's curse. Then again, she could've just as easily been referring to something else. Oscar's predicament was the work of the Witch of Silence, after all. Her overwhelming expertise in such things made the prince's curse difficult for another witch to detect without careful inspection.

As Tinasha munched on cookies and considered requesting the recipe for them, she asked her friend, "Do you think you can break it?"

"That's a tricky one... It might actually be impossible. The Witch of Silence's handiwork, right?"

"Yeah. I've been trying to analyze it, but I feel pretty stuck," Tinasha admitted.

The cookies were good, with just the right amount of sweetness. Tinasha truly waffled a little over whether to ask for the recipe. As an expert potion maker, Lucrezia was incredibly good at creative cooking as well.

The Witch of the Forbidden Forest poured more liqueur into Tinasha's glass. "What exactly are you analyzing?" she inquired.

"His hair and nails. Words, too," Tinasha admitted.

"I think you should use blood and semen. Those are probably the most affected."

"I see."

Lucrezia went to her workshop in the back of the house and brought back two small bottles. She tossed them casually to Tinasha.

"Here, take these. Consider it an apology for what I did."

Taking the little vials, Tinasha was shocked to see they contained the two substances in question. She put down the cookie she'd been eating.

"You extracted these? You really need to do something about this distasteful hoarding problem of yours."

"Well, since I had the chance, I thought I might make a clone while I was at it. It was woven into the dream's spell."

"What do you think my contract holder is? You didn't take anything else, did you?"

"Just these," Lucrezia purred. Tinasha was deeply suspicious but accepted the bottles anyway. She magically transferred them somewhere safe, to ensure they wouldn't be broken.

As Lucrezia watched her friend grumble to herself, she pressed the liqueur bottle to a faintly flushed cheek.

While Tinasha gave the impression of a cool, collected beauty, Lucrezia was a bright, flirtatious woman. Hordes of men had fallen for her friendly smile, and she'd kept many lovers over the years.

With a neatly manicured red-painted fingernail, Lucrezia poked Tinasha's hand. "When you get back, give him an honest apology, okay? I think you're very important to him. My spell wasn't designed to make you appear in it. All it did was reflect his own desires."

"Whose fault do you think it is that we're fighting?" Tinasha asked.

"Your stubbornness?" Lucrezia quickly replied.

She was half-right. Tinasha gave up debating it and took a sip of liqueur.

After cooling her head, Tinasha did admit she felt guilty. She hadn't lied, but she could've phrased it more gently. It was true she was important to him…however, it was just as true that she couldn't accept such feelings.

Regret needled at Tinasha like a thorn, and she looked out the window to gaze up at the moon. She thought about how that same moon was shining down on Oscar…and her eyes fluttered closed.

When he woke up the next morning, Oscar noticed his body felt oddly sluggish, and his bones groaned at his every move.

Whether it was the backlash of Lucrezia's spell or his own lingering bad memories of the previous night, he couldn't be certain. Lying in bed, Oscar was considering taking a bath when there was a light rapping at the balcony door.

Such a knock could only mean the arrival of one person. Oscar threw on a jacket and said, "Come in."

Immediately, the black-robed witch entered, but she didn't move past the balcony door. Oscar snorted lightly. Tinasha seemed to be feeling rather awkward.

"Come here," Oscar said, beckoning to her, and she walked over to him reluctantly. She opened her mouth a little as if to say something, and he reached for her and pulled her onto his lap.

From Tinasha's spot on Oscar, she frowned down at him, put out. He stroked her cheeks and neck, almost like he was making sure that every part of her was there.

"I'm sorry," Oscar admitted.

Her eyes widened a little. Perhaps Oscar's apology had been unexpected. She looked down shyly.

"...I'm sorry, too," Tinasha murmured very softly. She clutched at his jacket tightly.

The witch hoped the day he would face her as an enemy would never come, even as he assumed the throne and she returned to her tower.

▌7. Breathing Life into Form

A thin layer of clouds covered the afternoon sun, and in a corner of the training grounds, Tinasha and Suzuto were sparring.

Suzuto's speed and strength weren't poor for a soldier, but to a seasoned warrior, he lacked a certain element of surprise. As a result, Tinasha could predict and parry Suzuto's thrusts with ease.

He grew impatient with the witch as she fended off his cuts by merely adjusting her stance, then throwing his whole body into a downward thrust. His opponent did not even meet the attack with her sword.

Tinasha crouched into a low lunge, holding firm against him as she just barely dodged his blade. Then, with a dancer's elegance and the sure speed of a fighter, she brought her sword within a hairbreadth of his neck and held it there.

"All right, this is as far as we go," Tinasha declared.

"I—I lost again…," Suzuto lamented.

"You need to either learn how to read further ahead or get faster," the witch offered.

Suzuto looked crestfallen as Tinasha sheathed her sword. The witch's blade was her own, not a borrowed one. It had been crafted to be thinner than a standard blade. In battle, Tinasha often carried a magic-infused sword, but this was an ordinary one meant for practice.

Tinasha touched her hair, making sure it was all still bound up in a braid. She felt someone place a hand on her head and looked over her shoulder to see Oscar standing there.

"Why are you here?" she asked.

"I wanna get a workout every now and then. Can we spar?"

"No. From the very bottom of my heart, no." Tinasha glanced behind him and saw the lady-in-waiting girl pop up; she must have come along to wait on him. The witch waved expressionlessly at the girl, whose name was apparently Miralys. Evidently embarrassed, Miralys turned red and bowed her head. Tinasha smiled at the reaction.

"Even if you want to work out, you can't spar against anyone because of the protective barrier."

"Oh, I guess that's true. Can you lift it temporarily?" Oscar asked, making the powerful magic sound like it was nothing too troublesome.

"It would require a lot of effort, so I'd prefer not to. But there is a shortcut built in," Tinasha explained.

"You thought of everything, huh?"

Tinasha showed Oscar her right palm. After concentrating only a little, a small cut appeared on her pointer finger.

Oscar looked at the blood oozing out and frowned. "What are you doing? You're bleeding."

"I am," answered the witch. Tinasha floated up and rubbed her finger along the back of his ear. She murmured to him, "While my blood is on your body, the barrier will relax. That said, it will still repel strong magic... Think of it like a net. This a dangerous bit of info, so don't tell others about it."

"Got it," Oscar agreed. Tinasha was still floating in midair, and he hugged one arm around her waist.

Als came over to the two and bowed to the lord. "Your Highness, are you here for practice?"

"I haven't sparred in a while. Would you be my partner?" Oscar inquired.

"Gladly," Als replied.

Oscar set the witch down and took a sword from Als. Released, Tinasha stood next to Miralys to observe.

It was hardly a surprise to Tinasha at this point, but Oscar was fascinatingly strong. So much so that, while she had looked on sourly at first, a cold laugh bubbled up within her partway through the duel.

Normally, Als was the one putting countless soldiers through their paces during practice and winning against all of them, but now it was Oscar gunning for that position. Members of the Farsasian army watched respectfully as their future king defeated General Als and Officer Meredina rather easily. Tinasha, who was usually no match for Als, watched the spectacle with her arms crossed.

"Anyone else wanna go?" Tapping the flat of his blade against his shoulder, Oscar made an appeal to his many spectators. None stepped forward in response to the challenge, however. Likely because they knew they stood no chance.

Oscar's eyes were dancing when Tinasha met his gaze, and the witch was suddenly struck by a very bad feeling. She gathered magic, preparing to teleport away, but before she could, Oscar beckoned to her.

"Tinasha, come forward," he requested.

"I refuse!"

"Wow, instant rejection," Oscar quipped.

"Because I'll get nothing good out of it," Tinasha retorted.

"It'll be good training," he wheedled.

The witch simply stuck out her tongue, turning him down. Oscar eyed her with amusement for a moment before seemingly hitting upon something. The prince set his sword down.

"How about I let you use magic?" he suggested.

"Do you want to be burned to a crisp?"

"Most of it will still get repelled, right?"

It was true. The barrier would repel strong offensive magic capable of striking a mortal wound in one blow, even if it came from her. Even so, there were still all kinds of other spells that could knock people out fairly easily.

Tinasha wondered if Oscar knew how mages without a vanguard fought on the battlefield.

She looked into the prince's eyes and saw they were brimming with a dauntless confidence. Suddenly, a heady mix of hope, curiosity, and resignation washed over her. Until now, there had never been anyone who could hope to kill any of the witches, let alone Tinasha, the most skilled in warfare.

This man standing before her had a chance, however. He could very well kill her.

Tinasha made up her mind and answered Oscar's assured look with one of her own. "Fine. But I have a condition."

"What is it?" Oscar asked, eager.

"Use Akashia."

Silence fell across the training yard.

The royal sword, with its total magical resistance, was the enemy of all mages. With a single stroke, it had once cut down a mad mage endowed with enough power to bring a country to ruin. This match was sure to be something explosive. Whispers abounded through the crowd.

Oscar, however, seemed unfazed by the condition. "I don't mind, but it's not blunted."

"I'd be surprised if it were… In exchange, allow me to bring out my own personal weapons," Tinasha said.

"Sure," Oscar agreed, grinning with anticipation. He ordered Miralys to go fetch him Akashia.

About ten minutes later, both the prince and his witch were ready. Their match was to be held in an area slightly larger than the grounds normally used for practice fights.

Akashia in hand, Oscar faced off against Tinasha, who held a short sword in one hand and a dagger in the other. When she'd come down from the tower, she'd asked her familiars to bring these weapons along just in case.

Oscar eyed her choices with surprise. "Two-weapon fighting?"

"Essentially, yes. Normally, I'd keep one hand free, but it'll be pointless to use magical obstacles against that sword of yours."

"I see."

Both of Tinasha's weapons had been imbued with magic, but that wouldn't have much effect against Akashia. She'd chosen them simply because she was used to wielding them, though she hadn't done so in a long time. She adjusted her grip on the weapons' hilts.

"Anytime you're ready," Oscar provoked.

Afraid of getting caught up in any magic, the soldiers had given the two a wide berth. Even so, everyone present at the training grounds awaited the start of the fight with great anticipation.

Tinasha slowed her breath and gathered her thoughts. Oscar's blue eyes were staring her down.

"Then I'll take you at your word... Give me everything you've got," Tinasha declared, and on her final word, she launched seven balls of light into the air. Oscar's eyes narrowed a fraction. On an exhale, the witch murmured "Go," and the spheres assailed Oscar at varying speeds.

Two came for him from the front and the right, but Akashia readily dispelled them. The third changed its path before he could slice through it, arcing its way behind the prince.

Without a hint of hesitation, Oscar advanced, cutting down two more orbs that flew in from the left. Instantly, the witch's sword thrust in from the right. The blow was aimed at Oscar's neck, but he parried it away with Akashia's hilt.

Unfortunately, the prince felt a pain in his left ankle at the same time. The sphere that had been chasing him from behind had collided with his leg while he'd been fending off Tinasha's attack.

Doing his best to push the pain from his mind, Oscar dodged a lunging dagger attack. Tinasha's attacks were equal parts relentless and elegant.

Oscar blocked the thrust with a burst of force and put some distance between himself and his opponent. He then cut down another ball of light headed his way. The last slipped through Oscar's guard, however, colliding with his right shoulder. Pain and numbness traveled down his arm.

"*Wind*," Tinasha cried, giving the prince no chance to catch his breath. Conjured blades of air sped toward Oscar from all directions.

Putting his injured ankle through more abuse, Oscar jumped to the left. Using Akashia to offset the blades that aimed for fatal spots, he slipped through the rest with only a few cuts on his skin to show for it.

It was a succession of attacks like nothing he'd experienced before, and Oscar began to feel an elation take hold of his body.

His mind felt sharp and aware. Somehow, the prince could tell that air filled with magic was slightly different. Normally, Oscar couldn't sense

magic at all, but his vision had suddenly been honed, and now he could sense where the energy was amassing and what path it might take once it appeared.

The blades of wind had been a decoy for an invisible rope that attempted to go for Oscar's back, but Akashia cut through the transparent thing easily enough.

Tinasha smiled as she watched her spell get scattered. Oscar certainly had some natural aptitude. His intuition wasn't bad, either. In fact, he seemed to be growing stronger by the second.

Cutting through the air with the sword in her right hand, Tinasha loosed a blast of scorching wind from the spot she had seemingly torn. The heated blast raced in Oscar's direction, with Tinasha only a hair behind her own attack. Oscar cut through the eddy of hot wind, and the witch leaped to his left-hand side, hurling her dagger at him.

An ordinary person wouldn't have been able to respond to such an attack pattern; Tinasha had known that when she'd thrown her dagger. That was why she was dumbfounded to watch Oscar catch the weapon by its hilt so easily.

"Return," Tinasha commanded gently, and the dagger soared back from Oscar's hand to its owner's.

"What's this?" Oscar asked, surprised.

"That's just the kind of weapon I have," Tinasha answered.

Oscar looked astonished but recovered quickly, moving in closer.

Tinasha guarded a downward stroke of Akashia's with two blows from the sword in her right hand. With Oscar loosing such swift attacks, faster than even those of General Als, the witch had her hands full deflecting them with no room to spare for concentrating on magic. She leaped back to get some distance, but Oscar closed the gap just as quickly. Frustrated and annoyed, Tinasha fended off Akashia.

That's when the flat of Oscar's sword grazed her elbow.

Tinasha felt a cold sensation as the magic in her body began draining from the spot where the blade made contact. Quelling her ramping fear, Tinasha thrust her dagger toward Oscar's chest.

Before the tip could reach his body, Oscar lifted his sword and deflected the strike. Tinasha's blade collided with Akashia and shattered like glass against stone.

"What?!" Tinasha exclaimed. She kicked off the ground, teleporting beyond the reach of the Mage Killer.

After reappearing, she raised both her hands. "C-can we end it there?"

Glancing at her left hand, the witch saw that her dagger's blade had been reduced to splinters and was now utterly useless.

"You're not hurt, are you?" Oscar asked.

"Not really," Tinasha answered as she used magic to heal the little cuts that dotted Oscar's body. Despite the two combatants now sitting in the shade, the soldiers had apparently gotten rather fired up. They had gone back to their training drills with renewed enthusiasm.

"That's good. I don't really want to hurt you," Oscar said gently.

"You'll get yourself into trouble saying things like that," Tinasha retorted, dodging Oscar's hand as he tried to place it on top of her head. Finishing the healing, Tinasha sat back down next to Oscar. She gazed at the hilt of the dagger lying in the grass.

Unfortunately, the damage to the blade was irreversible. Many plain weapons could be used as a medium for spell casting, but this dagger had been rather unique in that magic had been embedded in its structure. That was exactly why Akashia had shattered it. Tinasha tucked the hilt into the front of her outfit.

"Were you going easy on me?" Oscar asked.

"Not particularly. Incantations and concentration are both required for more complicated magic. To be honest, I don't want to fight you at close range ever again," Tinasha answered, remembering the sensation of Akashia touching her skin.

She'd thought of it as just a simple sword unaffected by magic, but she hadn't expected it to steal her own magic energy from her at just a touch. That meant that she couldn't cast spells.

Most likely, Oscar didn't know about that. If he did, he'd probably use a

different fighting style. Shattering the dagger had been an alarming consequence, but Tinasha still didn't have any desire to tell Oscar just how strong
an effect the sword had on her.

Remembering something important, Tinasha reached out to wipe away
the bit of her blood that was lightly smeared behind Oscar's ear.

While they sat side by side, mulling over things they couldn't share with
each other, Oscar watched the witch's every move. Her profile looked somber beneath the shade of the tree.

"I really don't want to kill you," he said.

"You're naive," Tinasha replied, her dark eyes emotionless. She offered
Oscar a tiny smile, however.

Oscar ran his fingers through her silky black hair, carding them slowly
through the strands. He felt that something about the dark color of the
witch's locks seemed to embody the loneliness she felt.

"Do you want to die?" Oscar asked.

Tinasha tilted her head, confused. She stared at Oscar with a cool, clear
expression. Something about the gaze very nearly betrayed her desires,
but whatever it had been disappeared after a single blink, and she smiled
broadly. "No. I still have lots of things to do... Like breaking your curse."

"You could just marry me."

"I refuse! Think about our age difference!"

"You'll be a spirit sorcerer your whole life with that attitude," Oscar said,
standing up and offering Tinasha a hand. She took it.

When he helped Tinasha to her feet, Oscar was overcome with a desire
to pull her in close, to rip her away from that distant place in which she had
resided for so long.

The first time they met was truly anticlimactic.

True, she was breathtakingly beautiful, but because she looked like a girl,
the way she laughed and got angry seemed very innocent.

He found that funny and enjoyed that about her. Of course, she also provided invaluable help with his curse, but he felt like he'd never be bored with a companion like her.

That was why he wanted to make sure no harm would ever come to the fragile-looking slip of a thing.

It didn't take him very long to realize that wasn't what she was, however.

She drilled it into him over and over; she was a witch—she was fundamentally different.

No matter how close by she was or how calmly she smiled at him, no matter how much kindness she showed others, she could never devote herself to the humans around her. She always stood alone in a place distant from all others.

After realizing that, he wanted to know the truth of everything about her.

Her smile, her angry face, her cruelty, her pride, her kindness, her loneliness.

He sought the truth that dwelled within all of them.

Perhaps if he could touch the inner truth of this witch…he'd long to cherish her.

"I mean, to be honest, I was pretty damn shocked. Miss Tinasha was incredible, but so was His Highness. Is he even human?"

Als and Meredina were sitting at a table in the castle courtyard during their lunch break. Als stuffed a piece of bread into his mouth as they discussed the mock battle from the other day.

"I'm glad I saw it…," Als continued, "but at the same time, I feel like I've lost my confidence… I don't think I could ever win."

"Against who?" Meredina asked.

"Either of them."

Meredina's childhood friend was acting unusually insecure, but she smiled and took a sip of tea. "Don't go doubting yourself now. It'll be bad for the soldiers' morale to hear you say things like that."

"I guess," Als replied.

"That's what happens if you use magic in melee combat. And she was going easy on him, wasn't she?"

"I don't know about that, but it looked like she was only using quick, flexible spells. Hmm, I guess a regular mage wouldn't do that, so that makes me feel a bit better, at least," Als reasoned.

"You think so?" Meredina asked.

Als poured tea into his cup. Meredina took a bite of one of the cookies she'd brought.

"I've never seen one of our mages using a sword," Als said. "Normally, mages let swordsmen handle the front lines, while they launch large magic attacks from behind. The enemy uses mages to defend against that. I don't think there are many mages like Miss Tinasha, attacking and defending with a sword to compensate for not putting up a barrier."

"At the magical lake, she used an ordinary wave of huge magic to burn everything around us to ash," Meredina pointed out.

"That just means she knows how to fight the more traditional way, too. I guess a lifetime of centuries provides a different perspective."

Meredina smiled at Als's words. Before, she'd had a bit of an inferiority complex about the witch, but as she'd gotten to know Tinasha as a person, those feelings had faded. Perhaps Meredina's change had been because she'd caught sight of the witch, who seemed to have everything, casting a long, lonely shadow. Seeing the witch like that had made Meredina feel like Tinasha shouldn't have to look so sad—at least while she was in the castle.

With a bittersweet smile, Meredina took up her cup. "She was testing His Highness…or maybe teaching him? That's how I interpreted it."

"You think?" Als asked.

"Yes. She wanted to show him what type of moves a mage like herself would use in a real fight," Meredina explained.

Glimpses of a terrible, heartrending sorrow sometimes flashed in the eyes of that woman who had lived for many lifetimes. Her eyes seemed to convey that, while she balked at getting involved with humans, she wanted to leave something behind. Perhaps what Tinasha wanted to entrust was something she could give to Oscar.

Als evidently hadn't seen what Meredina had in the battle. With his chin resting on his hands, he looked up at the sky. "She said before that she didn't really want to give away her hand, though."

"Couldn't she have changed her mind? I mean, she started smiling halfway through." Meredina drained her cup with a bitter smile.

The weather was excellent. The castle walls encircled the sky, and clouds drifted slowly across the enclosure.

※

In a rare occurrence, Oscar's father, the king, asked Oscar to meet him in the royal family's salon that adjoined the audience chamber.

Told it was an emergency, Oscar came over in the middle of his work wearing a quizzical look. His father handed him a letter.

"What's this?" the prince asked.

"An envoy has come from Cuscull, a minor country to the north. He's asking to meet the Witch of the Azure Moon."

Two things struck Oscar about that, and he decided to inquire about the less important of the pair first. "I've never heard of that country."

"It appears to have gained independence from Tayiri a year ago. It's a small nation, but it's investing heavily in magic research."

"Magic…"

Tayiri was the northernmost major nation in the mainland, and it shared no border with Farsas. Such distance meant that state visits only occurred between the two sovereignties around three times a year.

The most pervasive characteristic of Tayiri was its belief in independence. It was also well-known as a land that frowned heavily upon magic. Children born with an aptitude for spells were banished as soon as their talent emerged. It was also not unheard of for them to be killed, depending on the region.

An internal faction within Tayiri declaring independence and founding a nation dedicated to magic reflected poorly on the power of the ruling state, which was likely why any news of the event had been quashed. It would've been far more surprising if Farsas *had* known of Cuscull's founding.

Oscar nodded in understanding, then asked about the more pressing doubt he had. "So how do you think they know Tinasha is in Farsas?"

Most of the witches weren't open about their whereabouts, with Tinasha being the sole exception.

That said, the only widely known fact was that she lived in the tower. It wasn't as though she'd left a note on the door saying where she was whenever she went out. Though it had been officially revealed to those within the castle that Tinasha was a witch, it was still a tightly kept secret beyond the walls. The rest of Farsas was unaware of the truth. How could a distant, newly founded country have learned of Tinasha's true identity?

King Kevin shook his head in response to his son's question. "I don't know. It just says they want to meet her."

Oscar fell into thought for a bit. Tinasha was probably in his study at the moment.

"Got it. I'll meet with them first," Oscar declared.

The king gave a little nod, like he'd anticipated that reply.

The envoy from Cuscull was a short, somewhat unpleasant man. He wasn't ugly, but his eyes were narrow slits, not unlike a reptile's. A vicious aura also seemed to emanate from every pore of his body at all times.

Though unsettled by the visitor's smile, Oscar made sure not to let it show on his face.

The man introduced himself as Kagar. "Please forgive my sudden intrusion. If you would be so kind as to introduce me to the esteemed witch, I will promptly take my leave."

Oscar responded to Kagar's polite greeting with a bit of audacity. "A witch? Sorry, but we don't have anyone like that here. I'd like to know who told you that."

"Please dispense with the jokes. I don't wish to occupy your valuable time, Your Highness," Kagar said with a grandiose flourish of his hands and a sly smirk. "A little while ago, a pack of fools from Druzan attempted to revive the demonic beast. If they'd succeeded, it would've meant serious trouble for every nation on the mainland. Fortunately, the witch's heroic actions appear to have prevented this. However, if word were to get out that someone with the power to kill a demonic beast had allied with a single country…

Well, it could quickly become a very real problem." Kagar's haughty attitude made no secret of the threat he was making, and Oscar narrowed his eyes.

The envoy knew of the demonic beast incident, even though it had been kept confidential, and he was trying to exploit Tinasha as Farsas's weakness. It was a bold move to be sure.

Oscar's problem quickly became how to dispose of this ambassador from a newly founded nation. He'd never wanted Kagar to meet Tinasha, and meeting the man had done little to change that attitude.

What Kagar said next quickly changed the prince's mind, however. "She's here in the castle, isn't she? Lady Aeti. Oh, I believe she's going by Lady Tinasha now, correct?" Kagar glanced over at Oscar with both triumph and conceit in his eyes.

Shortly before Oscar met with the envoy, Tinasha had come to the study, discovering it absent of the crown prince. Miralys was there instead. The lady-in-waiting sounded utterly flustered as she stammered out an explanation. "Um, His Highness was just summoned out of the room. Would you like to wait here for him?"

"Oh. No, that's all right. I didn't really have a reason to come by anyway," the witch answered crisply.

Miralys leaped to her feet, looking panicked. "But, um, you should still wait here…"

"It's fine; I know my place. I'm his protector and nothing more than that… and I'm aware of your place, too," Tinasha said smoothly.

Miralys paled. "Um…wh-who told you that…?"

"No one. I can tell by looking at you. I'd wager that Oscar is the only one who doesn't know."

Such a thing happened often in court and wasn't a matter of particular concern. The witch smiled reassuringly, but Miralys cowered in fear. Tinasha felt a little sorry for the girl, but she had another job requiring her attention.

She returned to her quarters and resumed her analysis of Oscar's curse.

A complicated spell pattern of several interlocking rings floated up from the scrying bowl Tinasha kept in the center of the room after she'd waved her hand over the basin's surface.

To that, the witch added a carefully pronounced incantation. Little by little, the spell began changing shape in response to the whispered magic words.

The labor seemed endless, but Tinasha had continued working on it in bits and pieces since her arrival at the castle. Rounds of trial and error and research, and she was almost in reach of the Witch of Silence.

Tinasha concentrated on her curse-breaking work, only idly waving a hand when someone called her name, even though no one else was present in the room. She waited for a good stopping point, then put the analysis spell on hold.

"Act a little more surprised," came the pouting voice of a woman standing by the window. Her light-brown ringlets shone gold in the daylight. Surprisingly, a magical or perhaps ornamental dagger was fastened around her waist.

"Yeah, yeah. So why are you here, Lucrezia?"

"I found a book that might be useful to you, so I brought it!"

Tinasha took the book her friend handed her. It appeared to be a rather old volume. Flipping through a few pages, Tinasha saw it was a detailed treatise on spells and words.

"…Thank you."

"You're welcome."

While her friend could be capricious at times, Tinasha was grateful for the help. She put the book on her desk and started to brew some tea for her guest. Lucrezia sat down in a chair and watched her.

"So you had a mock battle or something with that contract holder of yours?"

"…How do you know about that?"

"Some soldiers in the courtyard were talking about it."

"Ah, you were eavesdropping."

Lucrezia rested her chin in her hands and her elbows on the table. She made no attempt to hide her appalled expression as she stared at Tinasha.

"What were you thinking, exposing your skills to him like that? Do you have a death wish?"

"He said something similar," Tinasha replied.

"Even without any further training, that guy is incredibly strong. If he gets any stronger, it'll be a problem for me, too," Lucrezia scolded.

"I'm sorry."

Indeed, as Lucrezia was also a witch, she didn't want the wielder of Akashia to grow any more powerful. No one knew what the future held for the witches. With the lifetimes of experience between these two women, that much was obvious.

Tinasha took a seat as well and let out a deep sigh. "For some reason, I'm so tired lately…"

"Rest more."

"I know, but that's not it…"

Observing the emotion wavering in her friend's dark eyes, Lucrezia gave a resigned look. "If it's too much of a burden to stay neutral, just give up or something."

Tinasha had no answer to such a suggestion. Choosing silence, she stared at her own palms. Even she herself didn't quite understand why she'd felt like fighting Oscar.

It was just that she did feel, if only a little bit, like it wouldn't be so bad to have someone capable of killing her, should the need arise. If Oscar was to be that person, she was all right with it.

Perhaps she was just feeling fickle, or maybe she really was getting tired. She kept waiting for news that never came. Tinasha still refused to give in, however. Such a concession would mean all her time as a witch would be for naught.

Lucrezia stared at Tinasha. For a short while, there was a silence between them. When the Witch of the Forbidden Forest opened her mouth to say something, there came a knock at the door.

"Miss Tinasha, is now a good time?"

Lazar entered at Tinasha's approval, looking flustered. He recognized Lucrezia and froze in shock. She took gleeful notice of his reaction and waved at him teasingly.

"Did something happen?" asked Tinasha.

"W-well…a visitor has come demanding to meet with the Witch of the Azure Moon."

"With me?" Tinasha pointed to herself.

Lucrezia let out a low whistle. "Ooh, sounds sketchy."

"It certainly does, but I'll go and take a look. What about you?"

"I think I'll wait here for it to blow over and give the castle a nice little show."

"Don't pull any pranks," Tinasha warned.

"Of course," Lucrezia replied with a beautiful and calculating smile.

※

"Aeti."

Tinasha was stupefied to hear Oscar suddenly address her by that name when she arrived at the antechamber. After a span of several seconds, she answered, "Yes?"

Oscar scowled at the reply, having heard all he'd needed to. "So that really is your name?"

"…It's my childhood name. Did the visitor use it?"

"Yeah."

This unexpected development threw Tinasha for a loop, and she shook her head.

Only once since becoming a witch had she ever called herself by that name. It had been shortly after she'd just transitioned, before she'd holed herself up in her tower. Few relished speaking the names of witches, and none alive recalled the one she'd been given in Farsas seventy years ago. What could it mean that someone who knew her old name had come to see her?

Tinasha pondered a number of possible explanations, but none of them sounded particularly appealing.

"If you don't want to see him, I'll send him away." Oscar patted her head, clearly troubled himself.

Shaking her head, Tinasha replied, "No, I'll see him."

She reached for the door leading to the audience chamber.

Kagar let out sigh of admiration upon catching sight of Tinasha. He fell to his knees and bowed as low as he could. Tinasha surveyed him haughtily.

"It is an honor to meet you, Lady Aeti."

"Stop calling me that," snapped the witch.

"I apologize. May I address you as Lady Tinasha, then?"

"You may," she said.

Kagar got to his feet and opened his arms wide before her, as if really trying to play up his part. "With the foundation of Cuscull, we have restored the rights of the mages who suffered oppression in Tayiri. We have made it our foremost mission to set magic at the foundation of their citizenship—working to utilize and develop their skills. Lady Tinasha, I have heard that you are the only person who commands myriad, powerful old magics that have otherwise fallen into disuse. Would you please come to our country and lend your support to our further development?"

Hearing that, Oscar's face clouded over. He didn't try to hide his displeasure. Although he'd previously professed not to care about Farsas having a witch, it was clear Farsas wanted Tinasha's power, too.

The witch calmly listened to the emissary's request. "You said you have heard that about me. From whom did you hear it?"

"You'll know once you come to Cuscull."

"Is it the same person who told you my name?"

Kagar merely laughed at that, not giving an answer.

"How did you learn I was here?" Tinasha probed.

"Well, we have talented mages in our country as well…"

"I see," the witch replied, sighing. A cruel smile flickered across her face. Such an overpowering grin was enough to enchant all who beheld it.

Kagar shrank back slightly at the sight.

Tinasha's lips parted, and an icy voice spilled from between them. "I am here as this man's protector. No more and no less. It is only because of that agreement that you have been able to meet me. Why do you think I would just listen to the word of a mortal who hasn't even climbed my tower, much less be obliged to provide any sort of assistance? Do you think witches possess the sort of mercy that compels them to do something for those with neither readiness nor strength of their own?"

Kagar's lips trembled with rage. Until now, he had believed himself to be superior. Like a cornered mouse, he moved to strike, preparing to lash out with his words, but Tinasha never gave him the chance.

"Begone." She turned on her heel, a declarative action that she would suffer no further audience, and came to stand next to Oscar. Stroking her hair, Oscar threw Kagar a sharp glare.

Kagar turned an imploring, frustrated gaze on them but ultimately said, "I understand. I will leave for today. But you will become a citizen of Cuscull someday; I can assure you of that. I look forward to the next time we meet."

The witch left the room without granting the envoy a response.

Kagar left the audience chamber and gnashed his teeth violently. He'd been so confident that he could bring the witch back. That was why he'd been so audacious in using a long-forgotten name. He thought that once she heard it, the drive to know who Kagar had learned it from would lure her to Cuscull for sure.

He recalled what his lord had said to him before he left the country.

"We're not in a rush, so don't worry about it. Do not mention me."

Judging by those words, Kagar would likely go unpunished for returning without the witch. Even so, he hated the idea of going back and having to honestly admit that he'd been incapable.

At the very least, Kagar wanted to separate the witch from that impudent contract holder of hers.

Kagar glanced out the window and spied the courtyard. There, in the shade, a woman in officer's attire was dozing. A vicious smile spread on Kagar's face at the scene.

From the audience chamber, Oscar followed a few steps behind the witch as they made their way back to his study. Both of them wore extremely sour expressions. Each and every nasty thing Kagar had said clung to them like a stubborn stain.

As he attempted to swallow his lingering irritation, Oscar suddenly heard a woman coo "Is it over?"

A witch appeared next to Tinasha, who glanced at her friend and answered bluntly, "It's over. That was awful."

Lucrezia shrugged while Oscar's eyes widened considerably over the surprise of seeing her. "You were here?"

"It's only been a few days since I saw you. How have you been?" Lucrezia asked, giving him a wave without even the tiniest trace of guilt.

Oscar gave her only a wan smile in response. "Thanks for half killing me."

"Whaaat? Didn't you have a good time? Should I have let you keep your memories?" Lucrezia purred.

"Are you looking for trouble?" demanded Tinasha, her voice tight. Despite the apparent threat, Lucrezia seemed to be enjoying herself. Visible sparks of magic flickered and collided between the two witches.

Oscar frowned, shaking his head. "You'll destroy the castle. Stop."

No one had ever heard of a fight between witches before. If something like that happened, no building would be left standing. Tinasha tutted at Oscar's warning and cut off her magic.

Lucrezia listened to the story of the envoy with rapt fascination. She tapped a red fingernail against her forehead. "Cuscull, huh? I've never heard of it, either."

"It was originally just some small territory, apparently. But one day, mages started pouring in, and it declared independence," Oscar explained.

"Something's fishy," said Tinasha.

"…I agree. Come to think of it, haven't you sensed ripples of strange magic coming from the north every so often lately?" Lucrezia asked Tinasha, her pointer finger in the air.

Tinasha was silent, then shook her head.

"Really? Maybe it's because I live farther north than you do. The eddies are weak, but I do feel them occasionally. They're fluctuations of magic, like the ripples from a magical lake."

"A magical lake…," Tinasha repeated, biting her lip as she sank into thought. For a moment, Lucrezia gave her an incredibly pitying look. From behind the two women, Oscar caught sight of it, but Tinasha was too lost in contemplation to notice.

Oscar was about to say something when the three rounded a corner in the hallway and saw Als standing there. Meredina was right behind him. Als stared at Tinasha and the unfamiliar beauty standing next to her, then noticed Oscar behind them and attempted to bow.

That's when something none had seen coming occurred.

Silent and swift, Meredina drew her sword and stabbed at Tinasha.

"Wha—?!" Als froze in shock for a second.

Oscar moved to help but couldn't reach her in time.

Before Lucrezia could erect a protective wall, the tip of Meredina's sword reached Tinasha.

Just as everyone had thought it too late, Tinasha casually, yet quickly, drew Lucrezia's waist dagger and used it to deflect the sword coming right for her. Meredina's sword fell to the floor, and she was left defenseless as Tinasha slid the blade of the dagger toward the other woman's throat.

Meredina was helpless to defend, but a counterattack came from Als, who drew his own sword reflexively to intercept. He batted away Tinasha's dagger and pushed Meredina behind him. The tip of his weapon nearly leveled itself at Tinasha before Als stopped himself.

Als had suddenly found Akashia thrust before his neck.

"What do you think you're doing?" An anger-laden voice lashed out at Als. He froze up, realizing he'd made an unintentional mistake.

Just when he was about to sink to his knees, his childhood friend let out a bloodcurdling shriek from behind him. "Foul hag, deceiving people's hearts! You should leave this country for good!"

"Meredina!" Both Oscar and Als rebuked her at once. It was obvious who she was referring to.

Tinasha looked down at Meredina from behind her long eyelashes.

Although Tinasha was wearing her witch face, there was no trace of a smile anywhere. Her doll-like, perfectly crafted features were devoid of expression. Her eyes, the color of darkness, were alive like the water's edge.

"...I have been accused of that many, many times... But I have never once warped anyone's heart to my whim. Perhaps you're merely frustrated with yourself?" Tinasha said. Unlike her expression, which betrayed nothing, the witch's voice was charged with feeling.

Such a mix of emotion was carried by her words that those listening were unsure whether it was sadness, anger, or something entirely different coming through.

Tinasha bit her lip. In a quiet voice, she managed to say, "I've never wanted…anyone's heart."

Her voice was trembling, but it was a clear denial. For a moment, a flash of pain lit up Tinasha's dark eyes, and Oscar caught it.

Stowing Akashia, Oscar reached to pull Tinasha into his arms. He gave her slender back some light pats.

She said nothing.

Lucrezia was concerned about her friend, but when she saw Oscar embrace Tinasha, she turned her attention to Als and Meredina. She glared at them with hatred in her narrowed eyes. "That woman is being controlled. Her mind has been tampered with, apparently by someone with a fair amount of skill."

Lucrezia waved a hand casually, and Meredina collapsed. Als managed to catch her before she hit the floor.

With his back to her, Oscar asked Lucrezia, "Can you heal her?"

"Why should I?" she retorted acidly.

"Please," he pleaded.

Lucrezia was extremely reluctant, but after dragging her heels, she made an obvious sound of displeasure and said, "It's going to cost you."

"Please do it," Tinasha urged, and Lucrezia let out a huge sigh.

Lucrezia, Meredina, and Als left for the treatment, while Tinasha and Oscar remained in the hallway. Oscar placed his hands on either side of the witch's face, tilting it upward. She blinked once, then smiled. She seemed happy, but Oscar knew it wasn't real. The smile was a mask, a guise she wore to appear as mortals did.

Oscar refused to pity her, however. He didn't think it was right to ever feel that way toward her.

"When was the last time you cried?" he asked.

His face was reflected back in her dark eyes. "I don't remember," she answered, still smiling.

8. This Breath Comes from Beyond

Tinasha knew that a never-ending stream of months and years could rot a person away.

No matter how one tried to bear the passage of time, even the bearing would become a chore eventually.

Such people could even come to forget the concept of pain, an essential part of what it was to live as a human.

It begged the question, what had become of Tinasha herself? She'd lived for an eternity by relying only on her own strength of will.

Did she still have it? Had it become something else?

Perhaps she was fooling herself into believing she still possessed it?

What if it had just become a rote chore?

If it had, Tinasha thought it best to simply die already. Should she have died on that day?

※

The night of the meeting with the Cuscull envoy, Tinasha came down with a fever. Lucrezia tended to her, explaining that it had been brought on by psychological fatigue.

As agreed, Lucrezia healed Meredina, grumbling all the way, and also spent the night caring for Tinasha. Oscar could only guess at the things the two witches spoke of that eve.

All he knew was that when Tinasha awoke the next afternoon after Lucrezia had left, she seemed refreshed and back to her usual self.

"So you're telling me we've lost track of that gross envoy?"

"He's already vacated the inn where he was staying. It's possible he's left the city, too…"

Oscar frowned. Sitting at his study desk, he crossed his legs while he listened to Lazar's report. A short while prior, Als and Meredina had visited the study to formally apologize for what had happened the day before. Recalling how haggard Meredina looked despite having no memory of the incident stirred up an angry flame in Oscar.

"I'd bet anything he's the one who did that to her, but we have no proof. We should open up an investigation into Cuscull," Oscar declared.

"I'll send out a familiar. It'll be harder for him to avoid magic detection than a regular person," Tinasha said, grimacing as she poured tea. Lazar looked at her anxiously.

Taking a cup, Oscar glanced up at his witch. "You could rest for a little longer, you know."

"I'm completely fine, really," Tinasha assured.

"I don't feel very convinced," Oscar replied. The steam from his teacup tickled his face. He opened his mouth and filled his lungs with the wonderful aroma.

Tinasha watched the prince from her spot next to him. Oscar sensed she wanted to say something to him and looked up at her. "What is it?"

"Well, I was just wondering if you could give me two hours of your time after you finish your work?"

This was the first time she'd ever made a personal invitation like this. Oscar wondered what had gotten into her, but he didn't bother asking. Instead, he replied, "I don't mind, but for what?"

"To vent my anger," she replied.

"…"

"Bring Akashia," she added.

"…All right," agreed Oscar.

Tinasha grinned at him and left, while Oscar let out a little clueless sigh.

At some point, Tinasha had drawn a small transportation array in a corner of her room. Oscar followed her instructions and stepped onto it, upon which he was teleported to a familiar circular hall. The walls around him were a faint azure hue and perfectly smooth. Looking up, he saw the central atrium; anything beyond that was too distant.

"The first floor of your tower?" he asked.

"Correct," Tinasha answered, waving her hand lightly to dismiss the transportation array from sight.

"Why here?" Oscar wondered.

"Here, the walls absorb all magic that hits them, so my wards are at full capacity, rendering your protective barrier virtually ineffective. Also, well, I don't really want anyone to see us," Tinasha admitted, clad in a mage's black robe. She walked some distance away from Oscar. As she did, she gestured to him to indicate that he should step back, too. He obeyed and moved a few paces away.

"Starting today, for one month, I want you to spar with me here for two hours every day. I'll try my hardest not to die, so give me your best shot," Tinasha said.

Suddenly, she grabbed hold of thin air. A sword materialized in her right hand.

Oscar was stunned for a millisecond, then he finally realized what was going on and smiled nervously.

Tinasha stretched out her left hand, and blue flames flared up in her palm.

"Let's begin," she said, kicking off the ground.

This was certainly one way to blow off some steam.

Although Tinasha had said she didn't go particularly easy on Oscar when they'd had their mock battle, that was a case of matching her fighting to his. Today, Oscar had learned firsthand just how hard it was to fight her while she attacked from a safe distance.

"Well, it's the first day, so I suppose this is to be expected," Tinasha observed after she finished healing Oscar's wounds. Utterly drained, he'd flopped into a chair on the top floor as soon as she'd brought them up there. Oscar accepted a glass of water Litola had poured. He looked up at the witch as she dabbed his face with a damp cloth.

"Can I ask why we just did that?"

"Hmm… There are a lot of reasons, and I can't tell you everything, though I suppose if I had to explain… I want you to have lots of choices."

"Choices?"

"No matter what happens from here on out, I don't want you to feel like there would have been another way if only you'd been stronger. I want you to be able to decide which path you want to take from among a wealth of choices. That's my reason," Tinasha said, petting Oscar's head the same way he often did to her.

She stroked him very slowly, doting as a mother would.

Oscar wondered if perhaps it had been Tinasha herself who had suffered the pain of some mistake because she hadn't had enough choices. Mulling it over for a moment, the prince felt his assumption was likely correct.

Every day after that, Oscar trained with the witch.

It was only for two hours, but because he got hit with a considerable amount of magic, he slept like the dead to recover from the fatigue of it all. She'd heal his wounds, of course, but evidently, nothing could be done about his exhaustion.

He probably hadn't undergone such intense training since he was a boy—when he'd first understood what the curse meant and desired only to be strong. The witch educated him thoroughly on how to fend off long-range attacks from powerful mages, as well as the midrange attacks from mages who were more skilled at other kinds of battle, all on his own. There were times she fought him one-on-one, and other instances when she deployed her familiars as her vanguard, varying the types of attacks.

"You really should be able to see magic by now," Tinasha pointed out, stopping her casting as he wrenched his legs, which were entangled in invisible vines, apart. "You could see it back during the mock battle, couldn't you? Don't let it affect your mental state."

"That's easier said than done... I can't see it; I can just feel it," Oscar answered. Even now, he could tell there was something wound around his legs but couldn't discern what it was at all. He looked down at himself, attempting to take a step forward but unable to move.

"You have the raw talent to be a mage, but...I don't think you could. You're not quite cut out for it."

"Could I or couldn't I? Which is it?" Oscar asked flatly.

Tinasha shrugged and undid the binding spell on him. "It's been almost two hours. Let's call it a day here. You should get some sugar and some sleep."

As if upon her command, a wave of real exhaustion pressed in on Oscar, and he suddenly felt very sleepy.

"Oh, wait, don't fall asleep here," Tinasha cried in a panic. Even though Oscar heard the words, he didn't reply and instead closed his eyes.

...When he awoke, he found himself lying on a bed in a dark room.

It was not his castle bedchamber. The wounds on his body had all been healed, the blood had been cleaned away, and he'd been changed into fresh clothes.

Rousing himself, he looked out the window to see the moon shining out over the wilderness. There was no other room as high off the ground as this one. This had to be the witch's bedroom on the top floor of the tower.

Turning back, he saw a sliver of light spilling from the door leading to the next room. He pushed it open to see the witch standing in the center of a large chamber, facing away from him. She'd changed her look from how it had been earlier that day. Now her hair was all bound up, and she was wearing an enchanted robe with a large slit up the left side.

She waved her hand over a scrying bowl, chanting to the sigils that floated up from the water. She appeared to be concentrating raptly and did not notice that Oscar had emerged from the other room.

He crept up behind her and caressed her exposed leg while kissing her slender shoulder.

It was only then that Tinasha seemed to notice him. She looked up over her shoulder and smiled. "You're awake?"

Tinasha looked so calm and composed that Oscar pulled his hand away and frowned. "You're too defenseless," he complained.

"I was concentrating… I'd notice if an intruder came in."

"I don't mean that. If someone feels you up, you should get mad at them."

"You're the one who felt me up, and you're going to say that…? Then just don't touch me…," Tinasha grumbled. "I complain to you plenty if it tickles or if you're getting in my way. I'm already used to you doing that to me. If it bothers you so much, then you should be the one restraining yourself."

Oscar went silent, and Tinasha left the room. Five minutes later, she came back bearing some hot fruit wine with sugar added.

"I sent word back to the castle," she said.

"Ah, sorry you had to do that." Oscar accepted a glass and took a sip.

It was quite sweet. Dizzyingly sweet. The one sip made Oscar's head jerk up.

"Drink it," the witch hurled back at him, as if she'd anticipated his reaction. Reluctantly, he brought the glass to his mouth again.

Oscar managed to swallow half of the death-by-sugar drink before setting it down. Not allowing Tinasha to scold him, he brought up a new topic. "So what is magical power and magic anyway?"

"That's a very basic question…," Tinasha muttered.

"Well, I don't know the answer."

Tinasha sat down on a box placed by the window. The moonlight illuminated her, casting a hazy shadow of her figure on the floor.

"Magic is interfering with phenomena by way of using magical power that is drawn from an individual's will."

"…I didn't understand a word of that."

"Let me finish…," Tinasha said, looking exasperated. She snapped her fingers, and the lights went out in the room. The space was now as dark as it was outside.

"Say I decide to make this room bright… Then I'd light it. Whether I use magic to manifest light or I ignite a lamp, the end result is the same. It gets bright," Tinasha explained. She then snapped her fingers again. Light was restored to the room instantly. "This is what it means to interfere with magical phenomena by way of your own willpower. In other words, it's already what humans do normally just going about their lives. Magic does it—not with your physical body or speech—but with magical power."

"Oh, so that's what you meant," Oscar replied.

"To delve a little deeper, there are many rules governing what sort of interference the physical body can accomplish—dropping an object from above, moving something by exerting force, and so on. But at the same time, rules like that also exist for magic in the world. However, while spatially these rules are the same as those in the visible world, hierarchy-wise, there are a few places where they differ, so normally they don't function in nature. They just exist. Are you with me so far?"

"Yeah." Oscar nodded, pouring a glass of water to chase away the sweet aftertaste.

"Mages use magical power to pull those rules toward us and interfere with natural things around us. So while you can't move a heavy rock via physical interference no matter how hard you push against it, it's easy to move it if you use a pulley-and-lever system. Mechanisms like that are equivalent to spells in magic. If you cast a spell and move it with magical power, you've accomplished a greater thing than if you hadn't used a spell, even with the same amount of magical power. The more complicated the spell, the harder it is to cast it, but you can reap greater results." After she explained, she snapped her fingers again. A spell pattern of intricately intertwined red threads appeared before her eyes. This must have been a spell configuration.

She dismissed it with a wave of her hand and continued. "We're only aware of a few of the rules for magic, but there are probably more yet to be discovered. Even for those we do know, the magic that results will be completely different depending on the spell configuration used... Do you understand?"

"More or less." Oscar did understand the basic ideas, but he'd suddenly felt like he'd been transported to a lecture hall. "What decides if you have magical power or not?"

"We don't know if it's determined by one's body or soul, but it's entirely hereditary. Bloodline appears to carry some importance, but it's not a guarantee. People with magical power have it from birth, and those who don't cannot acquire it through training."

"What about me?" Oscar asked.

"…You have it."

"I never knew."

Among the direct royal lineage of Farsas, there had never been a mage. Tinasha had said bloodline was no guarantee, but even so, hearing that Oscar had magical power was a surprise. Perhaps there had been a Farsasian royal before who'd had magical aptitude but died never knowing it.

With a grim half smile, Tinasha pointed to Oscar's sword. "But as long as you carry Akashia, you cannot use magic. It keeps you from concentrating the magical power inside your body. My protective barrier on you is a complex enough spell that it can coexist with Akashia, however."

It finally dawned on Oscar what she meant when she said she'd prefer not to lift the barrier because it would require a lot of effort. She was right—normally, a sword that nullifies magic should not be able to coexist with a spell that protects the user from all forms of attack. Oscar was struck by a keen sense of gratitude for just how much of her craft she'd poured into pulling off that spell.

"That said, because you have magic, you should be able to see it. Maybe the reason you can't is because you think you're incapable? Tomorrow, try focusing your awareness on it more," Tinasha instructed.

"…Got it," Oscar agreed.

Tinasha got off the box she was sitting on and came to stand in front of him. With a cute flourish, she turned out her palms to him. "So what do you want to do? Go back to the castle? Or if you're hungry, I can make you something."

"You can cook?" Oscar asked, somewhat surprised.

"Sure I can. How many years do you think I've been living alone?"

"Like, a thousand?"

"If you're serious, I'm going to blow you up tomorrow," Tinasha griped, giving him a dangerous smile that looked like she'd blast him to bits right then and there.

As he often did, Oscar placed a hand on the witch's head. "All right then, I want you to make me something."

"Okay," Tinasha replied, whirling around and disappearing into her kitchen.

They were halfway through their month of training.

Tinasha didn't make Oscar explode the next day, but she did surround him in a sea of flames.

The ring of fire Tinasha set rose high around him on all sides. Just standing in its midst made sweat pour off his body, and he felt like he could pass out from the heat.

"Escape before you collapse or get burned to a crisp," the witch declared, looking down on Oscar from high up in the air. Her tone was as light as if she were saying, *Come back before sundown if you're going out to play.*

"It's pretty damn hot…" Oscar groaned, sending a testing swipe out at the wall of flames. The wall retreated from Akashia, and a fissure formed for a second, but the flames closed themselves back up once the sword had retreated. In an instant, the wall looked the same as it had before, and the witch offered him some advice. "Don't just slash like you always do, look at the flow of magical power. Find the spot that's the linchpin of the spell."

"You say that, but…," Oscar muttered, trailing off.

One thing he'd learned in the past two weeks was that once Tinasha decided to teach him something, she did so mercilessly. She was careful not to go too far, but her methods were still harsh enough that it seemed a wonder he hadn't died yet.

The results spoke for themselves, however. Oscar felt like he was truly improving. His swordsmanship had been superior to Tinasha's to begin with, and he already had combat instincts. His guardian witch seemed to craft very specific lessons for Oscar, and he was absorbing techniques for fighting mages like a sponge.

"I'm not telling you to use your mind's eye. Use your real eyes. The magical configuration should be visible within the flames," Tinasha instructed.

"Got it," Oscar answered. He was about to pass out if he didn't keep it together. Wiping sweat off his brow, he stared at the wall of fire. While the color and shape of the flames flickered and changed, it maintained its true essence, vibrating hypnotically.

Oscar slowly inhaled, then froze. He wiped his mind blank, deciding to trust only what Tinasha had told him.

Letting out a controlled breath, Oscar closed his eyes. When he opened them…fine threads the same color as the flames had seemingly emerged. They formed a huge arc, circulating inside the wall of fire in the shape of a spiral.

Oscar craned his neck to survey the burning circle. Right behind it, there was one spot where the lines were most concentrated. He drew Akashia and approached the flames, then slashed lightly at that point as if he were undoing it.

The sword tip touched the linchpin, and the instant it was cut apart…the circle of flames petered out, as if extinguished. All that remained was the boiling heat.

"Very good," Tinasha complimented.

Oscar sheathed Akashia and looked up to see the witch applauding happily.

Oscar's progress with learning how to see magic was rapid. It was so quick that Tinasha even asked if Oscar needed the remainder of the month to practice. Once he learned to perceive spell configurations as well as magical power that wasn't in spell form, his training turned from lessons to more practical combat scenarios.

"Hmm, I'd really like to have you fight a human," Tinasha murmured, leaning against the wall after Oscar easily defeated the demonic spirit she'd summoned for him to practice with.

Oscar used a cloth to wipe the demonic spirit's blood from his sword. "Don't make this sound like you're putting two bugs together to try to get them to fight," he chided.

"I've never done that…"

"I have."

"Unbelievable… You're the crown prince. Why were you outside doing something that vulgar…?" The witch chided with a disapproving frown, then waved her hand to dispel the slain body of the demonic spirit.

Oscar put Akashia back in its sheath. "If you need a human opponent for me, why not get one of our mages to do it?"

"What nonsense are you spouting? If a normal mage went up against you, they'd have nightmares and sleepless nights. I need to find you an opponent who isn't duty-bound to you."

Just then, a white light flashed into the tower hall. The entrance to the tower had opened. A number of shadows stood outside the door, most likely challengers.

"You left the door open?" Oscar asked.

"Huh, looks like I did. Oops, not good," Tinasha observed, straightening up reflexively and going over to join Oscar in the center of the hall.

Outside were five men whose garb made them easily recognizable as adventurers. They entered cautiously and were surprised to see Oscar and Tinasha. "What are you two doing here? Come to take a stab at the tower?" one asked.

Oscar and Tinasha exchanged glances, both unsure how to respond. Then, the witch broke into a mischievous smile and clapped her hands together. Oscar had a fair idea what she was thinking but prayed he was wrong.

Without making a sound, Tinasha flew up into the air. She surveyed the five stunned visitors from on high.

Two swordsmen, one mage with a bow in midrange gear, one mage with long-range gear, and one mage for defense. The witch grinned devilishly. To her, the timing could not have been more perfect.

"Welcome to my tower. I'm happy you've made such a sudden appearance."

Her greeting caused a stir among the guests. Down below, Oscar had his head in his hands.

One swordsman pointed his blade at Tinasha and asked, "Are you really the witch?"

"Yes," Tinasha answered. "Have you come with some business for me?"

"Will you grant our wish?"

"If you've got the strength," she replied, causing the men to murmur among themselves.

Another young swordsman from the group stepped forward. "Will you really grant any wish? I mean, you look really beautiful, so if I said I wanted you, would you agree?"

"I don't mind."

"Tinasha!" yelled Oscar angrily. Giggling, the witch alighted next to him.

"However, I did say only if you've got the strength. Normally, you'd have to climb to the top floor of the tower, but today is a special exception." The witch snapped her fingers, and the open door slammed shut. Left with no way back, the men stiffened.

Tinasha pointed one ivory finger at Oscar and announced silkily, "Defeat him. If you do, I'll grant you anything you desire."

Nervous excitement filled the men upon hearing such a promise. They probably thought this would be easier than taking on the infamous tower said to eat those fool enough to challenge it.

An archer mage stepped forward. "One against one?" he asked.

"No, all of you against him," Tinasha declared, floating into the air again and bringing her lips to Oscar's ear. "I'll make it so no one dies. Go ahead and fight to your heart's content."

"Why, you…," Oscar started.

"Good luck!" Tinasha sang out, looking truly entertained.

Oscar had the distinct feeling that he'd become a bug. There was little to do about it now, however. He took hold of Akashia.

That was the men's cue to ready themselves for battle as well. Oscar looked up at the witch from her spectator's spot high above, then eyed the young swordsman—the one who'd asked for Tinasha as his wish.

"I guess I'll start with him," Oscar mused.

Tinasha clapped her hands. With that as their signal, the battle began.

In the blink of an eye, Oscar had closed the distance with the swordsman. With Akashia, he broke right through the barrier the defense mage had set on him. It all happened at what should have been an impossible speed, and the man's face froze in shock.

"Wha—?"

He was aghast in the face of unavoidable death. Without hesitating, Oscar knocked the man's sword away and then sliced across his torso. Instead of getting bisected, though, the man's body disintegrated like smoke just before Akashia could touch it.

Tinasha had probably judged that to be a mortal wound and transported him away. The four remaining men were in an uproar over their companion's quick removal from the board. The other swordsman of the group regained his composure and shouted, "Don't get careless! Attack all at once!" He swung his sword down at Oscar.

It was a long, sweeping stroke, infused with strength and momentum, but Oscar met it effortlessly. Ignoring the swordsman staggering from the recoil of the prince's block, Oscar leaped in front of the mage, who was trying to nock an arrow, and sliced through him.

Disbelief was written on the mage's face as he was teleported away, but Oscar didn't even bother to watch it happen. He fell back for a beat. The swordsman was back on his feet, and Oscar rushed him.

"Are you the witch's damn familiar?!" the swordsman cried.

"Please don't say rude things about people's contract holders," Tinasha's exasperated-sounding voice called from above. If Oscar heard the witch's words, he didn't react. Instead, he met the blade that came at him with his own, eyeing the mage who'd begun chanting a spell all the while. On the fifth clash, he knocked the man's sword aside and then swung Akashia down on his opponent's shoulder. The swordsman disappeared.

It was then that the mage finished his incantation, and a blast of powerful wind was launched at Oscar.

"Take that!" For the mage, the magic must have appeared a killer move.

Oscar merely reached out his right hand and crushed the core at the center of the eddy. In an instant, the swirling gusts dispersed.

The mage was left aghast at such an unexpected feat, and Oscar edged closer to him. From behind, another mage sent out an invisible binding spell, but one flash from Akashia cut it down. The mage began reciting another spell in a panic, but Oscar thrust his sword at him, and he disappeared like his comrades.

Looking back, Oscar saw the final mage sprawled on the floor, and he placed his sword tip against the man's neck. "It's over."

There was a beat, and then the final challenger was transported away. The witch's voice rang out, clear as a bell. "That was over too soon."

"You need better taste in opponents," said Oscar.

"Sorry," she apologized as she fluttered back to the ground in high spirits. Oscar sheathed Akashia, then caught her slender body in his arms. Tinasha smiled as she patted down Oscar's mussed-up hair. "You exceeded my expectations with how well you did. Let's put an end to this here."

"You sure? We've still got five days left."

"There's no real point in continuing. Thanks for all your hard work," Tinasha said, sliding out of his arms and onto the floor.

Eyeing her lithe form, Oscar murmured, "If I fought against you at your full power, could I win?"

It was something the prince hadn't really considered before.

If such a day ever came, he'd be going up against the most powerful witch. Oscar had only asked the question idly, but Tinasha bent her head doubtfully, then looked up at him with eyes filled with loneliness. "Don't you think…it would be boring to know that now?"

She cast her long black eyelashes down. There was a transparent glimmer in her dark orbs. A smile played at her tiny lips, and in that moment, she looked both like a girl and like a witch who'd lived for many a lifetime.

This appearance of hers somehow felt distant to Oscar…or perhaps it was trying to be. Someday, Tinasha really could vanish.

Lost in his musings, Oscar held his breath without realizing it for a moment. Patting the witch's head, he managed to suppress his worries over things to come. "I won, so grant me a wish."

"All right, just make sure it's something I can manage. You did work very hard this past month. As long as it isn't marriage, I'll do it."

"Don't ruin my fun." Oscar pouted.

"I've learned my lesson." Giggling, Tinasha opened a transportation array to take them both back to the castle. She held out a hand to Oscar. Her palm was small and creamy white.

It seemed to shine as Oscar laid his own hand over it. When he intertwined his fingers with hers and squeezed lightly, she gave him a smile tinged with both relief and sadness.

9. Tonight, Under the Moon

The rainfall mixed with the blood on the cobblestones.

Kagar's strength had slowly been eroded by the cold, damp storm, but he was more concerned with it erasing the spots of blood that dotted the ground. He looked back to check for his opponent, but there was no sign. It had been like that for a while now—he was being pursued by someone who would not show themselves.

"Dammit… Is this the witch's doing…?"

When Kagar tried to leave the Farsas castle city, someone had attacked him. He thought it must've been someone Tinasha had set on him, but the assailant had only launched a few intermittent attacks, toying with him. The sun had set, and there weren't many people around. Kagar pressed a hand to his bleeding side.

"If only I could use a transportation array…"

Ever since he sustained the first wound, Kagar could cast almost no spells. That first hit must have placed some sort of sealing magic inside his body. He rounded the closest corner, almost slipping on the slick street.

No sooner did he turn onto the next street than a white light flashed before him.

"…Huh?"

Suddenly, his vision dimmed, and he collapsed on the spot.

Kagar saw a rapidly spreading pool of blood and his own leg lying severed on the ground.

"Ah… Aaaaaahhh!" he shrieked, his panicked cries echoing up the alley.

Then, he heard the sound of footsteps splashing through a puddle. A petite young woman was standing beneath the curtain of rain. She wore no cloak, her wet silver hair glittered like a knife, and that alone attracted Kagar's notice. He stretched out a hand to her, his vision blurry.

"Sa...ve..."

"You want me to save you? You don't seem to realize who's killing you." Her voice was cruel. By the time Kagar realized what she'd meant, it was far too late.

The envoy was speechless as he realized that the one tailing him all this time, the far superior mage, was this very girl.

Indelible hatred blazed in her eyes. "How dare you so shamelessly show yourself here. Your lord killed him, you know, in front of me. Even if I redo it all, your crime will stand forever. Do you understand?"

Two red orbs glowed in the darkness. There came the low growl of a beast. The creature that appeared behind the silver-haired girl held only death in its visage. Kagar knew that his end was imminent and let out a scream.

"L-Lord Lanak... Ah, guh..."

His hoarse cry for his lord soon became a twisted mix of shrieks and gurgles. Amid the strong stench of blood and the sounds of chewing...the girl brushed back her wet silver hair and turned to head toward the castle.

※

"My familiar was finally able to slip in through a hole in Cuscull's barrier. They've amassed a sizable number of mages there, including many spiritual sorcerers."

All those listening to the witch's report in the study looked upset. Lazar and Miralys stood pale-faced against the wall, while Oscar toyed with a porcelain figurine as he listened. It was obvious from his expression that he found this entirely undesirable.

"With so many mages, do they plan to mount a war?" Oscar inquired.

"I can't say for certain. Apparently, they're also attempting to summon demons."

"How many regular soldiers do they have?"

"The same as their number of mages. It's around two hundred. Not a huge amount, but my familiar couldn't break into the palace, so there may very well be more."

Normally, a castle was occupied by twenty to thirty mages. Major nations could have up to fifty, but there had never been a country with two hundred standing mages.

Oscar picked up on something in what Tinasha had said. "You said palace. Do they have a monarchy?"

"It appears they do. I don't know who the king is, but it doesn't look to be the lord of the former territory."

"If it's a country based around magic, then their ruler is probably a mage, too." Oscar crossed his hands behind his head and rested his feet on his desk. He normally wouldn't assume such a lazy pose and only did so when thinking over something difficult. "For now, and I'm sorry about the trouble, but could you send out scouts periodically? I don't think this is going to end peacefully."

"Understood," Tinasha replied.

Oscar had a bad feeling but couldn't do anything about it at this stage. He brought his feet down to the floor and picked up the documents he'd yet to deal with. Then he remembered something else and looked back up.

"Oh, I nearly forgot. Apparently, Ettard isn't feeling well."

Old General Ettard was the oldest military man in Farsas and one of the symbols of the nation's leadership. Standing up against the wall, Miralys looked gloomier by the second.

"Miss Miralys, you came here on General Ettard's recommendation, didn't you?" Lazar asked with concern in his voice after noticing the girl.

"Yes... We're only distant relatives, but he still did his best to help me. It's all thanks to General Ettard that I'm here now," Miralys admitted. Her light-blond hair looked dull and lank, perhaps because of how depressed she was. Though her face still had childish edges to it, she was very beautiful. In a few years, she was sure to turn the heads of every person in the castle.

Miralys had arrived less than a year ago under the good offices of General Ettard, and she was only sixteen years old. It was a great opportunity to learn royal etiquette. With such experience, she'd face few hardships in the future. Likely because she was the crown prince's attendant and often in his study, Tinasha taught her how to brew tea, and Lazar taught her matters of the court. She was growing and maturing by the day.

Oscar gazed at his attendant, his chin resting on his hands. "You can go visit Ettard whenever you want. I'm sure he'll be glad to see you."

"Th-thank you very much," Miralys said.

"It probably comes with the territory now that he's so old, but apparently, he's having a hard time waking up lately."

The gloom in Oscar's words caused the witch to respond quietly, "That seems pretty sudden. Als must be worried."

"Yeah, the old man's always had a soft spot for Als. I owe a huge debt to him myself," Oscar replied.

Before coming to the castle, Als had visited Ettard's mansion frequently to learn swordplay. When he was younger, Ettard had been the foremost swordsman in the country, and he had spared no effort in teaching what he knew to children. He'd often instructed a young Oscar on the fundamentals as well.

Over ten years ago, after Ettard learned of the curse, he told Oscar amid swordplay pointers, "Your Highness, despair eats away at people. Your will must be unfaltering. The results will fall in line with that."

What he said affirmed the power of honesty and determination. Even now, Oscar often recalled that lesson.

The prince looked up and met the witch's gaze. "Don't die until after I'm gone, got it?"

Tinasha looked a little shocked, then gave him a pained grin.

Three days later, Ettard died in his sleep.

He left no close family behind. After a solemn and subdued funeral, his estate was distributed, according to his will, among those with whom he'd been close. With permission from the king, Als assumed Ettard's position regarding the knowledge of the witch's curse placed on the prince.

The young general, who now stood at the head of the military officers in both name and substance, sighed regretfully after listening to Oscar tell the long story. "I never guessed you have such a curse on you…"

"It's annoying, right?"

Two days after Ettard was safely buried, Als came to the study to pay his respects. Over tea with Oscar, Lazar, and Tinasha, Als was informed of Oscar's circumstances, and the soldier offered his heartfelt condolences. He glanced at Tinasha from across the table. "Doesn't that mean things look pretty bad if Miss Tinasha doesn't agree to marry you?"

"Yep, end of the royal line," Oscar agreed.

"I'm not marrying him!" Tinasha cried.

Oscar and Als seemed oddly in sync, while Tinasha was anything but. Her face was tight with annoyance. "I'm analyzing the curse as we speak!"

"You don't need to try so hard," Oscar said lazily.

"Don't try to dampen my enthusiasm!"

The witch looked ready to bite Oscar's head off, and Als eyed her curiously. "What don't you like about His Highness?" he asked point-blank, as his lord appeared to have almost no flaws.

Such a question appeared to be something of a direct hit to Tinasha. She'd never been asked that before, and her eyes grew wide. "I... If you're asking me what, then... What don't I like?"

"Don't ask me," said Oscar.

Lazar, who'd been drinking his tea in silence up until that point, piped up. "Isn't it how he loves to tease people? That's a pretty bad habit."

"That might be it," agreed Tinasha.

"Quiet, Lazar...," Oscar warned, glaring at him coldly, and Lazar shrank meekly.

Sensing this conversation could become a quagmire, the witch interjected, "However, we have over half a year left in our contract. I'm sure I'll figure this curse out."

"Let's hope so," Oscar said vaguely, then nodded.

Tinasha had the sense they weren't seeing eye to eye on the subject, but it was likely better not to overthink things. Rolling her eyes at Oscar, she got to her feet.

When she did, her leg bumped against the table, and the sugar bowl fell off the edge. The dish made a *tink* as it hit the floor.

"Oh... I'm sorry."

"Are you all right?"

Tinasha leaned down to pick up the bowl. Fortunately, only the lid was broken. With a wave of her hand, the scattered sugar rose up and went back into the dish like before. She handed it to Lazar and started picking up the pieces of the shattered lid by hand.

Oscar watched her, looking quizzical. "You're not going to fix it?"

"You can't restore something that's broken. Even though you can stop time, you can't rewind it. If the pieces were bigger, I could repair it, but it's not possible after it's been shattered... Sorry."

"No, I don't care. Don't cut your finger."

Als looked on at the sight, sighing to no one in particular, and said, "So even magic isn't infallible."

"That's the truth of all living things." The witch laughed.

Als nodded, impressed...then caught sight of the clock on the wall and leaped to his feet. "Whoa, I've gotta get out on city patrol. Lately, people have reported sightings of a demonic spirit."

"In the city? I haven't heard anything about that," said Oscar.

"Well, nothing's for certain. All we know is that it *might* be one. It's pure hearsay. Someone saw something that looked like a stray dog with red, glowing eyes. Chances are high they were mistaken, and we haven't had any reports of injury," Als explained with a shrug, and Tinasha's brows furrowed.

"That's concerning. If that really is a demonic spirit, it's either pretty smart or someone's controlling it. There may be no reports of injury because they did a good job making sure none would be found," the witch hypothesized.

Oscar, Als, and Lazar all exchanged looks. Oscar crossed his hands behind his head. "Maybe, but we still don't have any proof. Report to me if you find anything. If there really is a demonic spirit, we'll bring it to light," the crown prince ordered, standing up to get back to work himself.

A dream of a past long gone that would never come again.

The girl had fallen asleep curled up on her warm bed but realized that, at some point, she'd been taken from it. Blinking sleep-heavy eyes open, she saw she was heading down a dim corridor.

"...Aeti, did you wake up?" came a kind voice. She was being rocked comfortably in someone's arms. She looked up at the boy carrying her.

She knew him well; he was closer to her than anyone. She smiled in relief. "What's going on?"

"Something good's about to happen. I knew you had to see it."

"Something important?"

"Yeah, very important. As important as you are."

She burst out laughing at his sweet words. She wasn't yet at the age where such flattery could really affect her.

Still, she knew he did care for her, and she loved him dearly. It was true that he was more important to her than anyone. Feeling relieved, her eyes grew heavy again. "But I'm still sleepy."

"You can sleep."

"...Sleepy..."

Once again, her eyes drifted shut.

The two made their way down the long corridor.

The sun had just begun to set when Oscar reached a good stopping place in his work and went to Tinasha's room to get her approval on the Cuscull investigation. He rapped lightly on the door, but there was no response.

"Tinasha, are you there?"

He touched the doorknob, and it opened easily. It clearly wasn't locked. Instead, Oscar saw a barrier erected at the entry. He hesitated a little but then stepped through. Fortunately, most likely because he was her contract holder, the magical blockade allowed him to pass with no discomfort or ill effects.

As soon as Oscar entered, he saw Tinasha. She was dozing in a chair next to a scrying bowl with sigils floating up from it. He nudged her shoulder, but she was clearly too exhausted, not even responding.

"Don't sleep in a chair…," Oscar chided quietly.

He picked her up. Normally, she weighed nothing at all, but because she was unconscious and not using magic, there was weight to her. Still, she was light. She stirred once but didn't wake up.

He looked down at the witch in his arms. "So defenseless."

Her slim, soft body.

Usually, he tried not to think too much about it, but now that he'd touched such an alluring creature, a desire to make her his own roared within Oscar. He wanted to kiss her porcelain-white skin and leave a mark. It didn't matter if it was possible, he simply wanted to have her. A feeling akin to lavish impatience smoldered deep within his chest, but Oscar knew this feeling didn't indicate what he truly wanted.

Tinasha had entrusted him with not her heart or body but her life—and had done so rather carelessly.

He could kill her at any time.

The idea that she was doing it knowingly was something Oscar disliked. That she could be doing so unconsciously seemed endearing to him, however.

Oscar wondered when he'd gotten so attached. He shook his head at himself, aware that he was just as bad as his great-grandfather.

If she weren't a witch… No, Oscar refused to think that way. If that were the case, they likely never would've met, and he didn't want to so casually toss aside how Tinasha had lived and the decisions she'd made based on that experience.

She seemed perfect, but she was unstable.

He didn't want to know every detail of her past. It was fine if she never told him.

What Oscar wanted was not her heart, nor body, soul, or life. Rather, he wanted her to feel attached to him. Oscar desired for Tinasha to take his hand and say that he was more precious to her than anything. Just like a child might've. He knew it was foolish, but foolishness didn't seem like such a bad thing to Oscar.

Oscar brought the witch to the bed and laid her down carefully, so as not to wake her. When he tried to retract his arms from underneath her, she suddenly shot up. Her eyes were wide with astonishment, or perhaps fear, as she looked up at Oscar.

It was the first time Oscar had seen Tinasha look this way, and it startled him. Instinctively, he laid a hand on her head. "Tinasha."

"Oh... Oscar...?"

"Yes."

In his arms, she let out a deep sigh, and he could feel the tension draining from her. He released her, noticing she seemed pale, but her eyes still burned with the same light they always did.

"Sorry. I had a bad dream...," Tinasha explained.

"Because you were sleeping in the chair. If you're going to sleep, rest properly," Oscar instructed, again placing a hand on her head. Tinasha offered him a smile, though it seemed somewhat weak.

The witch blinked up at him, her eyes shining. "Did you need something?"

"No, it can wait. You get some rest," answered Oscar.

The Cuscull situation wasn't so urgent that he needed to push her for answers when she wasn't feeling up to it.

Oscar ruffled Tinasha's head, messing up the ink-black strands.

To himself, he whispered a wish for nothing to harm the witch, even in her dreams.

A cup of tea was set before Oscar in his office, not by his protector witch but by Miralys, his lady-in-waiting. Oscar thanked her and took the cup. "Where's Tinasha?"

"I believe she's in her room. Busy...analyzing? Or something like that."

Whereas before, Oscar hadn't known if Tinasha was working on the curse analysis or not, things seemed to be proceeding more smoothly ever since Lucrezia's evil prank. Perhaps Tinasha had gotten some help. In recent days, she was often holed up in her room, focused solely on her task. Oscar knew it was for his sake but still sipped at his tea feeling disappointed. Fortunately, it tasted exactly the same as the tea the witch would have brewed, and he had no complaints.

Lazar came in with some documents. Oscar muttered to no one in particular, "More? I want to hurry up and finish this so I can go bother Tinasha."

"Stop that, Your Highness. If you go too far, she'll get angry with you."

"Even so, our contract has an expiration date. I want to do what I can before it runs out."

After Tinasha left, Oscar could just climb the tower again, but she'd probably be mad at him for that.

Then, Lazar clapped his hands together like he'd just remembered something. "That's right, His Majesty summoned Miss Tinasha earlier, so she's not in her room now."

"Father did? Why did he call her in?"

"I'm not sure…"

Normally, Oscar's father took no interest in the witch. What business did he have with her, then? Even if it had to do with their visitor from the other day, it was odd he would go straight to her without involving Oscar at all.

The prince silenced his thoughts before they began spiraling for too long and got up. "What room are they in? I'll go, too."

"What? No, I don't think…," Lazar started to say, but he wasn't given the chance to finish.

Oscar strode out of the study, and Lazar followed after him in a panic. Dumbfounded, Miralys watched them both go.

Ignoring the soldier stationed at the door, Oscar approached the entrance to a hall deep within the castle. Inside were the king, the royal council members, Chief Mage Kumu, and General Als—all the key players in Farsas. Each had their gaze fixed on the witch, who stood in the center. Tinasha looked over her shoulder to see Oscar, and her eyes grew wide.

Stone-faced, Oscar marched into the room and stood in front of her protectively.

"Father, what business do you have with my guardian?" he asked, a barely suppressed edge to his voice.

King Kevin was slack-jawed for a second but soon gave a strained smile. "I do have business with her, but it's not what you're thinking. I only wished for some advice."

"Advice?" Oscar asked, puzzled.

"About your future bride."

When Oscar heard the word *bride*, all he could think of was Tinasha. No one else came to mind, and he didn't want to consider anyone else.

As if anticipating such a thought, the king continued, "The woman who will become your queen needs to have strong magical resistance, right? Which is why you're bothering the witch."

"I'm not bothering her," Oscar objected.

"He is," Tinasha added flatly. Oscar was overcome with the urge to turn around and pinch her. Such an action would only derail things even further, however, so he refrained.

The king went on. "Then what would you think if there was someone else who had such resistance? You only have to make her your queen. I am asking Miss Tinasha to ascertain if the girl in question has the required strength."

"And who is this mysterious girl…?" Oscar asked.

It was clear King Kevin was referring to someone besides Tinasha.

Oscar frowned in confusion, and Tinasha answered, "It's barely enough, but I think she has a chance. It should work as long as she's supported with a little magic. It appears she can't use magic herself, so once I'm free, I'll formulate a support spell and pass it to Kumu. Please enchant her with it once she's pregnant."

"Tinasha?" Oscar cut in, curious. The conversation was about him, but he was the only one not part of the actual talks. Oscar turned to see Tinasha looking at him, composed as ever.

He saw no hint of an answer in the witch's eyes but deduced the identity of the candidate almost immediately.

"Miralys?"

"Correct," Tinasha affirmed.

Ettard's distant relative. Though she'd come to the castle to learn etiquette, it had been highly unusual for her to be suddenly assigned as the crown prince's lady-in-waiting. In reality, she'd been placed near him as a potential future queen from the start. Oscar was the only one who never knew.

All of a sudden, Miralys appeared in a corner of his study awaiting orders patiently. Oscar had thought so little of her. Dumbstruck, he asked Tinasha, "Did you know about this?"

"I was only told about it now. I could tell she had magical power sealed away, though. In terms of pure magic, she has a little more than a court mage, so I had a hunch she was a potential bride for you. Apparently, she's from a family lineage that passes down magic through their bloodline in an unusual way. Once the previous generation dies, the next inherits that magic… Ettard must have known about that and brought her to the castle."

With the trick revealed, Oscar at last understood. Accepting it was another matter entirely, however. He threw a little glare at his protector. "Why didn't you tell me?"

"Because I knew you'd make that face if I did."

"But I'm making it now even though you didn't tell me."

"I guess you are…," Tinasha said, bringing a hand to her chin thoughtfully, as if she'd only noticed for the first time.

Oscar wanted to keep arguing, but his father interjected. "That's enough. Everyone is only doing what they must for your sake. Where do you think that attitude is going to get you? Why are you so arrogant as to think you can solve this all on your own?"

"I don't intend to solve it on my own. It's just…," Oscar tried to protest.

"You still have plenty of time. Don't refuse outright. Get to know her properly."

The king stood up, an indication that the conversation was over. He evidently would not be entertaining any objections, as he left the room swiftly. Oscar considered going after him but heard the sound of a lock clicking and realized that Tinasha had already disappeared, too. He turned to face Lazar, who seemed at loose ends.

"…Couldn't they have waited just one second?!" Oscar cried.

"Your Highness… I understand how you feel, but please stop…," Lazar murmured obediently, teary-eyed though his shoulders were shaking with rage.

※

In the week that followed, Oscar got to know Miralys, while Tinasha didn't visit the study once. The barrier she'd placed on Oscar kept him safe enough, and her research on the curse didn't require his presence. It felt as though Tinasha had only been there with him to make tea, and she'd let Miralys assume that role completely.

Many castle residents relaxed now that the witch was making herself scarce. Those who knew her well felt the castle was emptier without her, however. Sylvia and the other mages all looked disappointed, though they didn't speak of it openly.

Oscar was no exception. A clawing irritation mounted in him every day he spent without his protector.

"Who can I complain to about this situation...?" he lamented, elbows planted on his study desk.

It was very rare to see the prince in such a state. Lazar gazed at him sympathetically, while Miralys looked ashamed. Gathering her resolve, she stepped forward. "Um, Your Highness, I'm really very sorry..."

"No, don't worry about it. There isn't much that can be done."

He didn't intend to blame an ignorant bystander. He wanted to complain to his father and the others who'd made this decision without him. Most had probably insisted that Oscar couldn't make a witch queen.

Before this choice had been made, Tinasha always helped Oscar out with other matters unrelated to her job as his protector—complaining the whole way, of course. Oscar hated that some people were so narrow-minded as to not assess her fairly. He'd thought his father understood until he'd presented Oscar with a different bride.

Without realizing he was doing it, Oscar let out a long sigh.

"Even her..."

Tinasha hadn't been fazed at all at the presence of a new potential partner for Oscar. He hadn't dared to hope she'd get jealous, but it was a little discouraging that she hadn't displayed any sort of attachment toward him. Tinasha had grown to be more open with Oscar since the day they first met, but he supposed that, in the end, he was just someone passing by in her life.

"...I guess I'll just do my work," Oscar said, his voice languid.

"I do appreciate that about you, Your Highness..." Lazar did his best to comfort the prince.

"Rest assured, I'm good and pissed about this."

"Then let's get this taken care of... Do you want to talk to Miss Tinasha? She's gone back to her tower today, so let's set up a time."

Lazar was Oscar's childhood friend. He'd been with the prince for a very long time and knew him extremely well. Nodding, Oscar accepted the stack of documents.

"Don't you pay it any mind, either. Just act the same as normal. Sorry you got dragged into my issue." Oscar told Miralys while his eyes remained fixed on the papers.

"I-I'm really sorry...," she apologized meekly. She really was sweet and lovely. Oscar understood why some had thought he'd have a change of heart with her around, but for him, there was none comparable to the witch.

Oscar recalled something he'd heard earlier about the lady-in-waiting. "Oh right, apparently your magic is sealed away. Who sealed it?"

"My mother. I inherited my powers when my grandmother passed away, but my mother had some magic, too... And Master Kumu reinforced the seal."

"I see. So it's double-sealed."

Oscar had been worried that his training to see magic had been ineffective. This seemed to be a rather extraordinary case. Likely, it was only because Tinasha was a witch that she was able to see through such powerful magic restriction.

The thought that something about all this wasn't quite right continued to needle at Oscar's mind, however. Unfortunately, all that proved to be good for was wasting precious time. He discarded his thoughts, took care of his most crucial work, arranged for the rest to go to his father, and left the castle before nightfall.

※

"Hey, are you free?"

"Does it look like I am?" Tinasha replied dryly to Lucrezia, who had suddenly appeared sitting on one of the tower's windowsills as Tinasha chanted an incantation for analysis. She looked up from her scrying bowl and gave Lucrezia a little grin. "I suppose I should be thanking you. I'm making good progress. I think I almost have the whole thing analyzed."

"What? Really? I salute your hard work and talent."

"I do take my work more seriously than you do," Tinasha said, pausing her efforts to order Litola to bring the tea settings and hot water. It was a perfect time for a break, so Tinasha started brewing some tea for her friend. "Next time, tell me how to make those cookies."

"Of course. It's not a difficult recipe," Lucrezia said, getting down off the windowsill and sinking into a seat quite naturally. Twirling a light-brown curl around her finger, she watched her friend prepare the cups. "You don't have to work so hard, you know. Just give him a child."

"Are you serious? Besides, I've already been relieved from that duty."

"Oh?" Lucrezia sounded surprised, and Tinasha explained about Miralys. During the explanation, the tea leaves reached prime steeping time, so Tinasha began pouring. Lucrezia listened to the story in shock.

When at last she'd heard the whole tale, the visiting witch cast an incredulous look at her friend. "What in the world? Isn't that a bit suspicious? She just happens to show up right then, while you were still there."

"She *is* there on someone's suggestion… She's a nice enough girl. I've been monitoring her," Tinasha reasoned.

"What will you do if there's someone pulling the strings here?" Lucrezia asked.

"I'll handle them if they show themselves. There's nothing any common mage could do to him now anyway."

Tinasha's words spoke to her faith in Oscar, but Lucrezia immediately made a face. "If you know that, then there's all the more reason for you to grab the reins."

"By reins, do you mean Oscar's?" Tinasha asked.

"I'd really prefer it if you didn't train him to be so dangerous and just let him loose into the wild."

Lucrezia had apparently struck at something Tinasha didn't appreciate, and she let out a little groan. She hadn't told Lucrezia the details of what she'd taught Oscar, but her friend evidently knew all about it already.

Beneath Lucrezia's cold stare, Tinasha shook her head dispiritedly. "It'll be fine. He's not the kind of person to throw his weight around recklessly."

"No matter how put together he is, he's still just twenty years old. You shouldn't put him in the same category as a dried-up husk like you," Lucrezia chided.

"D-dried-up husk…?"

"Quite dried-up, in a sense."

The remark left Tinasha unsure how best to respond. Unable to think of a reply, she merely set a cup of tea before Lucrezia. Contained within the creamy-white porcelain was a light-crimson liquid. A refreshing scent wafted up from it, and Lucrezia broke into a smile.

"I really love the tea you brew," she said.

"Thank you," Tinasha replied, sitting down to join her friend before putting both elbows on the table and resting her chin on her hands in a display of poor manners. Her thoughts turned again to the issues plaguing her contractee. "I think it's a good thing for him to have more options. Don't you think it's better for him to get to choose his wife? I'd feel bad for him if I was the only option."

"Are you being serious?" Lucrezia asked.

"This really isn't the time to be joking," Tinasha responded flatly. Such a clueless reply nearly drove Lucrezia to scream.

Apparently, Tinasha really had no idea that Oscar saw her as just another person. He didn't fear her like so many others did, nor did he gaze at her in reverence and longing, as Regius had. Tinasha believed that her worth lay only in her power as a witch and that Oscar only cared about her because of what she was. It seemed Tinasha really didn't know herself at all.

Choosing not to point out such things, Lucrezia held her tongue. Instead, she gave her friend some more substantial advice. "Remember this: You were human before you were ever a witch."

Tinasha gave no verbal answer but flushed shyly.

Immediately after Lucrezia departed, Tinasha returned to her research with renewed focus. She was so absorbed that she didn't look down at Litola until after the familiar had called out to her many times over.

"What is it?" Tinasha finally asked.

"As I said, you have a challenger," replied the little doll-like thing.

Frowning at the words, Tinasha replied, "The entrance is supposed to be closed."

"He came via transportation array. It's Prince Oscar."

"What?"

The witch was so shocked that her analysis spell pattern very nearly dissolved. Hurriedly, she set a spell to anchor it. "Are all the tower's mechanisms working?"

"They are, but..."

"Tinasha!" Oscar cried, slamming the door open violently.

"Whoa!" Tinasha met the sudden arrival with an indescribable expression.

"What's with that reaction?" Oscar asked.

"You just set the record for fewest challengers and the record for shortest time all at once... This really exceeds all human limits."

"I don't care about that."

He sheathed his sword and took the witch up in his arms like a child, though perhaps a bit rougher than that. He looked into her astonished eyes. "Why won't you come to see me?"

"Because I'm busy," Tinasha answered, glancing at the scrying bowl next to her. Oscar followed her eyes and saw a spell pattern of intricately entangled red strings glowing faintly as it floated above the basin sitting atop a pedestal.

Oscar knew better than anyone what the hovering magical arrangement meant and, with irritation in his voice, replied, "You don't have to rush."

"I want to get it done while I can," the witch calmly fired back. Something about her tone spoke of the distance between her and humans. It was a gap that had grown wide over Tinasha's many years. Oscar closed his eyes instead of sighing, then put the witch down. She stumbled a little as she landed on level ground, and Oscar reached out to steady her.

"You shouldn't push yourself so hard," he cautioned.

Whether it was training him or researching the curse, Tinasha was acting like she didn't have much time left. Before, she'd often taken time to relax and read books in the lounge. Evidently, something must have changed.

Tinasha smiled, her eyes crinkling up. "I've lived for so long already. It's too late now." There seemed to be no dark shadow of unhappiness in the witch's eyes as she spoke, which came as a relief to Oscar, if only a little.

"I get anxious whenever you're not around. It makes me want to leave the castle…"

"What nonsense are you talking about? Have some self-respect," Tinasha quipped lightly as she had done many times before, but then, she noticed Oscar's face and frowned.

Oscar hadn't said it as just a joke. It was clear something was deeply troubling him. Tinasha floated up a little until she could look Oscar in the eye. "Try to consider how your father feels. He's thinking of you here."

"I don't like the way he's doing it."

"Even so. He feels responsible for the curse the Witch of Silence placed on you. That's why getting yourself stuck with a witch for a wife would be a bad idea. Your father doesn't want you any more involved with witches than you already are."

"My father and I are different, and you and the Witch of Silence are different."

"Oscar…," Tinasha scolded him, and the prince felt the need to concede. He made a conscious effort to cool off.

Dark eyes met Oscar's gaze.

"All right. I'm sorry," he said, admitting he was in the wrong. Tinasha gave him a relieved smile, alighting on the ground and pointing to the scrying bowl. "The analysis is almost done. Once it is, I'll come back to the castle. You can tell me anytime if you find someone you want to marry besides Miralys; I'll ensure you have that freedom."

"You're almost done? You've really made that much progress?" Oscar was rather surprised.

"Yes, I've been giving it my best effort," Tinasha said, waving a hand toward the scrying bowl, and the spell pattern began slowly revolving in the air. Over the witch's head, Oscar scrutinized the eerie yet delicate sigil.

"What do you think of Miralys?" he asked.

"I think she's an obedient, good girl. I *am* monitoring her, though, just in case. You don't need to worry—I'll handle it if something happens."

"Aren't you the one always yelling at me to keep my guard up?" Oscar inquired rhetorically.

"What are you saying? You should trust her," replied Tinasha with a gentle tone. Veiled beneath her words was a clear lack of attachment to Oscar, something the prince hated.

There was still time yet, however. Nothing needed to be rushed. Oscar remained strangely confident.

Tinasha flung out both hands and recited an incantation at the spell pattern for a little while, but nothing happened. After catching her breath, Tinasha simply stared at the complex magical sequence floating above her scrying bowl. Her sigh of disappointment filled the room.

"The nonsense I'm about to say must never leave this room," declared Tinasha, quite suddenly.

"What is it?" Oscar asked.

"The 'blessing' the Witch of Silence put on you and your bloodline... It's really beautiful. It's woven together very prettily, with an intricate and delicate arrangement of spells. I can only admire how well-made it is. Nothing about it appears extraneous."

"I see," Oscar replied. He looked closer and saw that, indeed, the spell pattern was composed of twenty circles accompanied by little threads. It truly did appear to be one cohesive work of art. He had never looked at his own curse in such a way before and gazed at the complicated configuration.

Next to him, the witch shook her head a little. "When you look at it, you realize it's an expression of both love and hate. It's very...frightening."

"Frightening...?" Oscar fell silent. He didn't know what Tinasha meant.

Which part was love and which hate? What about it was so scary to Tinasha?

Even if he asked, he trusted Tinasha not to answer, so instead, he wrapped his arms around the uneasy-looking witch from behind. He hooked his chin over the top of her head, and she craned her neck to look up at him. He could tell she was giggling a little.

"Whenever you reach a stopping point, make us some dinner," Oscar said.

"Okay, okay," Tinasha replied.

⁂

A rare bit of sun peeked through on a particularly cloudy day.

Als didn't care about the weather, however. He was sitting on a chair in the courtyard and had been sinking deep in his worries for a while now. He just sat there with his legs crossed and a gloomy look on his face.

For the past few days, he'd been moping and fretting over something, but he couldn't find anyone to talk to about it. It wasn't something he could talk over with Meredina, his usual confidant, and there was no one else with whom he was comfortable discussing it. He couldn't even decide if it was something to mention to others in the first place.

Lost in thought as he cracked his knuckles, Als caught sight of something red in the corner of his eye and looked up. It was a small dragon carrying a paper package of some sort in its mouth.

Half rising to his feet, Als was about to yell to the dragon when a woman's voice called out the very name he nearly had.

"Nark!"

Her voice carried well, like a slender flute. A black-haired witch floated down from one of the upper ramparts bordering the courtyard. Recognizing her, Als couldn't help but cry out, "Miss Tinasha!"

She looked in Als's direction with some surprise, hearing her name called so suddenly. "What is it?"

"I've been looking for you but couldn't track you down..."

"I-I'm sorry," Tinasha admitted, landing on the ground and stepping over to him. Nark settled on her shoulder. "Is something wrong?"

Wordlessly, Als took the witch's hand and led her over to a shaded area somewhat separated from the castle walls. Nark deposited the paper package in its master's hands and calmly flitted off. After watching the dragon fly away, Als broached the subject in a whisper. "It's about Miralys... I looked into General Ettard's estate, but nothing related to her came up. Yes, he personally introduced her to me as well, but I'd never heard of him having any distant relatives. It's been bothering me for a while, but then he fell ill, and I wasn't able to confirm it with him..."

Miralys seemed in every way to be just an ordinary girl, but her origins were murky. Still, everyone had readily accepted her because she was attached to Ettard, a senior adviser. Now that he was dead, previous doubts began surfacing at the forefront of peoples' minds. Whether she became queen or not, a satisfying answer was needed.

Tinasha listened intently and let out a little groan once Als had finished speaking. Hesitantly, she explained, "I've kept quiet on this because I thought Oscar would make a fuss. The truth is, right after coming to this castle, I looked into whether any woman anywhere on the entire mainland could be his wife... I turned up none who could survive the curse save for witches."

"Could that be because Miralys's grandmother still had the family magic when you did the search?"

"I didn't filter by age. If I had, every witch would've been completely excluded. Even without such parameters, my inquiry turned up no woman who holds the amount of magical power Miralys does. It's the reason I've been curious about her, too," Tinasha explained.

"Have you told anyone else about this?" asked Als.

"I haven't. I thought I should let Oscar go into this without any preconceptions, since it's still a good chance for him to have a proper bride," replied Tinasha.

Als looked to the sky in a beseeching manner. He never expected a witch to be so dense—or maybe clueless was a better word. This beautiful witch's strangely thoughtful actions were only further muddying the situation.

Tinasha, with no idea as to what Als was really thinking, crossed her arms and fell into thought. "There's something else. Even if there's some sort of catch to her being here, I don't know if the target is the Farsas royal family or to get me out of here. Deciding on a plan would be far easier if we knew which."

"Ah, I see," Als said, recalling the envoy from Cuscull who'd shown up two months ago. If there was some mastermind behind that man and Miralys, they wouldn't be able to do anything to the royal family unless they first removed Tinasha from Farsas.

Als began pondering what the goal of such efforts might be when he suddenly noticed a girl standing in the shadows of a pillar, facing the courtyard. She was gazing out on the grounds in a daze, seemingly unaware that Als had spotted her.

After checking to make sure the girl wasn't looking their way, Als turned to the witch and gave her a roguish grin. "Miss Tinasha, I believe I have an idea."

"What is it?" asked the witch.

"Let's find out if the goal is you or His Highness," Als said, then drew her slender body to him with a hand around her waist. With his other hand, he tipped up her chin. Her eyes widened in shock for a second, but she grasped the situation quickly enough and closed her eyes somewhat ruefully. She wound her creamy-white arms around his neck.

Als brought his face to her smooth porcelain cheeks. To anyone watching from the castle, it should have looked like they were kissing. After making sure the girl had dashed off in a panic, Als let go of Tinasha, who immediately began laughing aloud.

"You're terrible," she said.

"It came with some perks. Two birds with one stone," Als replied, winking at her. Both Als and Tinasha knew that the girl concealed in that shadow had been Miralys. Thus, they had pretended to be lovers in front of her. If Miralys's ultimate goal was Oscar, then she wouldn't do anything, but if it was Tinasha, she'd likely make some kind of move related to Tinasha's lover being a general of the kingdom.

Als slapped his own shoulder. "I hope this clears up some things for us."

"Will it be worth the dangerous game we just played?" Tinasha wondered, grinning at Als like a mischievous child.

It was obvious enough that Tinasha thought of this as someone else's problem, and Als gave a shrug. "I think His Highness will kill me if he finds out..."

"What about Meredina?" Tinasha teased.

"..."

Als fell silent, and the witch giggled and floated up into the air. She brought her lips close to Als's ear. "I'll let you know once I get an answer."

"Please do."

The witch promptly disappeared into thin air. Relieved of the burden he'd been carrying deep in his heart, Als headed for the training grounds with a spring in his step.

He was completely unaware that there was someone on the third-floor passageway who had witnessed the whole thing.

"Als! Where did you go?"

Meredina was waiting right outside the entrance to the corridor that led to the training grounds, and once she caught sight of him, she flung the cloth she'd been using to polish her sword at him as hard as she could. Als caught it in one hand.

"Sorry, sorry. I'll head right to training," he said, guessing at the reason for her action.

"His Highness is waiting for you. Did you do something?"

"What?"

"He is *not* in a good mood. He's going to put you through the wringer."

It took less than a second for Als to understand what was happening. He could feel the blood draining from his face.

As Als contemplated his potentially imminent death, a clueless Meredina dragged him to the training grounds.

In her chambers, Tinasha was working to unravel the curse when she received a summons from Oscar and went to his rooms. She thought of entering via his balcony door as she usually did, but as long as he had a real fiancée in Miralys, she thought it better to put a stop to such acts. She stood in the hallway and knocked on the door normally. A reply from inside came back right away, bidding her to enter.

"Oscar, did you need something?" Tinasha asked, entering with curiosity in her voice. He was standing by the window and beckoned her over without saying anything. Without so much as a hint of caution, she approached to stand at his side. He looked down at her expressionlessly.

"What did you do today?" Oscar asked.

"The usual. Working on curse analysis and listening to reports from my familiars. Oh… Nark went out on an errand. He picked up some rare tea leaves from Lucrezia. I'll make them into a tea later," Tinasha recounted. She smiled amiably at Oscar but realized his stony expression hadn't changed at all. "What's wrong?"

Tinasha touched his face, moving to float up. Oscar grabbed hold of her wrist, pulling her close to him. She lost her balance in the air and crashed into him.

"Hey! What's going on? Ah!"

Just then, Tinasha heard a metallic *clink*. She looked at the hand he'd caught hold of and saw a broad silver bracelet on her wrist. She was puzzled for a second, but all too soon she realized what it was.

"D-don't tell me this is…"

"Sekta, a sealing ornament passed down alongside Akashia. It's made of the same material."

Tinasha tried to amass magical power in her hand, but it dispersed without taking shape. It couldn't be formed into a spell configuration, either. Such an effect, and the very idea that such a fearsome object existed, was enough to send a bolt of fear down Tinasha's spine.

"Oscar!" she cried, looking up at him reproachfully as she was unable to comprehend why he was doing this. When she saw the look in Oscar's eyes, she stiffened. There was clear anger there, the first she'd ever seen in the prince.

For the first time since Tinasha had become a witch, she felt true terror from the bottom of her heart.

She was rendered immobile, and Oscar tipped up her chin until she faced him. He glared right into her dark eyes. "I knew you didn't get it, but I had no idea it was this bad. I planned on waiting patiently, but even I have my limits."

"Oscar…?" Tinasha asked, aware her voice was trembling. She wanted to look away, but Oscar's hold on her face was firm. She blanched and felt dizzy.

His low voice swept over her body. "Tinasha, I didn't bring you here to let another man have you."

At last, she finally grasped what was happening. Oscar must have seen what had transpired earlier.

Tinasha opened her mouth to explain, but before she could, Oscar picked her up. He threw her a chilly glance, and she froze. He began walking with her in his arms, and she felt her vision dim.

Arms holding her up. The sensation of being carried. A long-gone, irretrievable memory surfaced.

It was hard to breathe. Fear dominated her body.

"...Oscar... Stop... Put me down...," she murmured, but her pleas went unheeded. He laid her on the bed, then held her wrists down.

Tinasha was shaking with childlike fear as Oscar whispered, "You don't understand anything, so I'm going to teach you until it sinks into your bones."

He lifted his head to see that her face was as pallid as a corpse. Her dark eyes looked unfocused. She was just staring into space, shivering minutely. He let out a little sigh and lightly patted one ivory cheek, but she remained frozen, as if she hadn't seen his character break.

"...Stop... I don't like this...," she whispered.

"Tinasha?"

She wasn't acting right. Oscar lifted her torso and wrapped an arm around her back to support her.

Tinasha slapped away his hand.

A nearby water jug on the table exploded into pieces. Uncontrolled, raw magic began swirling in the room.

Uh-oh, Oscar thought just as Tinasha twisted and ducked away from him. Now facedown on the bed, she used her trembling arms to push herself up and whirl on him.

Her eyes as she fixed her gaze on him again were those of a wounded wild animal.

A furious rage filled her dark eyes, but not to kill. It was the urge to protect herself.

The bracelet on Tinasha's right hand continued to diffuse her magic, but even without the ability to cast a spell, she still possessed an immense amount of magical power. That energy bubbled forth through the bracelet, completely uncontrolled and ran amok through the room. It sent random things flying and crashing into the walls, destroying them one after another. A shard from a broken vase flew toward the bed and bounced off Oscar's protective barrier.

It was like being in the middle of a storm. Despite the danger, Oscar didn't take his eyes off Tinasha. Anyone else would've been too frightened to meet her gaze, but he met her eyes and leaned forward with no hesitation to reach out for a white cheek.

"Tinasha."

He touched her tense face. His warmth was steady and real. Upon feeling that warmth, the witch's eyes widened.

"Ah..."

Instantly, her fury dispersed, and the maelstrom of objects ceased. Oscar reached out for her with his other hand and pulled her into his arms. He patted her back gently.

"Sorry. I only meant to startle you. I shouldn't have done that," Oscar admitted.

"...No, I... I'm sorry," Tinasha responded, now seemingly embarrassed over her deadly impulses. She reached out with still finely trembling hands to clutch hold of his shirt. "I'm sorry... Really..."

"The fault is mine," Oscar said, and Tinasha raised her head. She still looked pale.

She stared at him, puzzled. "Why?"

Snorting despite himself at how innocent and childlike she looked, he hugged his witch tight.

"What? You beat him up?"

"Sorry."

"You should be telling that to Als...," Tinasha said, at her wit's end as she sat on Oscar's lap.

"I told him that if he had something to say, he should just say it."

"There was no way he would! Not with all eyes on him like that!" protested Tinasha.

"He told me he had nothing to offer in his defense," Oscar explained.

"Als needs to choose his words better!"

Oscar hooked his chin over the indignant witch's head. He touched her hand to check on it and noted that she'd finally stopped trembling.

"I didn't cause him any serious injuries. We had about ten matches back-to-back. Worst he's got are bruises."

"I'll go heal him later…," Tinasha declared. As Oscar held her in his arms, he thought it looked like she'd returned to normal.

Oscar had only intended to get a little angry and threaten her, but he seriously regretted what a stupid thing he'd done after seeing Tinasha's unexpected reaction. It had only ever been his intention to cherish her, but he'd gotten his priorities backward and wound up hurting her instead. This was a lesson engraved deep in his heart, one he'd never repeat.

Concealing his inner thoughts, Oscar instead just poked Tinasha's cheek. "Still, don't keep information like that from me. Miralys does really seem insanely suspicious."

"Augh, so you think so, too…?" Tinasha asked, her eyes cast down despondently. She'd given him a brief report about all the things she'd learned about the curious lady-in-waiting. "I mean, it's possible she's just being used… And she's so cute and everything. I didn't want to destroy the chances of you falling for her."

"Listen, you…," Oscar said, heaving a huge sigh and digging his fingers into her temples. "I'm trying to tell you that you don't understand anything!"

"Ow-ow-ow!" Tinasha yelped, flailing around, and Oscar let her go. He watched her clutch her head painfully with tears in her eyes and felt an indescribable wave of exhaustion come over him. If this kept up, how many more times would he have to tease her? Perhaps it was best to just get this all over with now.

"Hey, come with me," Oscar said, lifting her up under the arms and setting her on her feet like a doll. As he left the room, he called for Lazar.

"Did you call for me? Ah—the furnishings are all broken… What in the world…?"

"Don't worry about that. I need to see my dad. Oh yeah, bring Miralys, too."

"At the moment, His Majesty is in the audience chamber discussing his birthday ceremony with the royal council."

King Kevin held an annual royal birthday ceremony as an opportunity to deepen diplomatic relations with other countries. Farsas was the largest nation in the mainland, as well as the most stable in terms of both military might and cultural accomplishments. In respect of such achievements, aristocrats and government officials from neighboring nations gathered in Farsas on the king's birthday.

"Oh yeah? That's perfect. That's where I'll be going, then," Oscar declared.

"What?!" Lazar exclaimed in reply.

"That's enough. Go look for Miralys—and hurry."

Flustered, Lazar took off, and Oscar grabbed a very bewildered Tinasha and set out.

"Oscar, what are you going to do? If we're going to look into Miralys's background, we shouldn't let her know what we're doing."

"I'm going to take care of that, too, but I'm starting with you first."

"What? Why me? All I've been doing is working to break your curse…," the witch said, sounding just like a child dreading a lecture. Oscar led her to the hall, and the two burst in. All eyes were immediately drawn to the sudden arrival of the crown prince and his witch.

"Allow me to interrupt," said Oscar, finally letting go of Tinasha's hand and striding right up to his father, who was seated on a high throne. Entirely confused, the royal council and magistrates retreated to stand along the walls. With nothing to do herself, Tinasha stood fixed where she was.

After only a few moments, Lazar entered with Miralys in tow. Unsurprisingly, she looked around the room uneasily before coming to stand behind Tinasha. The king looked thunderstruck at his parade of sudden visitors.

"What is this? What's going on?" demanded the king.

"It seems a lot of people are laboring under some kind of misunderstanding, so I'd like to take this chance to clear everything up," Oscar stated. He then turned back to look at Tinasha, who only tilted her head at him. It was clear she still hadn't a clue what was happening. Refusing to break eye contact with her, Oscar raised his voice so everyone present could hear him. "I don't keep Tinasha with me because I have no other choice. I'm doing it because I like her. It's pointless for you to parade other girls in front of me. Really, it's just a hassle. I don't intend to choose anyone but her."

At that, the hall fell silent. Some members of the royal council looked stunned, while others frowned hopelessly.

The king brought one hand to his mouth and sighed, as if he'd fully anticipated his son's announcement. Miralys's face was a frozen mask as she stood stock-still.

None appeared more floored than Tinasha herself as she stared at Oscar in blank amazement with her jaw wide open. "What?"

Oscar sounded frustrated as he replied, "Do you really not get it? I've spelled it out so many times. It doesn't matter if I have one choice or a thousand. I'll always choose you. So stop trying to spin it as something else; it's getting annoying."

Tinasha was left completely speechless by this turn of events. All the color drained from her beautiful face before she turned a bright red. Oscar watched it happen with amusement.

Content to leave the matter at that for the moment, Oscar then turned to Miralys. "That's how I feel. Sorry, but I don't plan on marrying you. And as for your origins, I'll be carrying out an investigation after you've been temporarily removed from the castle. If nothing fishy turns up, you can come back as an apprentice lady-in-waiting."

"U-um, Your Highness, I really haven't…," Miralys started to protest.

"It's just to be on the safe side. I'm not going to lock you up, although you will be monitored," Oscar said, signaling with his eyes to a magistrate who quickly approached the girl. She wore a startled expression as the magistrate tried to walk her out of the room.

At that moment, Tinasha suddenly snapped out of her strange state, muttering, "Huh… Just now, the castle wards…"

The sound of something shattering echoed throughout the room. Oscar and Tinasha whirled back at the same time, but Tinasha was the one closer to Miralys.

The witch broke into a run, her arms outstretched. She grabbed the magistrate by the scruff of the neck before he could leave the room.

A white flash of light seared Tinasha's eyes. It was a simple and finely honed spell designed to tear its target apart.

With practiced motions, Tinasha attempted to throw up a defensive wall but quickly realized she was still wearing the bracelet.

"Oh…"

"Tinasha!" Oscar shouted, moving to wrap himself around her. Unfortunately, the light proved quicker…

A burning pain lanced through Tinasha's eyes. Her vision a mess of red, Tinasha cried out, "Oscar! Run!"

It all happened so quickly that most were at a loss for understanding what had really occurred. All anyone knew for certain was that Tinasha had pulled the magistrate down, Oscar had tried to stop her, and now she was bleeding in his arms.

Only Oscar and Tinasha understood what it all meant. Only them…and Miralys.

Oscar glared at the girl. "You…"

"Sorry, but I can't allow myself to be removed from the castle. I still have business here," Miralys boldly asserted with a fearless look in her eyes. The obedient, fearful girl was gone. Magic sparked at her fingertips, and her light-blond hair turned translucent silver.

Miralys's eyes blazed as she fixed her gaze on Oscar. "If only you'd stayed unaware just a bit longer, I could've left you out of it for a while. But I suppose this is as good a time as any."

"I guess you used your powers to take off the sealing ornaments Kumu put on you… What's your game here?" Oscar demanded as he tended to the woman in his arms. The magic attack had left Tinasha's skin lacerated in a line from her leg to her left eye. If Oscar hadn't pulled her back in time, the attack might have torn into her organs. As Tinasha drew shallow breaths, Oscar reached for the bracelet, and the royal sealing ornament hit the floor with a *ping*.

"Sorry, Tinasha… Can you heal it?" he murmured to his protector.

Had she been able to use magic, she likely wouldn't have sustained any wounds at all. Oscar felt like he was going to go mad with remorse thinking about what would happen to Tinasha's blood-spattered eye.

In a hoarse voice, she answered, "I'll...be fine... You need to...run..."

As Tinasha spoke, her wounds began healing. Watching the lacerations on her white cheeks disappear, Oscar felt some of the deepest relief in his life, but that was why he refused to listen.

"You get out of here. Go get treated by Kumu," he urged.

It was his fault she'd gotten injured. There was absolutely no way he was going to leave her and run.

Exhaling, Tinasha returned to her feet. She glared at Miralys through her right eye. "No... She's aiming for you, Oscar. That's why she hurt me."

"I wasn't really aiming for you," Miralys admitted to Oscar. "It just would've been satisfying if I'd happened to kill you along the way. I mean, if you hadn't stabbed him, maybe he wouldn't have gotten killed."

"He? Who are you talking about?" asked Oscar.

Miralys's lips curved up in a smile, but her eyes held unwavering anger.

Something about Miralys's words and the color of her hair reminded Oscar of someone. "Are you...the girl who was with that mage?"

When the mage Oscar confronted at Ynureid was in the castle city, he'd had a silver-haired girl with him. Miralys was that girl. She'd changed her hair color and infiltrated the castle.

Tinasha wiped the blood off her lips. "The one from the festival? You didn't have any magic back then. What happened?"

"Haven't I already told you?" Miralys said, raising her right hand. A spell formed there, and as Tinasha saw it, she flung out her hands.

There was the ear-ringing sound of magic colliding. Gloom infused the girl's voice as she spoke. "Our family passes down magic through the bloodline. He died...so I've inherited his powers."

Miralys lashed out with a ray of white light, which Tinasha withstood behind a protective wall she erected. Despite blocking the attack, the witch had a feeling this was going to be annoying.

There was something headed for Oscar and Tinasha. Its presence had been a constant ever since the castle wards had been shattered. Whatever it was, its bloodlust was palpable. Tinasha knew the others couldn't handle this situation and said to them, "There's no time. You need to evacuate now…along with him."

Oscar was covered in Tinasha's blood from when he'd shielded her, and the efficacy of his protective barrier was dropping sharply. Miralys had likely heard at the training grounds about the trick to weakening the defense Tinasha had placed on him. It certainly explained why she'd attacked Tinasha first. Miralys must've known that as long as Oscar's barrier was up, she couldn't take him on.

"Really… We've been completely underestimated," Tinasha spat. She was still sore all over. It would take some time for her slashed eye to heal completely. For the moment, she was going to have to fight using only her good one. She exhaled, then used magic to shut out the pain that would have otherwise slowed her down.

When Tinasha looked up, she saw a new combatant had entered the fray.

"…So the eyewitness reports from the castle city were true?"

A silver wolf loped in silently from the corridor. Too ominously beautiful to be a stray dog, it was none other than the demonic beast Tinasha thought she'd defeated back at the magical lake.

The beast was much smaller than before, roughly the same size as a regular wolf, but its aura of fiendish, swirling magical power was the same. The witch snorted at the sight of the red jewel embedded in the beast's forehead.

"You used the core to regenerate it? How very clever of you."

"He did it, not me. It was pretty careless of you, not collecting all the pieces of the core," said Miralys.

"I'm speechless. I suppose I'll just have to clean up my mess," Tinasha replied.

The situation for the witch was hardly ideal. She'd numbed her pain but could still only see out of one eye. She could move, but not without extreme discomfort. Worst of all, she'd lost a fair amount of blood. Tinasha wasn't sure how far she could go in such a state.

The witch was confident in her ability to crush any opponent… Unless that opponent was a demonic beast.

Seventy years ago, she'd battled the monster while shielding soldiers. While they were wholly outclassed against the creature, at least they'd chosen to put their lives on the line. Now the battle was to be in the middle of a castle filled with court ladies and magistrates. Tinasha would have to choose her actions very carefully, lest the castle turn into a sea of blood.

With several different spells in mind, Tinasha made to move forward, but a man grabbed her shoulder and held her back. Before she could speak, Oscar stepped in front of her. The sight of his broad back brought her to her senses, and she yelled, "I told you to get back! She'll forcibly teleport you away!"

"You're the one who needs to get a grip on the reality of the situation. You can't be on the front line with that eye." Oscar spoke in an uncharacteristic tone. His words were bereft of naïveté. Oscar's was the low voice of a man on a battlefield.

Reflexively, Tinasha gasped slightly. With all the authority of a ruler, Oscar asked, "What did you train me for? Let me right this wrong for you."

"Oscar…"

"It'll be fine. I'll figure something out."

Oscar had not been born with such dauntless confidence. It was the result of many bloody struggles and the ceaseless effort he'd put into everything since he was a child. He was one who bore the responsibility of a prince and the burden of a terrible curse placed upon him when he was only a boy.

Tinasha's hot breath caught in her throat. It wasn't her injuries that caused the tingling sense of exaltation to surge within her. This was a human emotion she'd almost forgotten. Breaking into a grin, Tinasha said, "Now you've gone and said it. If you're that confident, let's win with room to spare. No injuries allowed."

"Don't just up the stakes. I'll be happy with any outcome, so long as you don't get hurt," Oscar replied.

Akashia in hand, Oscar focused his gaze. He wasn't looking at Miralys but, instead, the silver wolf at her feet. The smaller form of the demonic beast let out a low growl as it waited to pounce and devour its prey. The girl accompanying it gave a heartless smile.

"Always so confident. But just how much longer can you act so care-free? ...Go."

The demonic beast leaped off the ground at Miralys's command. It descended into a pounce toward Oscar's right arm, and the prince readied Akashia. In that same moment, Miralys uttered an incantation.

"Incinerate that which has form at my hand! Flames! Go forth from my palm!"

"...Let it be defined," Tinasha murmured, casting a short incantation of her own. An intricate defensive wall coalesced within the room, demarcating the rear of the hall from where the battle had erupted. At the same time, a smaller wall sprang up around Miralys. The flames she summoned turned back on her in an instant.

"Ngh, dammit!" Miralys spat, forcibly shattering the reflective barrier the witch had placed around her. Tinasha tried to launch an attack in that same instant but got dragged backward and lost concentration on her spell. The jaw of the silver wolf just barely grazed the tip of Tinasha's nose.

"Gah, that was close...," Tinasha managed to say.

"I'll move you around; just make sure not to fall over," said Oscar without sparing a glance at Tinasha. He refused to take his eyes off the demonic beast. The creature's movements had already been unnaturally fast while it had been gigantic. Now that it was smaller, it darted about so quickly that even Tinasha couldn't keep up.

It seemed quite apparent that Oscar could, however. The witch muttered to him, "That wolf has amazing magical resistance and magical penetration abilities. I can't attack it or defend against it without using incantations. I'm virtually defenseless against that thing when we're fighting in such close quarters."

"And yet you were going to go up against it alone," Oscar quipped.

"I was going to knock down some walls and give myself more space," Tinasha shot back.

"That's a last resort. If we really can't fight it any other way, knock down as many walls as you want. What about Miralys?"

"I can kill her anytime."

Such was the difference in power between a mage and a witch. However, there were a great many things Tinasha still wished to learn from Miralys.

What had her goal been in coming to the castle? Who'd killed the mage she'd been with? These unanswered questions meant the ideal outcome was capturing the silver-haired girl alive.

Unfortunately, Miralys seemed to be well aware of their power difference and retrieved a small bag from an internal pocket of her outfit. She scattered the contents of the satchel on the ground—crystal balls that rolled on the floor with a cracking sound.

Oscar frowned in confusion. "What are those?"

"Oh, those are magic spheres. Each one contains a spell. They save you the trouble of having to recite incantations in the middle of a fight. I used a few of them, too, back when I was fighting the larger form of the demonic beast," Tinasha explained.

"I'm not deluded enough to think I can take a witch head-on. That's why he prepared these a long time ago. You know, he really wanted to be your ally, but now he's no longer with us. So...I don't really care if you die," said Miralys.

Some of the scattered magic spheres began emitting a white light. Catching sight of that, the witch let out a fierce grin. "That's some big talk, little brat."

Tinasha flicked her hand. Several tiny magic arrows formed in midair, then shot toward the light-emitting spheres with deadly precision.

Before the little conjured projectiles could pierce the glassy globes, all the arrows suddenly changed direction. Four went toward Oscar and Tinasha, while two went in the direction of the demonic beast as it leaped upon Oscar.

Tinasha instantly dispelled them, her beautiful face twisted up with rage. "*Trajectory distortion!*" she cried.

Angered that her spell had missed its marks, Tinasha charged toward Miralys with her left eye closed. Seeking to give chase, the demonic beast evaded Oscar's swipe of Akashia and bounded after the witch.

At that moment, Tinasha manifested a dagger in her right hand. She tried to throw it at Miralys, but the girl caught sight of the maneuver and shouted, "*Split open!*"

The remaining magic spheres on the floor scattered in all directions.

Dozens of them flew about the room, with Miralys at the center of their orbit. Some appeared able to fly directly to their targets, while others utilized trajectory distortion, rushing at everyone with unavoidable attacks.

Tinasha withstood their barrage from behind a magical wall she'd quickly summoned, but sensing something, she jumped back.

One sphere had rolled to her feet, and a strange gas issued from it. Tinasha felt dizzy and clutched at her face.

"…This is…"

The demonic beast didn't fail to notice the witch staggering and leaped toward her, but Oscar proved faster. He grabbed Tinasha's arm and pulled her back. Slashing at the silver wolf's claws, Oscar retreated even farther, the witch wrapped in his free arm.

"You all right? What was in that ball just now?"

"…A natural poison, mostly likely. Evidently, she meant it when she said he'd intended to negotiate with me."

Almost all of the nearly one hundred magic spheres were designed to buy time or avoid a direct confrontation in some way. Some of them probably contained things that acted as magic-sealing ornaments. One or two likely wouldn't have much effect but collectively could quickly become very annoying. Pressing a hand to her forehead, which had broken into a cold sweat, Tinasha murmured a low incantation.

"For now, I've stopped time for my body. A natural poison can't be lifted with magic."

Perhaps the original goal had been to negotiate with Tinasha while she was incapacitated. Unfortunately, they had the demonic beast to contend with, too. If Oscar hadn't been there, it might have gnawed off one of Tinasha's arms.

The witch eyed the silver-haired girl, whose face was a screwed up in anger as she pulled a dagger out of her arm.

Tinasha whispered to Oscar, "How are you doing?"

"It's what I'd expect from a beast. It's hard to catch. I'm fairly sure I can wound it, but it's tough to get a hit."

"That's because you're using Akashia. No matter how strong its fur's magical resistance is, Akashia can cut through it. That's why it has to dodge you."

"It switches targets to me sometimes, too. Adapting to its changes is a bit tricky."

"I'm sorry I'm a burden. We need to turn things around as soon as possible," said Tinasha.

"I'm fine with handling it by myself, but… What do you have in mind? If you have a strategy, let's hear it."

Oscar's rather casual attitude in the face of such danger wasn't a bold front but, rather, the result of battle-forged experience.

No matter how skilled he was, however, Oscar was still just a human with a sword. Fighting the demonic beast was no small task. Tinasha desperately wanted to aid him with magic, but the creature's silver fur made that difficult.

"…Oh," the witch suddenly said on reflex.

"What is it?"

Tinasha instantly recalled a trivial detail. She reached inside her magic outfit and drew out a small crystal ball. "It's always good to help people. And…to have a contract holder who neglects his health."

"Tinasha, we need to move."

Oscar leaped to the side with the witch in his arms. He swung Akashia at the beast that threatened to sink its jaws into them, but it caught the slash with its fangs and sprang up into the air.

The shifting rounds of offensive and defensive maneuvers between Oscar and the demonic beast were so swift that neither Tinasha nor Miralys could find a moment to insert themselves between the two. Tinasha marveled at Oscar's ability to fight evenly against one of the most formidable magical creatures in history, even with the royal sword on his side. Sadly, it was a losing battle for the prince. The beast was dictating the pace. If it decided to change its focus or move to another location, things could take a turn for the worse very quickly.

That was precisely why Oscar and Tinasha needed to make a decision that shifted the momentum before the enemy did.

"Oscar, which plan do you like—one where the castle gets half destroyed or one where the castle is intact but you'll be in trouble?" Tinasha proposed.

"The second one. That's hardly a choice at all. Do it," the prince replied.

"Leave it to me, then. Let's go with the classic simple approach. Buy me some time," Tinasha ordered, clasping Oscar's left hand for a moment before moving to stand behind him.

Immediately understanding what Tinasha meant, Oscar nodded and stepped forward. The two formed a basic pattern of vanguard swordsman and rear-guard mage.

Normally, Tinasha would defend with her sword and defensive walls, but she left all of that to Oscar and fell back. Then, she began chanting a spell that would turn the tide of this struggle in their favor.

A deep and powerful magic swirled at Tinasha's back. Feeling his protector's power acutely on his skin, Oscar stared down the silver wolf and the girl behind it.

He'd been locked in a duel with the beast for a while now, and it had continued to make use of its speed to avoid Oscar's attacks. There was a chance Oscar could get a hit if he charged the monster, but then the beast might attack Tinasha.

Oscar adjusted his grip on his sword, and Miralys laughed. "Your protective barrier is weakened. I wouldn't push it if I were you. You'll get your throat torn out."

"You seem to be laboring under some misunderstandings. I've gone a long time without that protection," Oscar shot back.

It was true that his witch had granted him an unparalleled level of magical defense, but even before receiving such a boon, he'd emerged victorious through countless dangerous situations with only his sword at his side. Oscar's search for a way to break his curse had led him across many hazardous and ancient locales. Ultimately, he was prepared to confront the Witch of Silence herself.

"I don't know what you're after. I'm almost grateful you've brought the demonic beast along. It still owes a debt that's gone unpaid for seventy years," Oscar taunted.

With a thumb, he wiped the witch's blood off his cheek. The wolf seized its opportunity and leaped. Its jaw was open wide to clamp down on his throat, but Oscar stood firm.

"Flames! Incinerate him!"

Akashia's blade met sharp teeth, sending silvery sparks flying. After a moment's pause, Miralys launched a gout of flames after Oscar.

In response, the prince merely managed a full swing of Akashia with the beast still firmly fastened onto the sword. The creature's silver fur caught the scorching blast, and the beast was slammed to the floor. Immediately righting itself, the demonic beast let out a furious howl.

Miralys glared at Oscar with a look of disgust. "How very unexpected, using the beast as a shield."

"Sorry. I never was one for manners," Oscar replied.

If his father had heard that, he might have let out a deep sigh, but the king had thankfully long since evacuated. Although Oscar hadn't been able to risk looking back to confirm that himself, so long as Tinasha was behind him, he trusted no one else would come to harm.

All he had to do was focus on the fight.

"No injuries allowed, huh? That's a lot to ask, considering I got a hole torn in my stomach the last time." From her defensive-only position, Tinasha couldn't break the stalemate between Oscar and the demonic beast, yet she was still planning to orchestrate some sort of upset.

Oscar wouldn't let her go to unreasonable lengths, however. She was still injured, after all. He glanced down at his left hand—the one Tinasha had held.

"All right… Here we go." Oscar shifted Akashia to his left hand.

Miralys gave a little frown. "What are you doing?"

"Not to worry; I'm ambidextrous," he answered.

Anticipating that in the future he might have to fight Tinasha for her hand in marriage, Oscar trained himself to wield a sword equally well with either hand, though he'd hidden this from his protector. After making sure of his grip, a daring smile stole over his face.

Just as Oscar's eyes were fixed on the beast, its own eyes were trained on him. Perhaps the beast knew that, with Tinasha in the state she was, only this man was a true match for it.

An irregular magical creature born from the magical lake.

"Come on, then... I'll give you a place to die," Oscar called to the beast that wielded fury like a weapon.

Tinasha's incantation filled the air. Miralys lifted her hands and spoke the words, *"Formless twilight, warp!"*

A sigil appeared from thin air and sped toward Oscar. At the same time, the beast launched itself forward into a charge.

Magic swirled and howled toward Oscar. He took a big step forward and lunged with his sword. A flurry of wind blades slashed at his body, but Oscar paid them no mind as he took another step toward the wolf. Aiming for the demonic beast's gaping maw, he struck out with Akashia, but before the blade could pierce the beast's body, sharp fangs clamped down on it.

For a second, they appeared to be at an impasse.

Suddenly, a little crystal ball was thrown into the fray. It traveled through the air toward the gap in the beast's fangs. The tiny thing sank deep into the beast's body and burst open.

The silver wolf's body shook from the force of the spell, but its jaw remained tight along Akashia's edge.

"What did you do?!" Miralys wailed shrilly.

"A certain someone got on my case about not getting enough sleep." Tinasha only offered a vague reply.

Within the crystal ball the witch had received as a thank-you for healing the boy in the castle town, she'd instilled a compulsive sleep spell. The demonic beast's incredible magical resistance extended only to its silvery fur. Spells loosed internally could take hold of the creature.

The wolf quivered but remained standing. It brought its claws to bear, ripping into Oscar's left arm.

Even at the sight of his own blood, Oscar remained steadfast. He took another step forward and jabbed his sword, with the demonic beast still biting down on it, into the floor with all the momentum he could muster.

A crystal ball lying on the floor collided hard with the wolflike beast, promptly cracking and exploding. All the magic that had been contained within the sphere slid off the silver fur of the creature before pooling on the ground and vanishing.

Rage clouded Miralys. "What did you just…?!"

"Pretty unlucky for the beast that it has to fight me at this size."

Oscar put all his weight and strength into his left arm. Rage and hatred blazed in the beast's red eyes while its limbs continued to buckle.

As though immune to the monster's threatening snarls, Oscar brace a foot on its exposed stomach. Desperately, the beast's claws raked at the prince, but Oscar only frowned, ignoring the wounds.

"Sorry, but you really caused a lot of trouble for her," Oscar muttered to the sleep-weakened monster.

The battle with the demonic beast did succeed in buying Tinasha some time, as she'd requested, but that alone wasn't enough. If Oscar was going to stand by her side, he knew he needed the skill to defeat an enemy like this.

Supporting his injured arm, which had gone numb, with his other, Oscar put more weight on his bloodied sword. As his own strength warred with that of his opponent, the prince slowly began to win out.

Akashia thrust deep into the demonic beast's wolflike head. Its writhing limbs spasmed.

"You're just about done. Go to sleep now," Oscar said.

The creature had very nearly been pierced through by Akashia.

Miralys paled at the sight. Hurriedly, she kicked up a crystal ball from off the floor. "*O thing of form, incinerate—*"

"I won't let you do that," Tinasha interjected. The witch's incantation had at last concluded. Inside Tinasha's hands was a small pool of darkness, a freezing chill billowing forth from it.

Miralys was at a loss for words at the sight. "What is that…?" she managed.

The most powerful witch—the Witch of the Azure Moon. An overwhelming being with the strength to alter the course of history.

Tinasha gave a brilliant smile. "*…Erase all meaning.*"

The darkness spread, and in an instant, the hall was steeped in black, silencing everything.

Sight, hearing, magic, spells—anything and everything appeared to have been wiped away.

The universe seemed lost; time and space were a faint memory. Only a freezing wind swept through, icing over all that stood in the nullifying void. It entered the body through the breath and shattered soundlessly.

It was a pure blackness that sought to steal away all thought and sense of self. Oscar broke into a bitter smile from within the sudden darkness.

"Next time, give me a proper challenge."

No matter what else was lost, the feel of the royal sword in Oscar's hand was solid and sure. He couldn't rightly tell if it had entirely impaled the creature, however, so he didn't unsheathe the blade from the beast that had become its new sheath.

A woman's voice whispered in Oscar's ear. "As long as I'm with you, you shall never know defeat."

The words, a promise from the witch, were surprisingly sweet.

When the darkness receded, all that was left before Oscar and Tinasha were the frozen and shattered core of the demonic beast and a room full of broken crystal balls.

Miralys was nowhere to be found. Oscar searched the empty hall.

"Did you erase her?" he asked.

"Don't be ridiculous. She got away," the witch answered, approaching Oscar and making a face at the wounds riddling his body. She promptly started healing the worst of them, the one on his left arm.

"I shattered the beast after nullifying its resistance, but any mage would've realized right away that it would be the end for them if they got sucked into a spell like that. So she made her escape," Tinasha explained.

"You let her go? Do you know where she went?" Oscar inquired.

"I've been monitoring her this whole time. It looks like she teleported somewhere close to the treasure vault."

"The treasure vault, huh? I was just there to get the sealing bracelet."

"How about I dispose of that for you?"

Ignoring her complaint, Oscar picked up the bracelet and put it in his breast pocket. Tinasha reached out to the cuts on his face, but he stopped her. "I'm fine. You need to heal yourself."

"It will take time for my eye to heal… It requires some fine-tuning. I'm all right for now; it doesn't hurt."

Tinasha's left eye was all closed up, the sight of which made Oscar's stomach knot in discomfort. Choosing not to let that show, he instead kissed her swollen eyelid.

"If it leaves a scar, I'll take responsibility and marry you," Oscar declared.

"I will hang you from the tower," Tinasha retorted.

Oscar petted the witch's head, and her good eye narrowed like a cat's. After enjoying it for only a moment, Tinasha fixed her mussed-up hair and manifested a little spell in her right hand.

"Looks like she's stopped at the treasure vault. I'm going to go after her, so you clean up here."

"Hey, wait," Oscar called, reaching out a hand, but Tinasha was already gone. She must have known that, with the demonic beast dead, Miralys alone was no match for her. Oscar looked up at the damaged walls and ceiling of the room, letting out a sigh.

Tinasha was grateful she'd followed Oscar to the treasure vault on occasion in the past and knew where it was.

After teleporting to the coordinates, Miralys knocked out the guard soldiers and pushed the door open.

The huge space was a jumbled mess of dazzling treasures, though it did have a certain kind of order to it. With no time to spare, the mage used her magic to search the environs. It didn't take long for her to find a little stone box tucked away, which she picked up.

She opened the lid and saw that contained within was a red jewel. It was round, slightly larger than a palm, and inlaid with intricate markings on the surface. Miralys trembled as she beheld the faintly glowing object.

"This is it…," she whispered.

With this at last in her hands, she had no further business in Farsas. She turned to leave the treasure vault but suddenly stopped dead in her tracks.

Waiting for her at the entrance was the strongest witch. Both of Tinasha's hands already held a huge spell formation. Until now, she hadn't been able to cast proper spells, having been preoccupied with the demonic beast. Miralys shuddered at the sheer, overwhelming power difference between them.

Tinasha looked to the box in the girl's hands. "I don't know what you're trying to make off with, but I won't let you. Hand it over."

The witch's powerful warning made Miralys lick her dry lips. She rallied herself, body on the verge of seizing in fear. "Sorry, but I need this, no matter what... You could never understand."

"I believe that's for me to decide once you've told me the full story," Tinasha answered coldly, and Miralys gritted her teeth. This opponent couldn't be sweet-talked. That much was obvious after Miralys had seen her former companion try and fail to do so several times over.

Miralys smiled, her lips curling in a sneer. "Even though you have no intention of listening to what we have to say, I may as well tell you, since I've got the chance. You're about to be reunited with that delusion you've been searching for. So you can go right ahead and suffer alone... Madame Queen-to-be."

"What...?"

None alive should have known to address Tinasha in such a way.

Caught off guard, Tinasha faltered for a moment, and Miralys seized that opportunity to run. Box in hand, she opened a transportation array.

The silver-haired girl quickly found an invisible vine winding itself around her legs, however.

"I can't allow you to escape," Tinasha said, casting a capture spell. Another vine snatched away the box Miralys was carrying, while yet another bound her tight. Miralys cast a spell aimed at her bindings: "Cut apart!"

The magical bonds scattered. Unfortunately, Miralys's own spell had been too powerful for her, and blood spurted from her body. Despite the pain, Miralys refused to give in, reaching out after the box. She quickly found herself tossed to the ground by a blast of the witch's power.

Her goal, so little a prize, was now forever beyond her reach. Miralys bit her lip, cursing her fate. Miralys wondered why the witch couldn't understand that this was something so precious that she had to protect it at all costs. There was something she had to get back, no matter the price, no matter what she had to sacrifice…

The silver-haired girl's vision blurred beneath a stream of tears. She stretched out her hand.

Miralys wondered how things could've been different if she'd been stronger, and her consciousness grew dim while magic surged within her body.

"Stop!" Tinasha warned, but it was far too late for Miralys to hear.

With her last thoughts, she begged for her message to be heard.

"Valt… I'm sorry…"

Recalling the face of one who would never return, Miralys closed her eyes.

When Oscar arrived at the treasure vault with a company of guards, Miralys's unconscious body was lying on Tinasha's lap.

The girl's face was deathly pale, and her silver hair seemed curiously duller. Oscar stared at her closed eyes. "Is she dead?" he asked.

The witch shook her head. "Her body is alive…but her soul is gone. She converted it into power and…disappeared."

Oscar examined the girl's face again. There were tear tracks on her skin.

Her thin arms were extended, grasping at something. A small, white stone box lay nearby.

♜ 10. Unnamed Feeling

It felt like she could sink into the soft bed for miles, or maybe that was only because she was so thoroughly exhausted. Staring up at the ceiling, Tinasha blinked over and over. She focused her eyes on one of her hands as she lifted it up into the air.

"I guess this is how it is…"

It had been a long time since she'd injured an eye. When she'd fought the former highest-ranked demon, it had almost lopped off her leg, and that had been quite the pain to heal, too. Neither that nor the damage to her eye had been lethal, but both had been severe enough to impede Tinasha in battle. Had she been forced to fight alone with only one eye, things could've gotten dicey.

Putting what-ifs behind her, Tinasha felt like it'd been ages since she stood at someone's back in a fight.

The last time Tinasha had done anything like that was little more than a distant memory now.

Without realizing it, a smile came to the witch's lips.

"He really is a strange man…"

Tinasha's contractee was in the middle of dealing with the repercussions of the battle with Miralys.

I'm off to chew out my dad, he'd said.

More than anything, the whole incident had been defined by its mysteries. Miralys had entered the castle as Ettard's relative, a fact that suggested memory tampering. Now that both Miralys and Ettard were gone, the truth of just how it came to happen would remain shrouded in darkness.

Just as Tinasha let out a little yawn, there was a knock at the door.

"Tinasha, are you awake?"

"Yes, come in," the witch replied, sitting up as her visitor arrived sooner than expected.

Oscar entered and quickly approached to thoroughly examine Tinasha's body. "Looks like you're...healing well?"

"Why was that a question? I told you I'm healing. Do you want to test it out?"

Tinasha placed a hand over her right eye. Oscar waved to her left eye and finally seemed relieved after seeing it respond. He sat next to her on the bed and ruffled her hair. "Sorry about everything. I caused you some trouble."

"I think we both caused our share of trouble for each other this time. Miralys wanted to get to me, after all. By the way, what was that orb she was trying to make off with?" Tinasha asked.

"It's...not a treasure native to Farsas. It's something my mother brought. I don't know what it could be used for. My dad might know, but he wouldn't tell me."

"Something your mother brought?" the witch repeated.

That changed things. Tinasha deliberated over whether she should ask about the one possibility that occurred to her, but Oscar was a formidable enemy in a different way than Lucrezia was. Chances were high he wouldn't answer if Tinasha simply asked him. The witch would have to be careful about how she proceeded before Oscar's contract was broken.

A more pressing matter was what Miralys had said to Tinasha before she'd died.

Miralys alluded to something about Tinasha being reunited with the delusion she'd been searching for... If that referred to the person the witch was constantly seeking, she very well might be close to the end of everything.

"...Lanak," Tinasha said, speaking a name she hadn't uttered in ages. Then, she fell into deep thought until she noticed someone staring at her and frowned. "What?"

"So do you want to give up and marry me?" Oscar pestered.

"I…"

Recalling Oscar's declaration before the battle, she pressed both hands to her flushed cheeks. The prince really did say the most ludicrous things.

Exceedingly bold—and unbelievably kind. Even knowing she was a witch, Oscar still lent her a helping hand and tried to protect her as naturally as he would anyone else. It truly was a strange demeanor, but that's just the kind of person Oscar was.

Tinasha's heart grew warm—but with an emotion that felt alien to her. She swallowed the girlish feeling and smiled. "I absolutely will not marry you. You should give up."

"I refuse. And besides, didn't you say after I climbed the tower again that you'd grant me a wish as long as it was something you could do right away?" Oscar pressed.

"Did I say something like that? I think that's better left forgotten…," Tinasha replied, turning her head to the side. She wanted to run away before Oscar had the chance to say anything else. As she turned, he touched her gently.

"How about this: Just recognize that I like you. That's my wish," stated Oscar.

"…What?" Tinasha replied, rather dumbfounded.

What a very strange contract holder she had. She didn't understand what he could gain from such a thing. What would change between them if she looked at him slightly differently? Nothing, so long as she was a witch.

Tinasha was about to rebuke him for spouting nonsense…but instead, she smiled faintly. "Fine. From now on, I'll reject your proposals fully aware of your intentions."

"Listen, you… Well, it's fine. I can wait," Oscar said, seemingly content.

"Please don't."

Oscar reached out and pulled Tinasha onto his lap. Instead of answering her with words, he placed a kiss on her left eyelid. Snorting a little, she leaned into his arms. They were comforting and warm, and she closed her eyes.

Even if he left himself with only one person to choose, she'd send him an infinite amount of options until he forgot all about that.

That was what it meant to contract with a witch. It was an unholy blessing that crept out from the shadows of forgotten history.

For this reason, she would never let the darkness of her past reach him.

She would never let the delusion she sought overtake his own path.

She would one day release him with no sadness in her heart.

This was her vow.

Tinasha looked up and glared at Oscar. "Let me go now. I'm already sleepy."

"Yeah, I'm beat from today, too. Let's fall asleep together."

"Go away! I'll throw you into your room with teleportation!"

Tinasha floated into the air and escaped from Oscar's arms, but he only laughed, his blue eyes gazing at her.

Dusk was overtaking the sky. The deep-blue hue was breathtaking.

The master of the royal sword. He who was an unshakable warrior was also the holder of a contract with a witch.

That was why, someday, once this all came to an end…he'd do her the favor of killing her.

This is the story of the final year of the Age of Witches.

It is also an epic fairy tale—the unnamed story of the fifth witch and a royal prince.

Afterword

To new readers and old, thank you for picking up *Unnamed Memory*. My name is Kuji Furumiya.

This story began as a web novel posted on my personal site in 2008 and has now been published in its final, edited form. When it was first posted, there weren't many web novel sites yet, and I took my time fine-tuning the text before releasing millions of words all at once into a random corner of the Internet. Looking back on it now, that seems to me to be the height of madness.

This humble novel has, quite unexpectedly, been read and critiqued by so many people, and after many twists and turns, I'm finally able to work as a novelist full-time. I'm truly grateful that I have another chance to tell you all how this long tale began.

This is the story of a cursed prince and the strongest witch in a world where magic is a part of life.

Peeling back a layer, the true story is that of a protagonist with a mind of steel who declares, "You don't have to break the curse; just marry me since it doesn't affect you. That way everything's settled." Then, the witch insists, "I refuse to marry you, and I *will* break the curse!" From there, the story becomes one of how their back-and-forth ends up changing the history of the entire world they live in.

Many things lead up to that change.

Mysterious murders, secret plots, international friction, and hidden truths of the past. How will the two of them face such struggles? For the conclusion to all of those, as well as how the love story will play out when the witch's awkwardness stalls any progress that's made, please keep reading this series until its end!

Now I'd like to take this opportunity to thank some people!

To my editor, who approached me about adapting this story into a published novel, as well as supporting me since my debut: Thank you so much! I'm sorry for subjecting you to so many selfish requests! I'll keep working hard so you can keep playing *Gacha*!

To chibi, who handled character designs and made such gorgeous illustrations: I'm deeply impressed by how real you made the world feel and how beautifully you drew all the characters. Thank you so much! I look forward to seeing more of your art in the future!

Tappei Nagatsuki also wrote me a really cool endorsement for the published version of the book! I've known him since my web novel days, and I'm eternally grateful that he agreed right away when I approached him for a blurb. It's so cool... Really cool... I'm very lucky!

Finally, I'd like to say that it's thanks to all of you who've been following this story for over ten years now that this new tale featuring our two protagonists has come to be. I'll be sure to pour my everlasting gratitude into the story so that you can enjoy this unnamed tale again. Thank you so much!

Kuji Furumiya
(Yuki Fujimura)

Extra

Colorful clothing hung throughout the little tent. Amid the exotically scented interior, Oscar selected a pure-white dress and tossed it to the witch at his side.

"Try this one on next. It'll look good on you," he said.

"What? Ugh, what do you think you're doing…?" Tinasha answered, pulling a face as she took the dress into the back of the tent to change.

While normally these two would have been shut up in the castle study at this time of day, today they were perusing a street merchant's tent that had been set up in the castle city plaza. This had been their compromise.

Oscar had insisted, *"My senses are so dulled, I have to get outside."*

While Tinasha had shot back with, *"I won't let you go. Think of your position."*

In the end, they'd donned disguises and ventured into the city together. Oscar seemed to be having a great time dressing Tinasha up.

The witch emerged from the back, tugging on the hem of the dress with an exasperated look. She glared up at her companion. "Here, I'm all changed. Are you satisfied?"

The high collar framing her tiny face looked like flower petals, and the billowy skirt accentuated her slender body and flared out like a blooming bud. She looked mystical, and Oscar broke into a grin. "It looks good on you. I'm gonna buy this one, too; then we can head back."

"This is so hard to move in; when am I going to wear it? Why have you been buying me clothes anyway?" Tinasha asked.

"I think it's nice to change things up once in a while," Oscar replied.

The crown prince's daily routine was packed with all sorts of responsibilities to attend to, and he never got a chance to take a break. He was aware that such things were his duty but still sometimes felt strangely low-spirited and in need of diversion.

When such moods took him, he usually felt better after spending some time with his protector. Perhaps the reason was that, while Tinasha respected Oscar as her contractee, she didn't care very much at all about the status and responsibilities that came with his royal position.

Catching a glimpse of herself in the full-length mirror, Tinasha tied up her long hair to match the dress. "If you're quite done, let's go back. Lazar is probably in tears by now."

"I really wanted to take my time picking out clothes for you, though... Next, I planned to select accessories," Oscar said.

"We're leaving! I've had enough, and I'm tired!" Tinasha cried, signifying that she was almost at her limit.

Oscar placed a hand on top of the petite witch's head. "All right. Honestly, it was a surprise you put up with it for this long. I thought for sure you'd have made your escape by now."

While Tinasha had worn a scowl the entire time, she'd still accompanied Oscar on his diversion. He wondered what whim had possessed her to suffer through it, but she turned her face aside. In a clear voice, she answered, "I know very well how hard you work each day."

Oscar's eyes widened a little.

Without a doubt, Tinasha was the one person who, more than anyone else, saw Oscar as just a man. Even when the world revered him as royalty.

That was why he loved being with her and why he wanted her to think of him as he did her.

"I see... In that case, wanna get married? I'd love to dress you up like a bride."

"I do not! All right, it's time to go home! Right away! No detours!" Tinasha declared, holding out a hand to Oscar. He accepted it with a grin. Even the return trip to the castle didn't bore him.

On Sale

Unnamed Memory II

Kuji Furumiya Illustration by chibi

Lanak, the man who suddenly appeared before Tinasha, is her fiancé—the one she's spent centuries searching for. After four hundred years, he's resurrected the Magic Empire and crowned himself as its king. That alone has not satiated his desires, as Lanak now plots to conquer the entire mainland.

Oscar's and Tinasha's chosen paths begin to diverge...

A fierce battle to the death is brewing between powerful magic that seeks to rule the land and the wielder of the royal sword.

Shocking twists of fate and heartrending tragedy whip into a maelstrom in this thrilling second volume!

Spring 2021!

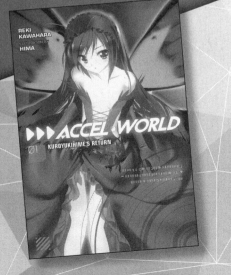

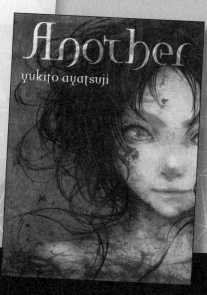